Hunting for a Highlander

By Lynsay Sands

Hunting for a Highlander
The Wrong Highlander
The Highlander's Promise
Surrender to the Highlander
Falling for the Highlander
The Highlander Takes a Bride
To Marry a Scottish Laird
An English Bride in Scotland
The Husband Hunt
The Heiress
The Countess
The Hellion and the Highlander
Taming the Highland Bride
Devil of the Highlands

The Loving Daylights

Immortal Born
The Trouble With Vampires
Vampires Like it Hot
Twice Bitten
Immortally Yours
Immortal Unchained
Immortal Nights
Runaway Vampire
About a Vampire
The Immortal Who Loved Me
Vampire Most Wanted
One Lucky Vampire
Immortal Ever After
The Lady Is a Vamp
Under a Vampire Moon
The Reluctant Vampire
Hungry For You
Born to Bite
The Renegade Hunter
The Immortal Hunter
The Rogue Hunter
Vampire, Interrupted
Vampires Are Forever
The Accidental Vampire
Bite Me if You Can
A Bite to Remember
Tall, Dark & Hungry
Single White Vampire
Love Bites
A Quick Bite

LYNSAY SANDS

Hunting for a Highlander

An Imprint of HarperCollins*Publishers*

This is a work of fiction. Names, characters, places, and incidents are products of the author's imagination or are used fictitiously and are not to be construed as real. Any resemblance to actual events, locales, organizations, or persons, living or dead, is entirely coincidental.

For information, address HarperCollins Publishers, 195 Broadway, New York, NY 10007.

First Avon Books mass market printing: February 2020
First Avon Books hardcover printing: January 2020

Print Edition ISBN: 978-0-06-297503-4
Digital Edition ISBN: 978–0–06-285538–1

FIRST EDITION

20 21 22 23 24 LSC 10 9 8 7 6 5 4 3 2 1

Hunting for a Highlander

Chapter 1

"Whinnie! Whinnnnnnie!"

Geordie Buchanan opened tired eyes as that call was followed by someone trying to make the sound of a horse whinnying. For a minute, he didn't know where he was. Early-morning sunlight was streaming down at an angle that managed to reach him where he lay against the trunk of a tree, one of several he could see growing in rows in front and to the side of him. Seeing them, he remembered that he'd made his bed in the orchard behind the gardens when he'd returned last night. There hadn't seemed to be much choice; after weeks away he'd arrived back in the middle of the night to find Buchanan crowded with people. The great hall had been overflowing with sleeping servants and soldiers, as had the kitchen, but it was his uncle sleeping in a chair by the fire that had told him just how full the keep was. The man only slept in a chair below when he had to give up his bed to guests. Geordie had assumed that probably meant his own bed had been given to someone too.

"Whinnie!"

Geordie scowled at the annoying voice followed by another high-pitched attempt at a horse's whinny. The keep was apparently up and children were ready to play. He'd barely had the irritated thought when a young woman appeared halfway along the row of trees and turned her back to him to peer up into the branches. Geordie was just wondering if she was the person who had been calling out and whinnying when the sound came again from somewhere to the left and farther away.

"Whinnnnnie!"

The woman muttered what sounded suspiciously like a curse, and then bent down, reached under her skirts to grab the back hem of the long gown she wore and pulled it forward and up to tuck the cloth through the belt around her waist.

Geordie's eyes were widening at the tantalizing amount of shapely ankle and calf she was showing when she grasped the lowest branch of the tree and began to climb quite nimbly upward. She was quick about it, but had barely disappeared into the leafy haven the branches provided when two women appeared farther down the row of trees and glanced around.

Where the first woman hadn't noticed Geordie, these two did and sneered briefly as they took in the fact that he'd obviously slept out in the gardens. They didn't lower themselves to actually comment. Instead, they turned back the way they'd come and one said with annoyance, "She must have slipped past us and returned to the keep. Come on."

Geordie watched them go before allowing his gaze to return to the tree. He fully expected the woman to climb down now, but when several moments passed without any sign of her, he rolled out of his plaid, then shifted to his knees to begin pleating it. He obviously wasn't going to get any more sleep today. Besides, he had a sneaking suspicion that the lass was like a cat and now that she was up the tree, she couldn't make her way back down. He'd give her the length of time it took him to get properly dressed again, and then offer his assistance . . . if she hadn't fallen out by that time.

DWYN LOOKED OUT THROUGH THE BRANCHES OF THE TREE SHE was in, and over the rolling hills beyond the back wall of Buchanan. It was a beautiful area, she acknowledged, but not as beautiful as Innes. There she would have had a view of the ocean, not to mention a sea breeze to soothe her jangled nerves. The thought made her grimace. Before this trip, Dwyn had never met a person she didn't like. The people at Innes were always kind and friendly, at least to her. But the women she'd met since coming to Buchanan . . . Well, other than Lady Buchanan herself, there wasn't one other woman she liked. The other female guests here were a bunch of catty bampots, the lot of them, and they seemed to have decided to target her with their cruel taunts for some reason. The thought made her mouth twitch unhappily. Dwyn wasn't used to people not liking her, and wasn't sure what to do about it. These women were like no one she'd ever encountered. They were bored, and had chosen to entertain themselves by picking on her.

"Good morrow, lass."

Dwyn blinked at that greeting, and then leaned forward to peer down through the branches at the man who had spoken. He'd positioned himself right below her, and Dwyn's eyes widened as her gaze slid over him. He appeared big from this angle, all shoulders, but she couldn't tell how tall he was from her position. He was handsome though, his eyes a fine pale blue, his nose straight, his mouth having a larger lower than upper lip, and his hair was long and dark, with a bit of wave to it.

"Can I help ye down, lass?"

His words startled her out of gaping at him, and Dwyn shook her head. "Nay, thank ye."

"Nay?" He looked surprised at the refusal, and then frowned around at the orchard briefly before tipping his head back to look up at her again. "Are ye sure, lass? I'm pleased to help ye, do ye need it."

"Nay. I'm fine. Thank ye," Dwyn murmured, and followed her refusal with lifting her head to gaze out past the wall again, hoping he'd take the hint and leave.

He didn't take the hint. Dwyn realized that when the branch she was on began to tremble a bit and she glanced down to see that the man was now climbing up. Her eyes widened incredulously, and then she sat back abruptly as he swung himself up onto the branch directly in front of the one she was on. It was actually a little lower than the large branch she was sitting on, but even so, Dwyn had to tilt her head back to look up at his face.

"Good morrow," he said again, offering her a smile. "Whinnie, is it?"

Dwyn had just started to smile in response when he asked that and the expression died before it had fully formed. "Nay. My name is Dwyn."

"Oh. My apologies. I thought they were calling Whinnie."

"They were," she said grimly, but didn't explain, and silence fell between them briefly. Dwyn did her best to pretend he wasn't there. Actually, she was mostly pretending she wasn't there either, but was back home at Innes, walking the shores with her dogs, Angus and Barra.

"Dwyn."

She turned reluctantly to peer at him.

"Who is yer clan?"

"Innes," she murmured, turning away again. "Me father is Baron James Innes."

"Innes is on the North Sea, is it no'?" he asked with interest.

"Aye, between the river Spey and the river Lossie. 'Tis beautiful lush green land," she added with a faint smile. "Innes is really situated on a large inlet off the North Sea called Moray Firth, and between that bordering it on the north, the Spey river on the west and Lossie river on the east, but curving down around the bottom o' Innes, 'tis nearly an island."

"It sounds lovely," he admitted.

"'Tis," she assured him. "And as Da says, having the water nearly surrounding us aids greatly with defense. A good thing, since Da's more a thinker than a warrior. Which is why we're here, o' course. For all the good 'twill do."

Geordie's eyebrows rose at that. "I do no' understand. Just why are ye here at Buchanan?"

The question brought her gaze around with surprise, and then she scowled at the man. He'd seemed mostly nice up until that point. "There is no need to be cruel, sir. I ken I've no' a chance with all the other women here being so beautiful, but ye need no' point it out quite so boldly."

He seemed confused by her words and said, "I did no' realize I was being cruel. I've no idea why any o' ye are here."

She considered that briefly and then supposed it wasn't perhaps something that Laird Buchanan would talk openly about. Still, gossip usually traveled quickly in keeps, and she was surprised that he didn't know. Dwyn wished he did though. It was all rather embarrassing to have to explain. But it looked like she was going to have to. Dwyn drew in a deep breath to begin, and then paused when the action made her breasts rise perilously in the low-cut gown her sisters had insisted she wear. Grimacing, she pressed a hand to the tops of the round mounds to keep them down as she quickly blurted, "The other women are here hoping to catch the eye of one of the still-single Buchanan brothers and lure them into marriage."

"What?" he barked, his eyes shifting swiftly up from her breasts to her face with disbelief.

There was no mistaking his reaction as anything but shock, she decided. He truly hadn't known the purpose of the visitors presently filling the Buchanan keep. Perhaps he was one of the soldiers who usually patrolled the Buchanan lands so didn't spend much time at the keep to hear the gossip.

"Surely ye jest?" he asked now.

Dwyn smiled wryly as she shook her head. "Nay. There are at least seven beautiful women presently wandering the keep and grounds, waiting for the three still-single brothers to return to Buchanan and select a bride."

"Seven?" he asked.

"And their escorts," she added. "Of course, a new woman or two seems to arrive every day so there may be eight or nine by the nooning, or sup."

When he just sat there seeming lost in thought, Dwyn left him to it and turned to peer out at the hills again. He obviously meant her no harm, and it was nice to talk to someone who was not nattering at her to sit up straight, and stick out her chest, or alternately pointing out her faults and making fun of her. Honestly, she'd never realized women could be so cruel until this trip.

"Why would these women seek out the brothers for marriage?"

Dwyn glanced around at that question, and noted that the man appeared completely flummoxed by the news she'd imparted. Shrugging, she said, "Presumably because they're all without a betrothed and their fathers wish to make an alliance with the Buchanans," she said, and then frowned and added, "Although I do know at least one of the women *is* betrothed. Apparently, Laird Wallace is willing to break the contract in favor of a Buchanan son, should one of them be interested."

"Why?" he asked again, this time sounding even more amazed, and she could understand his shock at this news. It was uncommon to break a betrothal. The family would lose the dower that had been promised in the contract.

"Because the Buchanans are becoming quite powerful what with the sons each marrying so advantageously. The siblings are all very close, and each now has their own castle and warriors." She shrugged. "What man wouldn't want to be a part of that and have that kind of power at his back?"

"Hmm." He was silent for a minute, displeasure on his face, but then glanced at her and raised his eyebrows. "And yer one o' these seven beautiful women?"

Dwyn grinned with amusement. "Hardly."

That made his eyebrows rise in question. "Then why are ye here?"

Dwyn drew in another breath that nearly dislodged her breasts from her gown and covered her chest again with irritation. Holding them down with one hand, she tugged her neckline up with the other as she reluctantly admitted, "Well, that is why me father brought me. He has no sons to pass the title down to, and me own betrothed died ere coming to claim me. Father is hoping to make a match to help protect us from our neighbors, the Brodies, who want to add Innes to their holdings, but . . ." Giving up on stuffing her breasts any farther back into the gown, she let her hands drop with disgruntlement as she finished, "I fear he will be disappointed. The Buchanans are no' likely to even notice me among so many beautiful women."

"Why?" he asked, but she didn't think he was really paying attention when he asked the question. His wide eyes seemed to be transfixed on her overflowing bosom.

Smiling wryly, she said, "Because I am overlarge and very plain in looks, sir." When he continued to stare at her chest, she added dryly, "'Tis why my sisters stuffed me into this ridiculously small gown. They are hoping that the Buchanans will be too busy ogling me breasts to bother to look at me face."

He wrenched his gaze up at that, his face flushing slightly, and murmured, "My apologies, m'lady. It was no' well done o' me to—"

Dwyn waved his apology away on a sigh that had her nipples peeking up over the neckline, and she muttered impatiently and returned to trying to tame her breasts and force them back into her gown. Honestly, this was going to be an embarrassing stay if her breasts kept popping out like this. Fortunately, the dress she'd worn when she'd arrived here yesterday had not been quite as tight as this one and she hadn't been spilling out at every turn. Obviously, she needed to change when she returned to the keep.

"No need to apologize," Dwyn growled now, more annoyed than embarrassed. "This was my sisters' plan, after all, and it would seem it works. Perhaps one of the brothers will be so enamored of me breasts that they won't notice me face. Men do seem to like breasts," she added thoughtfully. "I think it must reassure them that their bairns will be well fed or something."

Geordie restrained the laugh that wanted to slip out at her words. It wasn't a bairn he was imagining suckling at her nipples as he looked on them. Damn, but the good Lord had been generous with her bosom. Shaking his head, he forced his gaze back to her face and examined her features.

Dwyn Innes was not a beauty. At least, not an obvious beauty. She had a nice face, a straight little nose, a mouth that was neither full and luscious, nor small and mean, but somewhere in the middle, and her eyes too were neither too small nor large. They were perhaps average, but the color was a beautiful clear blue that actually seemed to sparkle when she was amused, he'd noticed.

And then there was her hair. Dwyn had it pulled back tightly from her face and set in a bun at the back of her head that was as overlarge as her breasts, but it was a beautiful pale gold with darker highlights that he would have liked to see down and flowing around her face. Geordie imagined that now, but in his mind she wasn't wearing the gown with its plunging neckline. Instead, she was naked, lying in the grass below the tree with her long hair spread out around her lush body.

Geordie shifted uncomfortably on his branch as his body responded to that imagining, his cock now waking from rest and beginning to poke up at his plaid. Leaning forward slightly, he rested his arm across his lap to hide it and then stilled as he realized the pose placed his face closer to hers, just inches away, in fact. Close enough to kiss, he thought suddenly, and then reached quickly for her when she jerked back in surprise and nearly tumbled backward off her branch.

"Careful, lass," Geordie warned, his voice coming out a husky growl. Releasing her once the risk of her falling passed, he straightened and suggested, "Mayhap we'd best climb down now."

"Aye," she agreed, her face a little flushed, and then without another word, she placed one tiny slippered foot on the branch next to his leg, braced one hand on the large branch she sat on and began to push her bottom off it.

"Dwyn!"

That shout from below startled both of them, but Dwyn physically started and he saw the way her eyes widened in alarm as her foot slipped from the branch and she began to fall. Geordie didn't even think, but leaned down and caught her about the waist, then dragged her back up and onto his lap. They both froze then, neither seeming to even breathe as another pair of females appeared under the tree and stopped to look around the orchard with obvious exasperation. They were both tall and pretty with dark hair and appealing features that were presently somewhat vexed.

"Oh, where has she got to now?" the lass in a pale pink gown muttered with irritation.

"No doubt, hiding," the second woman, dressed in a pale blue gown, responded on a sigh. "Ye ken how shy she is."

"Aye, well, she must work past that, Aileen, if she ever wishes to marry. Hiding is no' going to get her a husband."

"Oh, let her have some peace, Una," the lass named Aileen said wearily. "The single Buchanan brothers are no' here at the moment anyway, and we have harassed her enough what with taking in her gowns until she can hardly breathe, and constantly pinching her cheeks trying to give her some color. Besides, that bitch Lady Catriona and her friend Lady Sasha have both been tormenting our sister horribly. I do no' blame her for wanting a moment to herself."

"Aye," the lass named Una agreed grimly, and then growled, "They are calling her horse face now, did ye hear?"

"What?" Aileen said with dismay.

"Aye, and they have taken to taunting her by calling her Whinnie instead o' Dwyn too."

"I thought I heard them call her Whinnie, but then decided I just misheard and they were saying Dwynnie."

"Nay," Una assured her. "And they follow it up with whinnying sounds too. I'd like to scratch their nasty eyes out for picking at her."

"They are like she-wolves scenting the weakest in the herd, separating them and then attacking," Aileen said sadly. "I wish Dwyn would fight back."

"She is too nice for that," Una said, somehow making *nice* sound quite disgusting. "And do no' even bother suggesting it to her. She'd just make us feel bad for being angry at them and say they were obviously unhappy to act so and needed our sympathy."

"Aye," Aileen agreed with a faint smile, following when Una moved away from the tree. "I swear she'd have sympathy for the devil did she meet him."

"Probably offer him mead," Una muttered as they disappeared from view and their voices began to grow fainter.

Dwyn remained completely still at first as the voices faded

away. She'd barely dared breathe once her sisters had appeared beneath them, but now that they were leaving, she realized she couldn't move anyway. Her back was pressed tight to the chest of her savior, the arm around her waist like a band of steel under her breasts, holding her in place . . . And pushing her breasts up out of her top again, she realized with dismay. There was more than a little nipple now on display in the oversmall gown, although Dwyn didn't think that had been the man's intent. She didn't even think he probably realized what was happening. Did he?

Dwyn turned her head and tipped it so that she could glance back at him. Much to her relief, his head was turned, his eyes pointed in the direction her sisters had taken as he waited to be sure they left. Just as she noted that though, he glanced down toward her and then froze, the arm around her waist tightening briefly and sending her breasts farther out of her gown until the nipples were almost completely on display.

They both remained still for a moment. Dwyn was blushing fiercely and struggling to find something to say to ease her embarrassment when he suddenly lowered his head and pressed his lips to hers. Dwyn stiffened in amazement as his mouth brushed over hers once, then twice. When he nipped at her lower lip, drawing on it and tugging gently, she opened for him. The moment her lips parted, he released the lower one and covered her mouth again with his. This time she felt his tongue slide out and Dwyn gasped with surprise as it snaked in to fill her mouth. That reaction melted away, replaced by a warm rush of excitement though, as his mouth slanted over hers, his tongue thrusting and exploring.

Dwyn found herself responding, or trying to. She hadn't a clue what she was doing, and at first tried to keep her own tongue out of his way as her mouth moved under his, but he merely chased it. When his tongue rasped against her own, Dwyn moaned and stopped retreating to thrust back. Her hands came up to clasp his arm under her breasts, her nails digging into his skin as she kissed back with all that she was worth.

This time it was him who moaned, and for a moment the kiss became most demanding and hungry. It was as if he was trying to devour her, Dwyn thought faintly, and found she wasn't at all alarmed at the prospect. Tearing one hand from his arm, she reached up to slide her fingers around his neck, her body straining and twisting in his hold to press closer, and then he suddenly broke the kiss and lifted his head.

For a moment he just stared down at her, his heated gaze sliding over her flushed face and then down over her exposed breasts. Dwyn followed his gaze, noting that the circles of dusky rose flesh had contracted and darkened around the small buds that had hardened and were now rising out of the center like flowers seeking the sun.

She'd just noted that when the man holding her abruptly shifted his hands, caught her by the waist and turned Dwyn to set her on her branch again. The moment her bottom landed on the hard wood, he grabbed the front of her gown and tugged it up to cover her properly. He didn't let go of the cloth at once though, but froze, still holding the material, the backs of his fingers warm against her nipples, which were responding most oddly to the unintentional touch.

Panting breathlessly, Dwyn stared at his dark hands against her pale flesh. But then he groaned, drawing her gaze up to see that he'd closed his eyes and appeared to be in some distress.

"I— Are ye all right?" she asked shakily, her gaze shifting from his pained expression to his fingers still inside her top and back. "Did ye hurt yerself lifting me? I know I am heavy. Did ye—" She paused, her own eyes widening slightly when his suddenly flashed open. He was looking at her like she was sweet meat and he hadn't eaten in days, Dwyn thought faintly, and then he abruptly removed his hands and was gone. She blinked at the empty branch in front of her, and then leaned forward and looked down in time to see him land lightly on his feet on the hard-packed ground. He snatched up a sack that lay against the trunk and walked away.

Dwyn watched until he was out of sight and then sat back with a shaky sigh. Well, wasn't that . . . She shook her head slightly and reached up to press her fingers to her still-tingling lips. That had been . . .

"Oh, my," Dwyn breathed. She'd just had her first kiss, and it had been quite wonderful. At least, she'd thought so. She didn't think his walking off like that was a good sign though, and wondered what it meant. Perhaps she shouldn't have let him kiss her. Not that she'd had much choice, she assured herself. It had been somewhat unexpected, and her precarious position in his lap—

Oh, give over, her mind argued at once. She hadn't wanted to stop him, not once his tongue was in her mouth. Then she'd wanted him to continue to kiss her, and still did, she acknowledged with a grimace. Truly, she wished he was still there, holding her in his lap, his mouth moving on hers, his arms around her. But she wished he'd done more. She wasn't sure what exactly, but . . . Her hands rose and closed over her breasts almost protectively. They had tingled and hardened as he'd kissed her, and were oddly sensitive now, the brush of her palms over them even through the material of her gown making them tingle all the more.

Lowering her hands quickly, Dwyn turned to peer out over the land beyond the wall and tried not to think about the odd sensations now swirling through her body. Or who the man might be. And whether he might repeat the experience should they encounter each other again while she was here.

Chapter 2

"BROTHER!"

Geordie nodded at that greeting from his eldest brother, Aulay, as he reached the high table, but then turned to lean over and press a kiss of greeting to his sister-in-law Jetta's cheek.

"Geordie! We have been wondering where you got to," Jetta cried as she leapt up from her seat to embrace him warmly. Pulling back to peer up at him, she added, "We were not expecting you until today, but the stable master said your horse was in its stall when he went out this morning."

"Aye," Aulay agreed, taking his wife's place to hug Geordie next. Clapping him on the back, he asked, "Where did ye sleep last night?"

"The great hall was so crowded I knew we must have company, so I took meself out to the orchard," Geordie answered, his gaze sliding to the guests at the table who were now eyeing him eagerly. All but two, he noted. The women he had first seen in the gardens chasing after Dwyn with their taunts were looking a bit dismayed and chagrined. He suspected they were recalling the sneers they'd cast his way on seeing him sleeping out there and now regretted it.

"A good thing," Aulay said, regaining his attention. "I fear ye would have given the Innes lasses a scare had ye gone to yer own room."

"Innes?" He glanced at his brother sharply. "Dwyn?"

Aulay's eyebrows rose slightly, but he nodded. "Aye. Dwyn, Una and Aileen. Their father, James, slept in his traveling tent in the bailey, but we gave the girls yer bed last night."

Geordie hadn't noticed any traveling tents set up in the bailey as he'd crossed it to the keep, but it had been late, and dark, and he'd been exhausted enough that he hadn't really looked around much. That didn't matter to him though. His attention had been caught by the knowledge that Dwyn had slept in his bed last night, her lovely hair spread out on his pillow, her body warmed by his linens and furs.

Realizing his own body was responding to the image in his mind, he shifted the bag he held in front of him to cover his growing groin. "I just came to let ye ken I was back. I'm heading to the loch now to clean up."

"I'll come with ye. We need to talk anyway," Aulay announced, following on his heels when Geordie turned and started away.

"I'll join ye too."

Geordie glanced around at that eager cry, just catching the exasperation that flashed across Jetta's face at being left to handle all their guests alone, before his gaze found his uncle Acair on his feet and hurrying after them with a speed that belied his age. Geordie's gaze slid back to his sister-in-law with apology, but she smiled faintly and waved them off, then paused with surprise when Aulay suddenly turned and hurried back to kiss her. It was no quick peck, but a long, deep kiss that left his wee wife flushed and breathing heavily.

Geordie shook his head and continued walking, and Aulay caught up as they reached the keep doors. The three of them were silent as they crossed the bailey to the stables to fetch their horses. It wasn't until they'd reached the loch and dismounted that Aulay finally spoke.

"I suppose ye noticed that most o' our guests are female," his brother started as they dismounted.

"Aye," Geordie agreed as he tied his mount's reins around a low-lying branch.

"How could he not notice?" Uncle Acair growled as he took care of his own mount. "We've got women crawling out of the woodwork just now. There's no' a room in the keep that a man can find a moment's peace without giggling females following to ask questions." Speaking in a high voice meant to imitate the women, he asked, "Which o' the three brothers is most handsome, do ye think? Who is strongest? What kind o' woman do ye think this one would like? Or that one? Do they have all their teeth? Which one is best at battle?" Shaking his head, he said in his own voice, "'Tis damned annoying."

Finished with his horse, Geordie turned to his brother, one eyebrow raised.

Grimacing, Aulay avoided his gaze and muttered, "It appears you, Rory and Alick have become somewhat sought after."

"Sought after?" Acair hooted with amusement. "They're being hunted, the three of them." Turning, he speared Geordie with a look and said, "I'd run like the devil if I were you, lad, else ye'll find yerself run to ground and shackled to one o' those lasses back there."

"Uncle," Aulay growled with irritation. He then turned a scowl Geordie's way, and said, "Do no' even think about running. I have been stuck with a keep full o' females for several days now and want them gone. But they're no' going anywhere until you and yer brothers pick one each, or at least decide ye do no' want any o' them and make it known."

Geordie grunted at that, and moved to the water's edge. Once there, he quickly shed his plaid. He started to remove his shirt next, but paused and turned back to Aulay. "How the devil did they all end up at Buchanan?"

"Ah." Aulay grimaced. "Well, ye remember when the lasses decided to have that visit a couple months back?"

Geordie nodded. It was hard to forget. Jetta had sweetly but determinedly told him, Aulay, Rory, Alick and Uncle Acair that they were not welcome and to make themselves scarce while their sister and their brothers' wives, as well as Jo Sinclair and Annabel MacKay and her daughters, visited. Aulay had taken her at her word, put his second, Simon, in charge of the men and he, Geordie, Uncle Acair, Rory and Alick had all left for the hunting lodge.

They'd soon been joined by the rest of the brothers as well as MacDonnell, Sinclair and MacKay, who had escorted their wives to Buchanan, only to be sweetly kicked out by the women.

It had got damned crowded in the lodge, and they'd ended up talking, laughing and drinking the nights away, and then spending the better part of the days nursing hangovers. There had been little actual hunting in the end. But the alcohol had been needed to make the floor seem less uncomfortable at night, and it had been a good time in the end.

"Well," Aulay said now, "it seems they got talking about the three o' ye—you and Rory and Alick—and fretting about how they wished the three o' ye were settled and happily married too. They apparently came up with the idea that they should help ye with that."

"Good Christ," Geordie breathed.

"Aye," Acair agreed grimly.

"So?" Geordie asked when Aulay didn't continue. "What did they do? How the hell did we end up with a castle full o' women?"

"Apparently, they made a list o' all the women they knew who had lost their betrothed and were available. They then whittled the list down to all those who were the eldest child without a brother to inherit land or title, and finally they wrote letters to their fathers, pointing out the advantages of the daughter marrying a Buchanan."

"Advantages?" Geordie asked with amusement. "I do no' have a pot to piss in. What advantage is that?"

Aulay scowled at his comments. "Ma and Da left ye coin and a bit o' land just like they did our siblings. Ye ken it's waiting fer ye the minute ye ask fer it."

"Aye, but a bit o' coin and land is no' a home to bring a wife to," Geordie pointed out with exasperation.

"That's the beauty o' it," Aulay said with a grin. "When they got the responses from the interested lairds, they then wrote back and gave terms. Only the lairds who were willing to make one o' ye their heir and name ye the next laird were invited to bring their daughters fer ye to meet."

"And the fathers of all those women in the keep were willing?" he asked with disbelief.

"Geordie, we are Buchanans, a strong and proud clan, but now add that Niels and Edith are laird and lady o'er the Drummonds, Saidh and her Greer are laird and lady o' MacDonnell, Conran and Evina are laird and lady o' the Macleans, and Dougall and his Murine are not only laird and lady o' Carmichael here in Scotland, but also Danvries in England . . ." He paused briefly to let that sink in and then added, "And that does no' even include the Sinclairs and the MacKays, who are friends to us all, or Evina's cousin, Gavin, who is like a brother and son to her all at once and is now laird of the MacLeods. Any one o' them would certainly call up their men to help if any o' us needed aid." He pointed out, "Not only do we now hold considerable influence, we would have no less than eight strong and wealthy clans at our back if under attack."

"Aye," Acair said now. "Many would like to join our circle and enjoy that kind of safety. Especially men who were no' gifted with male heirs and seek to protect their daughters and lands from greedy neighbors who might like to take either or both by force."

Geordie shook his head. When put like that he could see why the fathers were interested in arranging a marriage. Still . . . "Ye canno' mean to tell me that the women did all this writing back and forth in that one weekend?"

"Nay. They sent the first messages that weekend, and then Jetta wrote the other women every time she got a response and they wrote back with suggestions about what to do next, and so on." He raised his eyebrows. "Have ye no' noticed I've had to send one o' me men out almost every damned day for the last couple o' months with messages from Jetta to the various women?"

Geordie had noticed that before he left, but had just thought it nice that Jetta was getting along so well with all of the women. Sighing, he shook his head. "I'd like to say it was kind o' Jetta and the others to go to all this trouble . . ."

"But?" Aulay prodded when he paused.

"But I do no' want to marry yet," he said simply.

"Geordie, ye're nine and twenty years old now," Aulay pointed out.

"Aye, but I have been so busy helping everyone else . . . First we were rushing this way and that for Murine and Dougall, and then Edith and Niels, and then . . ." He grimaced. "And I've spent the last six weeks helping Evina get Gavin set up at MacLeod."

"How did that go, by the by?" Aulay asked now.

"Good," Geordie assured him. "The uncle ran the place into the ground with his gambling and such, so the people were more than glad to welcome Gavin as their proper laird. I think the thyftbote Evina's father had taken for Gavin in exchange for his silence on what Garret MacLeod did to Lady MacLeod helped. It should go a long way toward repairing the damage the uncle did. And Evina and Conran are going to help young Gavin find his feet as laird."

Aulay nodded, and then placed a hand on his shoulder and squeezed until Geordie met his gaze. "I ken ye've spent a lot of time the last several years helping the family, and I'm sure ye probably feel ye've lost out on some time to sow yer wild oats. I'm no' insisting ye marry right away. But it'll no' hurt to take a gander at the women and see if any o' them interest ye. Ye could always agree to a contract stipulating the wedding does no' take place for six months, or even a year from now, so ye have some time to sow those oats," he said, and then pointed out, "This is a golden opportunity fer ye, Geordie. Do ye choose any one o' the women at Buchanan just now, ye'd no' just be gaining a wife, but a keep and people o' yer own."

"Aye," Geordie murmured, and then frowned and asked, "How far away is Innes?"

Aulay's eyebrows rose with surprise, but he answered, "About as far away as MacDonnell, but 'tis northeast rather than straight north."

Geordie nodded thoughtfully.

"I did no' ken ye knew the Inneses," Aulay said after a moment.

"Oh, I do no'," he said, tugging his shirt off now, and tossing it to lie on his plaid.

"But when I said the Innes lasses slept in yer room last night, ye mentioned Dwyn," he pointed out with confusion.

"Nay. I do no' ken her," he assured him firmly.

"Ah, Dwyn," Acair sighed from Geordie's other side as he removed his own plaid. "Now there's a good wee lass with a fine pair o' bosoms to keep a man warm at night."

Geordie scowled at his uncle, but his words had brought up those bosoms in his mind. Dear God, when he'd looked down after her sisters had left the area, and seen her beautiful breasts pushing out of her gown above his arm . . . He swallowed as he recalled the sight. His mouth filling now with saliva as it had then, and his tongue tingling at the thought of rasping over the sweet nubs of her dusky nipples and sucking them into his mouth. Geordie still wasn't sure how he'd stopped himself from simply closing his hands over each full globe and kneading her sweet flesh. But he had.

Nothing could have stopped him from kissing her though, and damned if Dwyn hadn't kissed him back. The lass had been awkward at first, obviously unskilled, but she'd learned quickly, and the soft mewls and moans of pleasure she'd given him from just kissing had nearly pushed him into doing much more. When Geordie had started thinking about how to get her out of that tree without having to stop their kissing, so that he could tear her gown away, lay her in the grass and drive himself into her welcoming heat, he'd known it was time to put an end to things and get the hell away from her. He'd done that so abruptly . . . He hadn't even stayed to help her down from the tree, he realized with a frown.

"Well, ye say ye do no' ken her, but 'tis looking like ye want to," Aulay said dryly.

Geordie glanced at him with confusion, and then followed his gaze down to his groin where his cock was up, and waving around with excitement at the thoughts that had just been running through his mind. Cursing, he turned and strode into the icy water of the loch, then dove under the surface. Dwyn wasn't someone he could sow his oats with . . . but he wished she was.

"Well, now," Acair drawled as they watched Geordie swim away from shore. "Despite his claiming he's no' ready to marry yet, I'm thinking our boyo might be interested in wee Dwyn."

"Aye," Aulay agreed dryly. "So ye might want to refrain from commenting on her fine bosoms again. He did no' look pleased when ye mentioned them."

"That, or mayhap I should woo the lass meself," Acair said with a slow smile.

"What?" Aulay turned on him with surprise.

"Well, I'm a Buchanan too, lad. And unmarried as well as without a keep. I've a decade or two o' good years left in me and could muster up enough energy to plant a bairn or two in a woman's belly." Grinning suddenly, he added, "At least, that'll be me story to convince Geordie he has competition. 'Tis always good to make a lad think he's no' the only option a woman has. Makes him appreciate her more. Think on how it was with Dougall when the boys were all hankering to save Murine through marriage."

"Aye," Aulay said thoughtfully, and then shook his head. "So long as ye explain the way o' things to Mavis. Else the woman might kill ye both in her jealousy."

Acair stiffened. "Ye ken about Mavis and me?"

"O' course."

Acair frowned over that and glanced to Geordie. "Do ye think Geordie kens?"

"I doubt it," Aulay said after a moment, and then admitted, "I only ken because Jetta sorted it out and told me. I do no' think she's mentioned it to him. She'd protect yer privacy."

"Good," he said with satisfaction. "Then I'll pretend to woo the lass."

"What about Mavis?" Aulay asked. "Will ye explain things to her so she's no' jealous?"

Acair considered that briefly, and then shook his head. "Nay, 'tis best no' to tell her. Just in case Geordie does ken about her. He'll expect her to be jealous and me Mavis canno' lie to save her soul. Besides," he added dryly, "she's been a mite testy with me o' late, and I'm thinking it canno' hurt to remind her that I have other options too."

Aulay raised both eyebrows at this and shook his head. "Ye'll do as ye like, but it's me experience that there's nothing makes a woman more bitter or dangerous than being scorned by a lover. So I'd watch meself around her if ye do pretend to woo Dwyn."

Shrugging carelessly, Acair stripped off his shirt and followed Geordie into the water.

"There you are!"

Dwyn didn't bother to glance up from the book she'd been reading when her sisters burst into the bedchamber. But she gasped in surprise when Aileen snatched the book from her hand. Sitting up abruptly, she cried, "Do no' lose my page!"

"Oh, I willna," Aileen said with exasperation, slipping the bit of linen Dwyn kept as a place marker out of the front of the book, and laying it between the pages.

"Honestly, Dwyn," Una muttered, grabbing her hand and dragging her off the bed. "We've traveled days to get here and win ye a husband, and what do you do? Ye hide in the bedchamber and lie about reading books all day."

"'Tis crusading poems by Gille Brighde Albanach," Dwyn explained, watching worriedly until Aileen set it carefully on the table. "We do no' have that at Innes."

"We do no' have men there either. At least, no' the kind ye could marry, and that's what ye're here for," Una said firmly. "Now let me look at ye."

Sighing, Dwyn stood still under her sisters' inspection, unsurprised when they both began to frown.

"What are ye doing wearing that gown?" Una snapped.

"'Tis the only gown that I can breathe in without me bosoms popping out," Dwyn growled unhappily.

"Well, that is too bad. 'Tis what ye wore to travel here and is filthy. You canno' wear that to the evening meal," Una said firmly. "Aileen, fetch her a clean gown. That rose-colored one looks nice on her."

"Oh, nay," Dwyn cried, her eyes going wide with alarm. She'd tried on all her gowns once she'd managed to sneak back into the keep. Not one of the damned dresses fit, but the rose gown was the worst. If she took more than a shallow breath in it, her breasts popped up and out like a vole sticking its head out of its hole to look around.

"Oh, yes," Una said firmly. "It looks good with yer coloring. Speaking o' which—"

"Ow!" Dwyn jumped back and glared at her sister when she suddenly pinched her cheeks painfully.

"I was just trying to give ye more color," Una said with exasperation.

"Do no' be mad, Dwyn," Aileen said quietly, rushing over with the rose gown. "We are just trying to get you a husband. We both feel so bad that we are betrothed while you—"

"Fine," Dwyn interrupted on a sigh, and shook her head as she began to undo the lacings of the gown she was wearing. Her sisters, both younger than her, acted like it would be the end of the world if she did not marry. Neither of them could understand her attitude on the subject, and why she was not doing all she could to find a husband, but she knew her value. She was a good woman, and she wasn't ugly, at least she didn't think so. But she also wasn't pretty, not the sort of pretty to draw the eye when pitted against the much lovelier women here at Buchanan anyway. The only way she was likely to get a husband was if someone came to Innes and stayed for a while for some reason. Once they got to know her . . . Of course, that wasn't likely to happen, so she had resolved herself to being an old maid, or perhaps taking herself off to a nunnery someday in the future. But since it meant so much to her sisters, she would wear the rose dress . . . and hope she didn't faint from lack of air, or alternately humiliate herself and her family by having her breasts pop right out of it.

"There," Aileen said moments later as she finished helping with the lacings and stepped back to examine her critically.

"The dress looks lovely," Una said finally. "But . . ."

"Her hair," Aileen said for her, and the other girl nodded.

"Oh! No, wait!" Dwyn cried, reaching up to cover her head.

"Nay. Ye have lovely hair, sister. Ye should show it, no' keep it all pinned up on top o' yer head like— Oh," Una said with surprise as she pulled several pins from Dwyn's hair and the golden strands unraveled and fell down her back.

"My," Aileen breathed. "'Tis so long. When did it get so long?"

Una shook her head and moved away. "I'll get the brush."

"'Tis glorious, Dwyn," Aileen said solemnly, grasping several strands and pulling them out to the side before letting them feather away. "Why do ye never let it down? I do no' think I've seen it down in years, no' even when I've come to harass ye awake in the mornings."

"I never let it down," Dwyn said on an exasperated sigh. "'Tis curly and it gets terrible knots do I no' keep it up in a bun."

"'Tis too heavy to curl anymore. Now it just lies in lovely waves," Una announced, returning with a brush and handing it to Aileen to hold while she took out the thong that held Dwyn's hair in a ponytail. Once she had her long hair lying flat along her back, she began to brush it, but asked, "If ye do no' like it so long, why do ye no' cut it?"

Dwyn grimaced at the question. "Mother made me promise never to cut it. She said I would be grateful one day, but . . ." She shrugged.

"Oh, Catriona and Sasha are going to eat their own tongues when they see Dwyn like this," Aileen said with excitement as they took in the results of their efforts a few moments later.

"Aye," Una said with satisfaction, and then met Dwyn's gaze and said, "Ye look pretty."

Dwyn just shook her head. Her face was the same, it was only the frame that had changed. Her hair was just another distraction like her breasts. The only difference was, at least she could hide her breasts behind her hair if they popped out now.

Chapter 3

"Dear God in heaven."

Geordie glanced up from his ale at that exclamation from his uncle, and followed his gaze to the stairs where three women were descending. It took him a moment to recognize Dwyn's sisters, Una and Aileen. He didn't recognize the woman with them, but his gaze narrowed with interest as he took in her long, flowing hair. It was quite glorious, reaching down to her knees, a shiny curtain of pale gold that seemed to have a life of its own as it swished around her.

"With those breasts against his chest and that glorious hair wrapped around him, a man would be in heaven," Acair growled, and was suddenly on his feet, crossing the hall.

Geordie frowned, his gaze shifting to the blonde's breasts, and his eyes widened when he recognized that bosom. Large, full breasts were presently doing their best to escape the rose-colored gown they'd been stuffed into and he knew at once that it was Dwyn. Geordie then lifted his gaze to her face, almost embarrassed that it was her breasts he'd recognized first.

"Dwyn looks nice with her hair down, but why is Uncle Acair acting so strange?" Jetta asked next to him.

"He's decided to woo Dwyn," Aulay drawled with amusement.

"What?" Jetta asked in surprise.

"What!" Geordie exclaimed at the same time.

Aulay shrugged, his gaze focusing on Geordie as he said, "Ye said ye did no' ken her and were no' ready to settle down, and he's a single Buchanan male too. So he's decided he might like a keep o' his own."

"Oh," Jetta said with a frown. "I had not thought to include him, because, well, what about Mav—"

"Mavis," Aulay said abruptly, smiling over Geordie's shoulder, and he turned to find the older woman standing behind him, a pitcher of ale in hand and a hurt expression on her face as she watched Acair bow and raise Dwyn's hand for a kiss. The bow, incidentally, nearly rested the crown of his head against Dwyn's bosom, Geordie noted with displeasure.

"Oh, Mavis," Jetta said sympathetically, and he glanced around to see the old woman rushing away toward the doors to the kitchen, the full pitcher still in her hand. Jetta followed after her with concern on her face, and Geordie turned a scowl on his brother.

"Do no' look at me," Aulay protested, raising his hands. "I have done nothing."

"Ye ken Acair and Mavis—"

"I do," he acknowledged. "Though I did no' think anyone else knew."

"*Everyone* else knows," he said heavily.

"Aye, well, they are no' married, any more than you and wee Katie were."

"What does that mean?" Geordie asked, stiffening.

"Nothing," Aulay said at once, and sighed. "'Tis just that affairs with servants rarely last long, and Uncle Acair is a nobleman just as we are. There is no reason he canno' marry and become laird o' Innes if he wishes."

"Mavis is no' just a servant," Geordie argued. "She's been like a mother to us since our own mam died. Before that even. She was always like a second mother."

"But she was no' our mother, and she is no' married to Acair," Aulay said solemnly. "He is free to woo who he wishes."

Geordie opened his mouth to respond, but then paused as his uncle spoke beside him.

"Here ye go, lass. Ye just sit down here beside me and I'll have a servant fetch ye a drink."

Geordie turned to scowl at his uncle and asked spitefully, "Why do ye no' ask Mavis? She was here with ale just a moment ago."

"Well, she's no' here now, so— Katie, love!" he called, smiling past Geordie. "Prey, fetch this lovely lady a beverage, there's a good girl."

Geordie glanced over his shoulder in time to see the dark-haired maid rush away toward the kitchens. He turned back to peer at Dwyn. She seemed a bit flustered by his uncle's attention; her gaze was lowered shyly, but her face was almost the same color as her gown, and there was no missing the relief on her face when her sisters rushed up from speaking to their father farther down the table and took up position on her other side. They had to make Lady Catriona Lockhart and Lady Sasha Kennedy shove down the bench to create room for them, but the sister named Una had no compunction about making the request. Geordie was quite sure the other two women were about to protest—both of them got spiteful mean looks on their faces—but then, noting that he was watching, Catriona smiled and elbowed Sasha, urging her to the side before leaning to whisper in her ear. Sasha's eyes darted his way and then away and she moved along the bench.

Geordie grunted and made a note to himself to warn Alick and Rory about the pair. They were both lovely on the surface, but he'd pity any man who married either of them, and he was damned if he'd have one of those vipers in his family. What kind of woman made a sport of taunting and harassing another one? His brothers' wives would hate them.

"Here ye go, m'lady."

Geordie tore his gaze from Dwyn's flushed face, and glanced to Katie when the maid set a mug of ale before the lass. Seeing him watching, the maid offered him a sweet smile that he automatically returned, but it was Dwyn and Uncle Acair who thanked the girl before she hurried off.

"Geordie?" Aulay said now.

He saw Dwyn's eyes widen slightly as she heard his brother address him by name, and realized only then that he hadn't bothered to introduce himself in the tree that morning. He offered her an apologetic grimace for it, and then turned reluctantly to his brother, raising an eyebrow in question.

"Have ye had a chance to meet any of the ladies since arriving?"

A small sound of distress drew his gaze back around to Dwyn. She'd obviously heard the question and was afraid he might disclose what had happened between them that morning. Geordie gave her a reassuring look and then turned back to his brother. "Nay. Although I did see Lady Catriona and Lady Sasha in the orchard. They were chasing after one of the other women, taunting her, and then stopped to sneer at me when they saw me sleeping under a tree."

"Oh?" Aulay eyed the women briefly. "Good to know."

"They're Lowlanders," he pointed out with disgust. Lowlanders were nearly as bad as the English to his mind. You couldn't expect much from them.

"Oh, now, there's nothing wrong with Lowlanders," Uncle Acair said. "Just look at our lovely Dwyn here. She's a Lowlander too and a fine figure o' a woman."

Geordie frowned as he realized that was true. Innes was in the flatlands to the east of the mountains that made up the Highlands.

"Aye, and Innes is on the North Sea. Surely that makes up for not having our lovely mountains," Aulay suggested, offering Dwyn one of his rare smiles. Although they'd become much more common since the arrival of Jetta in his life, Aulay was still not used to company in his home. This was no doubt a trial for him, but he was making an effort, Geordie thought, and then glanced around as a maid responded to his uncle's wave and rushed over with a platter of food.

"Here ye go, lass." Uncle Acair turned to take the platter and held it in front of Dwyn. "What will ye have? Or shall I feed ye?"

When Dwyn's face flushed with embarrassment, Geordie scowled at his uncle. "Can ye no' see ye're embarrassing the lass? She can feed herself."

"Young men today, eh, Dwyn?" his uncle said lightly. "No romance in their soul. You stick with me, lovey. I'm a man who kens how to treat a woman."

Geordie glowered at the man, and then glanced around with a frown when he was suddenly elbowed in the side. Seeing that Aulay had shifted over into Jetta's empty spot and that he was the one who had jabbed him with his elbow, he raised his eyebrows. "What is it?"

"Ye growled," he murmured, keeping his voice down.

"What?" Geordie asked with disbelief.

"Ye did," Aulay assured him with amusement. "Ye growled at Uncle Acair like a dog whose bone is threatened. Are ye sure ye do no' ken Lady Innes?"

Mouth tightening, Geordie stood up.

"Where are ye going?" Aulay asked with interest.

"I'm no' hungry. I think I'll take a walk about the bailey," he muttered.

"Ye're no' going to get to know the women that way," Aulay pointed out with exasperation. "Me wife brought them here for ye, the least ye can do is talk to one or two and see if ye're the least bit interested."

"I am getting to know them," he assured him. "And I've already eliminated two. I would no' even want the Lockhart and Kennedy lasses in our family let alone me bed."

"Really? They are that bad?" Aulay asked, glancing along the table to the two women in question.

"Aye," Geordie assured him. "And if Rory or Alick pick them I'll no' be attending family occasions in future either." On that note, he stepped over the bench and strode quickly away from the table. He didn't slow until he was out of the keep and crossing the bailey. But he couldn't as easily escape the memory of his uncle making a fool of himself over Dwyn. The man was more than twice her age, by God. Which, he supposed, wasn't that unusual. Many an old man married much younger women. But Dwyn was a passionate little bundle and deserved a virile young man with a passion and energy to match her own. Someone more like him.

Cursing under his breath, Geordie started to walk more quickly, and then stopped when he heard his name called in a soft feminine voice. Geordie didn't question his disappointment when he saw that it was the maid Katie, but merely waited patiently for her to reach him.

"Lady Jetta suggested I pack ye some food fer yer walk in case ye get hungry," the lass said a little breathlessly, holding out a large sack to him. "I put some peaches, bread, cheese and meat in there fer ye."

"Thank ye, lass. Ye're a good girl," Geordie said on a sigh as he accepted the bag.

Katie beamed at the compliment and slid a little closer, her hand coming up to brush his chest gently. "Would ye like me to come with ye, m'laird? We could go to the loch fer a night swim."

Geordie raised his eyebrows at that. "I thought ye were spending time with Simon?"

She shrugged slightly, her hand gliding down his chest to his stomach and continuing lower. "I do on occasion, but I'm no' right now."

Geordie caught her hand just as it dropped below his waist. "Thank ye fer the kind offer, lass. But I think I'd just like to be alone with me thoughts right now."

Katie made a moue of disappointment, but released him and stepped back. "As ye wish, m'laird."

"Thank ye fer bringing me the food, lass," Geordie murmured, and then watched her make her way back to the keep doors before turning away. He paused then, unsure where he should go. He usually enjoyed a swim in the loch of an evening, but another swim didn't really appeal to him just now. He didn't feel like riding his horse either. Or seeking out one of the female servants or village lasses to pass time with.

Geordie glanced down at the sack of food in his hand, and then turned to walk around the keep toward the gardens in the back. He'd eat and then roll himself up in his plaid and make an early night of it. That seemed a good plan. He hadn't really got a lot of sleep last night before Dwyn and her pursuers had woken him shortly after dawn. He also hadn't had anything to eat that day. He'd avoided the nooning meal and spent the afternoon practicing at battle with the men in hopes of avoiding the women overrunning his home, only to find that they'd tracked him down there and were watching him cross swords with man after man.

Dwyn, he'd noticed, was the only female at the keep who hadn't been among them. For some reason that had disappointed Geordie and he'd soon grown tired of sparring. Sheathing his sword, he'd avoided the women again and collected his horse to ride out to the loch to wash away the dirt and sweat he'd accumulated from his efforts. He'd then dressed and returned for the evening meal, but hadn't had even a bite of the food circulating before irritation had sent him from the table.

His uncle was acting like an ass around Dwyn, Geordie thought irritably, but then pushed the thought away. It was like to give him indigestion. Best just to push any thoughts about his uncle, Dwyn and any of the other women from his mind and concentrate on relaxing so he could sleep after he ate.

"HERE NOW, LASS. EAT. YE'VE HARDLY TOUCHED YER FOOD. A bird eats more than ye have."

Dwyn tore her gaze away from the keep doors Geordie had disappeared through several minutes ago and forced a smile for the kind man at her side. She was sure Acair Buchanan was just paying attention to her to make her feel good, and while she appreciated the thought, she really disliked being made the focus of attention. Unfortunately, the way he was hovering over her and giving her loud compliments seemed to be gaining the interest of everyone else in the keep. The other women here to meet the single Buchanans were whispering and giggling among themselves while watching her with condescending smiles, and her father was looking concerned. As for everyone else . . . Well, she'd noted the strange looks the people of Buchanan were sending toward her and Acair Buchanan, and got the feeling that they either didn't like, or didn't approve of, the attention he was giving her.

"So, what do ye think o' our Geordie?"

Dwyn glanced to the older man with surprise at that question, and felt herself flush. "Oh. I— Well, I've only spoken to him once."

"Did ye now?" he asked with interest. "And when was that?"

"This morning," she admitted, ducking her head to peer down at the food on her trencher.

"This morning, eh? And where was this?"

"In the orchard," Dwyn murmured, toying with the chicken leg Acair had put in her trencher. "I had climbed a tree to escape—well, to find a moment alone—and he . . . I think he thought I was stuck up there," she realized suddenly as she recalled his offers to help her down. Shrugging, she added, "He climbed up and we talked a bit, and then—" Realizing she was babbling a lot more information than she probably should, Dwyn snapped her mouth closed.

"And then what, lass?" Acair asked gently.

Dwyn swallowed, and then said, "And then he climbed down and I continued to sit there for a while."

"So, there was no—"

"Acair?"

Frowning, he broke off his question and glanced around.

Curious as to who had saved her from what she suspected might be an embarrassing question from a man she feared was far too discerning for her good, Dwyn glanced around as well and saw Lady Buchanan moving toward them. Once Jetta had their attention, she stopped walking, smiled crookedly at Dwyn, but then waved Acair over to her.

"Excuse me, lass. I'm needed, I guess," Acair murmured, and stood to move to the pretty dark-haired lady.

Dwyn watched as the couple talked. She couldn't hear much of what was said, but caught the name "Mavis," and something about crying, and then Acair followed Lady Buchanan to the kitchens.

"Did ye lose yer beau?"

Dwyn turned to peer at Catriona at that taunt. Her sisters were down the table talking to their father, and Catriona and Sasha had slid closer, taking up the space again, she saw. Ignoring them, she turned to her food, but her appetite was suddenly gone.

"Well, cheer up, I'm sure he'll return, and at least *someone* is interested in you," Catriona said with a cruel gleam in her eye.

"Aye," Sasha added, leaning around Catriona to add, "And an old Buchanan is better than no Buchanan. 'Tis certainly more than I expected ye to manage, *Whinnie*."

"Ladies, a word. Please?"

Dwyn glanced around quickly at those sharp words from Aulay, but he wasn't looking at her. His steely gaze was focused on Catriona and Sasha as he stood up.

For a moment, both women looked frozen, but then Catriona stood, dragging Sasha up by the elbow with her. "Of course, m'laird."

Dwyn watched them go with wide eyes, and then noted that everyone was looking at her again. Flushing, she stood up as well.

"Where are they going?" Aileen asked, rushing back to her side.

"I do no' ken. Laird Buchanan said he wanted to speak to them," she said uncomfortably.

"Were they picking on ye again?" Una asked at once. "Did he hear?"

Dwyn shrugged helplessly, and started to move past them.

"Where are ye going?" Aileen asked with concern, catching her hand to stop her.

"To the garderobe," Dwyn muttered, tugging her hand free and slipping away from the table. But she didn't go to the garderobe. She bypassed the small door and weaved her way around to the keep doors instead.

Relief washed through her as she stepped out into the cool night air. She hated being the cynosure of attention, especially when she got the feeling she'd done something wrong but didn't know what, and that was how she'd felt under the disapproving eyes of the people of Buchanan.

Shaking her head, Dwyn descended the steps of the keep, and then wandered around the side of the building to make her way back to the gardens behind the keep. More specifically, she was headed for her tree. That's how she'd started to think of it. She'd climbed that tree three times now since arriving at Buchanan and it had served her well all three times. People never looked up. Dwyn had learned that years ago as a small child of five when she'd climbed her first tree. Her mother and the maids had looked for her for hours and she'd sat in the tree, watching, but never making a sound. Mind you, she'd got her bottom paddled when she'd finally made her way down and her mother had found her, but it hadn't stopped her from climbing back up that tree the next time she wanted to escape whatever was happening in Innes.

Of course, Geordie had looked up this morning, but she suspected he must have seen her climb up first. A small smile curved her lips as she recalled that he'd offered to help her down. She could hardly believe the man she'd been talking to and who had kissed her was Geordie Buchanan. Dwyn shook her head at the thought, and recalled his surprise when she'd explained why the house was full of guests. He hadn't seemed to know anything about what was happening, and she wondered now what he thought of the whole business of finding him a bride. She suspected not much since he wasn't being very cooperative. The man had made himself scarce all day and then walked out of the great hall at dinner.

Dwyn couldn't blame him. She wouldn't like half a dozen or more men and their families showing up at Innes purely in the hopes that she'd pick them to husband. Her sisters would probably like that, but she wouldn't. Dwyn liked a nice quiet life. She went about her business, doing what needed to be done and waving away any thanks or compliments she received for it. She didn't do it for gratitude or to impress people; she just did what she felt should be done because it was her duty.

The sound of a door opening drew her to a halt as she rounded the back corner of the keep. Dwyn glanced warily toward the door, half expecting to see one of her sisters or both, or perhaps even Lady Catriona and Lady Sasha, rushing out in search of her. Spotting the small, dark-haired maid who stepped out with a basket in hand, she offered a smile and then left her to her business and started along the garden path toward the trees at the back.

Dwyn loved a garden in the evening. The sun was low in the sky, and darkness was falling, but she could still see well enough to avoid trampling on plants or vegetables. Once at the back, she turned into the trees, moving past the peach trees to the larger cherry trees beyond them. She glanced around quickly once she reached her tree, and then quickly scrambled upward, but came to an abrupt halt and nearly tumbled back down when she went to put her hand on a branch and felt soft leather rather than hard wood. It was only a firm hand catching her upper arm that kept her from a nasty fall.

"Careful, lass."

Raising her head, Dwyn blinked at Geordie through the growing gloom and then hesitated. Like everyone else, she hadn't looked up, she realized, or she surely would have realized her spot was occupied and would not have climbed up.

"I'm sorry, m'laird," she said after a moment. "I did no' realize anyone was up here. I'll leave and—"

"Nay," Geordie interrupted, urging her up with his hold on her arm. "Ye're welcome to join me. It was yer tree first, after all."

When she hesitated, undecided, he added, "I have food."

Dwyn blinked in confusion at the words.

"Jetta sent one o' the maids after me with a sack o' food, but they packed enough bread, cheese, meat and peaches for two or three people," he said with amusement. "Ye're welcome to join me."

That decided her. Dwyn loved peaches and she hadn't eaten much at dinner, so she continued climbing until she could settle on the branch across from him. The very same branch she'd been on when he found her there earlier, she realized. And he was on the branch he'd claimed earlier too, she thought, and wondered if he'd kiss her again as she watched him untie a heavy sack that hung from a thick branch just above him.

"What would ye like first?" Geordie asked, setting the sack in his lap and opening it to peer inside.

"Whatever's on top," Dwyn said with a shrug, and watched as he reached in and pulled out a chicken leg. Smiling, she accepted the offering and took a bite as she watched him pull out a second leg for himself.

"Legs are me favorite," Geordie announced, adjusting the sack so that it was safe in his lap and not likely to tumble off.

"Mine too," Dwyn admitted after swallowing what was in her mouth. "Dark meat is always moist."

"Aye," he agreed, and then fell silent as they ate their chicken. He was done with his leg first, but waited until she finished and then held out his hand.

Dwyn hesitated, but when his fingers wiggled in a "give it here" motion she gave him the stripped chicken bone and watched him toss both her bone and his toward the wall. She saw them sail through the branches unhindered, but wasn't sure they'd made it over the wall until a wet splash reached her ears. They'd landed in the moat beyond the wall.

"Ah. Cheese and bread."

Dwyn glanced back toward him, but it had grown darker while they ate and he was just a dark shadow in front of her.

"Put yer hand out," he instructed, apparently understanding the problem.

Dwyn reached out, felt his hand bump hers, and then he placed a hunk of bread and a smaller hunk of cheese in her palm. She pulled them toward herself, murmuring, "Thank ye."

"Me pleasure," Geordie assured her, and she heard a rustle as he dug in the bag again.

"So, tell me, do ye often hang about in trees?" Geordie asked lightly as he resituated the bag in his lap.

She smiled faintly at the teasing question, but pointed out, "You were here first."

"This time," he agreed.

Dwyn shrugged, but then realizing he might not have seen that in the darkening night, she said, "Aye. I like trees. They do no' pinch me cheeks to try to force color into them, and make me wear dresses better suited to a lightskirt."

Geordie laughed at that, a very nice, deep rumble of sound that made her grin and shiver all at once. When his laughter faded, he said, "Una seems . . ."

"Pushy?" she suggested, and then added, "Bossy? Bold?"

"Aye," he chuckled. "She certainly had no problem making Catriona and Sasha move along the bench to make room for her and Aileen to sit beside ye."

"Aye," Dwyn agreed, and explained, "Una is very protective of me, which is strange, because I took over mothering her when her own mother died. I was always the one protecting her then. But now, the roles seem to have reversed and she natters after me like she is the mother."

"Ye said her own mother?" he queried. "Do ye no' have the same mother?"

Dwyn shook her head, and then said, "Nay. Me mother died when I was six."

"How did she die?" Geordie asked, his voice sounding solemn.

"Trying to birth me little brother or sister," she said sadly. "After me she lost several babes ere they were full ready to be born, but this one survived to the birthing. Unfortunately, the healer said it was turned wrong inside her. Mother labored for three days trying to push the babe into the world and just could no' do it. She died with it still in her."

"I'm sorry," Geordie said softly.

"So am I," Dwyn admitted solemnly. "She was a good mother and I missed her terribly. But about a year later Father married Una and Aileen's mother, Lady Rhona. She was kind to me. Una was born nine months after that, and Aileen followed two years later. Unfortunately, Lady Rhona died a couple days after Aileen was born. An infection, the healer said."

"From the birth," Geordie said without a hint of doubt, and then clucked his tongue impatiently. "So many women die while trying to bring new life into the world. 'Tis how most men lose their wives."

"And most women lose their men to battle," Dwyn pointed out quietly.

"But me brother Rory says many o' the women die unnecessarily. That it's ignorance and a lack o' cleanliness that cause the death."

"And ye do no' think death in battle could be avoided?" she asked dryly. "If you men were no' so eager to rush off to battle, we'd lose a lot less men."

"Aye," Geordie allowed. "But a good man canno' stand idly by and allow evil to grow and spread across the land."

They both fell silent for a moment and concentrated on eating, but once the cheese and bread were gone, she heard the rustle as he dug in the bag again, and then he asked, "How old are yer sisters?"

"Una is sixteen, and Aileen fourteen," she answered. "And both o' them act twice that."

Geordie chuckled and then said, "So ye've seen twenty-four years?"

Dwyn stilled with surprise, and then realized that he'd worked it out from what she'd told him. Clearing her throat, she said, "I will be in a month."

"Ah. Put yer hand out," he ordered, and when she did he found it and placed a round, cool peach into it, and then asked, "How long ago did yer betrothed die?"

"Seven years ago," she answered, and then raised the peach to take a bite. A soft "mmm" of pleasure slid from her throat as her mouth filled with the sweet juice and peach meat.

"Good?"

Dwyn opened eyes she'd closed in pleasure, and peered at his dark shape. His voice had sounded husky, and she wondered why, but said, "Aye. Very. Peaches are the loveliest fruit . . . Except for the mess they make," she added as she felt a trail of liquid slide down her hand. "I do no' suppose they put a scrap o' linen in the bag or something?"

"I'm afraid no'," Geordie said on a chuckle. "Ye'll just have to lick away the juices."

"That's no' very ladylike," she said primly.

"Lass, ye're up a tree," he pointed out with amusement. "Is that very ladylike?"

"'Tis if ye do no' get caught," Dwyn assured him.

Geordie burst out in laughter at that, and she smiled at the sound as she ate her peach. When the laughter faded, he commented, "Ye're an interesting woman, Dwyn Innes."

"Aye," she agreed easily. "Una is always telling me I'm a strange one."

"I said interesting, no' strange," he protested.

"Is it no' the same thing?" Dwyn asked innocently, and he chuckled again. They stopped talking then to concentrate on their peaches, and the night was filled with chomping and slurping sounds as they did their best to eat the fruits without getting completely covered with the sticky juice. At least, that's what Dwyn was trying to do, but her peach was so ripe and bursting with the sweet liquid, she feared she'd made a terrible mess. Certainly her hand was wet and sticky when she was done.

"Here," Geordie said suddenly when she'd finished. "Give me yer pit and I'll put the sack in yer hand in its place. Ye can use the sack to mop up the mess."

"How do ye ken I made a mess?" she asked archly. "Mayhap I managed to not make a mess."

"Aye, mayhap," he allowed. "But ye did make a mess, did ye no'?" he asked, and she could hear the grin in his voice.

"Aye," Dwyn admitted on a sigh, and held out the peach pit. "I think I even got some juice in me hair."

Chuckling again, Geordie found her hand in the dark, took

the peach pit and replaced it with the cloth sack. Dwyn quickly wiped her hands, listening as he tossed the pits the way of the chicken bones and the splashes followed.

"Tell me what it's like at Innes." His voice came out of the darkness, deep and soft as the night air.

"Innes," Dwyn sighed the name, wishing she was there. "'Tis flat compared to your Buchanan, but lovely just the same."

"What's lovely about it?"

"The water," she said at once. "I miss the water when I'm away from Innes."

"Do ye spend a lot o' time by the water?"

"Oh, aye, I take Angus and Barra and we walk the beach often."

"Who are Angus and Barra?" he asked at once, his voice sharp in the night.

"My dogs," Dwyn explained. "They're brothers, a mix o' boarhound and deerhound. They're both big boys."

"Boarhound and deerhound?"

She could hear the surprise in his voice and grinned. "Aye. Their mother was a deerhound me father gave me when I was fifteen. I loved her to bits, but so did one o' me da's boarhounds," she said dryly. "She had a litter three years ago and I kept two o' the boys. Da likes me to keep them with me when I leave the keep. As protection. They're both quite ferocious and protective o' me," she added, and then hesitated before asking, "Yer parents are both passed, are they no'?"

"Aye. Me father died in battle some years back, and me mother o' illness well before that." He was silent for a minute, and then added, "Mother's dying is why Rory became interested in healing. We all felt so helpless watching her ail and unable to help her, but he took it the hardest."

"He has become well known for his skills," she said, not hiding her admiration. Dwyn had some skill at healing, but Rory Buchanan was considered almost a miracle healer by many. He was much in demand with lairds from the Highlands to the Lowlands offering him a king's ransom to tend their ill loved ones. She'd heard even the English were starting to send requests, though he apparently didn't care to travel that far south. Peering at Geordie's dark silhouette, she asked, "I suppose that is why he is no' here?"

"Aye," he almost snapped, irritated by the admiration he heard in her voice for his brother. Realizing that he was acting like a jealous ass, he added in a more normal tone, "And Alick, our youngest brother, is with him. They should return shortly . . . unless they get word of what awaits them here," he added dryly. "Then they might find a need to stay away much longer to save themselves."

"Save themselves?" she asked with amusement. "Do men no' wish to marry, then? I understood all yer older brothers are married. Are they no' happy?"

"Aye, they are, and they have fine wives, all of them," he admitted solemnly, and then grinned and added, "I do no' think I've ever seen me brothers so content as they are now they've found their wives. And they are all busy making me nieces and nephews. Me sister, Saidh, has already had two sets o' twins, the first lasses, and the second a fine pair o' lads. And then Dougall and Niels each have a bairn and another on the way, and Conran's wife, Evina, is now with child too."

"Ah," Dwyn said, smiling faintly, but said, "And yet it does no' sound as though ye want marriage and bairns fer yerself."

"Do you?" Geordie countered.

Dwyn considered that seriously, before saying, "Most women do, I should think. We are raised preparing for the day we marry and have a home o' our own, a husband to care for and bairns to love and raise as we were raised."

"So ye do?" he asked.

She grimaced wryly into the darkness, but it was that very darkness that allowed her to answer honestly. "I am no' sure. I have many fears about that."

"What kind of fears?" he asked with interest.

"Well, I used to fear the marriage bed," she admitted, blushing despite the darkness, and then rushed on. "But despite that, I still liked to imagine a life with a husband who cares for me, and a dozen sweet children running about. But me mother and second mother both died giving birth, and I fear dying that way too," she confessed. "I suppose, sometimes I think mayhap I was lucky me betrothed died and did no' come to claim me. I might already have died on the birthing bed if he had."

Geordie was silent for a minute, but then said, "Ye said ye used to fear the marriage bed?"

"Aye, well." She grimaced. "'Tis said 'tis unpleasant and painful and such. Hardly something a lass would look forward to."

"But ye said you *used* to," he pointed out. "As if ye no longer fear it?"

"Oh." Blushing, she peered at his dark shape, and then feeling brave in the darkness, she admitted, "Well, yer kisses this morn made me think mayhap the marriage bed could no' be all bad. Whatever follows the kisses may be a bit o' a trial, but might be worth it to enjoy the kissing."

Geordie was silent so long Dwyn began to think she'd angered him with her words, which hadn't been her intention. In truth, she suspected her honesty had been in hopes that he might want to kiss her again, but that obviously wasn't going to happen. He'd seen how lovely the other women available to him were. Why kiss her when there were so many other, prettier—

Her thoughts died abruptly when his lips suddenly covered hers.

Chapter 4

Dwyn was so surprised that she froze like a hare spotting a hunter when Geordie's mouth first covered hers. It was so dark now she hadn't realized he had even moved. But that darkness didn't prevent his finding her mouth, and after a moment, she breathed out a little sigh against his lips as they moved over hers. It was just a feathering touch he gave her at first, his lips brushing, drifting away and then brushing again. It was quite sweet, and gentle, and Dwyn smiled under his mouth, her eyes closing as she leaned forward to press her mouth more firmly against his. The moment she did, she felt Geordie's tongue slide along her lower lip. When she parted to allow it entrance, he caught her lower lip between his and sucked gently, then let his tongue glide into her waiting mouth.

Moaning in response, Dwyn twined her arms around his neck and kissed him back, shyly meeting his tongue rather than retreat, and sucking on it as well, inviting it deeper into her mouth. She heard the low growl that came from his throat, and all the gentle teasing stopped abruptly as he tangled his hand in her long hair and used it to shift her head so that his mouth slanted over hers, his tongue now thrusting with demand, conquering rather than exploring.

Dwyn groaned in response. Forgetting they were sitting in a tree, she tightened her arms around his neck, and wiggled forward, trying to get closer. She was reminded of their precarious situation when her behind slid right off the branch and she started to drop. Before she could do more than gasp into his mouth,

Geordie curled his arm around her, catching her upper body firmly to his chest, but leaving her hips and legs dangling between his knees as he continued to kiss her.

With her breasts straining against his chest and a cool breeze gliding up her legs under her hanging skirts, Dwyn tightened her arms around his neck and moaned into his mouth. The long low sound seemed to invigorate Geordie and she heard him growl deep in his throat as his mouth became more demanding on hers, his tongue thrusting almost violently now.

When he suddenly broke the kiss, Dwyn moaned again, but this time with disappointment. She feared he was about to set her back on her branch and leave as he had that morning, but instead he shifted his hands to catch her by the waist and lift her as his mouth settled on her neck and began to nibble and suck the tender flesh. A startled gasp slipping from her lips at the tingling that sent through her, Dwyn tilted her head to give him more room to work, her hands clutching at his shoulders now.

"Put yer knees on either side o' me, lass." The words were mumbled against her throat as he nipped and suckled there, and Dwyn obeyed automatically, raising her legs to brace them on the branch on either side of his hips so that she was astride him.

"Aye, that's it," he growled against her skin, and she felt one hand clasp her bottom and squeeze as he urged her forward until she could feel something hard pressing against her core. It sent a startling rush of excitement and need pouring through her. They both groaned, and then Geordie used his other hand to urge her upper body back so that he could peer at her.

Feeling his warm breath on her chest, Dwyn glanced down, not terribly surprised to see that her breasts were doing a good job of escaping her dress again. Her white skin seemed almost to glow in the darkness, she noted, and then watched her breasts rise even farther out of her gown as his head bent toward them, drawing a gasp from her. His head blocked her view, but Dwyn felt his mouth move over one breast, nipping, and then sucking eagerly at the top curve, before dropping so that his tongue could run wet and warm along her neckline. It glided over the curve of one round globe, before reaching and pausing on the nipple now just poking over the top.

Dwyn gasped as she felt his teeth gently catch the hardening tip, and then moaned when he tugged, urging it farther out from under the cloth, but she released a long low groan when he began to suckle on it. His mouth drew hungrily on the sensitive nipple, sucking even as his tongue lathed, and Dwyn threw her head back and cried out, her fingers digging into the cloth covering his shoulders as the action sent excitement and pleasure whipping through her.

Geordie let her nipple slip loose then, and raised his head again, one hand moving to tangle in the hair behind her head as he drew her face down for another kiss. Dwyn kissed him back almost desperately, her wet nipple tingling in the cool night air, until his hand covered it, the rough skin of his fingers abrading it and sending more shocks of excitement through her as he palmed and kneaded her eager flesh.

When he broke their kiss again, and growled, "I want to see ye," she released a small laugh. It was too dark to see much of anything, Dwyn was sure, but didn't protest when he urged her upper body back until she leaned against the branch she'd been sitting on, her body now splayed before him.

"Beautiful," Geordie growled, and she glanced down with confusion to see that the moon was up now, lightening the darkness and leaving her pale skin visible where the rose gown didn't cover her. Both breasts were fully out, the neckline caught beneath them and pushing them together and up as if offering them to him.

When Geordie took up the offer and closed his hands over them both, squeezing and urging them even tighter together, Dwyn let her head fall back. She closed her eyes, only to have them pop open again as she lifted her head with confusion when he pressed a gentle kiss to first one nipple, and then the other, before tugging the cloth up to cover them.

"We should get ye back inside." The words were a pained growl that sounded almost reluctant, but that didn't ease her disappointment. Obviously, he hadn't been enjoying their interlude as much as she had, Dwyn supposed sadly, and then gasped in surprise when he caught her at the waist and set her back on her branch.

"I'll go first and help ye down," Geordie said, and suddenly slid out of sight.

Leaning forward, she watched him climb quickly to the ground and then peer back up at her expectantly. Dwyn hesitated, but then sighed and found handholds and started to climb down on her own, reassuring herself that surely it was dark enough he couldn't really see up her skirt as she feared.

She was halfway down and searching blindly for a lower foothold when she felt his hand on her ankle under her skirts. Dwyn froze briefly, until he shifted her foot to a branch, and then she made herself continue down, her heartbeat tripping when his hand stayed there, moving up the side of her leg as she climbed lower. She stopped again though when his hand reached her outer thigh.

"M'laird?" Dwyn said then, her voice shaky with the queer feelings racing through her.

Dwyn thought he groaned then, but the hand was removed. Releasing a small sigh, she started to move again, only to suck in a quick startled breath when he caught her at the waist and lifted her down. Her feet had barely touched the ground when he spun her around, urged her back against the tree and kissed her again. It was a quick, hard, almost punishing kiss, and Dwyn didn't even get the chance to recover enough from her surprise to begin to kiss him back when he suddenly ended it and stepped back.

"Ye'd best go in now, lass. They'll be looking fer ye." His voice was deep, and rough, and made goose bumps rise on her skin, but she murmured assent and whirled, her long hair flying out. Dwyn felt a brief tug at her head as she started away, as if her hair had caught on something, but then she was free. She didn't glance back as she hurried through the trees; she wasn't even really looking forward. Mostly she was looking inward, her mind pulling up his kisses and caresses and the feelings they'd engendered in her. If she'd been looking where she was going, she wouldn't have crashed into the man on the path.

Gasping, Dwyn stepped back abruptly and would have stumbled over her own feet had Aulay Buchanan not reached out to steady her.

"Careful, lass. 'Tis dark enough to make the uneven path treacherous," he said gently.

"Aye," Dwyn breathed, and offered a shaky smile as he released her.

"What were ye running from?" he asked before she could skirt around him and hurry away. "Were those lasses giving ye trouble again?"

Dwyn's eyes widened at the displeasure on his face, but she shook her head quickly. "Nay, m'laird. I was just . . ." She gestured vaguely behind her, unable to answer. She could hardly tell him what she was running from when she didn't know herself. There had been no reason to run. Geordie had not given chase or threatened her in any way. But once he'd stopped touching and kissing her and said she should go, she'd hurried away and then broken into a run as if the devil himself was chasing her. That was something she didn't understand herself. Especially since she'd really rather have stayed there with him. Perhaps if she had he would have kissed her again. Maybe he would have bared and touched her breasts again too, something she'd found incredibly pleasurable, which was rather surprising to her. Dwyn had never thought them useful for anything but feeding a bairn. She was learning a new appreciation for the silly large things, and beginning to understand that perhaps men didn't like them merely because it meant their bairns would be well fed.

Aware that Aulay was staring down at her, waiting for a response, she sighed and shook her head. "I just thought I should go inside before me father started to worry."

"Ah. I will no' keep ye, then." Nodding, he straightened and stepped to the side, but then added, "Howbeit if those lasses trouble ye again, ye've but to tell me. I've warned them to behave else I'll send them on their way, and will no' hesitate to do so do they bother ye again."

"Oh." Dwyn stared up at him wide-eyed. "That's . . . er . . . Thank ye, m'laird, but ye needn't . . . I mean, I would no' want ye sending them away on me account. What if one o' yer brothers desire them to wife?"

"If they do, they're no' the men I think they are," he assured her. "In fact, I suspect the two women are doing naught but taking up space here. I'd send them away altogether except I did no' wish to humiliate them that way. But I will if they ignore me warning and continue to harass yerself or any o' the other women."

"Thank ye, m'laird." Tipping her head, she smiled faintly and said, "Ye're a kind man, m'laird."

Aulay Buchanan snorted at that. "Away with ye, lass. I'm no' kind. Have ye no' heard? I'm a monster, more like to make women and children weep and scream than anything else."

Dwyn's eyes widened in surprise, but then she recalled the tales she'd heard of the fierce warrior and his ruined face. The tales were all exaggerated, she'd decided when she saw him. While the man had a scar that almost divided his face in half, it wasn't nearly as bad as she'd been led to believe, and she thought he was still an attractive man. That being the case, Dwyn snorted right back at his claim, and said, "Oh, aye, m'laird. Why, just look at yer wife. Lady Jetta is obviously terrified o' ye."

Aulay grinned at her teasing. "Me wife does no' have the sense to be afraid."

"Then we should get along well," she assured him. "Because I do no' fear ye either."

"And I hope ye never have reason to, lass," he said solemnly, and before she could think too hard on that, he added, "Now, ye'd best go in, Dwyn. Yer father and sisters will be looking fer ye."

Dwyn clucked with irritation at that, and moved around him muttering, "You Buchanan men, ye do like to order me inside."

She was so exasperated Dwyn didn't notice the way his eyebrows rose or that his gaze then slid to search the depths of the gardens as she walked away.

GEORDIE TURNED FROM WATCHING DWYN DISAPPEAR DOWN THE garden path and let a small sigh slide from his lips. She was a tempting little bundle. He could still see her lying back across the branch, her bare breasts arched upward invitingly, her pale skin glowing in the darkness. He could feel her soft skin under his fingers, taste her on his tongue, and again felt the urge he'd had then to drag her to the ground, throw her skirts up and plant himself in her eager body.

Dwyn would have been eager, Geordie had no doubt. There was no subterfuge with this woman. She'd admitted she'd liked his kisses, and had responded honestly to his every caress, shuddering, sighing and moaning in his arms, her nails digging into his shoulders and urging him on, unintentionally stirring his own desires to a fever pitch.

Aye, Geordie thought, Dwyn would have opened eagerly to him, spreading her legs and taking his hard shaft into her body, welcoming it and openly enjoying the passion he could show her. He had no doubt he could make her beg with her need and then scream when he gave her the satisfaction her body cried for. It was the after, when her need was slaked and her passion cooled, that the problems would begin. She would be full of regret and shame then, he was sure, and he hadn't been able to do that to her. But she would never know how close he came to taking her anyway. It had required determination and grit to set her back on her branch and cover those lovely breasts. And then when she'd climbed down the tree . . .

Geordie opened his eyes and peered up the tree again, recalling the view he'd had of her legs all the way to her knees before the shadows had hidden the rest of her naked legs and the spot where they met under her gown. He'd only grabbed her ankle to help direct her on her climb down, but once he'd touched her, he hadn't been able to make himself let go. He'd let his hand glide up that smooth, pale skin as she'd descended, and had even stepped under her skirts, his head lifting, eyes trying to pierce the darkness and his mouth filling with saliva as he contemplated kissing her inner knees, and then her thighs, and then tasting her . . .

Dwyn's shaky "m'laird" had startled him out of his dark fantasies, and he'd released her with a groan, and then had caught her by the waist and lifted her down to end his torment. Geordie hadn't been able to resist kissing her then though, but had allowed himself only a brief hard kiss before setting her away, knowing that if she'd responded even the least little bit, he'd have her on the ground with her skirts over her head in no time.

Geordie turned away from the tree, his hand rising to run over his face where her hair had flown up and caught in the stubble when she'd turned away. It had been strands of gold silk against his skin, and he'd instinctively caught it, briefly contemplating pulling her back to him, before his good sense had made him release the golden tresses.

His uncle's words returned to him. *"With those breasts against his chest and that glorious hair wrapped around him, a man would be in heaven."* As much as he resented the man even thinking about that when it came to Dwyn, his uncle was right. He couldn't imagine anything more heavenly than having a naked Dwyn astride him, her long golden hair hanging around them like a curtain and feathering across his skin as she rode him, her hot, tight body squeezing his cock and her generous breasts hanging above his mouth for him to suckle and lathe as she moved against him. But he'd also like to have her on her hands and knees before him, so he could tangle his hands in that long hair and use the golden strands as reins as he plunged into her from behind.

A painful aching drew Geordie's attention down to where an erection was pressing against the cloth of his plaid and he grimaced at how he was tormenting himself with his own thoughts. He briefly considered finding Katie or one of the other maids to ease his condition, but the idea held no appeal. He knew he'd close his eyes and want to pretend it was Dwyn he was thrusting into, and they'd talk and spoil the delusion. Of course, he could let them ease his discomfort with their mouth, Geordie thought. They couldn't talk then, and he could close his eyes and imagine it was Dwyn on her knees before him, her long golden hair curling around her breasts and her beautiful blue eyes peering up at him as she took him into her mouth and sucked, and licked, and—

"I'm glad to see ye obviously did no' use that on Dwyn, but ye might wish to find a more private spot for such sport."

Geordie stiffened at those words, his head jerking around to see Aulay approaching through the dark. It took a moment though for his mind to process his words, and then he glanced down and tore his hand away from the erection he hadn't realized he'd been pumping and let his plaid fall back into place. Christ, he'd been pleasuring himself like an untried lad as he'd enjoyed his imaginings. He hadn't done that in years. A lot of years. There was little need when there were always so many willing lasses around to tend to it.

"I am right? Ye did no' use that on Lady Innes, did ye?" Aulay asked now as he stopped before him.

"Nay, o' course not," Geordie growled with disgust. "She's a lady, no' a lightskirt."

"Aye. I'm glad ye did no' forget that," Aulay said. "But I gather ye're finding yerself more interested in her than ye realized?"

Geordie merely turned to walk deeper into the trees, contemplating his question. Oh, aye, he was interested, all right, and his aching cock was proof of that. In truth, Geordie had never met a woman who could set him to aching like she did . . . and he had no idea why she affected him so. Dwyn wasn't especially pretty. She wasn't plain though, as she seemed to think. But she was no raving beauty. And while she had large breasts, they weren't the first large breasts he'd encountered. He'd held and fondled many a set of fine bosoms, but had never been as enthralled by them as he was with Dwyn's. In truth, her breasts not only made him want to lick and suckle her there, they made him want to explore every inch of her with his mouth and tongue. He wanted to kiss and taste the backs of her knees, the inside of her thighs, and he wanted to lick her—

"Well?" Aulay asked, interrupting another round of his tormenting himself. "Are ye interested in her or no'? Because if ye are, ye'd best do something about it ere Uncle Acair beats ye to it."

"She's no' interested in Uncle Acair," he said with certainty, knowing she couldn't shiver and moan in his arms if her interest were elsewhere. Quite sure he was right about that, Geordie dropped to sit on the ground in the spot where he'd slept the night before and spread out to lie on his side, hoping Aulay would take the hint and go away.

Instead, his brother crossed his arms, eyed him from above and pointed out, "It does no' matter what her interests are if Uncle Acair goes to her father and negotiates a marriage contract. She'll marry who her father says as every lass must."

Geordie sat up abruptly at that, alarm coursing through him. "Did Uncle Acair say he planned to talk to her father?"

Aulay hesitated but then grudgingly said, "No' yet. But that is the next step if he's truly interested in wedding the lass and gaining a keep."

Geordie scowled with irritation at that. "Dwyn is a fine woman. She deserves more from a husband than an old man whose only interest is in her father's keep."

"Uncle Acair would hardly tell her that," Aulay pointed out dryly. "He's a good man. He'll treat her kindly and keep her busy with bairns. She'd be . . . content."

Geordie snorted at that. Content. How could a woman as passionate as Dwyn be content with an old man interested only in her keep? She was a smart lass. She'd sense that right quick if she hadn't already. But, he acknowledged, Dwyn wouldn't have a choice if his uncle negotiated a contract with her father. She'd have to marry him, and then Geordie was quite sure she'd make the best of things and become one of those pleasant, meek women who fade into their husbands' shadow, always doing their duty, never complaining and never really smiling or even frowning, just moving through life untouched by any real emotion.

It was where she was already headed, Geordie realized now. She hid away in trees or his room, reading. At least, that was what she'd done today. Uncle Acair had asked where she was when they'd returned from swimming at the loch, and Jetta had said Dwyn had asked to borrow one of the books from Aulay's study and had slipped away to her room to read.

Aye. Left to her own devices, Dwyn would fade away to a shadow, and the very thought made him angry. That would be a crying shame. The lass was a bundle of passion, ready to explode under the right touch, and he was quite sure his uncle wasn't the proper man to bring that about. She needed a younger man, someone with a matching passion. Someone like him.

But did he want to be the one to do it? In truth, Geordie did, and if Dwyn weren't a lady, he already would have. But she *was* a lady. Now he had to sort out if he wanted her enough to marry her. His aching cock was saying aye, but his mind was not so sure. He barely knew the lass. Besides, he really had looked forward to going out drinking and wenching with Alick when he came home. Neither of which seemed very interesting to him next to tumbling Dwyn just at the moment, he realized, and shook his head at the vagaries of his own mind.

Irritated with his own confusion, he dropped back to lie down again and said, "I'm tired, brother. I got little sleep last night and need to rest before thinking on things like this. Go away."

"As ye wish, brother," Aulay said solemnly, and then added, "Although I would suggest ye might like to visit the garderobe ere ye do. The great hall is so full o' bodies at night right now ye'll never get across to use it later should ye wake up with a need."

"Damn," Geordie growled, and sat up again, then lunged to his feet. When he saw that Aulay had started away, he said, "Wait and I shall walk back with ye."

"As ye wish, brother," Aulay said mildly, pausing to wait for him.

"There ye are! I should have known this is where ye snuck off to when ye left the table."

Dwyn lowered the book she'd just picked up, and merely

smiled at her sisters, not daring to tell them the truth and that she'd only just returned to the room to read.

"Ye're never going to get a husband this way," Aileen said, approaching the bed to sit next to her.

Dwyn shrugged at that. "It seems to me no' a single Buchanan was at the table when I left. Did they return after I slipped away?"

"Nay. Well, aye, Laird Buchanan and his uncle did, but Geordie stayed away, so I suppose 'twas better ye stayed away too," Aileen said.

"Aye," Una agreed grimly, and then announced, "Da does no' want ye encouraging the uncle. He says he wants one o' the younger men as laird at Innes. He'll no' give up being clan chief for someone his own age, so do no' even think about it."

"I was no' thinking about it," Dwyn said defensively. "Besides, I think Geordie's uncle was just being kind. I highly doubt he's interested in me for a wife."

"Oh, he's interested," Una said dryly. "The man could no' take his eyes off yer bosom the whole time he sat beside ye."

Dwyn frowned at this news, but then waved the subject away. "Aye. Well, I shall try to avoid him in future," she assured them, and then raised her eyebrows in question. "Are ye ready to sleep, then? Shall I put me book away?"

"There seems little else to do," Aileen said with a shrug, and then announced, "Lady Jetta mentioned that she received word today that Rory and Alick will be back the day after tomorrow so ye should rest up as much as ye can so ye look yer best when they get here."

"Oh," Dwyn murmured as her sister stood and began to undo her lacings, but she was wondering what the other two men would be like. Geordie was the older of the three—she knew that—so in her mind she imagined two younger versions of him, but she had no idea what they would be like in personality. She hadn't really discussed Geordie's brothers with him beyond how Rory became interested in healing. She would have to ask him about them tomorrow, Dwyn decided.

"Oh!" Aileen said suddenly, turning back to face her. "Lady Jetta is making arrangements for a feast the night after they arrive."

"To celebrate the men's return?" she asked.

"Aye, and there will be minstrels and dancing and everything."

Una added, "She was going to hold the feast the night they arrive, but Laird Buchanan pointed out the lads might be tired from their travels and it would be better to hold it the next night. But that is better anyway—it gives us the next two whole days to sort out what ye should wear to the feast . . . and how to fix yer hair," she added, eyeing Dwyn's long tresses. "Perhaps we could ask for a bath for ye the night before, wash yer hair and then separate segments and wrap them around bits of cloth so that ye have curls once it dried."

"Where would we get the bits o' cloth?" Dwyn asked with a frown.

Una shrugged. "I suppose we'd have to rip up one o' yer shifts."

"Or we could braid it after washing it," Aileen suggested. "That always looks nice when ye take it out after it's dried."

"Aye, it does," Una agreed thoughtfully.

"Oh! And we could gather some flowers the afternoon before, and weave them in her hair somehow. Perhaps in small braids at her temple that we then pull around back. It could be like a fairy crown," she added excitedly.

"Or I could put it back in its bun and do without all this fuss," Dwyn suggested with exasperation.

"Nay," they both said at once, and then began to chatter to each other about what they could do to "fix Dwyn up and make her pretty."

Rolling her eyes, Dwyn set her borrowed book on the table and glanced around for her slippers. Not spotting them right away, she made her way to the garderobe barefoot. She loved her sisters, but truly, they were causing her nothing but misery with their efforts to make her attractive. It just pointed out how unattractive they thought she was, which was oddly hurtful. Dwyn wouldn't have thought it would be. She'd always prided herself on being a sensible young woman who saw herself clearly. But while Dwyn had always accepted that she was plain . . . well . . . she hadn't felt plain in Geordie's arms. She'd felt beautiful . . . and desirable, and even powerful. She'd felt like she imagined a goddess must feel, like she could bring men to their knees and conquer the world with her body.

"Which is just ridiculous," Dwyn muttered to herself as she slid into the garderobe and closed the door. She hadn't even conquered Geordie. He was the one who had ended both embraces she'd enjoyed with him. But until he had, she'd felt glorious, Dwyn admitted on a sigh.

Chapter 5

"IT LOOKS AS THOUGH I HAVE A BIT O' A WAIT," GEORDIE SAID dryly as he and Aulay entered the great hall and he spied the people lined up by the garderobe doors.

"Aye. Everyone wants to use them ere they sleep," Aulay commented, and then said, "I doubt there is a lineup fer the one above stairs though. Use that one."

"Ye got it finished?" he asked with surprise. Jetta had been pestering Aulay to install a garderobe above stairs for weeks before Geordie had left to help Conran and Evina at MacLeod. And his brother had finally agreed just before he rode out. But it was a large undertaking. They'd had to wall off the end of the hall just past the last of the bedroom doors to make a large garderobe, then build the stone shafts that would carry the waste away to the moat below, which had been the more difficult part of the endeavor.

"Aye, we finished just in time fer the arrival o' our guests," Aulay said dryly. "Which, as it turns out, was why she wanted them."

Geordie thought Jetta was clever to have thought of it. From what he'd seen last night when he'd arrived and first entered the keep, there were so many extra servants and soldiers presently here that everyone had been forced to sleep on their sides belly to back, and even then there had been little if any space between the sleepers. There certainly hadn't been the customary path left to the stairs, and from there to the garderobes and kitchens. Nodding, he said, "I'll use the upper one, then."

"Do ye see me wife?" Aulay asked before he could move away.

Geordie glanced over the people in the hall. There was no one at the trestle tables. In fact, those had been taken down and the pieces were even now being carted over to lean against the wall.

"Nay," he said finally. "But I do no' see any o' the would-be brides or their families here either. They must have all retired fer the night."

"Aye," Aulay said, and walked with him to the stairs, adding, "A messenger arrived today. Yer brothers should be back the day after tomorrow."

Geordie arched an eyebrow at that as they started up the steps. "Why bother sending a messenger if they would be practically on his heels?"

"I gather the man was sent several days ago, but ran into trouble on the way. He was fine," Aulay added before Geordie could ask. "But his horse was killed and he had to walk quite a way ere meeting up with a slow-moving merchant who was kind enough to allow him to ride on his wagon with him. I loaned him a horse for the return journey."

"Rory was attending the labor o' Lady Ferguson, was he no'?" Geordie asked.

"Aye."

"Well, then, I hope ye kissed yer horse fare-thee-well ere ye sent it off," he said dryly. "Ye ken those bastards'll just keep it."

Aulay shook his head. "They'll no' start a war with us o'er a horse. He'll return it."

"Oh, aye. We have influence and eight armies at our back," Geordie said with a shake of the head.

"Exactly," Aulay said with a grin, and opened his mouth to say something else, but paused abruptly as a cry of pain reached them from the upper floor.

They were only a couple of steps from the landing, but both men hurried up them and looked along the hall to see what had caused that sound. Geordie's eyes widened, his heart slamming into his chest, when he saw Dwyn on the floor near the garderobe. Even as he recognized the spray of golden hair around her, she planted her hands on the floor and pushed her upper body halfway up and then twisted her head to peer back toward her feet, her long hair falling to curtain her breasts as they bulged from her top.

"Dwyn." Rushing forward, Geordie started to kneel next to her and then paused when he saw the broken glass littering the floor around her and noted the bloody cuts on her bare feet. Then he bent to scoop her up, asking, "Did ye drop a goblet, lass?"

"Nay. I just came out o' the garderobe and stepped on it," she said on a sigh, and he couldn't help noticing that her drawing the breath in and then pushing it out had her breasts creeping upward out of her gown again. He was beginning to love her gowns, Geordie acknowledged.

"Ye stepped on an unbroken goblet and it shattered?" Aulay asked as he reached them.

"Oh, nay. It was already broken and all over the floor when I came out," she explained quickly. "I meant I just stepped on the broken pieces. They were no' there when I went into the garderobe," she added with a frown, glancing down at the glass strewn across the floor. "Someone must have broken it while I was in there. No doubt they went to fetch a maid to help clean it up."

Aulay grunted at that and moved to Geordie's side to lift Dwyn's feet and examine them.

"I am sure they are fine, m'laird," Dwyn murmured with embarrassment. "And 'tis me own fault anyway. I should have put me slippers back on ere I left our room."

"There should no' be glass all o'er the floor either," Aulay said grimly, and then let her feet go and glanced at Geordie. "Bring her to our room. Jetta will want to get the glass out and see her bandaged."

"Oh, no!" Dwyn cried with alarm. "Just take me to me room and me sisters can tend it."

"Nay," Aulay said abruptly, and then added, "Jetta has been learning from Rory. She will insist on seeing to them herself, and if we take ye to yer room, she'll just go there the minute she learns what has happened. Better to go let her care for them straightaway," Aulay said firmly.

"Oh, that's . . ." Her protest ended on a sigh as Geordie gathered her closer to his chest and followed Aulay down the hall. He'd lifted his arm slightly as he pressed her against himself, so that her chest was against his. He'd had to. Staring down at her swelling breasts pushing out of her gown was affecting him as much as touching and suckling them had and he didn't want to embarrass his sister-in-law by walking into the master's bedchamber with his cock pushing his plaid out like a traveling tent.

"Just let me see that she is still dressed," Aulay said as he slid into the room. Jetta was apparently decent, because Aulay didn't even close the door, but simply warned his wife that they had company as he swung the door the rest of the way open and stepped out of the way.

"What is— Oh, Dwyn, you are bleeding," Jetta cried, hurrying toward them as Geordie carried her into the room.

"Aye. Someone broke one o' Mother's glass goblets in the hall and Dwyn stepped in it coming out o' the garderobe," Aulay explained.

"Oh, dear," Jetta muttered as she quickly glanced over Dwyn's feet, then she turned and rushed to a chest against the wall, and began to dig through it. "Set her on the bed, Geordie. Aulay, can ye ask a maid to fetch me boiled water? Oh, where are the bandages Rory prepared for me ere leaving? I know I put them in here somewhere."

Smiling faintly, Geordie carried Dwyn to the bed as Aulay left the room. He set her down gently, straightened, glanced around to see that Jetta was still digging in her chest and turned back to quickly tug up the neckline of Dwyn's gown to better cover her nomadic breasts.

Caught by surprise, Dwyn gasped, and then flushed bright red and muttered, "Thank ye," as he released the material.

"Me pleasure," Geordie said with a grin, but the truth was he would rather tug the material down. The woman was on a bed, after all. However, he wouldn't dare do something like that with Jetta just feet away.

"Here we are," Jetta said brightly, hurrying back to the bed, her arms full of bandages, a bag with what he presumed were medicinals and a spool of thread with a needle in it.

"Oh, surely I do no' need stitches," Dwyn said with alarm when she saw what the woman carried.

"I hope not," Jetta said solemnly as she moved around Geordie to set her items on the table next to the bed. "But one of the cuts is bleeding quite freely, and 'tis better to be prepared."

Dwyn groaned at that as Geordie moved down the bed to bend and examine her feet. He winced when he saw them. The bottoms of her feet looked almost shredded. There were several cuts still with bits of glass in them that would need to be dug out, and one with a very large shard of glass poking out.

Moving back to the head of the bed, he scooped up Dwyn, settled himself on the bed and then set her down between his legs and wrapped his arms around her waist.

Geordie expected her to be embarrassed and protest at once. Instead, Dwyn proved how clever she was by sighing unhappily and saying, "'Tis that bad, is it?"

Jetta smiled crookedly as she glanced from him to Dwyn, and then said, "It might be."

"A maid will bring up the water as soon as it boils," Aulay announced as he reentered the room then. "And I ordered that the glass be cleaned up. Apparently whoever broke it had no' even bothered to tell anyone so that it could be taken care of."

Jetta clucked with irritation at that as she knelt at the side of the bed to look at the bottoms of Dwyn's feet. "That is just . . ." Apparently unable to find a word to finish her thought, or perhaps unwilling to voice it, she muttered instead, "I shall certainly be wearing my slippers around here until everyone leaves."

"I'm certain wee Dwyn will too," Aulay said, casting her a sympathetic look, and not even seeming to notice that Geordie was situated behind her, holding her in his arms. At least, he didn't think so until Aulay said, "Ye may want to hold her by the shoulders rather than around the waist, brother. Ye're pulling the top o' her gown down."

Dwyn gasped and glanced down at her escaping bosom even as Geordie did. She immediately started to raise her hands to rectify the situation, but his hands were already there, tugging the material back up into place.

"Thank ye," Dwyn moaned. Covering her face with both hands, she shook her head. But she just as quickly dropped her hands and straightened her shoulders as she admitted, "I fear in their enthusiasm to help get me wed, me sisters took in me gowns and lowered the necklines so I canno' e'en breathe without me bosoms threatening to spill out. I see a long, embarrassing stay ahead o' me and will offer me apologies in advance fer the way I'll no doubt be unintentionally waving me naked bosom about at every turn."

Geordie grinned at the back of her head, quite liking her forthright attitude on the subject. The lass was a strange mixture, seeking out the solitude of a high perch in the tree or a book in her room, yet facing embarrassing situations head-on and without flinching. He couldn't think of another lass who would handle the difficulties she was having with her gowns with such resigned strength. Most would be blushing, and running from view. Even most of his sisters by marriage, fine women all, would not have handled it as well, he thought. Certainly, Jetta had begun to flush bright red and looked embarrassed for her the moment Aulay had pointed out what was happening. Although, he noted, the color was quickly receding and she was relaxing after what Dwyn had said.

And that was Dwyn's magic, Geordie realized suddenly. She could make a person completely comfortable around her with little more than a few words. She could also ease a potentially embarrassing situation for everyone the same way. Just by being herself. He had certainly relaxed quickly in her presence that morning. Geordie had climbed up the tree thinking he would have to soothe her and help her down. But he'd quickly realized there was no soothing needed, and instead he'd ended up staying to talk with the lass as his tensions had fled.

Well, until a different tension had claimed him when he'd found himself clutching her in his arms. She hadn't soothed that. In fact, her response to his kiss had merely increased the pressure building in his body. But nothing short of getting her naked beneath him and loving her was likely to rid him of that kind of tension.

"I guess I had best start," Jetta murmured.

Geordie pulled himself from his thoughts and focused on the woman in his hold. Peering down at the top of her head, he noted how the candlelight set fire to the pale gold strands of her hair, and had the strangest urge to bury his face in it. She had truly glorious hair, he decided, barely restraining himself from plowing his fingers into it and running them through the fine strands.

Dwyn's suddenly stiffening against him distracted Geordie then and he glanced toward her feet just in time to see Jetta straighten with the larger piece of glass held in her fingers.

"It did not go in as far as I expected," Jetta said as she set the piece of glass aside. "You must not have set your complete weight down on it."

"Nay," Dwyn murmured. "I tried to sidestep as soon as I felt the first bite of glass and set my foot down on that one, then simply fell to the side to avoid impaling meself fully."

Jetta glanced up at that, her gaze sliding up Dwyn's body to her hands and then back, pausing on her skirt. Following her gaze, Geordie saw the small slices in the skirt and knew Dwyn probably had more glass there. It looked to be about where her knees would have been when she'd fallen to the floor.

"Look away, husband, Geordie," Jetta warned.

Geordie turned his head to the side, but heard the rustle as Jetta lifted Dwyn's skirt to examine her legs. The clucking that followed told him that Dwyn's legs hadn't escaped the glass. "I cannot believe anyone could be this careless. 'Tis one thing to break the glass, but not to ensure it was cleaned up so no one got hurt . . . And in front of the garderobe too! The one place everyone will eventually visit."

"Did ye see anyone in the hall when ye came out, lass?" Geordie asked, keeping his face averted.

"Nay. Neither when I went in nor out," she got out between gritted teeth that told him Jetta was removing glass from her knees and it was as painful as he had expected.

"Geordie, please give Dwyn the candle so she can hold it for me. I need more light," Jetta murmured, and he glanced around and picked up the candleholder from the bedside table to hand it to Dwyn. Taking it, she set it on her skirts just above her knees, but Geordie noted that her hands were trembling. It was the only other sign of the pain she was suffering. Dwyn hadn't made a sound as Jetta dug glass out of her knees.

"There," Jetta said with a sigh a moment later. "Now I shall just put a little salve on."

They were all silent as Jetta quickly applied salve, and then she tugged Dwyn's skirt down and glanced around. "Aulay, mayhap you could hold the candle now so I can check Dwyn's hands."

Nodding, Aulay stepped forward and took the candle when Dwyn held it up. She then held her hands out to Jetta, and said, "They're fine, really. I think they're just a little dirty and perhaps bruised from landing on them so hard, but I do no' think there's any glass in them."

"I think you are right," Jetta murmured as she used a linen to clean her hands. "Aye. They are just bruised." Releasing her hands, she grimaced slightly and said, "I guess that just leaves your feet."

Both women took deep breaths then, and Geordie found his gaze dropping to Dwyn's chest. Much to his disappointment, her breasts barely crept upward in the gown this time.

"Better to get it done quickly," Jetta said determinedly, and shifted to kneel farther down the bed by Dwyn's feet.

Aulay immediately moved to the end of the bed and knelt to hold the candle as close to Dwyn's feet as he could without getting in Jetta's way as she bent to peer at the bottoms of them. Grimacing, she glanced to Dwyn and said, "I apologize in advance, Dwyn. This is not going to be pleasant."

Dwyn's head bobbed, and she squeezed Geordie's hands when he released her shoulders to grasp hers. They were all silent as Jetta worked, but Geordie was concentrating on Dwyn, noting every flinch or stiffening that signified pain. They all jumped, however, when there was a knock on the door.

Aulay moved silently to answer the knock as Jetta leaned back to her work again, picking the pieces of glass out of Dwyn's feet.

"I'm sorry to bother ye, m'laird. But we were looking for Dwyn and a maid said— Oh! Dwyn!" Una gasped, moving into the room when Aulay stepped back and she saw her sister on the bed.

"What happened?" Aileen cried, rushing around Una to hurry to the bed.

"I stepped on a bit of glass," Dwyn said.

"Oh." Aileen blinked, and then frowned slightly as she peered at Geordie seated behind her, his legs on either side of Dwyn's and his arms around her as he held her hands. The sister opened her mouth, no doubt to ask why he was sitting, holding her sister like that, and then paused, her eyes widening when Dwyn suddenly gasped and lunged forward, her hand jerking toward her feet as if to push Jetta away before Geordie stopped her.

"Oh," Aileen said again, but with understanding this time.

They all fell silent now as Jetta worked, the two girls wincing as they watched. Almost every time they did, Dwyn flinched or stiffened in his arms. It was a relief when Jetta announced she thought she'd got all the glass out and moved on to quickly washing away the blood, and then started to apply a soothing salve.

"Was the glass what the maid was cleaning up when we came out into the hall?" Una asked with a frown as she watched Jetta smear a dark, odiferous substance over the bottoms of Dwyn's feet.

"Aye." Dwyn sounded weary, Geordie noted with concern, and supposed it was the strain of suffering in silence that caused it.

"It looked like it was all over the floor in front o' the garderobe door," Aileen said with a scowl. "Ye should have come back fer yer slippers rather than try to traipse through it."

"I did no' traipse through it deliberately. It was no' there when I went into the garderobe, and I did no' notice it until 'twas too late on the way out," Dwyn explained patiently.

"Ye mean someone broke a goblet there while ye were in the garderobe?" Una asked now.

"They must have, though I did no' hear a bang or crash of it happening," she said.

"Ye did no' hear anything?" Aulay asked with surprise.

Dwyn shook her head, but then paused and tilted her head slightly before saying slowly, "I did hear a tinkling sound, like broken glass clinking together." She shrugged. "Perhaps the goblet was broken in one o' the rooms and someone gathered it together to dispose o' it down the garderobe, but it fell out o' whatever they were using to carry it."

Geordie recalled the way the pieces of glass had lain on the floor. They hadn't made a starlike pattern, but had covered the floor almost from wall to wall in front of the garderobe . . . as if they'd been sprinkled there. Glancing to Aulay, he noted his concern mirrored on his brother's face and felt his mouth tighten.

"There," Jetta said with a sigh as she finished wrapping Dwyn's feet with strips of clean linen.

"Thank ye," Dwyn murmured as Jetta got to her feet. "I'm sorry to have been so much trouble."

"You have been no trouble," Jetta assured her, and then moved forward to stop her when Dwyn raised herself as if intending to get up. "Oh, you cannot stand up, Dwyn. Your weight might split the cuts open and start them bleeding again."

"But I canno' stay here," Dwyn said with dismay.

"I'll carry ye, lass," Geordie announced even as he scooped his hands under her bottom and lifted and then shifted her forward so that he could get off the bed. It wasn't until he was standing that he noted the shocked looks on the women's faces, and the way Aulay's eyebrows were raised. It made him realize that his behavior was entirely too familiar.

"Me apologies," Geordie muttered as he slid his arms under Dwyn and lifted her off the bed. He had no desire to cause her problems or embarrassment, and acting comfortable touching her so intimately could do that. The least it would do was bring about questions from others.

"Wait!" Una said with sudden alarm as Geordie straightened with Dwyn in his arms. When he paused, she turned to ask Jetta, "How long must she stay off her feet, Lady Buchanan?"

Jetta paused in gathering her items together to tell Dwyn, "I shall want to check on you tomorrow, but I do not think you should walk on them for at least a couple days. Hopefully if you stay off of them for a bit, they will scab over enough to allow walking."

"Oh, no," Aileen said with dismay. "She will no' be able to dance at the feast."

"She might. That is not for three nights. Her feet might heal enough by then." Despite her words, Jetta didn't sound as if she believed it.

"'Tis fine," Dwyn said quietly.

Geordie glanced down, trying to see her expression, but Dwyn had her head slightly bowed and turned away. He couldn't tell what she was thinking. But when she added, "We should leave ye to retire," he took the hint and started for the door.

Aileen and Una immediately rushed ahead to open the door for him to carry her out.

"We are just down here, m'laird," Aileen said, rushing around him to lead the way. "We are in—"

"My room," Geordie finished for her with amusement.

"Really?" all three women asked at once, and Dwyn tipped her face up to look at him.

"Aye," Geordie assured her, smiling into her wide blue eyes and then letting his gaze sweep over her breasts. They were mostly behaving at the moment, with just the tiniest edge of the top of her nipples showing above the gown, but they were still lovely to look at and tempted him to do things he shouldn't, and couldn't, with her sisters there.

That thought made him shift his gaze to Una and Aileen. Both girls were beaming at him as if the fact that they were staying in his room was somehow a fine trick, and then Aileen turned and rushed ahead to open the door for him.

"Which side o' the bed would ye prefer, lass?" Geordie asked as he carried Dwyn into the room.

"The far side, nearest the window, please," she murmured apologetically, and Geordie grinned at her. He always slept on that side himself, so understood the attraction. However, his father had always said a man must put himself between his woman and any possible attack, so he'd have to sleep on the side nearer the door were they to marry.

Geordie stopped walking at the corner of the bed when he realized where his thoughts had taken him. Marriage to the wee lass in his arms. Despite his earlier assertions to his brother that he was not ready to marry, the idea was an appealing one. Were they married, he could join her in the bed and—

"Am I too heavy, m'laird? If ye're tiring, ye can just set me down here at the foot o' the bed. I'm sure I can pull meself up to the top without putting pressure on me feet."

Geordie blinked his thoughts away, and scowled down at Dwyn for the suggestion. "Ye're no' heavy, lass," he assured her, and continued around the bed. "I just had a thought that distracted me briefly."

"Oh," she murmured, and then drew in a breath that raised her breasts a little farther out of her gown.

Geordie glanced down at them, and then lowered his head and slid his tongue out to slide it across the curve of one soft mound along the neckline of her gown as he bent to set her in the bed. It was a swift action, one he was sure her sisters didn't see, but he was pleased by Dwyn's small gasp and the way her arms tightened around him as she shivered in his hold before he released her. She was also flushing prettily, her eyes wide and sparkling with the beginnings of desire, when he straightened and looked down at her.

Geordie smiled with satisfaction at her expression, pleased that he could affect her so easily. If her sisters were not there—

But they were, he reminded himself, and forced his face into a more polite expression as he moved toward the bottom of the bed. "Good sleep, ladies."

"Good sleep, m'laird," Dwyn and Aileen said together. But rather than the polite good-night, Una asked, "Do ye think Laird Buchanan will arrange fer one o' his soldiers to come collect Dwyn in the morning? She canno' walk below to break her fast," she reminded him.

Geordie paused at the door, a scowl tugging at the corners of his mouth at the idea of one of the Buchanan soldiers carrying his Dwyn around. He shook his head. "I'll tend to her meself. She was hurt in our home, after all. 'Tis the least I can do."

"Oh, how kind," Aileen said happily.

Una nodded. "Shall ye sleep in the orchard again? Should I come find ye there when she wakes?"

Geordie hesitated, but then shook his head. "I'll sleep on a pallet in the hall rather than out in the garden. Just open the door does she wish to go below or to the garderobe."

Dwyn's eyes widened with dismay, and she opened her mouth on what he was sure would be a protest, but he didn't stay to hear it. Opening the door, he slid out into the hall, and pulled it firmly closed behind him. Even through the door he heard the excited squeals from Dwyn's younger sisters inside the room, and could imagine them rushing to their sister in the bed as they hurried into speech.

"I think he likes ye, Dwyn!"

"Aye, he could no' take his eyes off yer bosom."

"And he's decided to cart ye about by himself so canno' find ye overly heavy."

"He's such a big man, her extra weight probably does no' signify to him. He could probably carry the three o' us at once with those broad shoulders and thick arms."

Rather than be flattered by the compliment, Geordie found himself scowling at what he considered an insult to Dwyn. While she wasn't a skinny lass, he liked her curves. She was like a ripe peach, soft and round, and Geordie did like his peaches ripe. They were the juiciest and most pleasurable to eat.

That thought led naturally to his wondering if Dwyn would be as juicy. He'd yet to test that, but had kept his caresses and kisses above the waist other than running one hand along her leg as he'd helped her down from the tree. Now, however, he couldn't help but wonder what he would have found had he let his hand slide up the inside of her leg and to the treasure trove between her thighs. Would she have been warm and wet for him? He was quite sure she would have been, and the thought started an ache between his own legs that made him glance down to see that he was sporting another tent below the waist.

Sighing, he turned away from the door. He had to fetch a pallet and bed down in the hallway. He'd be damned if he'd let anyone carry wee Dwyn around.

He'd barely had that thought when the door to the master bedroom opened, and Aulay emerged. Spotting him, his brother moved toward him, his expression grim.

Geordie didn't have to think hard to know what he wished to talk about, and the moment they were close enough to speak without needing to raise their voices, he murmured, "The glass looked deliberately spread across the floor."

"Aye," Aulay agreed. "It covered the floor from wall to wall for several feet, and certainly wouldn't have landed that way had it fallen from something."

"Nay," Geordie said solemnly. They were both silent for a minute, and then he said what both of them were thinking. "Someone set out to hurt Dwyn."

"It would seem so," Aulay agreed, his tone grim. "I hardly think whoever did it simply wished to catch just anyone entering or leaving the garderobe. They must have seen her enter and spread the glass to catch her unawares when she left." He paused briefly and then added, "I noticed the torch outside the garderobe was out too, so she was no' likely to see the glass."

Geordie glanced at him sharply at this news. He hadn't noticed that the torch was out. He'd had eyes only for Dwyn, but realized it had been darker at that end of the hall. There had still been light from the other torches to keep it from being too dark, but it had been just dark enough that she could not have seen the glass.

"Do ye think it was the lasses from Lockhart and Kennedy?" Aulay asked now.

"Probably," Geordie said tightly, and then scowled. "Ye should send them both away. They're no' the kind o' women we need in our family anyway."

"Aye, and I would if there was proof they'd done it, but . . ." He shook his head unhappily, and then added, "And we may be wrong. What if it is no' them?"

"Who else could it be?" Geordie asked with surprise.

"Well, Acair did a fair job o' making Mavis jealous today," he pointed out.

"Mavis would never do something like this to the lass," Geordie protested at once.

"Mayhap no', but jealousy can turn the sweetest lass into a virago, and 'tis no' impossible. And then there are five other women here beside Catriona and Sasha hoping to win a husband. One o' them may have been jealous enough o' Dwyn to harm her."

"Why? I did no' pay her special attention at sup," Geordie pointed out.

"Nay, but ye both disappeared from the table minutes apart, and the lass returned to the keep looking like she'd been tumbled," he informed him dryly. "Her hair was mussed, her lips swollen, and though I did no' notice it until seeing her in the light of our room, her one cheek was pink from yer stubble, plus she had love bites on both her neck and the top o' one breast." He arched one eyebrow. "While her sisters did no' seem to notice, I did, and 'tis possible others did as well."

Geordie lowered his gaze, thinking he would have to be more careful in future. He hadn't realized he'd marked Dwyn. A love bite on her neck and the top of her breast? He had been a little enthusiastic, nibbling and sucking his way down her neck and across one breast before concentrating on her nipple.

"I shall ask around and see if anyone saw someone in the hall with glass, but other than that the best we can do is keep an eye on Dwyn and be sure she is no' left alone," Aulay said now.

"I shall keep watch over her," Geordie assured him. "She needs someone to carry her around anyway, and I planned to do that. Speaking o' which," he added, raising his gaze again. "I'll need a pallet so I can sleep outside her room should she need the garderobe in the night."

Aulay nodded. "Come. We'll find one."

Geordie followed him, but his mind was on the love bites he'd left on Dwyn, and how he could have missed seeing them himself. Probably because his gaze always went directly to her neckline to see how much nipple was peeking out, he acknowledged. He really had to be more careful in future with her. No more love bites, or mussed hair. Mayhap he should carry a brush around with him. Geordie actually liked the idea of brushing her long hair. It would give him an excuse to touch it. Aye, he'd carry a brush around.

Chapter 6

"Come, join us, m'laird. Help us gather flowers."

Dwyn turned as Geordie did to peer toward the woman who had called out. Lady Catriona Lockhart looked lovely in a gold gown that set off her slim figure and pale complexion to perfection. She held a bouquet of bluebells to her lips and eyed him seductively over them. Dwyn sighed, sure he wouldn't be able to resist the invitation. She was more than a little surprised when he shook his head, and said, "I am only here today to carry Dwyn wherever she wishes to go, and aid the men with defending ye all should the need arise."

Catriona's mouth pursed with displeasure at his words, and she scowled at Dwyn. "I do no' ken why she came here anyway. 'Tis no' as if she can help gather wildflowers. She should have stayed at the keep with yer uncle. Then ye could have helped us. Ye'd have had a better time."

"Lady Innes came because she wished to enjoy the fresh air, and some o' our rare sunshine," Geordie growled at the woman with obvious anger. "And I go where she goes until she heals enough to walk on her own. So, had she stayed away, ye'd still no' have had me help. Besides," he added heavily, "I am having a fine time talking to her, and would rather do that than pick flowers with ye anyway."

Dwyn swallowed a sudden thickness in her throat at his defense of her, and smiled widely at Geordie when he turned back to face her. They had been talking the day before as he'd carted her about. Not at first. Both of them had been pretty quiet as he'd carried her into the garderobe first thing that morning; Dwyn because she was embarrassed at his having to carry her to attend to such a personal duty, and he, she suspected, out of deference to her. But once he'd carried her below stairs and sat her at table next to him, they'd started chatting and just hadn't seemed to be able to stop. After breaking their fast, he'd carried her to sit by the fire and the talking had continued.

They'd soon been joined by the other women, who had quickly taken over the talking end of things. But Dwyn hadn't minded so much; she'd simply sat back and watched the way Geordie responded to the other women, noticing that he was extremely polite, but not nearly as relaxed as when she and he were alone. That had pleased her. Sadly, they had not got the chance to be alone at all yesterday. With her needing to be carried, there had been no opportunity to slip out to the orchards or anywhere else. They'd spent the day in the company of others until Geordie had carried her up to her bed. She'd hoped he might kiss her again then, but her sisters had followed them up and their presence was somewhat inhibiting.

Today had started the same way, with his being quiet and she embarrassed as he carried her to the garderobe, but once at the table they'd begun to talk again. At first, it had been polite talk of the weather, and what time they thought his brothers might arrive that day. But once they'd finished breaking their fast, Geordie had insisted she needed fresh air and he was taking her outside. He'd carried her out to the gardens and to her tree. He hadn't let her climb up, but they'd sat under it and she'd asked about his sister, and brothers, and before long he'd been telling her tales about his youth with them. The stories had been terribly amusing, and Dwyn didn't think she'd ever laughed so much as she had at the naughty antics he and his siblings had got up to as children.

By the time Geordie carried her in to use the garderobe again, and to join everyone at the table for the nooning meal, he had moved on to telling her how his sister, Saidh, had come to be married to the MacDonnell. When Dwyn had expressed disbelief that his sister would dare take on seven brothers and beat them silly when they had ridden to MacDonnell to "save" her, Jetta had said she'd not doubted it for a minute and assured Dwyn she would understand once she met her. Aulay too had quickly backed up Geordie's tale, and even embellished on it so that the four of them had been laughing so hard they could barely eat.

Una and Aileen had been sitting on her other side and been included in the group and enjoyed the tales too, but Dwyn had not missed the scowls and dirty looks Catriona and Sasha had been casting toward her from down the table where they sat on the other side of Geordie's uncle Acair. The two women had rushed to sit next to her when Geordie had set her down. Next to her was as close as they could get to Geordie since Jetta and Aulay were on his right, but his uncle had forced them to move farther down the table to make way for he and Dwyn's sisters when they'd come to the table. The two women had been no more happy about that than they were now at Dwyn having Geordie all to herself, and she supposed she could understand. She was taking up a lot of his time and attention.

But it had been Geordie's idea to accompany the women out here this afternoon when Una and Aileen had mentioned their desire to find wildflowers to plait into Dwyn's hair as the nooning meal had broken up. Jetta had announced that she'd planned on sending servants out to gather flowers to strew in the rushes for the feast, and would accompany them for the task. The next thing Dwyn knew, Geordie was suggesting they should join the small group and enjoy some sun while the others found their flowers. The moment she'd agreed, the rest of the women had begun clamoring to join the party.

Had Dwyn realized they would want to accompany them, she would have refused Geordie's suggestion and claimed a desire to rest. But it was too late by then, so here she sat on a plaid in the middle of the clearing, as Geordie continued to talk about how his brothers had encountered their wives. The stories were almost too much to believe with various villains after the women, and the brave Buchanan men battling to keep them safe. But there were some very amusing parts to the tales too, such as Conran being kidnapped in Rory's place by mistake, and Dougall meeting his wife when she tried to escape her home on a bull named Henry.

"Ye have a beautiful smile, lass. Ye should do it more often," Geordie said suddenly, and Dwyn felt herself blush at the compliment. Her gaze slid to the flower he'd plucked from the small mound her sisters had dumped on the corner of the plaid. He was now twirling it between his thumb and fingers, but looking at her. When he leaned forward to brush the petals of the flower down her arm, she closed her eyes briefly as the gentle caress sent shivers down her back.

"Yer very responsive, lass," he murmured, repeating the act.

"I'm sorry, m'laird." Dwyn sighed the words and ran her hand swiftly over the goose bumps that his action had given rise to on her arm.

"Do no' apologize. I like it. A lot," he added in a near growl, and another shiver slid through her. He noticed, of course, and a purely male grin curved his lips.

Shaking her head, Dwyn whispered so that no one else would hear, "I do believe ye're a very naughty man, m'laird."

"Naughty?" he asked, his eyes twinkling with amusement. "And why is that?"

"Because ye ken what ye're doing to me, and not only persist, but ye're enjoying it," she said at once.

Her honesty seemed to catch him by surprise, and Geordie stared at her briefly in silence before reaching down to slip his hand under the hem of her skirt to clasp her ankle lightly. "And what am I doing to ye, lass?"

Eyes widening, Dwyn glanced anxiously around. Much to her relief, no one appeared to be looking their way.

"Hmm?" he murmured, letting his hand glide up to her calf under the gown.

Dwyn reluctantly turned her gaze back to him. But her breath was now reduced to short, shallow gasps as his touch sent warm heat gliding through her, and she couldn't have answered him had she wished. Instead, she bit her lower lip, and simply stared at him helplessly.

"Would that I could bite that fer ye meself, lass," Geordie growled, his gaze focusing on her bottom lip as he let his hand drift up to her knee.

Dwyn released her lip at once, but was wishing he could too. She was wishing she could allow him to continue running his hand up her leg as well, but was aware of the women around them, and put her hand down to clasp his through her gown, preventing it from moving farther.

"I think," she began, but paused as Jetta suddenly appeared at the edge of the plaid they sat on.

"Geordie Buchanan, I know you are not taking liberties with Dwyn out here for anyone to see." Jetta's words were hushed to prevent anyone else hearing, but grim for all that, and Dwyn peered at her with alarm.

"Oh, nay, he was—"

"About to unwrap her feet to examine them," Geordie interrupted calmly, his hand sliding out from under hers to clasp her calf and draw her leg out so that she sat with it now straight.

"Oh, aye. I am sure it was her feet you were thinking of unwrapping," Jetta said with a snort of patent disbelief. But she dropped to her knees on the blanket and smiled at Dwyn, and said, "Stick both legs out straight, Dwyn, so we can have a look. 'Tis probably better not to sit with them curled under ye like that anyway—'twill cut the blood off to your feet and they need the blood to heal."

"Oh, aye." Dwyn uncurled the other leg from under her so she sat with both legs straight. When Jetta began to unwrap her left foot while Geordie did the right, she pressed her hands to the plaid behind her and leaned back on her arms as she watched.

"They look better today," Geordie commented as he got the linens on her right foot unraveled. "But it might be good to let them have some air while we sit here in the sun."

"Aye," Jetta agreed as she finished with the wrappings on

Dwyn's left foot and examined it, then the one Geordie had unwrapped. "It might allow them to scab up, and speed the healing along."

"How is she? Are they healing?"

Dwyn glanced up with surprise, and shielded her eyes from the sun as she peered at her sister Aileen.

"Do ye think she'll be able to dance at the feast tomorrow night?" Una asked, joining them.

"It is looking like she may, and hopefully letting her feet air in the sun will help," Jetta said cautiously. "We shall have to see."

"Oh," Aileen said with concern. "But we are done gathering the flowers. At least, I think we are. I was just coming to ask if ye thought we had enough."

Dwyn turned to glance toward the cart they'd brought with them as Jetta did, and felt her eyebrows rise. The cart was pretty much full of flowers. There was more than enough to cover the great hall floor, she was sure.

"Aye, 'tis more than enough," Jetta said.

"I'll take her back to the keep on me horse. There is no room in the cart for her now anyway," Geordie pointed out. "We can sit in the gardens once there so that her feet can enjoy the benefit o' the sun."

Jetta relaxed and began to gather the used linens. "'Tis better I put fresh linens on when I rewrap her feet anyway. Rory says reusing bloodied linens can infect the wound."

"Help me gather our flowers, Aileen," Una said, bending next to Jetta to begin collecting the flowers they'd gathered. "That way Geordie and Dwyn can take the plaid to sit on in the garden."

When Dwyn started to try to help, Geordie leapt to his feet and quickly bent to pick her up. He knew he'd startled her when she gasped in surprise and grabbed for his shoulders as she stared up at him with amazement.

"I did no' even see ye stand up," she murmured as he started to walk toward where his horse waited by the cart. "Ye're very fast, m'laird."

"If that were true, lass, I'd have had ye naked and under me the first morning we met," he said with amusement before he could think better of it. Once he realized what he'd said though, he looked down at her face with concern.

While she had flushed a bit at the words, Dwyn didn't get flustered or squawk with outrage. Instead, she merely tilted her head as she peered up at him and asked with curiosity, "And would I have enjoyed it?"

Dwyn's question made him stop walking. He stared at her for a long moment with those words circling in his mind. Would she have enjoyed it? He'd like to think so. While he'd never taken a lass's innocence before, he knew he would have enjoyed it, and that he would have worked damned hard to ensure she enjoyed as much of it as she could too. Come to that, he was pretty sure she would have enjoyed the beginning. It was the ending he was more concerned about. Breaching her maid's veil. It was not supposed to be pleasant for any woman.

"Shall I put this on your horse for you?"

Geordie tore his gaze from Dwyn's face and glanced around to see Jetta beside them holding the plaid. His gaze slid to his horse, and then to Dwyn, and he asked, "Will ye hold it, lass? I did no' bring anything to fasten the plaid to me horse's saddle."

"O' course." She held her hands out and his sister-in-law passed the plaid to her.

"I shall see you both back at the keep," Jetta said, before moving away to begin calling to the other women still picking flowers.

Geordie started walking again the moment Jetta turned away, his legs eating up the distance quickly. The women were just starting to move toward the cart with their bundles of flowers when he set Dwyn on his horse and then mounted behind her.

"Where are they going?" Catriona asked resentfully. "Why is Whinnie riding with Geordie rather than in the cart like she did on the way out?"

Geordie was just stiffening at the insulting nickname when

he heard Jetta say, "Her name is Dwyn, not Whinnie. I suggest you try to remember that else you shall be invited to leave. And she is riding back with Geordie because he wishes it so. Besides, there is not enough room in the cart for her what with all the flowers."

Because he wishes it so. Geordie smiled at the words as he reached around Dwyn to gather his horse's reins, and then spurred the animal to a trot that took them quickly out of the clearing. Aye, he wished it so. At least, he had. Now though, with her back to his chest, and her bottom pressed snugly against his groin . . . Well, mayhap he hadn't been thinking ahead like he should have, Geordie decided with a grimace. Their arrival back at the keep could be somewhat embarrassing now that his body was responding to her closeness in the predictable way.

"Ye said Conran was kidnapped by his wife last summer."

Geordie glanced down at the lass in his lap, and recalled it had been the last tale he'd been telling her before Catriona had suggested he join the women in picking flowers.

"It was last summer, was it no'?" Dwyn asked now, turning and tipping her head to glance back at him.

"Aye," he agreed, returning his attention to his horse and the path through the trees.

"And yet ye've only just returned from aiding Conran and his wife to settle her cousin, Gavin, as laird at MacLeod," she pointed out. "How long were ye there? Surely no' this whole past year?"

"Nay," he said on a laugh. "I am no' that good a brother."

"I suspect ye just might be," Dwyn countered, and he wished he could see her expression to tell if she was teasing or not. If she wasn't, she thought highly of him indeed. Although, Geordie admitted if only to himself, he probably would have stayed a year had he been needed. Fortunately, that hadn't been necessary.

"Gavin only became laird o' MacLeod six weeks ago," he explained. "Conran, his wife, Evina, and Gavin had to petition the king, and get him to hear his case. That took some time. Mostly because none of them, not even Gavin, wanted to sit about at court awaiting the king's pleasure to see them. So, they wrote and requested an audience. Six months passed before they got a response, and then the date for the audience was three months after that. Once he'd listened to their case, the king sent one o' his trusted men out to MacLeod to demand the will. Conran, Evina and Gavin had to wait at court for him to go there and come back, which took longer than necessary because Gavin's uncle insisted on riding back with the man, and he brought a slow-moving caravan of soldiers and wagons rather than ride alone. And then they had to wait a couple more weeks for the king to actually see the will."

"Weeks?" she asked with dismay.

"When his man didn't return in the expected length of time, the king thought he'd met with foul play and sent a garrison o' soldiers out to find him and get the will . . . and then he went on a hunting trip."

"What?" Dwyn asked with disbelief.

"Aye," he said dryly. "Apparently, it was planned ahead o' time though, so . . ." He shrugged, jostling her a bit in his lap. "The worst part is they all arrived back at court—his man, the uncle and the garrison—the day after the king left. The garrison ran into their traveling party that morning, and rode back with them. But 'twas too late—the king was gone, so they had to await his return to have the matter resolved."

"Oh, dear," Dwyn said with amusement. "I suspect yer brother would no' have liked that. I would no' have."

"Nay, he didn't," Geordie admitted, and then asked, "But why would you no' have liked it?" He suspected he knew the answer, but wanted to hear it anyway.

"Because I canno' think of anything less pleasant than to be stuck at court for weeks on end, awaiting the king's pleasure. No' if 'tis full o' lasses like—"

Geordie grinned when Dwyn cut herself off. He was quite sure the lasses whose names she was thinking of but wouldn't say were Catriona and Sasha. From what he'd heard, the two women were often at court, which perhaps explained their behavior.

Court was a place of excess, where cruelty was common. He'd never cared for it himself either.

"Oh, look! There is Buchanan," she said brightly.

It was such an obvious attempt to distract him from what she'd stopped herself from saying that Geordie found himself grinning down at the top of her head and squeezing her affectionately with the arm around her waist. He only recalled the effect that would have on her neckline when he heard her mutter something under her breath and raised her hands to work at pushing her breasts back into the top of her gown. He glanced down as she pushed at the round globes, and it made him think of Cook kneading dough for some reason, which just struck him as ridiculous and made him laugh.

"'Tis no' funny, m'laird," Dwyn said, tossing an exasperated glance over her shoulder. "How would ye like it if yer brothers shortened all yer plaids so that yer pillicock kept showing?"

Geordie grinned at the fact that she would even refer to his cock, but was even more amused at the suggestion, and hoping to fluster her, he said, "Well, I guess that depends on whether ye'd be looking or no'."

"Of course I'd be looking," Dwyn said in somewhat distracted tones as she now tugged on the neckline of her gown, trying to pull it up to cover what she couldn't push in. "What lass with half a wit in her head would no' take the opportunity to see yer pillicock?"

Geordie burst out laughing anew at her honesty, and unthinkingly gave her another affectionate squeeze.

"Arggh!" she growled with frustration. "Do ye no' stop doing that I'll be giving the men on yer wall a fine show as we ride by."

That ended his amusement rather quickly, and Geordie scowled toward the men posted on the wall ahead. He then released her to yank her top up himself. It didn't really help much, he decided as he peered down over her shoulders at the tops of her breasts on display in the pale blue gown she wore today, so he took the plaid from her and let it drop open, then tucked it around and over her shoulders until she was fully covered up to her neck.

"Better," Geordie judged then, and Dwyn sighed and nodded as she leaned back into him.

"Aye. Much better. I feel properly clothed fer the first time since coming here," she admitted wryly, and then added, "I do love me sisters, but truly, this was no' their finest idea."

Geordie merely smiled. To his mind, it had been a brilliant idea. While he didn't care for everyone else being able to look on what God had gifted this lovely lass with, putting her beautiful breasts on display had certainly caught his attention. Although it wasn't the only thing that had caught his attention. There was much more of merit to the lovely Dwyn Innes than just her fine breasts. And he did find her lovely now. At first, he may have agreed that she was nothing special when it came to her face, but that was before she'd smiled. When she did that, her blue eyes widened and sparkled, her whole face lit up like a candle, and she was honestly and truly lovely.

One of the men on the wall hailed them as they rode across the bridge and Geordie slowed his horse to hear the news that his brothers were returned and in the keep. He thanked the man for the news, and then continued forward, riding to the corner of the keep rather than the steps.

Spying Drostan, the stable boy, running toward them, Geordie peered down at Dwyn as he tried to decide the best way to dismount. Should he scoop her up and dismount with her already in his arms, which might jar her? Or should he dismount and lift her down and swing her about to get her in his arms without her feet touching the ground?

Dismounting with her, he decided. There was less risk of her wounded feet brushing the ground that way.

"Are we waiting for— Oh!" Dwyn gasped when he lifted her into his arms, his seat on the horse making him hold her high enough he could have licked and kissed her breasts were they not covered with the plaid.

"Hold on to me, Dwyn," Geordie instructed gently, and waited until she'd wrapped her arms around his neck before lifting his left leg over the horse and saddle and then dropping to the ground. He managed the landing without too much of a jolt, but the plaid Dwyn had been holding on to fell to the ground.

"I'll get it fer ye, m'laird," Drostan said as he reached them, and rushed to his side to snatch up the fallen plaid. The boy's eyes went to Dwyn's feet as he straightened though, and he paused, clutching the cloth as his eyes widened. "Gor, m'laird. The lady's feet are cut up something awful."

"Aye, Drostan," Geordie agreed solemnly. "Dwyn, this is Drostan, a fine young man who works in the stables. He's going to be stable master one day when old Fergus retires."

As Drostan beamed at the prediction, Geordie continued. "Drostan, this is Lady Dwyn Innes. The finest lady ye'll ever rescue a plaid fer."

Drostan turned his attention to Dwyn and gave an awkward half bow. "M'lady. 'Tis a right pleasure to meet ye."

"Thank ye, Drostan. I'm right pleased to meet you too," Dwyn assured him.

Geordie smiled at the pair of them, and then glanced to the plaid when Drostan held it out. After a hesitation, he said, "Can ye bring it along and come with us fer a minute, lad? I promised Lady Innes she could rest in the orchard fer a bit and enjoy the sun, but I canno' hold her and lay out the plaid at the same time. I'm thinking I'll need some help to get her safely situated."

"O' course, m'laird," Drostan said eagerly, and fell into step with him as Geordie turned to head around the keep.

They hadn't gone far before Drostan tugged at his plaid to get his attention. Once Geordie glanced to him in question, he asked, "Can I ask how the lady got her feet so cut up? Or does it pain her to talk about it?"

"Asking is fine," Dwyn assured the boy before Geordie could respond. "Ye canno' learn anything if ye do no' ask, right?"

"Right," Drostan agreed, smiling.

Dwyn grinned at him, and said, "I fear 'twas naught but a silly accident. Someone broke a goblet in the upper hall and I stepped on the pieces o' glass when I came out o' the garderobe."

"They did no' warn ye or anything?" the boy asked with dismay.

"There was no one there to warn me when I came out into the hall," she explained.

"Oh. Well." Drostan scrunched up his eight-year-old face with disgruntlement. "What kind o' bampot leaves broken glass on a floor and does no' clean it up, or stay to warn others o' its presence?"

"Someone as silly as I was when I left me chamber in me bare feet," Dwyn said wryly.

"Going barefoot is no' silly," Drostan assured her. "I am always barefoot. Unless 'tis winter," he added. "But I'm always barefoot when 'tis warm like now. I would ha'e got cut up too had I no' seen the glass and walked into it. Nay, 'tis no' you who were silly, m'lady. Whoever did it was though. Or mean enough they just did no' care if someone got cut up walking through the mess they'd made." He tsked with disgust and shook his head. "I do no' ken what Scotland is coming to with that kind o' goings-on takin' place."

The boy had sounded like an old woman when he'd said that and Geordie felt a smile split his lips, even as he saw Dwyn grin. They shared their amusement with a look, and then Drostan said, "Well, I'm sure sorry ye're suffering fer someone else's folly, m'lady, and I'd be pleased to help in any way I can while ye're healing."

"Ye're helping right now by agreeing to bring the plaid and lay it out fer us," Dwyn assured him solemnly.

"Speaking o' which," Geordie said now, coming to a halt. "This is the spot, lad. Go on and lay out the plaid fer us, please. But try to make sure the bottom quarter of it is outside the shade cast by the tree—Lady Dwyn's feet need sun."

"Aye, m'laird."

Geordie noticed the way Dwyn glanced around as Drostan

quickly shook out the plaid and spread it on the ground. She seemed surprised that they'd reached the orchard already, but she smiled when she took note that he'd chosen to have the boy lay out the plaid beneath their tree.

"There ye are, m'laird," Drostan said, stepping back once he'd finished his task.

Geordie turned to inspect the lad's work and nodded with approval. "Thank ye fer yer help. Now ye'd best go see to me horse ere he wanders off to the stables on his own and upsets Fergus."

"Oh! Aye," Drostan gasped, and whirled around to hurry off.

Dwyn chuckled as she watched the boy rush away, and then turned her head up to Geordie. "Drostan is an adorable lad."

"Aye," Geordie agreed as he stepped forward onto the plaid, and then knelt before setting her down. "But do no' let Fergus hear ye say that, else he'll have a fit."

"Why?" she asked with amazement as she watched him settle on the plaid beside her.

"Because Drostan drives him mad," he admitted on a grin. "He says the lad talks from sunup till sundown and is like to drive him to drink does he no' cease his incessant chatter."

Dwyn threw her head back on a laugh at that, and Geordie found himself searching for something else to say to keep her laughing. He loved her laugh. It was so honest and open, not the silly twitters most ladies employed in an effort to appear ladylike. Dwyn laughed from the belly, or perhaps the heart. It was a sound full of life and joy, and made him want to wrap her in his arms and squeeze tightly. And if her breasts popped out during the squeezing, all the better.

That thought made Geordie smile again, and he wasn't surprised when his face muscles complained about the action by aching a bit. They were not used to the workout they'd been getting the last day or two, but especially today. Geordie knew for a certainty that he'd never in his life laughed or smiled as much as he had since meeting Dwyn.

"Oh, m'laird, I shall miss ye," Dwyn said with a shake of the head as her laughter began to ease.

Geordie stiffened, a frown tugging at his lips as her words raised alarm in every inch of his body. "Why would ye miss me, lass? I'm no' going anywhere."

"Well, nay," she agreed with amusement. "But once you and yer brothers pick brides from the selection Lady Jetta arranged, or reject all o' us, I and my sisters and father shall return to Innes." Shrugging, she added, "Much as I love me home, I have never laughed so much there as I do in yer company. I shall miss that, as well as talking to ye . . . and yer kisses," she admitted on a sigh. "Thank ye fer making this all so much more enjoyable than it started out. I shall look fondly on the memories ye've given me."

Geordie stared at her silently, not nearly as stunned by her honesty as by his mind's rebellion at the thought of her leaving Buchanan and returning to Innes without him. He didn't want her to leave. He didn't want the laughter and talking to end. He certainly didn't want the kissing to end either. In fact, he wanted more kisses, and he wanted more than kisses. He wanted Dwyn. He wanted her in his bed, naked and laughing until he turned that laughter to moans, and sweet groans and pleas as he loved her with his body and planted a bairn in her. He hoped it was a lass with the same honesty, and quiet beauty, he saw in Dwyn. But he'd be pleased with a lad too.

Dear God, he wanted to marry Dwyn, Geordie realized with amazement, but supposed he shouldn't be surprised. His interest in drinking and wenching had fled quickly after meeting her. He certainly hadn't taken the opportunity to find a willing woman last night, or even the night before when he'd been hard and hurting after sending her back to the keep. The thought of other women simply hadn't appealed to him. How was he to wench if the only woman he wanted to bed was the one sitting before him?

"M'laird? Ye've gone oddly quiet. Is aught amiss?" Dwyn asked with sudden concern.

Geordie dragged his attention from his thoughts to peer at her, letting his gaze drift over her blue eyes, and soft lips, then to the long plait her hair was in today. It was thick, and beautiful and well done as it had been the day before, but he wished her hair was undone and flowing around her as it had been the night she'd been injured. He wanted her naked here on his plaid, with her hair free and the sun shining down on her pale skin and light gold hair.

With that in his mind, Geordie shifted closer to her and caught the end of the plait where it lay on the plaid beside her hip.

Chapter 7

Dwyn stilled in surprise when Geordie suddenly plucked the end of her braid off the plaid and removed the thong at the end of the plaiting. But she laughed nervously and grabbed for his hands to stop him when he began to unravel the plaiting her sister Aileen had spent so much time on that morning.

"M'laird, what—?" she began with confusion, trying to catch his hands to stop him, but Geordie caught her hands instead and lifted his face to kiss her. He did not start out with gentle teasing caresses as he had when kissing her before; this time he went straight to the devouring kisses, his tongue thrusting out almost before his mouth had fully covered hers.

Dwyn opened for him without protest, her tongue meeting his, and then she moaned and slid her arms around his chest as he made love to her with lips and tongue. She felt his arms go around her as he kissed her, and knew his hands were in her hair, but didn't care so long as his tongue was thrusting and filling her as it was. When he broke the kiss and trailed his lips to her neck and she felt him tugging at the laces of her gown, she opened her eyes and then closed them again and took a relieved breath when he got them undone and her breasts spilled out, their constriction ended. That breath then came out on a startled gasp though when he suddenly pulled back to peer at her.

This was not like the night before. Then she'd had the darkness cloaking her in shadows. Now it was broad daylight, the sun shining down on what he'd revealed, but Dwyn remained still, allowing him to look. It seemed silly to cover them now. Besides, her breasts were constantly climbing out of her gown anyway. He'd surely caught peeks of what he was looking at now, so the only difference was he was getting a full unencumbered view.

"I want to see ye naked with nothing but yer hair fer cover," he confessed in a broken growl that had her heart hammering in her chest.

Dwyn hesitated. What he was asking for was more than he should of a lady. On the other hand, she knew she wasn't likely to get the request again from another. She didn't even want the request from another. She wanted Geordie. She wanted to give him whatever he desired, and she wanted him to give her the pleasure she'd already experienced with him. She wanted his kisses, and caresses, and she wanted him to suckle her breasts, and she wanted those memories to carry away with her.

Lifting her chin, Dwyn tugged her open gown off her shoulders and let it slide down her arms until she could draw her hands free of the material. Then she sat, uncertain what to do next. She could not stand and remove the gown altogether with her cut feet. Dwyn wasn't even sure she wished to go that far, so she simply met his gaze and waited, naked from the waist up and her hair loose about her shoulders and around her breasts.

Geordie stared at her for the longest time, as if he too wanted to hold these memories for later, and then he reached out and brushed his knuckles gently over one nipple. Dwyn gasped and stiffened, her back arching slightly, unconsciously offering her breasts to him, but she didn't close her eyes. She watched as his other hand rose and he palmed her breasts in each hand, squeezing and kneading the tender flesh briefly before his head bowed so that he could take one into his mouth. Dwyn's eyes did close then, and she moaned as he lathed and suckled at the hard bud, his mouth seeming to pull on an invisible thread that ran straight down to the spot between her thighs. When he switched to her other breast, she found there was another invisible string there that took the same path, and Dwyn squirmed on the plaid as her hands reached up to glide into his hair.

"I want more," Geordie groaned around her nipple, and she felt his hand release the breast he was suckling, but didn't realize where it was headed until she felt it against her calf under her skirt.

Dwyn gasped, and arched her back harder, pushing her breast farther into his mouth as his hand glided up along her leg to her knee. Geordie accepted the invitation, taking as much as he could of her breast into his mouth and suckling almost painfully before suddenly releasing it to raise his head and peer at her as his hand slid around to the inside of her knee and continued up her thigh, urging her leg to the side and spreading her for his pleasure.

"Are ye wet fer me, lass?" he asked, his voice rough and almost pained.

"I do no' ken," Dwyn whispered uncertainly. There was a strange liquid sensation in her lower belly as if small elves were inside there pouring molten gold down to a spot between her thighs, but she was experiencing so many different sensations just then, Dwyn wasn't sure what was going on. And then his hand pressed against the spot between her legs, and she gasped and jerked slightly under his hand at the sharp achy need his touch sent through her. She jerked again and cried out this time when one of his fingers slid between her slick folds to brush over the center of her building excitement.

"Aye, ye're wet," Geordie breathed, seeming pleased. Watching her face, he let his fingers dance over her moist flesh. His fingers were moving and sliding, rubbing and gliding, circling the tightening nub that was aching for his touch, but never giving it the direct contact her body seemed to be crying out for. Dwyn withstood it as long as she could, but then dug her nails into his shoulders, and gasped, "Geordie, please."

"Please what, lass?" he growled, leaning forward to nip at her raised chin with his teeth. "What do ye want? Do ye like this?"

"Aye," she groaned, lowering her head and turning her face against his in search of his mouth. Much to her relief, he kissed her then, his other hand releasing her breast to clasp the back of her head and move it as he willed. As his tongue thrust into her mouth, Geordie's fingers finally pressed against the bud they'd been avoiding.

Dwyn cried out into his mouth at the contact. She also clutched him closer, pressing her breasts against his plaid and rubbing them frantically against him as her body began to shake violently. Much to her dismay, Geordie withdrew his hand, his kiss suddenly becoming gentler, almost soothing, and then he broke it altogether and pressed a kiss just below her ear as he murmured, "I want to taste ye, lass."

"Taste me?" she whispered uncertainly, not sure what he was talking about.

"Aye, I want to see if yer as luscious as a peach like I imagined," Geordie breathed, his hand squeezing her hip under her skirts.

"Oh," she breathed, not sure what he was talking about, but hoping she was as luscious as a peach for him.

Dwyn didn't realize she'd spoken that hope aloud until he pulled back with a lazy chuckle and smiled at her as he said, "I love yer honesty, lass. And I'm sure ye are."

He kissed her again, urging her to lie back on the plaid as he did, and then he broke the kiss to shift lower and trail more kisses down her throat and collar. He paused to pay homage briefly to her breasts. Despite the excitement this caused in her, Dwyn felt her skirts sliding up her legs as he suckled briefly at her breasts, and then the material was gathered up around her waist and he left her breasts to shift between her thighs. Staring up at the tree overhead and panting, she let her legs fall open when he urged them wider, still unsure what he was up to until she felt him press his mouth to her core.

Dwyn's eyes widened with shock, her upper body rising half up off the plaid at the first lash of his tongue across her sensitive skin, and then she dropped back with a gasping grunt as he settled in to what he was doing. This was beyond anything Dwyn had ever experienced or even imagined, and she was quickly a trembling mass of sensation, her body jerking and hips thrusting under his mouth. She wanted to press her feet flat to the ground, and push up into his mouth as she'd done with her breasts when he'd been suckling there, and she wanted to scramble away and make him stop this mad torment. But she could do neither. Geordie had her pinned to the ground, her legs held open by his hands as his mouth drove her to the edge of her endurance and then pushed her over, casting her into a chaos that had her shuddering and convulsing, her eyes closed and mind completely unaware of anything but the sweet release that washed over her.

When the madness finally passed, Dwyn found herself cushioned in Geordie's arms, his hands moving soothingly over her back as he held her close against his chest and pressed kisses to the top of her head. She lay still against him for a moment as her breathing and the pounding of her heart slowed, and then cleared her throat, and whispered, "That was . . ."

She shook her head, unable to put into words what she'd just experienced.

"Ye liked it, did ye?" he asked, and she could hear gentle amusement in his voice.

"Aye," Dwyn breathed, and then tipped her head back to peer up at him. "Can we do it again?"

That brought an abrupt laugh from Geordie, and he hugged her tighter to him, and shook his head. "Nay, lass. No' now. I have to go talk to me brother."

"Oh," she sighed with disappointment, but when he didn't release her, she relaxed against him, and brushed her fingers over his chest. After a moment she became aware of a hardness pressing against her stomach, and glanced down to see the long column under his plaid. Dwyn may not have understood what he'd meant by tasting her, but she did know what she was looking at, and asked with awe, "Is that fer me?"

She glanced up in time to see him grimace, and then he offered her a weak smile and said, "Aye. I'm trying to make it go away so I can go speak to me brother."

"Oh," Dwyn said with understanding, and then asked tentatively, "Can I help?"

Geordie groaned at that, and rested his chin on her forehead as his arms tightened around her. "Ach, lass, ye're killing me here. Pray thee, just stop wiggling and asking questions and— Mayhap would help if we put yer dress back on properly," he decided suddenly, and sat up, taking her with him. Once he had her sitting upright, he reached toward the gown tangled around her waist, and then paused, a helpless expression crossing his face as his gaze slid over her naked breasts and then to her legs, bare all the way to perhaps an inch below the apex of her thighs, where her skirt now rested.

"Ye'll have to dress yerself, lass. I canno' do it. Do I touch ye . . ." Geordie shook his head woefully.

Dwyn's eyes widened at that, but she was already reaching for the top of her dress. She hadn't expected he would dress her; she'd expected to do it herself. But not with him watching, his hungry eyes roving over her breasts and making them tighten and harden with excitement as she recalled his kisses and caresses. Struggling to get her sleeves turned right side out, she glanced up at him to see that his gaze had dropped to her lap and her barely covered womanhood that he'd so recently kissed too, and Dwyn paused and scowled.

"M'laird, pray stop looking at me like I'm a peach ye wish to eat. Ye're oversetting me nerves and making me long to rip me gown off and climb in yer lap."

Geordie blinked, and then raised his eyes to her face. "Lass," he countered quietly, "while I most oft love yer honesty, this is no' a good time fer it. I am a hairsbreadth away from losing me control, pushing ye to yer back, tossing yer skirts up over yer head and thrusting into ye right here in the orchard like a lightskirt. I do no' want to take yer maiden's veil that way, and beg o' ye, please, just dress."

Dwyn hesitated, tempted to ignore his plea and reach for him, but his "like a lightskirt" comment held her back. She suspected her behavior here today already was no better than a lightskirt's. But he didn't seem to think so. She feared though that did she push him to the point of taking her here in the orchard, he would think her no better than one, and she didn't want that. The things he'd done to her, and the pleasure he'd shown her, had been glorious. Special. Like a gift. She didn't want it all tarnished and turning to dust in her mouth by going too far.

Sighing, Dwyn shifted on the blanket until her back was to him, and quickly untangled and donned the top of her gown. Her hands were still shaking from what she'd experienced, but she managed to tie her lacings despite that, and then she ran her unsteady hands through her loose hair. She was about to turn back to him when he was suddenly standing beside her and bending to pick her up.

Dwyn eyed his face solemnly as he straightened with her in his arms. "I thought ye wished to speak to yer brother?"

"I do. But I'll no' leave ye out here on yer own when ye canno' even walk," he said, turning toward the gardens.

"I could—" Dwyn paused and glanced around as the sound of a twig snapping caught her ear.

Geordie stopped as well, and they both stared along the trees, waiting for whoever had made the sound to appear. Instead, they heard the sound of someone moving quickly away.

"Ye do no' think someone saw—?" she began with concern.

"It does no' matter," Geordie said grimly, and began to walk swiftly through the trees to the path through the garden. And then he forced a smile and assured her, "All will be well as soon as I speak to me brother."

Dwyn nodded for his benefit, but didn't really believe it. If someone had seen what they'd got up to in the orchard . . . Well, she could be ruined, she supposed, but that troubled her little. She never left Innes as a rule, and they rarely had visitors, so she wasn't likely to be faced with her ruin there among the people who loved her. What bothered her more was that Geordie might be forced to marry her. To her mind that would be a terrible punishment for a man who had done nothing but show her the pleasure to be found between a man and woman. It was something she probably wouldn't have experienced otherwise.

Nay, whatever happened, she would ensure he was not forced to marry her, Dwyn decided firmly. She knew he didn't want to marry. She'd heard his brother Aulay telling his wife, Jetta, that the first afternoon when the laird had returned ahead of his brother and uncle from swimming in the loch. They hadn't realized she heard it. Dwyn had been approaching where they sat at the table to ask if she might borrow the book of crusader poetry when she'd overheard their conversation. She'd moved away then until they finished talking before approaching again to make her request. When Geordie had begun hovering over her and keeping her company after she was injured, she'd assumed his desire not to marry was why. She'd thought he was doing so to avoid the other women who were hunting for a husband. Dwyn was sure he'd felt comfortable keeping company with her because she'd already admitted she didn't expect him or his brothers to choose her, so he needn't fear her expecting anything of him.

Nay, Dwyn thought. She would not see him punished for being kind to her. If word got out of what they'd done this afternoon, and her father, or Geordie's brother Aulay, tried to force him to marry her, she'd refuse . . . she would protect Geordie Buchanan.

"GEORDIE!"

Feet slowing as he carried Dwyn around the front of the keep, Geordie glanced around at that call, relaxing when he spotted Alick ambling toward him, a wry smile on his youngest brother's maturing face. Geordie had seen Alick as a stripling for so long, it was surprising to note that his face had hardened with age, and his body had filled out, gaining muscle that matched his own. How had he missed this? he wondered, and then forced himself to concentrate as his brother began to speak.

"Rory sent me out to fetch ye back."

"Why?" Geordie asked with a frown. "Did ye run into trouble on yer journey?"

"Nay," Alick assured him quickly. "'Tis just that Jetta told him about a certain beautiful young lass who had a mishap with glass in the upper hall and asked him to look at her injuries to be sure they were healing well." His gaze drifted over Dwyn then, alighting on her bountiful breasts and pausing there briefly, before sliding on to the tops of her bare feet. Offering her a charming grin, he added, "Pray tell me ye're no' the lovely lass who suffered so. Me heart breaks at the mere thought o' ye enduring such pain."

Geordie noted the way Dwyn smiled at the flowery words, and found himself scowling at his brother. Turning abruptly away from him without even introducing her, he started toward the keep doors, growling, "Aye, this is the lass, and her name is Dwyn Innes. *Lady* Dwyn Innes, so stop ogling her like a pudding ye plan on eating and run ahead to get the door fer me, *little* brother."

"My, someone is grumpy today," Alick said with amusement as he moved past at a leisurely pace to mount the steps before him.

Geordie merely glowered at him in passing as Alick opened one of the keep doors for him to carry Dwyn inside. Pausing a couple feet inside the door though, he glanced around, frowning when he didn't see Rory or Jetta anywhere. "Where is he?"

"Probably gathering his medicinals," Alick said with unconcern as he moved up beside him on the side where Dwyn's bare feet hung over his arm.

Geordie debated what to do. Aulay was at the table and he wanted to speak to him, but he had no idea where Rory would want to look at Dwyn's feet. It could be her room, or Jetta might suggest taking her to the master chamber to tend them there again. He was trying to decide whether to carry her to the table or take her directly above stairs when Dwyn gasped and gave a startled laugh.

Glancing down he noted the way she was blushing.

"Ye're ticklish," Alick said with amusement, and Geordie

glanced to his brother to see that he had lifted Dwyn's foot by her big toe so that he could look at her injuries. Alick then shifted his hold to clasp her by the back of her foot and lifted her leg higher. His smile immediately died, and he murmured, "My, ye did do yerself some damage. Is the other foot as bad?"

"Most o' them are surface cuts," Dwyn said quickly as he raised her second foot to examine it as well. "I did no' even need stitches."

Disliking Alick touching her so familiarly, Geordie glowered at him, and then started walking again, deciding the table would do for now. He was impatient to speak to Aulay and get the wedding arrangements in place. He wanted to marry her quickly, today even, and would not be talked into waiting to hold some grand celebration once every one of his siblings and their mates could travel here. He'd resort to handfasting with Dwyn, if necessary, and marry her later, but he was not waiting to bed her. He simply couldn't. Not after tasting her passion in the orchard.

Geordie liked to think he was a good lover, but he'd never had a woman come apart under his attention as Dwyn had. The woman was as open and honest with her passion as she was in everything else, and he was nearly rabid with the need to bed her. But he was determined she understand her worth to him. He wanted her married to him, or at least handfasted, so that she understood how much he valued her, how much he wanted her, but also how much he was coming to care for her.

Pausing as he reached the head of the trestle tables, Geordie hesitated and frowned, unsure where to set her. He didn't want to set her on the bench and let her unbandaged feet rest in the rushes, but—

"Set her on the tabletop," Aulay said, seeming to realize the issue.

"Oh, nay!" Dwyn protested, but Geordie was already sitting her on the table so that her feet could rest on the bench.

"We canno' have yer feet in the rushes, lass," he pointed out solemnly as he slid his arms out from under her. "They're unwrapped and like to get infected."

Dwyn did not protest further, but merely sighed with resignation.

Pleased that she wasn't arguing or fussing, Geordie bent and kissed her nose. It wasn't until he straightened and noticed the surprise on her face, and then glanced around to see the interest on his brothers' faces, that Geordie realized what he'd done. Shrugging, he told Aulay, "I would have a word with ye."

"Aye." Aulay stood at once even as Alick settled on the bench next to Dwyn's feet and grinned up at her.

"No' yet," Geordie said, waving Aulay back to his seat. "After Rory returns and I carry Dwyn to wherever it is he wants to examine her."

"Alick can do that," Aulay pointed out.

"Aye," Alick said, popping up off the bench at once. "I'd be pleased to carry—"

"Ye're no' touching her," Geordie barked. "So get that out o' yer head and sit yer arse down." He waited until Alick had sat down, and then turned to Aulay to find his brother eyeing him with interest. When Aulay's gaze shifted to Dwyn, Geordie followed his gaze to her and he frowned when he saw the concern on her face. She was obviously confused by what was going on, and starting to fret.

"Everything is fine," he assured her in a soft voice. "Just rest here a minute."

When she relaxed a little, he waved at Aulay to follow and walked over to stand near the doors to the kitchen. Turning to face his brother, he opened his mouth, and then paused, searching for where to start.

Before he could figure it out, Aulay asked, "Have ye slept with her?"

"Nay," Geordie snapped, glad he hadn't and could answer that honestly. "But I'm marrying her."

"I'm glad," Aulay said at once, not seeming terribly surprised. "I like her. So does Jetta."

Geordie smiled faintly at the words. "She's a smart, sweet, honest and lovely lass who laughs as easily as most lassies weep."

"Aye," Aulay began. "Well, then, we should—"

"She's worth more than all the other women here combined," Geordie added.

"Her father—" Aulay tried again.

"I've never met a more sensitive lass either," Geordie informed him.

Aulay paused to frown at that. "Sensitive as in weepy, or—?"

"Nay," he said with disgust. "At least I do no' think so, else Catriona and Sasha's antics would have had her in tears. I meant something as small as a light caress down her arm can make her shiver and break out in goose bumps, and mere kisses can make her mewl and moan with need, and—"

"Aye, well, I would no' tell her father that," Aulay said dryly, interrupting his explanation. He paused briefly, but then asked, "Are ye sure, Geordie? Ye have no' kenned the woman long."

"How long did it take ye to decide ye wanted Jetta to wife?" Geordie countered.

"I take yer point," Aulay said wryly.

"It does no' take long to sort out whether a lass is a good woman or no'," Geordie said solemnly. "And once ye do, if ye're lucky enough to burn to bed her, I figure ye've found yerself a wife."

"Aye," Aulay agreed, and then straightened. "Then if ye're sure ye want to marry the lass, I guess we'd best talk to her father."

"Aye, I'm positive I do," Geordie assured him. "Tonight."

"What?" Aulay asked with surprise, and immediately started to shake his head. "Ye canno'—"

"I am," he said grimly.

"Geordie," Aulay began with exasperation. "Surely ye can wait the week or two it would take fer Saidh and our brothers to make their way here to—"

"Certainly I could," he admitted, though he wasn't sure that was true. Dwyn was like a fever in his blood. He *needed* to bed her. "But I do no' want to."

"Sometimes, ye canno' do what ye want," Aulay said firmly. "And if her father wishes to delay . . ."

"I suggest ye help me convince him no' to wait," Geordie said grimly. "Because while the wedding may wait, I canno', and I would really rather she be mine ere I take her maiden's veil . . . tonight."

"Geordie," he tried in a reasoning tone. "It will no' kill ye to wait a week or two to marry and bed the lass."

"Really?" Geordie narrowed his eyes. "Fine. I will wait a week or two . . . if you do."

Aulay stiffened, his eyes narrowing. "What mean ye by that?"

"I mean, if ye're willing no' to bed yer wife fer the week or two it takes fer everyone to get here, I'll no' bed Dwyn. Howbeit," he added firmly, "I suggest we both go to the lodge until the wedding day to ensure we both behave."

Aulay's mouth tightened grimly. "I'll talk to her father."

"Ye do that," Geordie said dryly, and turned to glance at Dwyn, frowning when he saw that Rory had arrived, as had Uncle Acair, and they and Alick were now all gathered around Dwyn, laughing, and chatting up a storm. And the lass was laughing too. Her hair was a wild tumble of pale gold around her face and shoulders that gleamed in the candlelight, her eyes were sparkling, and she wore the wide, relaxed smile of a woman who had just rolled from bed after being tumbled. She was ridiculously gorgeous, and his brothers were noticing. They were also noticing how the neckline of her gown dropped with her every laugh.

Growling deep in his throat, he started toward the table, but was brought up short by Aulay's hand on his arm.

"They are yer brothers and uncle. She is safe with them," his older brother said firmly, and then pointed out, "And we have a contract to negotiate."

"You negotiate it," Geordie said in a low grating voice. "I—"

"You will come with me for the negotiations. Ye can survive without Dwyn fer an hour or so."

"An hour?" he protested with dismay.

"This is yer life we are about to negotiate, Geordie," he pointed out. "And hers. Ye can spare an hour to see 'tis done right."

Sighing at that, Geordie glanced toward Dwyn as she laughed again.

"Aye," was all he said, but he followed silently as Aulay led him to the lower table where Dwyn's father sat talking to Una and Aileen.

Chapter 8

"TONIGHT?" BARON JAMES INNES SQUAWKED. HE'D BEEN MOST accommodating until this point in the conversation, nodding calmly as Aulay explained that Geordie would like Dwyn to wife. The man did not even seem surprised. He'd agreed with all the points Aulay had made, assuring them that Geordie would be his heir and the next laird, even saying that he grew weary of the task and would be pleased to share it with him until Geordie had a chance to get a feel for the place and the people and was ready to take over fully as laird. It was only when Aulay got to the part about the marriage taking place right away, that very evening, that James Innes had balked.

"Are ye mad?" the man asked now. "How would that look?"

"I do no' care how it looks. I want her. Now," Geordie said grimly.

James Innes narrowed his eyes on him, and then dropped to sit on the edge of Aulay's desk and shook his head. "Ye've fallen hard fer the lass, just like I did her mother all those years ago. The two are so much alike, I sometimes . . ." He sighed and glanced to Geordie. "It snuck up on ye, did it no'? Ye most like looked at Dwyn and thought she was a nice enough lass, a small wren, not displeasing to the eye, but by no means as lovely as a white swan, or as majestic as the golden eagle. And then she smiled, and laughed, and began to speak, and ye saw the swan hiding behind the wren. And did ye kiss her, or anything else, ye found the golden eagle and its mighty talons have got ye by the scruff o' the neck now."

Geordie remained silent, but blinked at the words. They

described things pretty well, except he would have said it was his ballocks the eagle had in its talons, and he liked it. In fact, he wanted more of it.

"Well." James stood up and straightened his shoulders. "I understand yer eagerness. I have been there meself. But I'm going to make ye wait until tomorrow night." He held up a hand for silence when Geordie started to protest, and pointed out, "Lady Jetta already planned for a feast tomorrow, and me daughter deserves a feast fer her wedding. She deserves to remember her wedding day fondly, and as special. No' as some rushed affair ere ye tumble her and take her maiden's veil."

Geordie forced himself to relax. Dwyn did deserve a wedding feast. He could wait one night and day to give her a celebration she might be able to remember fondly.

"Very well," Laird Innes said solemnly, correctly taking his silence as agreement. "Then let's get this contract drawn up and signed."

"THERE WE GO, THEN. THIS LEATHER SHOULD PROTECT THE LINEN that protects yer feet."

Dwyn smiled at Rory Buchanan as he finished wrapping a soft thin leather around the linens he'd already bound her injured feet with. They looked ridiculously big now he was done, but she could sit on the bench seat and set them in the rushes without worry of infection. Which was something at least.

"No more airing them out," Rory added firmly now. "I ken most people think 'tis good for a wound to be aired on occasion, but I've found it slows healing rather than aids it. And the risk o' infection increases, especially on feet." Straightening, he met her gaze. "And ye must still stay off them fer now, especially the right foot. Ye've a couple o' deep cuts there that are like to split open the minute ye put weight on it. They'll heal quicker do ye stay off them."

"Aye. I'll stay off them," Dwyn assured him when he paused expectantly.

"Will she be able to dance by tomorrow night?" Una asked as

Rory started putting his medicinals back in his bag. She and Aileen had come to join them shortly after Aulay and Geordie had disappeared above stairs with their father. The pair had hovered behind the men, paying close attention to everything Rory had said.

"Me sisters," Dwyn explained when Rory and the other two men turned to peer at the two brunettes eyeing them with concern. Gesturing to the taller lass wearing a cream dress today, she said, "This is Una, and—" she gestured to the shorter lass in a dark green gown "—Aileen."

A moment was spared for the men to offer up greetings and for Una and Aileen to respond, and then Rory answered Una's question.

"I'm thinking she will," he said cautiously. "At least for a dance or two." Turning back to Dwyn, he added, "I would no' overdue it though. And I'd advise ye to stay off yer feet until then. But keep the linens on until I look at them again. Do no' even take them off in bed."

"I will," Dwyn promised, but asked, "Can I sit on the bench seat now rather than the tabletop?"

Chuckling, Rory moved his bag of medicinals and then clasped her by the waist and lifted her off the table, to set her on the bench.

"Thank ye," she murmured as she swung her feet over the bench and turned to face the table. Her gaze struck on Catriona and Sasha as she turned, and Dwyn noted the looks being sent her way by the pair, but merely sighed wearily at the sight. Truly, the two women were always glaring at her, and she was growing sick of it. She knew they saw her as somehow usurping attention they wanted, but one would think they'd realize by now that it wasn't intentional, and that their own attitudes were not gaining them attention, at least not the kind they wanted.

"So," Rory said now, settling on her right while Una and Aileen took up position on her left. "All these lasses are hunting up husbands, are they?"

"They're hunting Buchanan husbands," Acair said dryly as

he waved to get a maid's attention and imitated drinking from a nonexistent mug. Presumably the maid understood the gesture for the request for drink it was. At least, the lass rushed into the kitchens then, Dwyn noted, and then glanced to Rory to see that his gaze was sliding over the women in the room. While Catriona and Sasha were seated at the table alternating between casting glares her way, and sultry smiles toward the Buchanan brothers, the other five women were standing in a group by the hearth, chatting and casting nervous glances toward the newly arrived Buchanan brothers.

"Most o' the ladies seem nice enough," Aileen offered quietly.

"Aye, all but the two down the table," Una added in a quiet growl. "A couple o' vipers."

"Why do they keep glaring at ye, Dwyn?" Alick asked.

Dwyn glanced toward the women in time to see Catriona stand and move off toward the kitchens, but then turned back and merely shrugged. "I do no' ken. They took a dislike to me from the start, though I canno' think what I did that caused it."

"Nothing," Una said firmly. "They are just jealous."

Dwyn laughed at the suggestion. "Of what? They are much prettier than me."

"Mayhap," Aileen said at once, "but people *like* you. Ye make everyone ye meet feel better just by being around them. Besides, ye have a bigger bosom than the two o' them put together."

Dwyn groaned and dropped her forehead into her palm. "Thank ye, Aileen. As if yer forcing me to wear tight, low-cut gowns was no' enough to draw every eye to me bosom, talking about it surely will."

"Well, 'tis true," Una said with a shrug. "And a lass has to make the best o' her assets."

"I like to think me mind and kindness are much larger assets than me bosom," she said dryly.

"Nothing could be bigger than yer bosom," Aileen said solemnly.

Dwyn wasn't surprised when startled laughs slipped from Geordie's brothers and uncle. To give them their due though, all three men quickly cut off their amusement and managed to avoid looking at her bosom when she glanced their way. Rory even gave her a sympathetic grin and said, "Younger siblings, eh?"

Dwyn grimaced and admitted, "'Tis me own fault. I as good as raised them, and am the one who taught them to be so blunt and honest."

"Honesty is a fine trait in a person," Rory assured her.

"Aye, but I am beginning to see there may be such a thing as too much honesty," she said, her lips twisting wryly.

"Ye raised yer sisters?" Alick asked, turning sideways on the bench seat and propping an elbow on the table to lean that way to see her around Rory.

"Aye," Dwyn said, and then paused to murmur thanks as a drink was set by her elbow. "Me mother died when I was six, and I was left to run wild until me father married Una and Aileen's mother. She did try to teach me to be a little lady. However, she died after Aileen was born when I was about nine and . . ." She shrugged, and took a sip of her drink before continuing. "Da had no idea what to do with three daughters." She smiled suddenly. "In truth, 'tis me father I feel sorry for. He seems bewildered by us more often than not. As for the three o' us, we rarely have company at Innes and so have got used to saying and doing what we wish. Hence," she added dryly, "why Aileen and Una have no compunction at all about talking about inappropriate things."

When Dwyn glanced at her sisters and saw the unconcerned expressions on their faces, she added, "I suspect we are very poor ladies in comparison to most women who were raised properly and with ladylike behavior drilled into them."

"Well, the three o' ye seem like fine ladies to me," Rory said staunchly.

"Aye," Acair agreed from where he hovered behind her. "'Tis refreshing to talk with lassies ye do no' have to watch yer every word around."

"Actually, 'tis no' that ye're no' ladies," Alick said slowly. "'Tis more like ye're family."

Dwyn lowered her glass from taking another drink and turned to look at the younger Buchanan with interest, noting that the men were peering at him thoughtfully as he continued. "While Saidh and Evina are more rough around the edges, Murine, Jetta and Edith all behave with a certain . . ."

"Decorum?" she suggested when he hesitated.

"Aye. Decorum," Alick agreed. "'Tis as if they pull on the mask o' a lady when in the company o' strangers. But they're much more relaxed around each other and family. You and yer sisters just seem to no' bother with the mask. Ye do no' give those silly little titters other ladies use, or hide yer irritation or joy rather than express true emotion, and ye mention openly things that everyone sees and leaves unspoken. Ye act as though everyone is family." He shrugged. "In truth, while I've no' kenned ye long, I feel comfortable around ye already. I feel ye accept me without judgment. Ye feel like family." He smiled. "I think Geordie's a lucky man."

Dwyn's eyebrows flew up with alarm at that claim. "Oh, Geordie is no' lucky. I mean, he's no interested in me that way. He's been very kind and kept company with me because o' me hurting me feet, but he's no' interested in marrying. I heard yer brother Aulay telling his wife that Geordie had said so."

"Aye, he did say that his first day home," Acair admitted when Rory and Alick looked disbelieving. "But he was no' very convincing and is most possessive o' ye, lass. 'Tis why I flirted with ye so shamelessly, to give him a poke and help him decide what he really wanted." He grinned and nodded when Dwyn turned to glance at him with surprise, and then added, "And it appears to have worked. He's in talking with Aulay and yer da right now, and I'm thinking the lad's definitely interested and we may be having a wedding here soon."

Dwyn frowned at the suggestion, and picked up her drink to gulp some down as her gaze slid to the upper landing. Acair might think Geordie had changed his mind, but he didn't know what had happened in the orchard and that it might have been witnessed. If Geordie had changed his mind, she suspected Aulay had changed it for him after hearing what they'd got up to. That was not something she wanted. Had Geordie wanted her to wife himself, that would be one thing, but she had no desire to have a man forced to marry her, and then resent her for it all the days of her life. Especially not Geordie, who had shown her such pleasure.

"Are ye all right, lass?" Rory asked suddenly, and when she glanced at him in question, he pointed out, "Ye're rubbing yer stomach. Is it paining ye?"

Dwyn glanced down at herself to see that she was indeed rubbing her stomach, but then it *was* troubling her a bit. Probably just a result of her worry, she thought, and took another drink.

"SO, WE'RE AGREED?" JAMES INNES ASKED. "WE'LL HAVE A CEREMONY here tomorrow, and hold a second ceremony and celebration at Innes for our people to witness?"

Geordie nodded impatiently. He was fine with that; he just wanted this over with so that he could go tell Dwyn he was marrying her. Or should he ask her? He wondered over that briefly, and frowned. Surely she'd be willing? He didn't want her to marry him only because her father had agreed to it. He wanted her to want to be married to him, and her response to him in the orchard made him think she would. But they hadn't known each other long, and she had mentioned those worries she had about dying on the birthing bed.

Geordie frowned as he recalled that. He didn't intend to allow that to happen. In fact, he decided he'd best press Rory into promising to stay with them during the last weeks of her every pregnancy so that he was sure to be there to attend it. If anyone could see her safely through giving birth to their children, it was Rory. Geordie wasn't losing her to the birthing bed. In fact, mayhap he should avoid spilling his seed in her. He could live without a child for a while. It was her he didn't want to do without.

"That's it, then," Aulay said, straightening. "If ye'll just both sign . . ."

Geordie glanced around to see Baron Innes bending to sign the marriage contract. When the man finished, he took the quill and signed his own name, the tension in him easing as he did. It was done. Dwyn would be his.

"I'll just go talk to Dwyn and tell her—" James Innes began.

"Nay," Geordie interrupted, straightening from the desk. "I will ask her first."

Baron Innes raised his eyebrows at that. "There's no need to ask, lad. The contract is done. She's yours."

"I will still ask anyway," Geordie insisted.

Dwyn's father shrugged. "As ye will."

Geordie turned to head for the door, aware that the other two men were following. He led the way out into the hall, and was headed for the stairs, when he noticed the activity down by the garderobe. Alick, Uncle Acair, Jetta and Dwyn's sisters, Una and Aileen, were all standing about outside the garderobe door, looking anxious. He was just wondering what was about when Alick glanced around and spotted him. The way his brother's eyes widened just before he rushed toward them, his hands rising as if to soothe a skittish horse, immediately sent alarm coursing through him.

"What's happening?" he asked sharply.

"'Tis fine. Do no' panic," Alick said soothingly. "Rory says she'll most like be fine."

"What?" he asked with alarm. "No' Dwyn?"

His expression was answer enough, and Geordie went to move past him, but paused when Jetta now reached them too, and patted his arm, her face a mask of concern. "Dwyn is purging, Geordie. But Rory does no' think the poison was deadly. Just one to make her ill."

"Poison!" he bellowed with alarm, and nothing could have kept him from hurrying forward then.

"Aye," Alick said as he, Aulay, Jetta and Laird Innes rushed to keep up with him. "'Twas in her drink. She complained her tummy was upset, and Rory grabbed a pitcher to refill her glass thinking a drink might settle her stomach, but then he suddenly stopped and sniffed her mug. The next thing we all knew, he'd jumped up, scooped up Dwyn and rushed away from the table. Both garderobes below were busy and he had to bring her up to this one. He was just in time too. She started retching just as I got the door open."

"It was in her mug, no' the ale?" Aulay asked behind him.

"As far as I ken," Alick said with a frown.

"Go and check," Aulay ordered, and Alick turned and hurried away to the stairs as Geordie urged Dwyn's sisters aside so that he could get to the garderobe door. He reached for the handle, but paused as he heard the violent retching coming from the other side of the door.

"She'll be embarrassed do ye see her getting sick like this," Una said quietly. "She does no' like to appear weak in front o' anyone."

"Aye," Aileen said sadly. "She's always had to be strong fer us, ye see. 'Tis why we are so determined to see her married. She was a good mother to us. She should have children o' her own, and a husband to care for her, instead o' always having to be the strong one."

The words struck Geordie like a blow, and he turned to spear her father with a furious gaze. "Dwyn was nine when yer second wife died. I knew she helped take care o' her sisters after that, but surely ye did no' leave her to raise them on her own?"

"Aye, he did," Una said, and he could hear the resentment in her voice. "She ran the keep too, and even took care o' listening to the villagers' complaints, and judging disputes."

"She also arranged our betrothal contracts," Aileen said quietly.

"Like Conran's Evina," Aulay said grimly.

"Dwyn wanted to do all that," Laird Innes said with exasperation. "She kenned I was busy cataloging the different plants on Innes property, and writing me music, and she was always a lass who needed to keep busy. She was like her mother that way."

Geordie scowled at the man, and turned back to Dwyn's sisters. "Did she oversee the men too?"

"O' course no'," Baron Innes said with irritation before either of his daughters could answer. "She was just a lass. My first took care o' the soldiers at Innes."

Geordie exchanged a grim glance with Aulay, and then became aware that the retching sounds had stopped and turned to knock at the door. "Rory? Dwyn? Can I come in?"

"Nay," Dwyn moaned, even as Rory said, "Aye."

"I told ye," Una said now. "She'll no' want ye to see her like this, m'laird."

Geordie scowled, and hesitated. He wanted to see that Dwyn was all right. But he didn't want to upset her when she was feeling poorly. It was Aulay who made up his mind for him.

"Begin as ye plan to go on, brother," he said solemnly. "Will ye be there to comfort her when she's ill? Or leave her on her own to save her a bit o' embarrassment?"

"Ballocks to that," Geordie growled, and pulled the door open.

"Oh, nay!" Dwyn moaned, covering her face when she saw him entering the garderobe. "Please, just let me die in peace."

"Ye're no' dying. I'll no' let ye," he said firmly, moving to kneel next to where she crouched in front of the low wooden counter with its hole in the center that she'd no doubt been purging through moments ago. Rubbing her back, he glanced to his brother and asked, "She is no' dying, is she? Jetta said you said she'd be fine."

"Aye, she will be fine. She just will feel like she's dying fer a bit," Rory said on a sigh.

Geordie's mouth tightened at that, and then he glanced to Dwyn. Her head was bowed, her hands over her face, and her long hair curtaining even that from his view. "Are ye done purgin', lass? Would ye like to lie down, mayhap?"

Dwyn was silent and unmoving for a moment, and then nodded on a weary sigh.

Geordie picked her up at once, bundling her close to his chest when she tucked her face into his neck. He suspected she was trying not to let him see her, but simply turned to the door. Rory moved in front of him and stepped out first, then held the door for him, and Geordie carried her out through the small crowd.

"I will get my medicinals from downstairs and mix up something that will hopefully help settle her stomach at least a little," Rory said, stepping up beside him as they moved through the silent group. "Which room do I bring it to?"

"Mine," Geordie growled, glaring at Dwyn's father in case he thought to protest. The man didn't say a word though. It wasn't until he'd reached the door to his room and Una rushed ahead to open it for him that he recalled the sisters were staying there anyway.

Murmuring a "thank ye," he carried Dwyn to the bed and then paused briefly before simply climbing onto it and settling to sit against the headboard with Dwyn in his arms.

Her sisters were the only ones who had followed him into the room. They both now stood at the foot of the bed, staring wide-eyed at them. He ignored them and simply held Dwyn, hugging her tight to his chest for several moments, before easing his hold so he could rub her back.

"There, lass," Geordie murmured as he ran his hand soothingly up and down her back. "Rory is fetching ye something to help settle yer stomach. Ye'll feel better soon," he assured her, though he wasn't at all sure that was true. Rory had said she would feel like she was dying for a bit, after all. Not that she would feel like she was dying until he gave her something to feel better.

"I'm sorry I'm such a bother," Dwyn mumbled against his throat, and Geordie grimaced as his body responded to the unintentional caress. Dear God, the woman was ill and he was still sprouting an erection from just holding her and having her lips at his neck. Thank God he had set her in his lap and her sisters couldn't see the proof of his insensitivity, he thought, and then realized Dwyn could probably feel that proof under her bottom and no doubt was disgusted with him.

Sighing, he pressed her to his chest in a half hug, and muttered, "Ye're no' a bother. And none o' this has been yer fault."

"Well, obviously I've angered someone," she pointed out reasonably.

"Everyone here likes ye just fine too," he assured her.

"Not everyone," she grumbled.

"Aulay and Jetta like ye," he assured her. "Aulay told me so."

"Did he?" she asked with surprise, and then said, "That's nice. I like them too."

"And I'm quite sure me other brothers and me uncle like ye as well. They all seemed to be enjoying yer company when I left with Aulay to talk with yer father," he pointed out.

She went still and silent for a minute, and then asked, "What were ye talking to me father about?"

Noting the curiosity on her sisters' faces, Geordie smiled wryly, but tried to think of a way to avoid answering that. This was not the moment for him to ask her to marry him. Fortunately, a knock at the door saved him from trying to come up with something to say that avoided the subject of marriage.

Una moved to answer it, and much to his relief Rory entered with a mug in hand.

"I decided a sleeping draught might be the best solution here," Rory announced as he approached the bed. "Nothing is likely to settle her stomach, but if she can keep this down long enough, she can at least sleep through the discomfort."

Geordie nodded at that and glanced down at Dwyn. "Can ye sit up, lass, and drink what Rory brought fer ye?"

Dwyn sighed against his neck, but reluctantly straightened and held out a hand for the mug Rory held.

"Ye might want to pinch yer nose, lass," Rory said before giving it to her. "With yer stomach as sensitive as it is just now, the smell may have ye retching again ere ye can even drink it." Glancing around then, he spotted the ewer and bowl on the table, and said, "Can one o' ye lasses bring the bowl over in case she canno' keep this down?"

Aileen hurried to the table, set the ewer aside and brought the bowl over to the bed.

"Go ahead," Rory said after taking the bowl from her sister. When Dwyn immediately plugged her nose, he offered the mug. They were all silent as she gulped the liquid down, and Geordie took the opportunity to look her over. Her face was pale, and there were tracks on her cheeks. Tears had obviously escaped her eyes as she'd purged. He wasn't surprised. Even muffled through the door, her retching had sounded violent. But she was still beautiful to him, Geordie thought, and then quickly took the mug from her when Dwyn suddenly froze, her eyes widening with horror.

Even as he set the mug on the bedside table, Rory was moving forward with the bowl Aileen had brought over. Geordie turned back just in time to support her shoulders and hold her hair back as she brought up the liquid she'd just taken in.

"How is she?"

Geordie lowered the hand he'd been rubbing the back of his neck with and glanced up wearily at that question from Jetta as he reached the trestle tables. "She's finally asleep, but 'twas a long night," he said quietly, and then shifted his gaze over the people at the table. It was morning, and the entire inhabitants of the castle appeared to be breaking their fast except for Dwyn and her sisters. Dwyn was sleeping. Her sisters were watching her while he came below to break his fast and find out what they'd discovered about who had poisoned Dwyn. His gaze stopping on Rory, he asked grimly, "What the devil was it she was poisoned with? She was retching all night."

Rory opened his mouth to answer, paused and then sighed tiredly. "I am too weary to recall the name o' the plant at the moment, but its only effect is to upset a person's stomach and set them vomiting."

"From what Alick said, it sounded like ye recognized the smell o' it in her mug," Geordie said quietly.

"Aye," Rory said dryly. "It has a very recognizable, sickly sweet smell that ye do no' forget once ye smell it, and with all the liquid gone, some o' the crushed leaves were in the bottom o' the mug, the smell faint, but there." He grimaced and added, "The taste is no' one ye're likely to forget either, but it can be covered with a drink that has a strong flavor o' its own."

"But it would not have killed her?" Jetta asked solemnly. "So someone just wanted to make Dwyn sick?"

"I guess cutting her feet was no' misery enough fer her attacker," Geordie said grimly.

"What?" Rory said with surprise. "I thought that was an accident?"

"Nay," Jetta said sadly. "The glass was not there when Dwyn entered the garderobe and Aulay and Geordie think it was spread on the floor deliberately so that she would cut herself on the way out."

"The glass was evenly spread wall to wall rather than in any kind of circular or star-shaped pattern," Geordie explained, not surprised Aulay had shared what they suspected with his wife. "And the torch by the garderobe was out."

Everyone was silent for a minute, and then Alick said, "Well, Geordie, the good news is that ye've picked a bride someone just wishes to torment and no' kill like the rest o' our sisters-in-law. That makes a nice change." When everyone turned to look at him, he said defensively, "Well, it is."

Geordie shook his head, and rubbed his tired eyes. He'd been awake all night with Dwyn. While she'd had moments where her stomach had seemed to settle briefly, as it had before he'd carried her out of the garderobe, those moments had been few, short and far apart. She'd spent the rest of the time retching, doing so long after there was anything to bring up. But the protracted retching had given her a headache, and begun to cause spasms in her stomach muscles. The additional symptoms had merely added to Dwyn's misery.

It had been terribly difficult to watch her suffer so and not be able to do anything but hold her, rub her back and keep her hair back from her face. Geordie had been more than relieved when she'd finally fallen asleep as the sun rose. He suspected it was simple exhaustion that had allowed her to drift off, but when she'd slept for an hour without waking to retch again, and her sisters had insisted he should break his fast first, he'd judged it might be over and safe for him to come below briefly. He'd known the lasses had wanted to refresh themselves and change before leaving the room anyway, and his absence would give them the chance to do that. Besides, Una and Aileen had gone for dinner the night before while he hadn't, and had managed to drift off to sleep on pallets Aulay had ordered brought into the room for them. With nothing to bring back up, and with Dwyn growing weaker as each hour passed, her retching had become much quieter. Even so, he didn't think he could have slept through it and didn't know how they had.

Running his hands through his hair now, he muttered, "I gather ye have no idea who poisoned her?"

"Nay," Aulay admitted with a scowl. "Everyone was entering the great hall then, and there were a lot of servants coming out with drinks. No one noticed the mug being set beside Dwyn." He was silent for a minute, and then added, "We have been thinking perhaps we should put the wedding and feast off at least until tomorrow night."

"Dwyn will no doubt sleep through the day," Jetta pointed out gently when Geordie opened his mouth to protest. "She will be in no shape for a wedding, let alone a wedding feast and the bedding tonight."

Geordie closed his mouth in defeat. In truth, he doubted he'd be in shape for a wedding, feast and bedding himself at this point. He was so exhausted his vision was blurring. Nodding, he stood abruptly.

"Where are ye going?" Aulay asked with concern.

"Back to watch over Dwyn," he said, stepping over the bench.

"But you have not eaten," Jetta pointed out with concern.

Geordie paused briefly, but then shrugged indifferently. "I'm too tired to be hungry."

He didn't wait for further protests, but walked away and headed for the stairs.

As he'd expected, Una and Aileen had changed and made themselves more presentable while he was gone. The two stayed long enough to assure him that Dwyn hadn't stirred at all while he was gone, and then slipped from the room.

The moment the door closed behind them, Geordie climbed into bed with Dwyn, shifted himself onto his side behind her so that he was spooning her and then wrapped an arm around her and quickly drifted off to sleep.

Chapter 9

Dwyn woke up feeling like something had crawled into her mouth and died there while she slept. On top of that her head was pounding, and her stomach muscles ached with every breath she took. But she had no immediate need to retch. That was something anyway, she thought grimly as she opened her eyes and peered around what she could see of the room. Bright sunlight was streaming in through the open shutters, falling on the gowns and shifts discarded in a pile in the corner, and the empty mugs on the bedside table.

A grimace claimed her lips when Dwyn spotted the mugs. One was the remaining half of the sleeping potion Rory had mixed for her after Geordie had first brought her back to the room she and her sisters were using. The other was a half-full mug of cider that she'd tried to drink in the middle of the night after going a half hour without retching. It was as much as she'd managed to drink before her stomach had rebelled.

Sighing, she closed her eyes briefly, and then frowned slightly as she became aware of a heavy weight along her side to her hip, and something warm against her back. Opening her eyes again, Dwyn shifted her head slightly on the pillow to stare blankly at the arm resting along her side that ended in a sun-darkened hand that was curved over her hip. She recognized that hand. She'd watched it twirl flowers between thumb and finger, hold reins before her, tug up the neckline of her gown and close over her breasts. The hand was Geordie's. She was in bed with Geordie.

Dwyn knew she should be shocked at that, but couldn't find the energy to stir the emotion let alone sustain it. Besides, he'd been there the whole time she'd been sick, holding her with care and concern while she'd retched, murmuring soft soothing words after and cradling her in his arms in the short intervals in between.

Geordie Buchanan was a saint, Dwyn decided with a weary smile. Her own father had never even visited her when she was ill as a child, staying far away from her at times like that lest he get sick himself, yet this man had tended her like a loving nursemaid. Of course, she'd been poisoned, which wasn't something he could have caught. Still, he had taken care of her, and that was what was important.

Reaching down, she covered his hand gently with hers, startled when his hand suddenly turned under hers and his large fingers slid between her smaller ones and clasped gently.

"Ye're awake." It was a sleepy growl by her ear, and Dwyn closed her eyes briefly at the shiver it sent through her.

"Aye," she whispered after a moment, frowning when her voice came out husky and broken. Her throat hurt to speak.

"How is yer stomach?" Geordie asked, concern entering his voice. "Do ye think ye could keep cider down?"

Dwyn grimaced at the mention of cider. She'd spent quite a while retching up the last bit of cider she'd tried to drink, and the memory made the drink completely unpalatable to her just then.

"Mead instead?"

Dwyn turned her head to see that he had rested his elbow on the pillow behind her and propped his head on his hand. It put his face above hers so that he could look down on her. He'd seen her grimace, she realized, and quickly turned her head away so that he couldn't look on the horror she must be at that moment.

"Mayhap mead," she whispered, unable to speak with full volume until she had something to drink. At least, she hoped liquid would soothe her sore throat and allow her to speak again.

Dwyn stilled with surprise when Geordie suddenly bent and pressed a kiss to her cheek. When he followed that by rolling away from her, she turned onto her back, and watched silently as he strode to the door and slipped out of the room. The moment the door closed behind him, she sat up and swung her feet off the bed, but paused when her wrapped feet hit the floor and she recalled that she was not supposed to walk on them.

Scowling, Dwyn glanced down at herself and then around the room. She wanted to wash her face and brush her hair. She'd like to change out of her wrinkled dress too before he returned, but she couldn't get out of bed and nothing was close enough to be useful. Breathing out an exasperated breath, she tugged up her neckline, and tried to brush out the worst of the wrinkles in her skirts, then she began running her fingers through her hair, trying to restore some order to it. She was still working on it when she heard the door open. Turning swiftly, she peered over her shoulder and saw her sisters entering.

"Geordie sent us to sit with ye while he arranges fer food and a bath fer ye," Aileen said with a bright smile as she hurried to the bed.

"How do ye feel?" Una asked, following their younger sister.

"Like horse dung," Dwyn admitted with a grimace, her voice barely more than a whisper.

"Oh." Aileen's smile faded a bit, but then she rallied and hurried away. "Well, you will probably feel better if ye wash yer face and brush yer hair."

"Aye," Dwyn agreed with relief, glad she didn't have to ask for a brush and the basin of water her sister was collecting and bringing back to her. Her throat was really sore and her voice broken. The less she talked, the better, until she had something to drink.

"Here." Aileen set the bowl of water on the bedside table and handed the hairbrush to Una, then turned away to rush back for a strip of linen and the soap that were on the same table the ewer and basin had sat on.

"I'll brush yer hair," Una offered, and climbed onto the bed to sit behind her.

"Geordie was most gentle and caring with ye last night," Aileen announced as she moved back with the other items.

"Aye," Dwyn whispered as Una began to draw the brush through her hair. "I remember."

"He's such a wonderful man, sister," Aileen said with awe as she dipped the linen in the room temperature water and then rubbed the soft soap on it. "I am ever so glad we came here."

Dwyn didn't respond to that; she didn't get the chance. Aileen had finished soaping the linen and was now washing her face for her. Did she speak, she was like to end up with a mouthful of suds. Feeling like a child, Dwyn tried to reach up to take the cloth from her and take over the job, but it was gone before she could.

"They delayed the feast and dancing until tomorrow so ye can attend," Aileen added as she turned to rinse out the linen in the water, and Dwyn's eyes popped open with dismay.

"Oh, but—" Her voice died there and she moved her tongue around inside her mouth, trying to build up enough saliva to swallow and wet her throat. Aside from painful, her throat felt dry and scaly, and she was sure if she could just moisten it, she would be better able to talk.

"Oh, stop," Una said from behind her as she continued to drag the brush through the tangles in her hair. "I ken ye want to protest that they should no' delay it on yer account and so on. But they have and that's that. Besides, ye deserve to enjoy a nice feast and dancing after all ye've been through here." She made a sound of exasperation and then pointed out, "First, someone got yer feet all cut up, and now ye've been made sick—"

"No one got me feet cut up," Dwyn managed in a raspy whisper. "That, unlike the poison, was an accident."

"Nay," Una assured her. "It was no' an accident. The Buchanans think someone deliberately put the glass there after ye went into the garderobe so ye'd get yer feet all cut up."

"It's true," Aileen said solemnly when Dwyn started to shake her head. "They have been talking about it all day, trying to sort out who could be behind that and poisoning ye."

Dwyn's mouth curved down unhappily at this news. She'd heard Rory saying that something had been put in her drink and that was why she was sick, but she hadn't realized that they thought the glass on the floor had been deliberate too. It seemed she'd really angered someone here, and the only people she could think of who disliked her enough to perhaps do something like this were—

"Laird Buchanan sent Lady Catriona and Lady Sasha and their families away," Una said with grim satisfaction, speaking the names she'd just been thinking.

Dwyn turned to glance at her. "They—?" She left the rest unsaid, mostly because she had no voice and it hurt to talk.

But Una understood what she wanted to ask and grimaced. "They canno' prove it, but suspect they were behind both attacks though."

"Aye, but that's no' the only reason he sent them away. In fact, he said without proof he would no' have sent them away, but Rory and Alick were no' interested in the lasses and they needed their rooms."

When Dwyn's eyebrows rose at that, Aileen explained, "They needed one o' the rooms fer a new lass and her family who arrived today, and Una and I are moving to the other room so ye and—"

"So ye can rest and recover more quickly," Una interrupted firmly.

"Oh," Aileen said with dismay. "Aye, so ye can rest."

Dwyn narrowed her gaze on the lass. Her sister's eyes were wide, as if she'd just realized she'd nearly said something she shouldn't have. Aileen never had been able to lie worth beans, but before Dwyn could question her about what she'd really been going to say, a soft knock on the door drew their attention.

"That'll be Geordie. He said he would fetch back food fer ye," Aileen said with relief, and rushed to the door.

Dwyn frowned, and stared after her sister, watching as she opened the door for Geordie to come in. He entered with a tray in hand that held a pitcher, goblets and a large platter of food. His eyes found her sitting up on the bed and a smile softened the grim expression he'd initially had on his face, and then he carried the tray to a small table and two chairs to the side of the hearth and set it down.

"They have brought out sweet pasties for the guests below, Una and Aileen," Geordie announced as he picked up the pitcher and poured the liquid it held into the goblets. "Yer father asked me to tell ye that and send ye down."

"I have no' finished brushing her hair," Una said, but was climbing off the bed as she did.

"I shall finish fer ye," Geordie announced, turning with both goblets in hand.

Much to Dwyn's amazement, her sisters nodded and immediately hurried out of the room, leaving her alone with Geordie. They even closed the door behind them, which really wasn't proper at all. She should not be alone in a room with a male with the door closed. It was just—Come to think of it, she'd been alone with him *and him in bed* with her when she'd woken up, Dwyn realized now, and began to frown. That definitely hadn't been proper.

"Here, Dwyn, drink."

Blinking, she turned from looking at the door to find Geordie in front of her now, holding out one of the goblets. She stared at it blankly, and then lifted her gaze to his face, still trying to sort out why she was being left alone in a room with him with the door closed. Her sisters knew better than that, as did their father, but he'd apparently wanted them below . . .

"Can ye hold it?" he asked with concern when she hesitated.

Dwyn reached for the glass with one hand, but then quickly added her other hand to help hold it when she found she was indeed weak. The retching had apparently taken more out of her than she'd realized, Dwyn thought with disgust as she raised the goblet to her lips and sipped tentatively. It was mead, as she expected, and delicious, but she was almost afraid to drink too much and start retching again, so she started with the sip, and then lowered the glass to wait a moment as she swished it around in her mouth and swallowed.

"Mavis is arranging for a bath to be brought up once the water warms," he announced, setting his own goblet down on the table. "It may take some time though."

Dwyn murmured in response to that, and then stiffened in surprise when he crawled onto the bed beside her. When he continued to move around behind her, Dwyn glanced around to see him pick up the brush Una had apparently left there. Eyes wide, she quickly turned forward as he began to run it slowly through her hair.

For a moment, she just sat there, feeling odd and a little uncomfortable with everything, but when he murmured, "How is yer stomach? Is the mead bothering it?" she glanced down at the goblet she'd lowered to her lap, and took a moment to pay attention to her stomach. It seemed to have accepted the mead well, she acknowledged, and said with relief, "It seems fine with the mead."

Her voice was still raspy and broken, and she wasn't surprised when he urged, "Try some more."

Nodding, she raised the goblet and took a larger sip this time, and again swished it around her mouth before swallowing. But when that stayed down and her stomach didn't rebel, she took a proper drink, and then another as Geordie continued to brush her hair.

"I love yer hair," he murmured after a moment, and she felt him lift it away from her neck and raise it out behind her. "'Tis so soft and fine. Lovely."

Dwyn stilled, her fingers tightening on her goblet, and then he let it fall back into place and asked, "Ye must be hungry. Would ye like to try a little food?"

"Aye," she said, relieved when her voice was a little less raspy this time and it didn't pain her as much to speak. The liquid was helping, Dwyn thought, and then glanced around with surprise when Geordie was suddenly shifting past her to stand. When he took the goblet and set it on the table, then bent toward her, she automatically raised her arms to wrap them around his neck as he picked her up.

"I think we'll start with something light and then move from there," he said as he carried her to the table. "Cook sent up broth to start with, as well as meat, cheese and fruit. But why do we no' see how the broth settles ere we try anything else?"

Dwyn nodded, but her hungry eyes were on the tray with the food on it and her mouth was watering at the thought of eating. The mead had eased her mouth and throat, but it had also made her aware of how empty her stomach was and the hunger gnawing at it.

Geordie set her in the nearer chair, and lifted a small wooden bowl of broth from the tray to set it before her, but then turned to head back to the bed to get her empty goblet and his full one. He was back quickly though, and took the opposite chair.

"Did yer sisters tell ye Jetta delayed the feast until tomorrow so ye could attend?" he asked as he poured more mead into her goblet.

Dwyn swallowed the broth and nodded. "Aye. 'Twas very kind o' her, but I feel bad that she did. I'm sure everyone else was disappointed, and 'tis no' as if I could have danced at the feast anyway," she pointed out.

"Ye might be able to. Rory is going to come up with the bath, and check yer feet while they prepare it. He's hoping they've healed enough ye can put weight on them again and can walk and dance. If no' tonight, then by tomorrow."

"Oh," Dwyn breathed, smiling at the thought. While she loved the excuse of needing to be carried to be in Geordie's arms, it could also be embarrassing when it came to things like using the garderobe. Fortunately, her sisters had helped her in the garderobe, but he'd still had to carry her there and set her on the wooden bench, and then carry her away after. Most embarrassing, she thought with a grimace, and hoped she wouldn't have to go again now that she was eating. At least, not until Rory had seen her feet, and hopefully said she could put weight on them again.

"How is yer stomach faring now?" Geordie asked, drawing her attention back to him. "Is the broth bothering it?"

"Nay," Dwyn said, relieved to be able to say so.

"Would ye like to try some meat, cheese and bread?" he suggested.

Dwyn looked at the food. Her mind was very aware she'd missed several meals and wanted the food, but her stomach was telling her it was starting to feel full from just the drink and broth. Sighing, she said, "Perhaps just a little bread and fruit. I'm almost full already."

"What about a pastie, then?" he suggested, drawing her attention to the fruit-filled pastries she hadn't noticed until he now pointed them out.

"Oh, aye," she said with a smile. "That would be perfect."

Nodding, he picked one up and set it before her, then began eating as well, starting with the meat, cheese and bread he'd first offered her.

They ate in silence for several minutes, and then Dwyn said, "Una and Aileen told me that yer brother sent Lady Catriona and Lady Sasha away."

Geordie swallowed the food in his mouth, before saying, "Aye. Rory and Alick were no' interested in them, and they were just taking up space and being unpleasant, so Aulay asked them to leave."

Dwyn watched him take another bite of the beef that had been sent up, but after watching him chew and swallow, she said, "Aileen said the rooms were needed, one for a new lass who arrived today?"

"Aye, Aulay mentioned another lady had arrived with her escort," he admitted, and then smiled wryly. "I think he mentioned the lady's name, but I paid him little attention. I shall ask him later and tell ye who it is though," he promised.

Dwyn nodded, but said, "Aileen said that they were taking the other room and leaving me here. Una said it was so that I could rest and recover, but that's no' necessary. I should be fine now, and it seems silly for us to be split up like that when you and your brothers could take the other room," she pointed out.

"Me brothers are sleeping in the barracks until more women leave," he said, reaching for a pastie now.

Dwyn was silent for a minute, but then said, "I got the feeling Aileen was going to give another reason for why we were being split up before Una interrupted to say it was so I could rest and recover."

Geordie glanced up at that, his eyes wide and almost guilty-looking, and then relief washed over his face when a knock sounded at the door. Standing abruptly, he hurried over to open it and then stepped back to allow Rory in. The healer was followed by two men carrying a large bathtub, and several women carting pails of water, half of which were steaming.

"How is your stomach accepting food now?" Rory asked, moving toward her as soon as he spotted her at the table.

"Good, thank ye," Dwyn answered, wishing she'd had more time to question Geordie before the man had interrupted. She had a feeling there was something she needed to know here.

"Good, good." Rory beamed at her as if she had done something to make herself feel better, when she suspected the truth was whatever had been put in her drink had obviously just moved out of her system.

"Should I carry her to the bed so ye can look at her feet?" Geordie asked, leaving the door to join them.

"Aye," Rory said at once. "Hopefully they are much improved too."

"Aye," he agreed, and scooped her up out of her chair to carry her to the bed. Once he'd set her down, both men went to work removing the leather Rory had put over the binding, and then unwrapping the linens too.

"Hmm," Rory said, raising her feet to peer over them. "They are much improved."

"Aye," Geordie agreed, looking them over as well.

Rory set her right foot down and began to press on the bottom of her left foot, and then glanced at her face in question. "Does that hurt?"

Dwyn hesitated, and then admitted, "'Tis a little tender in spots, but no' much."

Nodding, he set that foot down, raised her right again and began to press on it as he had the first. He paused when Dwyn sucked in a pained breath though.

"That one hurts," he said sympathetically and Dwyn grimaced, but nodded.

"Ye've made it bleed again," Geordie growled with displeasure.

"Just the large cut, and just a little," Rory said soothingly as he set the foot back. "It is healing, but no' quite ready. I think 'twill be fine by tomorrow though. She should be able to stand on it then."

"So, she canno' walk yet?" Geordie asked.

"She can put weight on her left foot, but should not use her right yet."

"So, she canno' walk," Geordie pointed out dryly.

"She can stand on one foot to dress though," Rory pointed out when Dwyn's shoulders sagged with disappointment. "Ye'll only need carry her to the garderobe and set her down inside the door. She'll no' need her sisters to help her in the room itself anymore."

Dwyn breathed out with relief at that news. It was almost better than walking when she thought about it. She could continue to enjoy being in Geordie's arms when he carried her around, but would now avoid the embarrassment of needing help in the garderobe. She could hop to the bench herself from the door, and stand on one foot while she pulled her skirts up. Aye, this was better.

"I shall leave the salve and fresh linens fer ye to replace on the still-tender foot after her bath, Geordie. But," he added, eyeing Dwyn sternly, "ye must wear yer slipper on the unbandaged foot for the next little while until 'tis completely healed. The cuts have all scabbed over or healed altogether now, and the chance of infection is small at this point, but better no' to take risks."

Rory waited until Dwyn nodded obediently, and then he stood. "I'll leave ye to yer bath, then."

"Thank ye, Rory," Geordie said, standing to see him out. He didn't just see him out, but followed him out into the hall. When the two men paused briefly to speak, Dwyn turned her attention to the bath being prepared for her. The men who had carried in the tub had left while Rory had examined her feet, as had a good half of the women after dumping their water in. The remaining women would soon be gone too, she saw as they emptied their pails into the quickly filling tub and turned to trudge out one after another, their empty pails swinging from their hands.

There were only two left in the room when Geordie finished talking to his brother and came back into the room, and one of them was already walking toward the door. The younger woman smiled from Dwyn to Geordie and then slid out through the door Geordie was holding open. Dwyn then turned to the older woman as she finished emptying her pails and made to start across the room. She returned the smile Dwyn gave her and then her footsteps slowed and she glanced uncertainly from her to Geordie and back, a small frown bringing lines to her forehead. "I should have arranged for one o' the maids to stay behind to help Lady Innes bathe. But I can help if—"

"Nay, 'tis fine, Mavis. I will help Dwyn with her bath," Geordie said quietly.

The woman's eyes widened, her jaw dropping with shock, and she swung her head toward Dwyn, who was just as wide-eyed and agape with shock. The two gaped at each other with dismay for a moment, and then Geordie said, "Thank ye, Mavis. Ye may go."

The woman looked as if she might argue, but then something in Geordie's expression gave her pause and she merely mumbled, "I hope ye ken what ye're doing, lad," and rushed from the room, leaving Dwyn to stare at Geordie, her face hot with what she felt sure was a blush as she watched him close the door behind the woman and then turn to move back toward her.

Forcing herself to close her mouth, she cleared her throat, and then said nervously, "Ye were jesting, surely, m'laird? I'm sure even now Rory is sending me sisters up to help . . ." She let the words trail away when he began to shake his head. "Ye were no' jesting?" she asked weakly.

Pausing in front of her, he took in her expression and said, "I want to marry ye, Dwyn. I want ye fer me wife. Agree to marry me."

"Aye," Dwyn breathed, and then blinked and shook her head when his face broke out in a smile and he reached for her. "I mean, nay, m'laird."

Geordie paused, surprise crossing his face. "Nay?"

"Ye do no' want to marry," she reminded him miserably. "And I'll no' let yer brother force ye to marry me just because someone witnessed what we did in the orchard and tattled to him. Ye'd hate me fer it if I allowed that."

Geordie relaxed and bent to clasp her by the waist to lift her up off the bed. "Kneel," he instructed as he lowered her again, and Dwyn automatically bent her legs to kneel as he set her back down facing him on the edge of the bed.

"No one tattled to Aulay," Geordie announced now, setting to work on her lacings. "At least, if they did, he did no' bring it up before I told him I wished to marry ye."

"Which ye did because ye feared someone had seen and would tell," she reasoned.

"Nay," he corrected gently as her neckline loosened. "Because I want to marry ye, lass."

Dwyn shook her head and caught the top of her gown to her chest as it began to fall away. "But ye do no' wish to marry. I heard yer brother telling his wife ye'd said that."

"I did no' when I first got here, that is true," he acknowledged. "But spending time with ye changed me mind."

Dwyn was so amazed at this news she simply stared at him as he stepped back and bent to pick up something. One of her slippers, she realized when he straightened and leaned around her to slip it onto the foot Rory had said she could now stand on. Once it was firmly on her foot, he straightened, clasped her by the waist and carried her to the tub.

"Stand only on yer slippered foot," Geordie reminded her before setting her down.

Dwyn kept her gown up with one hand, but reached for his arm with the other as she teetered briefly before adjusting to standing on one foot. Once she was sure she wouldn't fall, she released him though, and returned that hand to her chest to help hold her gown up.

"I canno' bathe ye with yer gown on, lass," he said huskily. "Ye need to let it go."

When Dwyn raised her head to peer at him with wide-eyed alarm, he smiled faintly and asked, "Where's the brave lass who bared her breasts to me in the orchard? She's the lass I admired so much I went to me brother and said I planned to marry her."

Dwyn stared at him briefly, a small battle taking place in her head, and then she straightened her shoulders and let her hands drop. The wrinkled gown immediately slid down her body to pool around her feet. Dwyn swallowed and raised her chin as his gaze followed the same path, gliding over her breasts, down over her stomach, to her hips and the spot between her legs where his kisses had given her such pleasure, before finally following her legs to her feet, one slightly up and back to prevent it touching the ground, and the other still in its slipper. Then his gaze followed the same path back up, before settling on her face.

Dwyn noted the hunger in his eyes and felt heat and tingling roll through her body in response. His voice was a low, rough growl when he said, "I'm going to lift ye up and ye need to slip off yer slipper ere I place ye in the tub."

Swallowing, she nodded once, and then braced herself as he stepped forward. Dwyn closed her eyes as his warm rough hands closed on the naked skin of her waist, and then opened them again as he lifted her. She reached instinctively for his shoulders to brace herself, and then stared past his head as she concentrated on getting her slipper off. A startled gasp slipped from her when something brushed one of her nipples and she glanced down to see that he'd raised her until her breasts were in front of his mouth. She watched silently as his mouth closed over one, and then closed her eyes as he began to draw on the nipple, sending a sharp shaft of pleasure through her.

Dwyn blinked her eyes open again when he released her nipple and ordered, "Hold yer hair up so it does no' get wet."

Reaching back, she gathered the long strands and lifted them, until he had lowered her into the tub. Then she let them fall over the edge of the tub where they wouldn't get wet. She expected him to straighten and leave her to her bath then, and he did, but only long enough to fetch the soap and strip of linen Aileen had used earlier to wash her face. Carrying them back, he knelt beside the tub and dipped both into the water, before pulling them out to begin working the soap over the linen.

"I'm sorry ye've been hurt and made sick, lass," Geordie said in a husky voice as he began to move the now-soapy cloth over her body, starting at her neck and shoulders, before moving lower. "But hopefully, with Catriona and Sasha gone, the attacks will end."

"Aye," Dwyn breathed, her eyes closing and head dropping back as he began to soap her breasts, his hands caressing even as they cleaned.

"Ye're so beautiful when ye do that," he growled, both hands on her breasts now and concentrating on the nipples, one with the linen, one without.

Blinking, she lowered her head with confusion. "When I do what?" she asked, and then gasped and threw her head back again when one of his hands suddenly dipped into the water to slide between her legs.

"That," he said. "Ye close yer eyes, and throw yer head back, yer beautiful neck stretched tight and yer mouth open just a bit. It makes me want to—" His mouth covered hers suddenly and Dwyn opened her eyes and pulled her hands out of the water to wrap them around his neck. She moaned with pleasure when his tongue thrust between her lips and then cried out into his mouth when his fingers slid between the folds guarding her sensitive nub and began to run circles around it.

Dwyn kissed him back desperately as he caressed her, her fingers plucking and tugging at his plaid. She wanted to touch his naked skin. She wanted to run her hands over his shoulders and down his back. She wanted to press her breasts to his naked chest and . . . Dear God, she wanted him to keep touching her, but wanted him to taste her again too. She wanted that explosive release he'd given her before. But she wanted to touch him there too, so that he exploded as well, and she wanted . . .

Dwyn cried out with dismay when he suddenly broke their kiss, and then watched him stand and give his plaid a tug that had it dropping away to the floor. She barely got to see him in just his shirt, and note that he had fine strong legs, before he tugged the shirt up and off. Her gaze moved immediately to his pillicock and her eyes widened incredulously as she saw how large and hard it looked. It was pointing accusingly at her, she noted, before he bent and lifted her out of the tub.

"Put yer arms around me, lass," Geordie ordered, and she did so automatically and then squeezed her eyes nervously closed as he stepped into the tub he'd just taken her out of. She didn't open them again until he'd settled in the water with her in his lap, the backs of her knees on one side of the tub, her feet hanging over but not touching the floor, and her back against the other side, her hair trailing on the floor. She could feel his hard erection against her bottom, and her gaze shifted to Geordie's face as he leaned back in the tub and looked her over as his hands returned to her body.

"One day I'd like to take ye to the loch and make love to ye under the waterfall," he murmured, his hands closing over her breasts again. "There's a little ledge on the wall under the falls I can set ye on while I love ye."

"Oh," Dwyn breathed, her eyes closing as she enjoyed his touch and envisioned what he was describing.

"Would ye like that?" he asked, shifting one hand between her legs to caress her there again.

"A-aye, G-Geordie," Dwyn gasped, her legs automatically spreading to give him more room, and one hand sliding from his neck to drop and cover his, urging him on.

He kissed her again, and Dwyn kissed him back with all she

had, her mouth opening, her tongue meeting his, her lips sucking and her chest twisting to press against his and slide soapy wet across the coarse hairs there. Her hips began to move, riding the hand caressing her, and her bottom was rubbing over the hardness beneath her. Dwyn heard water splashing out on the floor, but didn't care as she chased that release she'd experienced before. And then he slid one finger into her and she broke their kiss on a gasp, her head pulling back so she could look at him. Geordie held her gaze and eased the finger in farther, his thumb now rubbing over the center of her excitement.

"Relax yer muscles, lass. Let me in," he growled, easing his finger back out a ways before pushing back in, deeper this time, his thumb continuing to build her excitement as he did.

Whimpering, Dwyn leaned back against the side of the tub, her back arching, and legs opening and closing around his hand, hips moving into the caress. She tried to relax her muscles for him, but she was panting, her body tightening, the need in her becoming so intense she didn't think she could bear it.

"That's it, love. Give me yer passion," he murmured, splashing water over her breasts with his free hand to rinse away the soap, before bending his head to claim one nipple. Catching it between his teeth, he nipped lightly, then began to draw hard, adding to the pressure building in her, and Dwyn clutched at his head with her free hand, her other still covering his between her legs and trying to move it more swiftly against her and with more pressure. But he resisted, keeping his movements slow and steady until she thought she would go mad in search of her release.

"Geordie," she gasped desperately, and felt a second finger join the first, stretching her as they slid in. Releasing her breast then, he raised his head and watched her face, his expression a combination of grim determination and something softer.

"What is it, love? What do ye want?" he asked, flicking her sensitive nub with his thumb now. "Can ye tell me what ye want?"

"More," she groaned, and then, "You."

His determination broke from his expression and Geordie slid his hand into her hair and dragged her face up to claim a kiss, his tongue thrusting in time with his fingers as they moved faster and more firmly into her until she screamed into his mouth and began to convulse against him with her release. Dwyn was vaguely aware of Geordie breaking their kiss and resting his forehead on hers as his fingers paused inside her, but she merely held on tightly to him as the only stability in a world gone mad.

Chapter 10

GEORDIE KISSED THE TOP OF HER HEAD WHEN DWYN COLlapsed weakly against his chest. She was limp and breathing heavily, but moaned in protest when he eased his hand from between her legs, his fingers drifting across her oversensitized skin. She didn't even have the strength to clutch at his shoulders when he shifted her in his arms and stood up in the tub. She simply lay with her head in the curve of his neck, and her arms in her lap, as he carried her to the bed.

Her energy began to return again though when he laid her in the bed, climbed in with her and began to kiss her once more. Moaning, she welcomed his kiss, her body stretching against his as he half covered hers with his own. Much to his pleasure, her excitement returned as if it had never been sated and began to burn brightly again. She had recovered quickly in the orchard as well and had been ready to go again after he'd pleasured her there. Now she kissed him eagerly back, her hands moving over him with curiosity. He grinned against her mouth as she squeezed his muscled chest, and then ran her hands down over his stomach, before bringing them back up to find and focus on his nipples.

Geordie growled into her mouth when she plucked at them. Apparently taking that as encouragement, Dwyn concentrated there, toying with them until they hardened and grew as hers did when he did it to her. He was caught by surprise when she suddenly pushed at his chest. Unprepared for it, Geordie found himself rolled to his back on the bed. Before he could roll her back, she was kneeling beside him, leaning over him to claim one nipple with her mouth, and he sucked in a startled breath as her teeth grazed the oddly sensitive tip before she drew it into her mouth to suckle.

"Ah, God, lass," Geordie growled, peering at Dwyn's body as she licked and nipped at his nipples. She was on her knees, bent over him, her hair a pale gold curtain, shielding her from his view so that he had to lift it away to see her breasts dangling above his stomach.

Smiling, he released the curtain of hair, and reached under to find her breasts. Geordie smiled when she moaned around his nipple as he fondled and caressed her breasts. His smile died though when one of her hands found his erection and squeezed him with interest.

Growling, he caught her by the upper arms and dragged her up his body, so that she lay half on top of him, her hair drifting around their faces as he claimed her mouth in a searing kiss.

She was breathless and panting when he ended the kiss, but despite that asked with concern, "Did I hurt ye, m'laird?"

"Nay," he assured her, before rolling her onto her back again. This time he covered her fully. Holding his upper body off of her with his arms, he watched her face and ground himself against her, pleased when she gasped and let her legs open to cuddle him. He slid against her again, his cock gliding against her moist heat and making him grit his teeth.

Damn, he was hard as a poker, and wanted her more than he'd wanted any woman in his life. But he couldn't take her yet. Geordie was determined to give her as much pleasure as possible before he breached her. The tips of his fingers had pressed against her maid's veil as he'd pleasured her with his hand. Georgie had even pushed against it twice, but it hadn't broken, and he didn't know if it was because he hadn't pushed far enough in, or it was thick enough that it would take some force to break through. But he hadn't wanted to cause her pain just then, so he'd kept from further testing the situation. However, either way, Geordie suspected she wouldn't enjoy the breaching, and he wanted to make sure she enjoyed the before part as much as possible before getting to that. He wanted her to want him again, not fear the marriage bed, so he ground against her again, groaning with her as his cock slid over her.

"Geordie, please," Dwyn gasped, wrapping her legs around his hips and shifting against him. "I need—"

"Soon, lass," he growled, grinding against her again.

"But I want— Let me taste ye," she begged now, clutching at his arms. "Let me make ye want me like I want you."

Geordie froze at her words, tempted by them. The image they made rear up in his mind almost had him forgetting his good intentions and thrusting into her, but at the last moment, he pulled back, and then pushed away and slithered down her body to get his erection as far from her opening as possible. He didn't pause until his head was between her legs, and then he pressed her thighs farther apart to open her to his gaze, and ducked his head to press his mouth to her.

A smiled eased the grim expression on Geordie's face when she cried out and jerked under the first touch, and then he set to work, sucking on the soft folds guarding the jewel beneath, and then licking and sucking the hardening nub before thrusting his tongue where he wanted to put his cock. He didn't dally and enjoy it this time as he had in the orchard. This was purely to send her over the edge, and he quickly worked her into a frenzy and then added a finger to the mix. The moment she cried out and began to convulse, he raised himself up to kneel between her legs, caught her by the hips, lifted her and drove home.

Dear God in heaven, Geordie thought, sure he'd found paradise. She was so hot, and tight, her inner muscles squeezing him as her body shuddered with her orgasm. Dwyn hadn't even seemed to notice the tearing, though he'd felt the brief resistance before her veil gave way to him. Now he released her hips and fell forward, catching his upper body with his hands on either side of her shoulders, and bent to claim her mouth and silence her insensate babbling. Dwyn went briefly still, but when he eased himself back out of her and drove back in, she moaned into his mouth and began to kiss him back. When he did it again, she wrapped her arms and legs around him, her fingers clawing at his back and heels pushing at his arse and urging him on.

That's when Geordie gave up trying to be slow and gentle and began to thrust as he wished, pounding into her, his balls slapping against her, and a growl building in his throat as her body squeezed and milked him. When Dwyn came again, her inner muscles clamped down on him so hard he nearly came too, but Geordie managed to hold himself back by slowing his motions until her muscles eased. He didn't let himself go until she cried out into his mouth again as she found her third orgasm. Then he stiffened against her and broke their kiss, his head rising and her name slipping from his lips on a groan as he poured himself into her.

It was only as Geordie collapsed on top of her and then quickly rolled to the side, taking her with him, that he recalled his intention not to spill his seed in her. A frown claiming his lips, Geordie closed his eyes unhappily as he realized he'd failed Dwyn there.

"I do no' think we should marry, m'laird."

Geordie's eyes blinked open with amazement.

"No' until—" she began.

"Are ye mad, woman?" he interrupted with shock. "We *are* married. There's no thinking we should or no'."

"What?" She lifted her head to peer at him with surprise. "Nay, we just—"

"I asked ye to marry me. Ye said aye. And I bedded ye. We're handfasted. As good as married in the eyes of the law," he pointed out grimly.

"Aye, I said aye first," she agreed, "but then I said nay."

Geordie narrowed his eyes. "We are handfasted, Dwyn. And the contracts are drawn up. We are wed by law already, and the wedding for the church is tomorrow."

"What?" she gasped, pulling away to gape at him.

Geordie stared at her with a combination of bewilderment and anger. For God's sake, there were six women in the keep who would have been glad to marry him, and he picked the one who looked horrified at the prospect.

"But we canno' be, Geordie," she protested unhappily. "Ye do no' ken what ye're getting into, m'laird. Ye should ha'e been warned. Did me da tell ye what is happening at Innes ere he got ye to sign the contract? Nay, o' course he did no'," she answered herself before he could, and then added, "I'm sure ye can use that to get out o' marrying me do ye wish it."

Geordie stared at her miserable face, and sighed heavily with both weariness and relief as he realized that it was not that she didn't wish to marry him, but that she was sure he wouldn't want to once he knew . . . whatever the hell it was her father hadn't told him, he thought grimly. He hadn't a clue what that was, but supposed he'd better find out so that he could soothe her fears in that regard.

Easing her away from his chest, Geordie shifted himself up to sit with his back against the headboard, then caught Dwyn's upper arms and dragged her up to rest against his chest. Peering down then, he stared at her beautiful breasts, sighed as he felt his cock stir and pressed her head to his chest before grabbing some of her hair and shifting it to cover as much of her body as he could.

"There," he growled, once he couldn't see her curvy little body and get distracted. "Now, tell me what 'tis ye're so worried about."

"'Tis the Brodies," she said, raising her head to look up at him anxiously.

"Brodies," he muttered with a frown as the name tugged at a memory string in his mind. Nodding as it came back to him, Geordie said, "Ye mentioned them the first morning in the tree. They want to add Innes to their holdings, ye said."

"Aye," Dwyn breathed woefully.

Geordie almost smiled then. This was no problem at all, he thought, and tightened his arms around her in a hug as he said, "Well, lass, they canno' have it. Innes is yers, and ye're mine now. So Brodie is out o' luck."

She appeared surprised by his words. "Surely Innes becomes yours once we marry?"

"We *are* married," he growled. "And nay, it remains with you. I had it put in the contract. That way, should I die first, ye decide whether to marry again and canno' be forced to it by yer father or anyone else."

"But what if I die first?" she asked with a frown.

Geordie shrugged with unconcern, and then scowled as the thought sank in. Dwyn die? Leave him? And she could if his seed took and she got with child and died while trying to birth his son or daughter. Cursing, he leapt off the bed, and then turned to pick her up by the waist and swing her out in front of him so she dangled above the floor. He then began to lift her quickly up and down.

"M-m'l-laird," she protested, grabbing at his arms. "W-what are y-ye d-doing?"

"Trying to shake me seed out o' ye," he muttered, continuing to jostle her up and down. "I meant to withdraw ere I spilled into ye, but forgot. Well, I did no' exactly forget, I just did no' even think on it. Ye felt so damned good and I— Ow!" he barked, nearly dropping her when she suddenly slapped at his face. Catching her before her feet hit the floor, he scowled at her. "What was that for?"

Dwyn scowled right back. "Because ye're obviously hysterical or lost yer mind," she explained, and ordered, "Put me down."

"I canno'. Ye're no' supposed to stand with yer feet—"

"On the bed," she said with exasperation.

"Fine." Geordie heaved the word out on an irritated breath, and turned to set her on the bed, grousing, "But I've no' lost me mind or gone hysterical, and if ye die on the birthing bed because ye would no' let me shake me seed out o' ye, I'll never forgive ye." His eyes narrowed when she rolled her eyes at that. "Lass—"

"Ye canno' shake the seed out o' me," Dwyn assured him with exasperation, interrupting what would have been a fine lecture on the merits of respecting a husband and not rolling her eyes and such. But then she frowned and added, "At least, I do no' think ye can." She considered it briefly, and then shook her head. "Nay. Surely 'tis no' possible or there would be no bastards in the world. Women would just do some jumping after being bedded and . . ." She shrugged.

Supposing that was true, Geordie bent and scooped her up into his arms.

"What are ye doing now?" she asked with concern as he started across the room with her.

"I'm taking ye to the table. Lovin' ye's made me hungry," he muttered, and then paused as he reached the table and realized he could not set her in her seat. Her unbandaged feet would be in the rushes then. Shrugging, he set her on the table instead, and moved around her to look over what was left on the tray.

"M'laird," she said, twisting her upper body around to frown at him. "We have to talk about the Brodies."

"There's nothing to talk about, lass. We're married. Brodie canno' marry ye, and he canno' have Innes."

"Da did tell ye?" she asked with surprise.

Geordie shrugged, and started picking through the meat, shifting the top pieces that had dried out and selecting the still-moist pieces underneath. Turning, he offered her one, and when she took it, he said, "Yer father said Brodie has been trying to force a marriage for the last couple years."

"The last four years," she said grimly. "Ever since he learned my betrothed had died."

"I thought ye said yer betrothed died seven years ago?" he said, turning to peer at her in question.

"He did," she murmured. "But Brodie did no' ken who I was betrothed to, and only found out four years ago that he had passed." Dwyn grimaced. "The minute he knew, he began pestering Da about marrying me. His own wife died the year before that, and he tried to convince Da it would be a good idea to marry the two lands. But Brodie is a brutal bastard—he once beat his wife right in front o' us while we were visiting. It was the last time we visited," she added grimly.

When Geordie scowled at the mention of the abuse, she sighed and continued, "Brodie seemed to let it go when Da said no that first time, but then he showed up at Innes again a couple months later bringing it up again, and then a month after that. This last year though, he's been coming by more and more frequently and becoming more and more determined until he started coming by every week. And then he . . ."

Swallowing, she lowered her head again, and admitted, "He caught me outside walking the shore the one day, a month and a half ago, and tried to . . . force the issue."

Geordie stiffened. He understood exactly what she meant by force the issue. Brodie had tried to rape her to force a wedding. Rage coursed through him at the thought of anyone touching his Dwyn.

"He would have succeeded too if Angus and Barra hadn't been there," she said grimly, and explained, "My hounds had chased off into the woods after a rabbit just minutes before he arrived, but heard me scream and came back. They got in a couple of good bites before I called them off." She lowered her head unhappily. "He was bleeding and furious when he climbed back up on his horse, and he said he *would* marry me. One way or another he'd have Innes and me, and when he did he'd make me pay for what me dogs had done to him."

Shaking her head, she raised her gaze to his. "He was raving mad, Geordie, and even foaming at the mouth with it. He'll no' let Innes, or the opportunity to punish me, go so easily. Once he hears I am married, I think he'll attack Innes. That is what ye're in for do ye marry me."

Sighing, Geordie set down the meat he hadn't taken even a bite of, and moved over to step between her legs and wrap his arms around her. Pressing her head to his chest, he kissed the top of her hair, and said, "Dwyn . . . we are married. Why do ye think yer sisters were moved to another room and I was allowed to help ye with yer bath?"

She pulled back sharply and stared up at him. "Da knows we're . . . ?"

"They all know," he assured her. "We were supposed to marry at the feast that was planned for tonight. Then ye got sick and it had to be delayed." He grimaced. "I only agreed to the delay because we were no' sure ye'd be up to standing for the ceremony after being so sick. But I knew when I went below after we woke up that since we slept all day today, we'd most like be awake well into the night. And I knew I would no' be able to resist ye. So, I told them while I was below that I was handfasting with ye tonight and we'd have the ceremony tomorrow." He kissed her nose. "Yer da agreed."

"Oh," Dwyn breathed, looking surprised.

"So," Geordie said now. "Even if ye still do no' agree we're handfasted, I plan to marry ye all o'er again tomorrow in front o' the priest, me family and witnesses."

"But what about Brodie?" she asked with a frown.

Geordie caught her face in his hands and tipped it up so their gazes met. "I'm no' afraid o' Brodie, lass. And you should no' be either. Remember, you and Innes now have eight powerful clans at yer back. Brodie would be a fool to attack."

He started to lower his head to kiss her then, but she stopped him with a hand to his chest.

"I ken ye think 'twill be all right, Geordie, but there's something wrong with the man. The things he was saying when he attacked me . . ." Her mouth tightened. "There's something wrong in his head. He'll no' fight fair and come straight at us."

"Lass," he began soothingly, but Dwyn shook her head.

"Nay, Geordie, ye need to listen. He was twisted in the head ere the dogs attacked him, but surely it will be worse now. Ye need to ken what Angus and Barra did. They—"

"Hush," he murmured, placing a finger over her mouth. "Ye have me now. All will be well. I promise." He sealed that vow with a kiss.

For the first time, Dwyn didn't respond at once to the caress and he could almost hear the worry chasing around in her head. Displeased that anyone could come between them, Geordie redoubled his efforts to gain a response from her. Thrusting his tongue into her mouth, he found her breasts and began to caress and palm and fondle them.

Much to his relief, Dwyn finally moaned and began to kiss him back. The moment she did, Geordie released one breast to snake his hand down between her legs and begin stoking the fire there. Dwyn immediately gasped into his mouth, and reached down to clutch his hand, pushing it tighter against herself. But she broke their kiss and threw her head back on a cry when he slid a finger into her.

Recalling that she was newly breached, and unsure if that cry was one of pleasure or pain, Geordie frowned and stilled his hand to ask in a concerned growl, "Are ye sore, lass?"

"Nay," Dwyn groaned, shifting her hips and digging her nails impatiently into his hand. "Do no' stop, Geordie."

"Good," he breathed with relief, and began to caress her again, his eyes sliding over her full round breasts and the tight nipples pointing up at him as she leaned back on one arm, her back arching upward. Bending, he nipped lightly at one sweet bud, and said, "Because I've a mind to take ye like a dog takes his mate, lass. I want ye on yer hands and knees, with me behind ye so I can nip at yer neck, tangle me hands in yer hair and—" His words died, choked off in his throat when her hand suddenly released his and instead grabbed his cock, to squeeze lightly.

Dwyn didn't stroke him. He doubted she knew to do that, but she squeezed and growled, "Then do it, husband."

A smile slid over Geordie's lips as he realized she'd called him husband, but then she squeezed him more firmly, and added, "I'm aching and need ye."

"Christ, woman," he growled, retrieving his hand from between her legs, and knocking her hand away from his erection before slipping both hands under her behind and lifting her off the table. "Thank God I met ye before Rory or Alick did."

"It would no' have mattered," Dwyn assured him, wrapping her legs around his hips, and tightening them until he was rubbing against her with every step as he started to walk back to the bed.

"How do ye ken? Ye might have fallen for one o' them," he said, hoping she'd assure him otherwise. And she did.

"Nay," she said firmly. "I do no' look at them and want to see their pillicock."

Laughter bursting from his lips, Geordie tumbled onto the bed with her, and then raised his head to watch her face as he entered her. Dwyn groaned, her body stretching under his, head going back and eyes closing, only to open again when he remained planted deep inside her, but not moving. When she raised wide, questioning eyes to him, he smiled and said, "Oddly enough, wife. Neither do I."

Dwyn blinked, slow to realize that he was talking about not wanting to see his brothers' pillicocks when he looked at them, and then she burst out laughing too. Smiling, Geordie began to move then, his gaze sliding over his wee wife as he thrust into her. She was right where he'd wanted her, naked and laughing in his bed. His wife. Damn. All was right with the world.

DWYN RAN ONE HAND LIGHTLY DOWN GEORDIE'S CHEST, WATCHing his face for any reaction. A sigh slid from the depths of her body when she got none. He had fallen fast asleep the moment he'd finished loving her the second time after carrying her to the bed from the table. Or was it the third? She wondered over that briefly, but wasn't sure. All she knew was that he'd fallen dead asleep and she was lying here wide awake and restless. But he did look tired, she thought guiltily. Perhaps it took more out of the man to mate. Mayhap he poured all his energy into the woman along with his seed, and that was why she was so energetic while he was sleeping like the dead.

Sighing, Dwyn rolled away from him onto her back, and stared up at the royal blue bed drapes briefly, but then frowned as she became aware of another need that wanted tending. Grimacing, she glanced to Geordie and then sat up and glanced around. Her wrinkled gown was lying on the floor by the tub, as was one of her slippers, but the other slipper was next to the bed, she saw. It was for the wrong foot, but . . .

Shrugging, she leaned off the bed to scoop it up, and pulled it onto her left foot. It didn't feel quite right, but it was a soft slipper and would do, she decided, and then crawled to the end of the bed and along to the bottom corner closest to the door. Once there, she slid her leg down and got carefully to her foot. She then took a hop, grimacing at the noise she made. Pausing, she glanced back to the bed, but Geordie hadn't stirred. Letting out a relieved breath, she turned forward and took several hops this time, her hands out and pinwheeling for balance. She'd meant to just take three or four hops and stop to look around and check on Geordie again, but was afraid she'd lose her balance and fall so continued forward, picking up pace as she went in an effort to keep from tumbling forward. Even so she was a couple feet from her chest against the wall holding the door when she did tumble forward.

Fortunately, Dwyn was close enough to catch herself on the edge of the chest. Holding on to it, her body like a board leaning against a low wall, she glanced back to the bed to be sure Geordie still slept, then dragged herself forward to sit on the chest. Dwyn took a minute to regroup then, but finally heaved herself back to her foot and opened the chest.

The gown on top was a royal blue color, much like the drapes of Geordie's bed. Smiling, she pulled it out, and then grabbed a shift, closed the chest lid and sat on it to draw her naked foot up onto the chest with her so she didn't accidentally set it in the rushes. Dwyn then set the dress next to her and quickly dragged her shift on. Her sisters had lowered the neckline on her shifts so that she could wear them under the dresses with the lower necklines, but the rose gown was so low she hadn't been able to wear a shift under it. She was hoping to have better luck with the blue.

Finished with the shift, she shook out her dress in front of her, and then found the bottom and began to drag it over her head. Normally, she would have stepped into it, but she wasn't trying that on one foot. Tugging it into place so that it gathered on top of the chest behind her and dropped to cover her legs in front, she quickly did up the lacings and then peered down at herself. A thin line of her shift showed, but she pushed that down under the neckline of the gown, and then stood on her foot and looked down again.

"Good enough," Dwyn muttered, and then realized she'd spoken aloud and glanced toward the bed. Geordie hadn't moved.

Relaxing, she hopped the couple of feet to the door, one hand against the wall to balance herself as she went, and then opened it and hopped out. Much to her relief, the hall was empty. She could hear talking and laughing from below stairs and supposed everyone was still down at the tables. That made her wonder what time it was, but it was hard to tell. She didn't even know what time it had been when she'd woken up the first time to find herself fully clothed in Geordie's arms. If she had to guess, she would have said she thought it had been mid- to late afternoon. The sun had still been up and shining brightly then, and was still up now. Not fully though; while there had been enough light coming through the window to see around the room, it had been the dimmer light of a setting sun. So, she supposed it was probably time for the sup, or shortly after it.

Knowing that was as close as she was going to get to figuring it out on her own, she turned and hopped up the hall to the garderobe, using one hand on the wall to steady herself as she went. Much to her relief, she made it there without encountering anyone or falling over, and then hopped inside to tend to matters. She had come back out and paused by the door to carefully examine the floor to be sure there was nothing that might cut through her slipper or otherwise hurt her when she heard movement ahead of her. Raising her head, she spotted Geordie's brother Aulay even as he spotted her.

"Dwyn," he said sharply, and moved quickly toward her, a scowl twisting his scar so that he looked quite ferocious. "What are ye doing out here by yerself, lass?"

"I had to use the garderobe," she said with an exasperation that was as much at herself for the sudden fear his angry face caused in her, as at him for being short with her.

"Yer foot is no' bandaged," he pointed out in a growl.

"Nay, but I—"

"And where the hell is Geordie?" Aulay snarled with annoyance, scooping her off her feet without warning.

"He's sleeping, but—"

"Sleeping!" he barked. "Well, I shall wake him up, and—"

"Ye will no'!" she snapped, and when he stopped walking to look down at her with amazement, she warned, "M'laird, do ye no' stop snarling and growling at me like a vicious dog and start listening, I shall do what I do with me Angus and Barra, and put ye on yer side with me teeth at yer throat."

"Now, I should like to see that."

Dwyn glanced up the hall at those amused words and flushed as she watched Jetta walk toward them from the stairs. Sighing, she shook her head. "I am sorry. I should no' have lost me temper like that," she said to them both, and then turned to peer up at Aulay and added, "But ye should no' be angry at Geordie. I did no' wake him. Had I, I've no doubt he would ha'e bandaged me up and carried me to the garderobe. And I do no' want ye to wake him now, because I was rather hoping to speak to ye and me father together anyway, and without him there. I suspect he would interfere if he was awake."

"Ah," Jetta said with understanding, and then glanced to her husband. "Should I go fetch her father?"

Aulay was silent for a minute, and then let his breath out and relaxed. "Aye. And Rory too, please, wife. Send them to me study. I shall take Dwyn there. Rory can bandage her foot ere we talk."

Jetta nodded, and then offered her a reassuring smile before turning to hurry to the stairs.

"Who are Angus and Barra?"

Dwyn tore her gaze away from the departing woman, and met Aulay's curious gaze. Grimacing then, she admitted, "Me dogs. They're huge beasts. Deerhound and boarhound mix."

His eyebrows rose at that, and then he started to walk and asked with amusement, "Do ye really put them on their sides and bite their necks?"

"Aye," she admitted, and then explained, "They did no' like to listen much when they were young, at least no' to me. But they always obeyed their mother, and she used to grab them by the throat and force them to the ground when they misbehaved. I knew they were going to be big dogs, and I'd best get them used to listening to me while still small enough I could handle them, so one day when Angus was being difficult, I grabbed his legs, whipped them out from under him so he landed on his side and then leaned over him and bit his neck. Not hard," Dwyn added quickly, lest Aulay think her mean. "I just closed my teeth on him firmly, so he knew they were there. He stopped moving at once, but I waited until he relaxed and submitted as he did with his mother, and then let him up."

"And it worked?" he asked with interest.

"Oh, aye," she assured him. "Surprisingly well. He started obeying me at once like his mother. So I did it to Barra the very next time he would no' listen to me and they both became very good dogs." Dwyn paused briefly, and then admitted, "I do have to pull them to the ground and bite their necks again on occasion when they get rambunctious. But that's only about once every six months or so now. Thank goodness," she added with a wry smile. "Because they each weigh more than I do and, do ye stretch them out, are probably taller than me too. But they're very obedient pups for the most part."

"Pups?" he asked dubiously.

"They're not quite three years old now," she said.

"Hmm," Aulay murmured, and then asked, "And is that how ye brought Geordie to heel?"

"Nay, o' course no'! I—" Dwyn paused abruptly when she saw the sparkle in his eyes. Clucking her tongue, she said, "Ye were teasing."

"Aye," he said gently. "And I do no' think ye'd have tried it with me either."

"Nay," she admitted. "But it has proven a very effective threat with Aileen and Una. I just used it with you out o' habit."

"Surely yer sisters do no' really believe ye'd do such a thing to them, do they?" Aulay asked with disbelief, pausing in front of the door to his study.

"I do no' think they're quite sure whether I would, or would no'," Dwyn admitted as she reached out to open the door for him. When she looked back to see his doubting expression, she smiled faintly and said, "Ye'd understand did ye see the size o' Angus's and Barra's teeth. Me sisters canno' believe I put me face that close to their mouths without fear, so are no' sure what else I might do."

Aulay chuckled at that and carried her into his study.

Chapter 11

GEORDIE STIRRED SLEEPILY, AND TURNED ON HIS SIDE TO WRAP his arm around Dwyn, but blinked his eyes open when he found only empty bed. Frowning, he rolled onto his back and looked to the other side of the bed, but she was not there either. That realization had him jerking upright to quickly scan the room. Dwyn was not there.

Panic clutched at him at once. While Catriona and Sasha had been sent away, and they all hoped that would bring an end to the attacks on Dwyn, they couldn't be positive it would since they had no proof the two women were behind the broken glass and poison. Aulay had offered to put guards on Dwyn for the rest of her stay there, but Geordie had assured him that would not be necessary. He would stay by her side every moment of every day while she was here, and even after, once they left for Innes. Yet, here it was, not even twenty-four hours later, and he'd already lost her.

Cursing under his breath, Geordie scrambled off the bed and rushed out into the hall. When Aulay barked his name, he glanced over his shoulder, mouth open to explain that he'd lost Dwyn, but he whirled toward them when he saw her in his brother's arms. Her father was behind and to the side of them, he saw, eyeing him with raised brows.

Ignoring both men, Geordie sighed her name with relief and rushed toward them, asking, "What are ye doing up, lass? Why did ye no' wake me?"

"Perhaps she was scared off by that monster between yer legs, brother," Aulay said dryly, and then added with exasperation, "Could ye no' have at least grabbed yer plaid on the way out the door?"

Geordie ignored that too. He had eyes only for Dwyn, who was staring at his erection with a concern he didn't understand, until she asked worriedly, "Did ye damage yerself, husband? There's blood on yer pillicock."

Geordie glanced down at the dried blood on his cock, and almost laughed aloud. It was her blood from the breaching, and while he would have expected it to have been removed the second or third or even the fourth time he'd loved her, it had apparently merely mixed with their juices and dried on him all over again after each use. Or perhaps she'd continued to bleed after the breaching, he thought with a frown. It was possible. She had assured him she was not feeling any pain, but perhaps they shouldn't have been so enthusiastic and vigorous after the breaching. The thought made his erection begin to wane.

"Geordie?" Dwyn asked, real worry in her voice now.

Sighing, he raised his head, and offered a reassuring smile as he took her from his brother. "Nay. I'm no' hurt. The blood is yers, lass. The proof o' yer innocence."

"Oh." She flushed a bit at that, but then rolled her eyes. Whether it was from exasperation with herself for not realizing the source of the blood on her own, or because of the pinch of embarrassment she was now feeling as her father and Aulay saw the proof that he'd breached her, Geordie didn't know. He merely squeezed her affectionately, and kissed her nose, before demanding firmly, "Now, what were ye doing out here? And why did ye no' wake me up ere ye left the room?"

"I had to go to the garderobe and ye were sleeping so soundly I did no' wish to disturb ye," Dwyn said quietly.

"The garderobe is the other way," he pointed out dryly.

"I spotted her coming out of the garderobe, realized she was hopping around without her foot bandaged and had Rory come up to me study to bandage her up," Aulay said before she could respond. When Geordie glanced to him, he added, "And then her father and I lectured her on leaving the room again without someone to accompany her until we are sure the attacks on her person have ended. She will no' be hopping around without ye again. Will ye, Dwyn?" he added sternly.

Dwyn didn't seem at all upset by his brother's lecture, Geordie noted. In fact, she seemed more amused than anything, though she did promise, "I shall no' hop around alone."

"Well, then," Laird Innes said brightly. "Now that's settled, I guess we should leave these two to . . . er . . . Good sleep," he said abruptly, and turned to head for the stairs.

When Geordie raised his eyebrows at the man's odd behavior, Aulay said dryly, "I believe Laird Innes is a bit uncomfortable having his daughter's handfasted husband waving his manhood around quite so boldly. Especially with his daughter's blood on it. Speaking o' which, the sup has been over fer a while, and the women shall soon be retiring. Ye may want to take that—" he nodded toward Geordie's groin "—and yer wife back to yer room ere ye scandalize the lasses."

Grunting at the suggestion, Geordie turned and carried Dwyn back up the hall toward his room.

"Good sleep," Aulay called after them with amusement.

"Aye," Geordie called. "Good sleep to ye too."

"I am no' like to sleep this night, m'laird," Dwyn said apologetically as he carried her back through the door he'd left open.

"Nay," he agreed wryly, kicking the door closed. "After sleeping the day away, and then the short nap I had after bedding ye, I'm no' likely to sleep this night either."

"It was an hour at least. More like two," she corrected.

"What was?" Geordie asked with confusion.

"Yer nap after ye bedded me," she explained.

"Aulay and yer father were lecturing ye for two hours?" he asked with raised eyebrows.

"Well, I did no' leave the room right away, and I had to dress first, and then hop there and then Rory bound me foot again and . . ." She shrugged. "But I'm sure ye slept for a couple hours at least."

Geordie groaned at this news and sat on the end of the bed with her in his lap. "I will definitely no' be sleeping tonight, then."

"Nay," Dwyn agreed, and said apologetically, "And I fear I'm hungry and thirsty."

"So am I," he said, his gaze dropping to her breasts.

Dwyn chuckled at his expression, and leaned up to kiss him lightly on the cheek, but said, "For food, m'laird. I will be more than pleased to address the other hunger after that, but first I must eat. And I fear do we no' go down soon, we will no' be going. Once everyone lies down for the night, we'll no' be able to get to the kitchens," she pointed out solemnly.

Geordie frowned at that observation, knowing she was right. Once the castle settled for the night, they would be stuck above stairs, unable to fetch more food or drink later did they desire it. Considering his new wife's appetite for loving, he suspected he'd want food at least twice this night to keep up his strength, and he'd definitely have to replenish his fluids at least that many times too. Remaining in the room was not looking very attractive with those concerns on his mind.

Standing abruptly, Geordie turned and set her on the bed and then moved to gather his shirt from the floor next to the tub. As he donned it, he asked, "Would ye like to see the waterfall I mentioned?"

"Could we?" Dwyn asked with excited interest.

"Aye. 'Twas a full moon last night, so will be almost full tonight still and riding a horse should no' be a problem," Geordie thought aloud as he pleated his plaid. "We could go below now, before everyone retires, get some food from the kitchens, and a skin o' wine, and then take them with us to eat by the waterfall," he suggested.

"That sounds lovely," she breathed, and then frowned. "But we are no more likely to be able to get back to our room once everyone has retired than we are to get to the kitchens."

"Aye, but we could always nap in the orchard do we tire ere everyone else rises," he suggested. "That way we would no' be stuck up here without food or drink at least."

"Aye," she decided. "I'd like that, m'laird."

Smiling, Geordie donned his plaid, and then moved to gather his *sgian-dubh*, one of his daggers, and his sword. After sliding each weapon through his belt, he turned to walk back to her. His footsteps slowed when he noted where her gaze had gone though, and he glanced down to see that while the erection he'd awakened with had deflated while they were out in the hall, it was back and poking at his plaid again.

"I'm looking forward to making love to ye in the waterfalls," he confessed wryly, scooping her up. "And in the meadow where we picked the wildflowers, and under our tree in the orchard."

"Under our tree in the orchard." Dwyn sighed the words and nestled against his chest, but then lifted her head and asked, "Do ye think we could try in the tree?"

"No' if ye want to survive," Geordie said dryly, and then shook his head when she looked disappointed. Heading for the door though, he murmured thoughtfully, "Mayhap we could if I think o' some way to tie us to the tree so that if we fall out, we do no' fall far."

When Dwyn smiled widely at him, and kissed his chin, Geordie shook his head with amusement. He liked making Dwyn smile. He'd figure out something. He rather liked the idea of loving her in the tree. The image of her body lying back over her branch, her breasts bared as she straddled him on his branch, was an image burned in his mind. He'd like to see her like that again, but with her skirts up around her waist and him inside her. Aye, he'd think of something. But first he wanted to take her to the loch and make love to her under the waterfall. Geordie suspected that as sensitive as Dwyn was to touch, she would go wild with him inside her and the water pouring down over their bodies. That was another image burned into his brain, though only an imagined one. Dwyn on the small ledge he'd mentioned, her head back against the wall keeping her face out of the water, her back arched, breasts thrust up and nipples erect as water rained down over them while he stood between her legs, his cock buried in her lovely heat. Aye. He definitely wanted to go to the waterfall first.

"I LOVE THIS SPOT," DWYN BREATHED WHEN GEORDIE REINED IN his mount in a small clearing next to the loch. Her gaze slid over the falls spilling over the cliff, the water silvered by the moonlight as it tumbled into this end of the loch, and she gave a little shiver of pleasure.

"I thought ye'd like it," Geordie said, and the arm around her waist squeezed gently. "'Tis me favorite spot here at Buchanan."

"Then ye may jest like Innes, m'laird. Some days the sea is as wild and powerful as those falls, and others as gentle as a lamb, but 'tis always beautiful."

She felt him press a kiss to the side of her head, and then he lifted her off of his lap and turned, leaning down to set her on the ground.

"One foot," he reminded, and Dwyn lifted her still-bound foot before her slippered foot touched the earth. Grunting in satisfaction, he suggested, "Hold on to me mount to keep yer balance until I can carry ye to the water's edge."

Dwyn shifted the bag of food and drink she held to her right hand and clasped his saddle with her left as he dismounted and moved to the front of his horse to tie the reins to a low branch of the tree he'd stopped under. Her gaze moved eagerly around this small clearing as she waited. Dwyn could not believe she was so lucky. On the journey to Buchanan she'd been positive the trip was a wasted effort, and that she'd never draw the attention of one of the Buchanan brothers. Yet here she was, married to Geordie, experiencing passion she'd never imagined, and having late-night adventures in the most beautiful spots.

The only thing that could make it any better was if he loved her, but Dwyn was too sensible to fret much over that. Love was rare in a marriage, and she already had a great deal. Geordie seemed to like her well enough and enjoy her company . . . and he wanted her. She had no doubt of that. It was obvious in the way he couldn't resist touching or kissing her when nearby, in his passion as he loved her and even in the way his eyes burned when he looked at her. Aye, he wanted her, and that was miraculous enough for now.

Dwyn did hope that eventually finer feelings would grow between them. She felt sure her own emotions were already headed that way. At times, just looking at Geordie could cause a small ache in her chest she felt sure was love. She didn't expect he'd return the feelings in full, but hoped he'd come to care for her as more than a bed partner someday.

That being the case, now they just had Laird Brodie to deal with. Dwyn frowned and pushed the thought quickly away, not wanting to ruin a moment of the joy she'd found.

"I'm going to go lay out the plaid for us," Geordie announced, coming around the front of the horse with the plaid they'd collected from the orchard. They'd left it there when he'd carried her into the keep after "tasting her" there the day before. Recalling that, he'd run back to collect it after setting her on his mount. "Are ye all right to stand here a few more minutes?"

"Aye," she assured him. "I am fine, m'laird. I can wait."

He nodded, and then bent to press what she felt sure he'd meant to be a quick kiss to her lips, but the moment his lips touched hers, she opened to him, and the quick kiss turned into a passionate embrace that left her breathless and panting when he reluctantly broke it and rested his forehead against hers.

"Damn," he breathed suddenly, pulling back to look down at her. "I canno' get enough o' ye. Every time I touch ye, I just want to . . ."

His helpless expression made Dwyn smile and she admitted, "So do I, m'laird." And then grinning, she added, "Mayhap 'tis an affliction and will pass."

"Aye." Geordie cupped her bottom through her skirts and lifted her off the ground to grind his hips into hers. "I'm thinking in forty or fifty years 'twill pass."

Dwyn groaned as he pressed against her. "Pray, m'laird. Go spread out the plaid so we can do something about this need ye cause in me."

"Just as I feared, married no' even a day and already ye're a nagging wife," he accused in a teasing tone as he set her down.

"Demanding too," she assured him, reaching out to find his hardness and squeeze.

"One minute," Geordie promised, kissing the tip of her nose before he turned away and strode off.

Dwyn watched him make his way to the water's edge. He was just laying out the plaid when she heard a sound behind her. Before she could turn to find the source of it, a hand had slapped over her mouth, and an arm was around her waist, dragging her backward into the dark woods.

GEORDIE FLAPPED THE FOLDED PLAID OUT TO LIE ON THE GRASS, and then took the time to move to each corner and give it a tug to straighten it out on the ground as he considered what to do first. He wanted to make love to Dwyn in the waterfall, and had planned to set her down here just long enough to strip off her clothes and bandages, as well as his own clothes, and then carry her into the water. But the kiss he'd just shared with her had heated his blood so quickly he feared they'd end up mating here on the plaid first.

"Well, so be it," Geordie muttered to himself. With the appetite his wife had, and that he had for her, they could start here, move on to the waterfall after they'd rested and then maybe make their way over to the meadow where the ladies had picked their flowers. He'd had some pretty hot imaginings of loving Dwyn there too, and they could end the night back at their tree, perhaps even *in* the tree if he came up with a way to keep them from falling, he thought wryly, and turned to walk back to Dwyn where he'd left her. Only she wasn't there.

Geordie's feet paused, and he blinked at the spot where he'd left her . . . by his horse, which also wasn't there.

"What the hell?" he muttered with bewilderment. While Geordie knew that the noise of the falls would have prevented his hearing the horse leave, Dwyn wouldn't have ridden away with the beast without him. Where the hell were they? he wondered, and then spotted something on the ground by where he'd left his horse. Hurrying forward, he squatted and picked up the item, his heart lurching when he turned it in his hand and realized it was Dwyn's slipper.

His eyes searched the dark woods as he straightened, and then he withdrew his sword and started forward. His pace was cautious, until he heard a male shout followed quickly by Dwyn screaming his name, then he burst into a run.

"Shut up, bitch!"

Dwyn grunted as she was hit in the face hard enough to send her crashing to the forest floor.

"And what the hell's the matter with ye, Coll? Screaming like that. Ye'll give us away. We're supposed to be quiet, remember?"

"She grabbed me ballocks and twisted."

Dwyn raised her face off the ground, and glanced around as she spat out the dirt that had got in her mouth as she'd fallen. The man who had dragged her into the woods must be the one presently bent over with both hands covering his groin, she decided. Which meant the man standing straight up was the one who had hit her and started yelling. And he was complaining about the other one not being quiet? She snorted at that, and then stilled, her eyes narrowing warily when the standing man turned on her.

"Ye'll no' be looking so pleased with yerself when we get ye back to our camp, little lady," he growled, stomping toward her.

Dwyn tried to lunge to her feet and make her escape, but didn't even get upright before he grabbed her by a handful of hair and yanked her around to face him. Dragging her so close she could smell his foul breath, he snarled, "There's a good chance the men'll all get a turn at plowin' into ye once we have ye back at camp, lass, and I'm thinking Coll there's gonna want to show ye about as much care as ye showed him now we ken what a nasty lass ye are. So, unless ye want me to behave just as badly, I suggest—"

He broke off abruptly, his head swiveling to the side.

It was only then Dwyn heard the sounds of someone crashing through the woods toward them. Geordie had heard her scream, she thought with relief, and then began to struggle as the man holding her by the hair tried to drag her in front of him. Desperate to get away, she tried to reach down and grab him as she had the other man, but this one was ready for that trick and grabbed her hand with his free one so she kneed him in the groin instead. When his grip eased, Dwyn threw herself to the side. She was already scrambling away before she hit the ground, desperate to put as much distance between them as she could to avoid being used against Geordie. But Dwyn hadn't moved far when she heard the ring of swords clashing.

Glancing over her shoulder, she saw Geordie battling the man she'd just kneed. It took little more than three swings of his sword before he felled the man. It was only when Geordie started to turn toward her that she realized he didn't know there was a second man. She and the villain he'd just felled must have been blocking the second one from view, she thought, and shouted a warning even as a sword suddenly exploded out of the front of his lower chest.

She watched with horror as Geordie lowered his head to peer in shock as the blade slid back the way it had come until it disappeared into his chest. Dwyn fully expected Geordie to drop to the ground then as the first villain had done when he'd struck him a similar blow, although it had been a little higher on him. But Geordie didn't drop. Instead, he whirled on his feet with a roar, his sword coming up and swinging.

Judging by the man's wide eyes and gaping mouth, he hadn't expected that response from Geordie any more than she had, Dwyn thought grimly as she watched his head tumble from his neck and crash to the floor even as his body fell. Only then did

Geordie go down, dropping first to his knees, and then falling forward on the forest floor.

Crying out, Dwyn crawled quickly to his side. Her gaze slid over his back, but while her eyes had adjusted quickly to the dark forest where the moonlight didn't reach, all she could see were dark shapes. She could feel the blood soaking his plaid though when she placed a hand to it, and quickly grabbed up her skirt hem. She tried to tear it, but the material was too thick for that, and she had to feel around on Geordie for the dagger she'd seen him slide into his belt back in his room. Dragging it out, Dwyn used that to cut off a strip of her skirt. She then balled it up, and pressed it against the center of the spreading patch of blood, before slicing at her skirt again to get another swath of the material. Dwyn laid that over the ball of cloth she'd placed over the wound, then stuck each end under his arms before rolling him onto his back. She sliced away a third strip of her gown to ball up and press against the center of the blood patch on the front of his chest when she found it with her fingers. Dwyn then grabbed up both ends of the cloth she'd tucked under his arms and drew them together to tie them off over the cloth. She pulled both ends as tight as she could as she did it, putting her whole body behind the effort, relief sliding through her when she heard him grunt in pain.

Pain was good, it meant he lived, Dwyn thought as she finished tying off the cloth and bent over his face. Patting his cheek lightly, she said, "Geordie? Are ye awake, husband?"

"Aye," he groaned.

"Thank God," she breathed, and then ordered, "Stay that way!"

"Well, I'm no' likely to sleep with ye bellowing at me like that," he said, his voice weak, but with a touch of humor to it.

"Good, because ye're no' getting out o' marrying me good and proper in front o' a priest, Geordie Buchanan. So do no' even think o' dying on me," she growled, and then glanced around anxiously, trying to think what to do. She needed to get him back to the clearing and his horse. "Can ye get up, do ye think?" Dwyn turned back to him to ask.

He raised his head and shifted his hands to his sides to help push himself up, but then dropped back to the ground on a sigh. "I'm sorry, lass. I do no' think—"

"'Tis okay," Dwyn said at once. "Don't waste yer strength talking." She glanced through the trees, trying to judge how far she'd been dragged. Turning back to Geordie, she bent to press a quick kiss to his mouth, then pushed herself to her feet, muttering, "I'll be right back. Do no' die on me."

"Wife, wait," he gasped, but she ignored him and burst into a run. The clearing wasn't far at all, perhaps twenty feet, but when she didn't see Geordie's horse, Dwyn at first thought she'd somehow got turned around and come out at the wrong spot. But then she saw the plaid spread out under the moonlight and cursed. This was the right place. Geordie's horse was just gone.

Dwyn stood still for a second, her heart thumping and brain twisting itself up trying to sort out what to do. She had to get Geordie to help, and quickly, or she could lose him. His horse had been their best bet. She hadn't thought ahead to figure out how to get him on the horse when he couldn't even stand up, but she would have figured out something. Unfortunately, there was no horse to get him on.

"Oh God, oh God, oh God," Dwyn breathed, turning in a circle. She could lose him. She couldn't lose him. She loved him.

The thought made Dwyn freeze briefly. Love? Already? She wanted to scoff at the thought, but was very much afraid that she did already love Geordie Buchanan. The man was just . . . He made her feel alive. For years she'd felt like she was fading away, becoming just another piece of furniture at Innes. That had been happening for the last seven years actually, since the day that she'd learned her betrothed had died. She'd never met the man who was to be her husband, so had not grieved his passing for the man he was. Instead, she'd felt only panic and fear.

When they received the message with the news of his death, Dwyn had turned to her father with dismay and asked what they would do now. His response had been "not to worry, everything would work out," and she'd known then that he wasn't likely to try to find her a replacement husband. Her father was too comfortable with the way things were. He was too happy having her to run his keep, and handle his people. And she'd known she would live out her days at Innes, alone, without the husband and children she'd dreamed about someday having.

Dwyn was positive that if it weren't for Geordie she would have died a lonely old maid, running her father's home and people. Or perhaps living out her end days on the charity offered to her by her sisters, depending on what had been done with Innes if her father died first.

By the time the first letter had arrived from Buchanan, she'd already been a shriveled-up old maid in her head. Almost. But that first letter had sparked hope in her heart. However, her father hadn't shown much interest in it. In fact, he'd tossed the first away. It was Dwyn who had snatched it up from the floor where he'd tossed it after crumpling it up. And it was Dwyn who'd responded to the message in her father's name. She'd continued to respond to each successive message from Jetta Buchanan, telling herself it was a nice little fantasy to pass her dreary days so that she wouldn't get her hopes up, because she knew her father ultimately wouldn't agree to anything that might prevent her taking care of him. But then the message with the Buchanan terms had arrived. Dwyn had begun to tremble when she'd read that if a brother chose her to wife, Laird Innes had to agree and put in the marriage contract that the Buchanan brother would become the heir to Innes, and next clan chief.

Hope had flared to life in Dwyn, a brilliant fire in her breast. She'd known her father would like that. It not only wouldn't take her away from him, it would add someone else to take over more of his responsibilities, freeing him to pursue his own interests. She'd been sure that would appeal to him, and she'd been right. The next thing she knew he was responding that they would travel to Buchanan so that the sons could meet his daughter.

Dwyn had been over the moon . . . until her sisters had decided to help. She knew they really had wanted to help, that they'd wanted her married and happily settled like they were going to be with their still-living future husbands. They had not *tried* to make her feel inferior. But, in the end, that's what their help had done. Their determination to lower the necklines on her gowns to highlight her large breasts, which were her "finest feature," had reminded her that she had not been graced with the beauty they had, but was plain and unappealing. Their insistence on taking in the waistline of those same gowns until they were so tight that she could barely breathe so that she looked slimmer had just reminded her that she was not long-legged and slender like her sisters. And the lessons they'd insisted on giving her in how to be interesting and not a bookworm had reminded her that she was a dull little wren, not likely to attract a husband.

By the time they'd left for Buchanan, Dwyn was regretting ever answering Lady Jetta's first letter, and sure the trip was going to be a terrible waste of time. Things had not improved when she'd arrived and Lady Catriona and Lady Sasha had begun to peck at her, reinforcing what her sisters had unintentionally made her feel. She was plain, and boring and fat, and none of the Buchanans would be interested in her, they'd said, and then begun to call her horse-face and to whinny at her, and she'd thought the trip would not just be a waste of time but probably the most miserable time of her life.

And then Geordie climbed up into her tree and everything changed. He made her laugh. He made her burn. He made her feel desirable, and even desired. He made her feel powerful, like a goddess . . . and he was so kind and gentle with her. So careful with her at all times. Geordie made her see herself through entirely different eyes than her sisters and Catriona and Sasha did. He made her like herself again, and she loved him for that and much more. For his kindness to Drostan. For the way he helped his family. For his strength and character.

She loved him . . . and she had to get back to him now, Dwyn realized, pushing her thoughts away. She didn't dare leave him alone for too long. Time was of the essence here. She needed to get him to help as quickly as she could, and it seemed there was only one way to do it now that his horse was gone.

Mouth tightening grimly, Dwyn rushed over to grab the plaid and then turned to charge back into the woods.

Chapter 12

"YER HORSE IS GONE," DWYN GOT OUT ON A GASPED BREATH as she reached Geordie and started to lay out the plaid.

"Aye," he sighed. "I tried to tell ye that, but ye ran off too quick."

"The men must have loosed him," she muttered, pulling the plaid corners out.

"And slapped him to make him run," Geordie added. "Else he would no' have gone. He has probably returned to the keep. They'll send help if he has."

Dwyn glanced at him sharply at that. "What's his name?"

"Who? Me horse?"

"Aye, Geordie, what's his name?" she asked again.

"Horse."

"Ye named yer horse *Horse*?" Dwyn squawked with disbelief. "Do ye call yer dog Dog too, then?"

"I do no' have a dog," Geordie reminded her, sounding amused but weary.

"Ye do now. Two o' them, and their names are Angus and Barra, so do no' expect them to answer to Dog," she said firmly.

"Wife, what—?" His question ended on a grunt when Dwyn moved around to his side opposite the plaid and shoved with all her might to roll him onto his stomach. It put him half on the plaid, and before he could protest her shabby treatment of him, she rolled him again, onto his back this time. Much to her relief that roll put him in the center of the plaid.

"Dwyn," he said with a frown in his voice as she moved to his feet and began to tie the ends of the plaid together beneath his boots. "What are ye doing, lass? Ye need to make yer way back to Buchanan."

"I intend to," Dwyn assured him, "with you."

"Nay, lass. Ye—"

"Horse!" she called over his protest. "Horse!"

"Dwyn!" His voice was a raspy hiss, but it was his hand grabbing her ankle that made her stop and turn to him as he said, "These men may have cohorts out here, and ye could draw them to us."

"They do have others out here with them," she admitted unhappily, recalling the one villain saying there was a good chance the men would all get to have a turn at her. Giving up on the horse for the minute, she moved to the end of the plaid opposite his feet. Dwyn hadn't spread the whole plaid out; she'd left almost half of it bundled in a clump just past where his head now lay. There simply wasn't room in the woods to lay out twelve feet of plaid. Taking up the ends now, she tied them around her waist, knotting them to be sure they didn't untie and slip off. She then started walking in the general direction she thought Buchanan keep must be. At least, she tried. The man was much heavier than she'd expected, or perhaps heavier than she'd hoped was a better description. Dwyn had to lean all her weight forward to get him moving across the forest floor, but after a couple of false starts, she was able to drag him at a slow steady pace.

Of course, Geordie began to protest the moment he realized what she was doing, and insisted she leave him and hurry back to the safety of Buchanan without him. Dwyn ignored him at first, but when his voice began to weaken, she knew she had to do something. He was wasting strength he needed to survive.

Glancing back, she growled breathlessly, "Do ye really want to see me raped by a whole camp full of villains, m'laird? Because that's what one o' the men said would happen once they got me back to their camp, and that's most like what will happen do ye no' quit yer carping at me. They'll hear ye and catch us."

When Geordie snapped his mouth closed, she grunted with

satisfaction and turned her face forward. Dwyn was moving steadily at an angle she hoped would take them out onto the path they'd ridden to get to the loch. She knew it would be risky to drag him along the path, but the forest floor was full of branches and the exposed roots of trees and she didn't think it was probably doing his wound much good bumping him over those. Besides, they would surely move more quickly on the flatter path, and that was important. Dwyn was terrified he'd lose too much blood and die before she could get him to help. But she only had to get him to the edge of the woods around Buchanan castle. Dwyn was sure once they reached the clearing, the men on the wall would see them and send riders out. She just had to get him that far . . . and quickly.

Dwyn's thoughts died as she heard the snap of a branch behind her. Afraid she wouldn't be able to get Geordie moving again did she stop now, she continued forward, and merely glanced over her shoulder, but didn't see anything. She didn't hear anything else either, at least not from behind her. Instead, she became aware of the growing thunder of horses ahead and to her right. Sure they must be riders from Buchanan, Dwyn enjoyed a burst of energy that allowed her to move more quickly for a couple minutes, but not quick enough. Afraid the men would ride right past them, she stopped and quickly undid the plaid from around her waist.

"I'll be right back," she whispered to Geordie, and hurried through the trees toward the sound. Dwyn had meant to stop in the trees before she reached the path the riders must be on, just to make sure that the riders were from Buchanan, but it was so dark she couldn't tell where the trees ended until she raced out of them and onto the path. Stopping abruptly, Dwyn started to turn back and then froze, her hand coming up to cover her chest as she saw the horse about to run right over her.

It was much lighter on the path where the moonlight was not obstructed by trees, and Dwyn could actually see the dismay on Aulay's face as he sawed viciously on his horse's reins to keep from trampling her. The animal reared, his head forced to the side by the reins and his huge body following just enough. The beast's front hooves churned the air, brushing so close to her face she felt the breeze of their passing, and then they crashed to the ground just to the side of her. Chaos immediately erupted behind Aulay as the men following him were all forced to an abrupt halt as well. Some managed it, some had to turn their horses off the path to avoid a collision, and then Aulay leapt off his mount, and grabbed her arms.

"Are ye all right, lass?" he growled with concern.

Dwyn shifted her eyes to him, gasped, "Geordie," and then pulled away to run back into the woods. After the light on the path, the darkness of the forest at night left her almost blind, but she stumbled through the trees as quickly as she could, and found the wounded man by tripping over him. His grunt as she fell over him sounded beautiful to her, and Dwyn scrambled back to kneel next to him and feel for his face in the dark.

"Geordie? Aulay's found us. 'Tis going to be all right now. We'll have ye back at the keep in no time," she assured him, brushing her hands over his cheeks and forehead. "Ye just hang on."

Straightening then, she glanced to Aulay's dark shape as he knelt on Geordie's other side. "We have to get him back quickly—he's bleeding badly."

Aulay didn't ask questions; he merely scooped up his brother and turned to stride back through the trees. His men had followed, and now scattered, backing out of the way for them to pass. It wasn't until they were out of the woods that Aulay asked, "What happened?"

"We were attacked. Two men. Geordie killed them both, but took a sword through the chest before he dispatched the second one," Dwyn explained quickly.

"Were there only two?" Aulay asked, his voice grim as he moved to his horse.

"Aye, but they mentioned a camp and more men," she said on a sigh.

"Alick, take Geordie and pass him up to me once I'm mounted," Aulay ordered, pausing next to his mount.

Dwyn glanced around with surprise at the man who had been standing beside her when he stepped forward to take Geordie. She hadn't realized it was Geordie's younger brother until Aulay addressed him.

"Follow me back with Dwyn," Aulay ordered as Alick raised Geordie up to him. Once he had his brother settled before him, he glanced around and barked, "Simon, search the woods. Find this camp and bring back the men ye find."

"Aye, m'laird." The young soldier's fair hair shone under the moonlight as he immediately began barking orders of his own. Satisfied, Aulay turned his horse and headed back along the path, headed for the keep.

"Did Geordie's horse return to the castle?" Dwyn asked as Alick ushered her over to his own mount.

"Aye," he said as he mounted. Alick then bent to catch her about the waist and lift her up before him on the horse as he added, "The men on the wall immediately raised the alarm. Aulay and I were just helping to break down the trestle tables and joined the men riding out."

Dwyn nodded as he settled her in his lap and urged his horse around.

"How bad was the wound, Dwyn?"

She glanced around at the worry in his voice, and swallowed before saying, "Bad," in a weak voice.

As quiet as the word had been, Alick apparently heard it. Expression grim, he spurred his mount to a gallop. Even so, Aulay was still a good three horse lengths in front of them when they entered the bailey. By the time Alick reined in at the foot of the steps to the keep, Aulay had dropped off of his horse with his burden and was carrying Geordie up the stairs, barking orders as he went.

Dwyn slid off of Alick's horse the moment he stopped, and chased after Aulay, following him up the steps as quickly as she could.

"Dwyn," Alick shouted, and then cursed behind her. She heard his boots on the steps as he hurried after her, but was still startled when he scooped her up off her feet.

"Put me down, Alick. I want to see if Geordie is—"

"I'll carry ye, lass. Yer feet are bleeding again. There's a trail o' bloody footprints up the stairs," he said grimly.

Dwyn glanced over his shoulder, shocked to see there was indeed blood on the steps. It wasn't full footprints, but half a bloody print, and just drops of blood from the other. Turning back, she raised her feet to get a look at the tops of them, and saw that her slipper was missing off her good foot, and the linen unraveled and hanging down from her ankle on the other. She wasn't sure when she'd lost the slipper, probably when she'd been dragged backward so abruptly, but she hadn't even noticed. Nor had she noticed her linen wrappings unraveling.

Sighing, Dwyn let her feet drop and turned to look for Aulay as Alick carried her through the keep door Drostan was holding open. She wasn't surprised to find the people in the great hall all up and about. Alick had said they were just breaking down the trestle tables when Geordie's riderless horse returned and the alarm was called. She supposed the others had given up any idea of sleeping until the men returned and they knew what was about. Now the inhabitants of Buchanan watched silently as she and Geordie were carried to the stairs.

Dwyn heard her name gasped and glanced around as her sisters rushed forward from the crowd, her father close behind them. It was only then she realized it wasn't just servants and soldiers in the great hall; many of the visiting women and their escorts were below still too, and had been waiting.

"Oh, Dwyn, yer poor feet," Aileen moaned as she reached them and hurried along beside Alick.

"What happened?" Una asked grimly on her heels. "Geordie looks badly hurt."

"We were attacked." Dwyn sighed the words, her head swiveling to look toward Aulay again. She had no idea when Geordie had lost consciousness, but he obviously was now. His head was hanging over Aulay's arm, his face slack and pale as death.

"Was it Brodie?" Una asked sharply, and Dwyn glanced around, a frown claiming her lips.

"I do no' ken. They did no' mention Brodie," she admitted wearily, and then they'd reached the steps and Aileen and Una were forced to drop back behind them as Alick started to jog up the stairs.

Dwyn forgot them then, her attention wholly on Geordie's slack face as Alick carried her quickly up the steps and followed Aulay into Geordie's room as she heard Jetta say, "Set him on the bed, husband."

Dwyn glanced around the room to see that Rory was already there as well, fresh linens and his medicinals at the ready.

"What happened?" Rory asked, his eyes finding hers as he stepped back to allow Aulay to lay Geordie on the bed.

"He took a sword through the back. It came out the front," Dwyn said at once, knowing that was what he was asking. She then added, "His lower chest, mayhap his upper stomach. 'Twas too dark to see properly."

Rory nodded and then stepped back up beside Aulay to cut away the strip of skirt she'd tied tightly around his wound. He and Aulay then worked together to remove Geordie's plaid and shirt.

Alick carried Dwyn around to the other side of the bed, and set her down. She resisted the urge to crawl closer on the bed, and stayed out of the way, watching anxiously as they held Geordie upright to get his chest bare. She winced when she saw the wound to his back. It was a little more than two inches across, she saw, when Rory washed the blood away. He paused briefly then—she assumed to see how quickly the blood bubbled back up—and then grunted and pressed a wadded-up linen to it with one hand as he shifted to look at the front of his chest.

Dwyn immediately crawled closer then so that she could help hold Geordie upright as Aulay had to release him and step out of the way for Rory to look at his front.

"Well?" Aulay demanded as Rory washed the blood from Geordie's chest.

Rory glanced up and then frowned when he saw the way Dwyn was straining to hold Geordie upright for him. "Alick, climb on the bed and hold Geordie up. Dwyn, move closer to the edge of the bed so Jetta can start work on yer feet." Those orders given, he still ignored Aulay's question and started to do something to Geordie's chest that she couldn't see, and then she was distracted by Alick climbing up the center of the bed.

Dwyn shifted her legs aside for him, and then released Geordie and shifted her bottom over too to get out of the way as he took over holding him up. She continued shifting sideways until she reached the edge of the bed, and then glanced toward Geordie again as Rory murmured, "It missed his heart. However, I think it might have nicked one lung. He's lost a lot o' blood. No' as much as he could have though, thanks to Dwyn binding him up tight." He raised his head to glance to her and nodded solemnly. "Good job, lass."

She managed a smile, but her lips trembled with it.

"So that's what happened to yer skirts."

Dwyn turned at that murmur from Jetta to see that Lady Buchanan was now kneeling next to the bed, a basin of water on the floor beside her that she was dipping a fresh scrap of linen into. Dwyn shifted her attention to her gown then, and grimaced when she saw the state of it. Her neckline had dropped as usual to reveal the tops of her nipples—not surprising after what she'd been through—but she had cut away so much of her skirts they now barely covered her knees. Dwyn merely sighed at the sight, but she did think she probably wouldn't be at all bothered by the bedding ceremony if they ever had a wedding. Everyone had pretty much seen the better part of her anyway.

"I wish ye'd cut a little more off to cover yer feet though," Jetta said grimly as she gently clasped her feet and looked at one and then the other.

Dwyn considered curling her legs so she could look at the

bottoms of her feet, but decided she didn't want to know how bad they were. While she hadn't felt a thing while struggling to get Geordie out of the woods, they were paining her something terrible now and she knew she'd done them more damage running about the woods, and then dragging Geordie on the plaid. She'd had to dig her feet in to pull his weight and knew she'd been digging into branches and whatnot as she had.

"Will he live?"

Aulay's growl drew her gaze back to Geordie and she saw that Rory had finished cleaning and exploring his chest wound and was now threading a needle. He also was not answering Aulay's question, she noted with a frown. Or at least was taking an inordinate amount of time answering. Judging by Aulay's grim expression, that wasn't a good sign, she thought, and felt her heart drop just as a knock sounded at the bedchamber door.

She glanced toward it with disinterest as her father moved to answer, her mind still wrestling with what Rory's silence might mean.

"He'll live."

Dwyn glanced to Aileen, who had said those words solemnly beside her.

"He has to," she added. "Ye're no' properly married yet."

"They *are* married, Aileen," Una said firmly. "They handfasted, 'tis as good as married in the eyes of the law."

"Aye, but no' the church," Aileen said with a frown, and then her eyes suddenly went round.

Startled by her expression, Dwyn turned her gaze to see what had made Aileen react that way and stared blankly at Father Archibald as he entered the room. She was vaguely aware of her father greeting the man and closing the door, but most of her focus was on the Buchanan priest. Expression solemn, he crossed to the bed and murmured something to Aulay. Dwyn couldn't hear all of what he said, but caught the words *penance, anointing of the sick* and *viaticum,* and suddenly couldn't breathe. The priest was here to perform the sacraments for the dying, and while she knew it had to be done, it just seemed to her to push Geordie closer to death in her mind and she couldn't bear it.

"Is he conscious?" Father Archibald asked Rory.

"I am, Father."

Dwyn turned sharply to Geordie when he said that and was in time to see him lift his head.

"Do ye have the strength to give me yer confession, m'laird?" Father Archibald asked quietly.

When Geordie grunted in the affirmative, the priest glanced to Aulay. "Mayhap ye could move everyone to the other side o' the room?"

"All but Rory," Aulay said grimly. "He'll continue to try to save his life even while ye try to save his soul."

The moment the priest assented, Aulay started around the bed to help Jetta to her feet.

"Go ahead, Alick," Rory said quietly. "I'll work on his chest first."

Alick eased Geordie onto his back, and then glanced to Dwyn.

"I have her," Aulay said, and she turned just as he scooped her up off the bed. Alick immediately shifted to the edge of the bed and followed Aulay when he carried Dwyn to join the others now standing as close to the fireplace as possible without getting in it. They all turned their backs then, as if that would stop them hearing anything. Dwyn almost didn't. She was sideways in Aulay's arms and almost turned to watch Father Archibald and Geordie, but a stern look from Aulay made her turn her head to the fireplace as well. The silence on their end of the room was deafening; even so she couldn't make out what was said at the other end of the room. It was all soft murmurs in her ear, the priest's and Geordie's voices hushed. It seemed to her as if eons had passed when the priest said, "Lady Dwyn?"

Aulay turned at once and then carried her across the room when the priest gestured to them.

"Geordie would like to marry ye now," Father Archibald announced.

"Now?" Truly, Dwyn hadn't meant to squawk the word that

way, but this was not how she'd imagined her wedding. Dear God, she wore a dress that kept flashing her nipples and now barely reached her knees. Her feet were muddy and bloody. She had scratches on her arms and legs, and mussy hair from the branches that had caught at her as she'd dragged Geordie through the woods, and Dwyn was quite sure she had a fat lip from when one of her attackers had hit her. At least, it felt swollen . . . and split, she thought grimly as her tongue slid over it.

"Dwyn."

She shifted her gaze to Geordie at that soft growl, and Aulay carried her around to set her in the bed next to him. Dwyn immediately shifted closer to his side so he wouldn't have to raise his voice, which he couldn't do anyway.

"Ye're no' getting out o' marrying me good and proper in front o' a priest, Dwyn Innes Buchanan," Geordie got out in a weak, raspy voice. They were the exact words she'd barked at him in the woods. Well, except for her name, she acknowledged, and then his hand found hers and squeezed with little strength. "Marry me, lass. I love ye, and would have me name protect ye in case I canno'."

Dwyn felt tears fill her eyes at the words, and nodded soundlessly. She didn't hear or see Aulay call the others over, but suddenly they were surrounding the bed. Aulay, Jetta, Alick, Rory, Aileen, Una and her father. Their family. They stood witness as Father Archibald married her to Geordie Buchanan so that they were husband and wife, not just in the eyes of the law, but in the sight of God too . . . until death did they part.

Chapter 13

Geordie opened his eyes, stared at the drapes overhead and then turned his head to the side where Dwyn slept, only she wasn't there. That made him immediately cranky. His head was pounding, his mouth was dry and his wife missing. *Grand,* he thought grimly, and tried to sit up, only to find he didn't have the strength to manage it, and that trying caused a great deal of pain in his chest.

Cursing, he flopped back to lie flat and then peered down at the furs covering him. When his gaze caught on something dark on his face, and he realized he had a beard and mustache, his eyes widened incredulously and he wondered what the hell had happened. He was still trying to sort through the store of fuzzy memories in search of the answer to that when the door opened.

Turning his head sharply at the sound, he relaxed, and almost smiled when Dwyn came in. But before the smile could fully form, a scowl took its place as he realized Dwyn was *walking.* Hell, she was practically skipping, and looking pretty damned pleased with herself too. He opened his mouth to berate her for walking on her wounded feet, but all that came out was a dry and cracked sort of squawk. Geordie's eyes widened in alarm at that, but Dwyn had heard, stopped walking to gape at him and suddenly hurried to the bed with a squeal of delight.

"Ye're awake! Oh, I'm sorry I missed it, husband. I only left to use the garderobe."

Somewhat mollified by her joy at his waking, Geordie grunted when she threw herself on him. She landed with her head on his stomach, her arms hugging his hips. It didn't hurt so much as surprise him. As did the fact that the lass's breasts were pressing against his groin, and his groin didn't care. That was new, he thought with bewilderment, and opened his mouth to ask what was going on, only to emit another dry, cracked squawk.

The sound made Dwyn lift her head to look at him, and then she was up off the bed and standing next to him. The next thing he knew, she had caught him by the shoulders and managed to drag him up a bit so that his face was cuddled against her breasts as she held him there with one hand just long enough to shove a pillow behind his back. Raising him up again, she pressed him to her bosom and shoved another pillow behind him, and then did it a third time. Each time she did it Geordie stared at the tops of her breasts just visible above her neckline and inhaled her sweet scent, then frowned when he realized how little bosom there was visible above the neckline.

"There," Dwyn said after she'd stuffed the last pillow behind him. Settling her hip on the bed beside him, she then reached for a goblet on the bedside table and moved it to his lips, holding and tipping it to help him drink.

Geordie could have wept when the sweet, cool cider slid over his tongue and filled his mouth. It was the best damned thing he'd ever tasted, he decided, and would have gulped down the entire contents, but she wouldn't let him.

"Slowly, husband, until we see how yer stomach handles it," Dwyn cautioned, before tipping the goblet again. She tipped it four times in a row, but then set the goblet on the bedside table again and turned to look him over with bright eyes. "I should go fetch Rory. He made me promise to get him when ye woke, but . . ." Dwyn sighed and then bent to kiss him softly, before straightening to look at him again, as she said, "'Tis so nice to finally have ye awake again. I just want to look on ye for a minute."

Geordie smiled, and wanted to raise a hand to caress her cheek, but it flopped uselessly at his side when he tried. That brought a frustrated frown to his face until she reached over and clasped his hand, squeezing gently.

"Do no' fret. Ye'll get yer strength back quickly now ye're awake," Dwyn assured him, and then tears filled her eyes, and she admitted, "For a while there in the woods I feared ye were done for. I thought I'd be a widow ere ye even married me properly."

"The waterfall," Geordie breathed as his memories finally coalesced in his head, filling his mind briefly. Setting out the plaid. Turning to find Dwyn gone. Her scream from the woods that sent him running. The man she was struggling with when he found them. A short battle with him, and then he'd turned to Dwyn and a bloody sword tip was sticking out of his chest.

Geordie frowned at the memory. He had no idea where the second man had come from. He'd only seen Dwyn and the man she was trying to get away from when he'd run up on them. So the blow had more surprised him than actually hurt. He would have sworn at first that someone had punched him in the back, so was shocked when the blade appeared, slicing out of his chest. It had hurt a hell of a lot more when it was pulled out, and the moment it was gone, he'd turned on his attacker in a rage and—

Geordie grimaced as he recalled hacking off the man's head. His aim had been a little off. He hadn't intended to behead the bastard, just kill him, but—

"Ye remember, then?" Dwyn asked quietly.

"Aye," Geordie managed, though his voice was raspy. "How long?"

"Ye slept fer two weeks," she said solemnly. "Well, really, ye were awake but feverish most o' the first week, but then in a sleep so deep we could no' wake ye this last week. Rory said yer body had shut down to allow ye to heal, and ye'd hopefully wake soon."

She paused then, but he saw something flicker in her eyes and the worry pulling at her lips as she peered at him, and he asked, "What?"

Dwyn hesitated, but then admitted, "Rory said 'twas possible the sleep was due to yer brains boiling from the fever, and ye may no' be quite the same when ye woke," she admitted reluctantly, and then asked a bit anxiously, "Do ye feel any different?"

"Nay," Geordie assured her, but wondered if that were true. The lass was sitting there on the bed with him and he was feeling no urge to tup her. He was quite sure that never would have been the case before the wound and fever. He hadn't been able to keep his hands off her prior to that. Dear God, what if the fever had taken his manhood from him?

"Oh, good," Dwyn sighed out on a relieved breath, unaware of the worry suddenly plaguing him.

His gaze slid immediately to her chest to see if she'd unseated her breasts and her nipples might be poking out at him. Surely his interest would return then? But the neckline of her gown was so high there was no chance of them escaping. Before he could comment on that, she was up and heading for the door. "I'd best go let Rory ken ye're up. He'll want to see ye. I'll fetch ye some broth too while I'm below."

Geordie watched the door close behind her, and then glanced fretfully around the room, trying to tell if there was any damage to his mind. He didn't know. How would he be able to tell? Would he be able to? He was still fretting over the issue when the door opened again and his brother entered. Rory wasn't alone, he saw as he turned his gaze that way. Aulay was with him. Both looked relieved to see him awake.

"How are ye feeling?" Rory asked as he reached the bed, and looked him over.

Geordie grunted noncommittally and waited as Rory bent to listen to his heart, and then held his eyes open to peer at them briefly.

"Ye seem well," Rory decided, relaxing a bit. "Do ye remember what happened?"

"Aye," Geordie growled, and then turned to peer at the drink on the bedside table.

Getting the message, Rory held it for him to drink. He was

more cautious even than Dwyn though, and allowed him only two sips before setting the goblet back, and asking, "How does yer chest feel?"

"Like it had a sword shoved through it," Geordie said dryly, but then admitted, "No' as bad as I'd expect though."

"Ye were lucky. It slid between yer ribs rather than smashing through them, and it missed yer heart or anything else o' note. I worried at first that it might have nicked yer one lung, but if it did, it healed itself up well enough and quickly because other than when ye first arrived ye've no' seemed to have trouble breathing," Rory told him, and then added, "And too, ye've missed the worst of the healing since ye were out o' yer mind the first week and slept the second," Rory said solemnly.

Geordie nodded, and then asked reluctantly, "How will I ken if the fever damaged me brain?"

Rory's eyes narrowed. "Is there something specific ye're worried on?"

He hesitated, his gaze sliding to Aulay and away before he admitted, "I'm no' feeling like tupping Dwyn."

A startled laugh of disbelief burst from both men, but Rory stifled his quickly, and used his most patient voice when he said, "Geordie, ye just woke up, and ye're still healing from a terrible injury that could have killed ye. I'd be more surprised if ye *were* feeling up to tupping yer wife."

Geordie relaxed at that and asked, "Where's Dwyn?"

"She went to the kitchens to fetch ye broth as we came up," Aulay explained as Rory pulled the furs down and then the linens to reveal his bandaged chest. Moving around the bed, Aulay climbed on to kneel beside him and lifted him to a sitting position and then held him there so that Rory could remove the bandages that ran around his chest and back. It was obviously something he'd done many times. Rory hadn't even had to ask.

They were all silent as Rory examined his wounds. Geordie couldn't see the one on his back, but did glance down to see the one on his chest. The stitches made it look bigger than it was, and he was surprised at how far along the healing was. By his guess Rory would be able to remove the stitches in another week or two.

"'Tis doing well. Another week and a half, or more, and I'll take the stitches out," Rory announced, applying fresh salve, and then beginning to bandage him back up.

Geordie merely grunted at that and glanced to Aulay. "Did ye find the men's camp?"

"Aye. I set Simon to the task when we found you and Dwyn." Mouth tightening, he added, "They had cleared out by the time the men found it though, and they did it quickly. They left food cooking over a small fire and a half-skinned rabbit on a rock nearby. Obviously, one o' their men caught wind o' the search and gave the warning."

Geordie scowled at the news. "How many men? Could he tell?"

"From the food and the compressed grass where people had slept, he guessed there were probably six including the two ye killed," Aulay told him solemnly. "The men followed their trail to the edge o' our land, but then turned back."

"They should have hunted them all down," Geordie growled. "The bastards who had her told Dwyn all the men were going to have a go at her."

"She did no' mention that," Aulay said with a frown.

"Do ye need to use the garderobe?" Rory asked as he finished binding him up.

Geordie opened his mouth to say no, and then thought better of it. As weak as he was, he wouldn't be able to manage on his own once his brothers were gone, and big as he was, Dwyn couldn't get him there, so he muttered, "Aye. Mayhap."

"Good, then we can have Mavis send someone to change the bed while we take ye there," Rory said, and dragged the furs and linens the rest of the way off of him, revealing a large folded linen square across his hips. There was another larger one under his arse too, he noticed, and grimaced, knowing what it was for. He'd been on his back for two weeks, unable to use the garderobe. They'd been protecting the bed and beddings. On the bright side, neither linen seemed dirty, he noted as the two men dressed him in a nightshirt that fell to his knees. But then he hadn't eaten or drank for two weeks, and, for all he knew, they may have changed the cloths just minutes before he woke.

"I'll go ask Mavis to see to the bed, and tell Dwyn to take her time. There's no sense her coming up to stand about while the maids work," Rory said once they had him dressed.

Aulay nodded at that, but said, "Leave the door open," and then bent to scoop up Geordie.

"Oy," he complained as his brother started to carry him to the door. "I could walk with a little help."

Aulay snorted at that. "Ye could no' even raise yer arms or move yer legs to dress, Geordie. We'd have to pull yer arms over each of our shoulders and drag ye there."

"'Twould be less humiliating than being carted around like a bairn," he grumbled with disgust.

"Aye. So yer wife said many times as she was carried to the garderobe and back the last couple weeks," he said with a smile. "She grew quite impatient with no' being able to walk. I suspect had Rory no' said she could start putting weight on both feet again yester eve, she might have done him bodily harm."

"What?" Geordie asked with surprise. "But she was nearly healed before I was injured. Rory thought another day or two and she'd be able to take off the bandages and walk again."

"Aye, well, that was before she ruined them in the woods trying to save yer sorry hide."

"How badly?" he asked with concern.

"Her already healed foot took the worst damage. She somehow lost her slipper and Jetta and Rory think she must have impaled that one on a broken branch on the ground or something. She had a lot of slivers, cuts and a nice-sized hole between her heel and the meat under her toes. Fortunately, it did no' get infected like yer wound did. Her other foot made out better. The linen wrappings protected them for the most part, though they had unraveled and were hanging from her ankle by the time we got her back to the keep," he said, and then ordered, "Open the door."

Geordie glanced around to see that they'd reached the garderobe. He automatically tried to reach for the door handle, but his arm merely flopped down at his side when he took it from his stomach and lap where it was resting. Mouth tightening, he muttered, "Sorry."

"Nay. I'm sorry. I forgot," Aulay said quietly, and then turned slightly to catch the door handle with the hand under Geordie's legs. He tugged it open a bit with that hand, and then shifted quickly to slide his foot between the bottom of the door and the frame, then first dragged and then shoved it open with that foot so that he could quickly carry Geordie in before it swung closed.

By the time Aulay carried him out, Geordie had decided he was going to eat and do whatever else was necessary to regain his strength as quickly as possible. Truly, having to be helped to the garderobe was a humbling experience. He hadn't even been able to lift his own nightshirt.

"So, Dwyn was stuck abed with me the last two weeks?" he asked, to get both their minds on something else as Aulay carried him out of the small room.

"Aye. But she kept busy, sewing, visiting and constantly spooning broth down yer throat. I think if she could have breathed fer ye while ye healed she would have," he added with an affectionate smile.

"Ye've accepted her as family," Geordie said with satisfaction. While he'd known his brother liked Dwyn before the marriage, it was obvious he felt affection for her now too. That just seemed to validate his own feelings, which was nice.

"Aye. So have the women," Aulay assured him. "They've spent a lot of time up in yer room with her and her sisters, helping as much as they could with tending ye."

"The other husband-hunting lasses?" he asked with a frown, finding it a little disturbing to think of having that bunch of young, unmarried women helping tend him.

"Nay, our sister and our brothers' wives," Aulay corrected him. "I sent the other lasses away a couple days after ye were injured."

Geordie raised his eyebrows at that. "Have Rory and Alick picked brides, then, already?"

"Nay. And they were no' going to," he said dryly. "Both o' them barely left yer room those first few days. Rory was tending ye, and Alick was helping, both to tend ye and to carry Dwyn around when she needed to go to the garderobe and such." Grimacing, he added, "Keeping the women here when neither of the single Buchanans were paying them any attention seemed a waste. And then when the family started arriving we needed the bedchambers so I had Jetta send them all home."

"Sorry," Geordie said on a sigh as Aulay carried him back through the still-open bedchamber door. When he paused abruptly, Geordie glanced around to see that Mavis and a couple of maids were changing the bed and cleaning the room.

Mavis glanced over now and beamed at him. "Hello, love, 'tis good to see ye awake again at last. Ye gave the wee lass a fine scare there fer a couple days." When Geordie managed to smile back, she turned to Aulay and said, "We'll only be another moment. Why do ye no' set him down in one o' the chairs by the table and take a seat yerself. I ken Lady Dwyn'll be up soon with food and drink. The girls insisted she have something to eat while she waited for Cook to prepare a tray. She'll be along shortly."

Geordie saw Aulay nod and then his brother carried him to the table and chairs. Rather than set him in a chair though, he simply sat down with him still in his arms.

"Ye could put me in a chair," he growled with embarrassment as the maids glanced over at them.

"Ye could no' keep yerself upright," Aulay pointed out with a shrug that jostled him in his arms. It made Geordie feel like a damned toddler, and renewed his determination to get his strength back as quickly as he could.

Trying to ignore that he was sitting in his brother's lap like a child, he watched the women work for a minute and then murmured, "Mavis seems happier."

"Aye," Aulay said, keeping his voice just as quiet. "Acair explained he was only paying attention to Dwyn to help ye sort out yer feelings for her, and the pair made up."

Geordie scowled at the claim, but then let it go, too weary to be annoyed.

"HOW SHOULD WE ARRANGE THE VISITS?"

Dwyn glanced up from the stew she was eating at that question from Geordie's sister-in-law Murine. The lovely blonde was the wife of Geordie's second oldest brother, Dougall. She was also a very organized-type lady, she'd noticed. Murine was obviously intelligent and clearly enjoyed order in her life. Dwyn would guess that came from having the responsibility for both Carmichael in Scotland, and Danvries in England. Murine probably had to be much more organized than most to help run and take care of two keeps and all their people, Dwyn supposed.

"What do ye mean?" Geordie's sister, Saidh, asked now.

"Well, do we all go up at once?" Murine asked. "Or do ye think that might overwhelm Geordie when he's so newly awake? If so, mayhap we ladies should visit first, and then the men can visit after. Or the other way around."

There was silence for a minute, and then Edith, a pretty strawberry blonde, and the wife of Geordie's third oldest brother, Neils, turned to Dwyn and asked, "What do ye think, Dwyn?"

Setting her spoon back in her stew, Dwyn considered the question seriously, but then sighed and said, "I suspect he'll no' be awake fer long this first day, so ye may all want to come in for a quick word today, and then plan on longer visits tomorrow."

"Aye," the other women agreed together, and then they all glanced to the stairs as Mavis led two young maids down them. Each one was carrying something—Mavis had the linens, the maid behind her had dirty clothing and the third carried a tray with various items on it, mostly bowls and glasses that had held broth or cider or mead, a few of the liquids Dwyn had been dribbling down Geordie's throat for the last week while he lay unconscious.

The three women had barely disappeared through the door to the kitchens when another maid came out with a tray and hurried toward her.

"Cook put on some broth, mead, cider and a little stew in case he feels up to something more solid," she announced brightly. "And Mavis says I should carry this up fer ye."

"Oh," Dwyn said as she stood. "Well, that's kind, but I could manage, I'm sure."

"Nonsense, m'lady. I'm pleased to help ye. We all ken ye've had little sleep these last weeks while ye tended Laird Geordie. Besides, ye're newly back on yer feet. I'm pleased to carry this up fer ye."

Dwyn smiled faintly and nodded, not wanting to argue further. The girl seemed so happy to be given the task. But then everyone had been happy since she'd come below with the news that Geordie was awake. It was only then that she'd realized how worried everyone had been. Her husband was well loved by the people of Buchanan.

"We'll give ye a bit o' time to help him eat before we come up," Saidh said as she headed away.

Dwyn cast a grateful glance over her shoulder, and was smiling as she started up the stairs. She really liked Geordie's family. They had welcomed her with warmth and friendship, even including her sisters and father in that welcome. She hadn't spent much time with the men, but the women had spent a lot of time up in the room with her and her sisters as she'd tended Geordie. They were good people.

"Let me get the door for ye," Dwyn murmured, hurrying ahead of the maid to open it, and thinking it was good there were two of them and she hadn't tried to manage on her own. She'd have had to kick at the door for Aulay to open it, she thought as she held the door and then followed the maid inside the room.

Geordie was back in bed, but sitting upright with several pillows behind his back and a nightshirt on. He had a little more color in his face too, she noted, though he looked a tad grumpy. She wasn't terribly surprised at that and suspected he would be a cantankerous patient. Men rarely had much patience when ill.

"Set it on the bedside table, please, Katie," Dwyn murmured when the maid slowed and glanced to her uncertainly.

Smiling, the lass rushed over to set it down, and then turned that smile on Geordie and murmured, "'Tis good to see ye awake and recovering, m'laird," before turning away and heading for the door again.

"I'll leave now ye've returned," Aulay said, moving toward Dwyn as she approached the bed. "Just give a shout does he need to make another trip to the garderobe, or do ye need him moved for any reason."

"Thank ye," Dwyn said sincerely, reaching out to squeeze her brother-in-law's arm as he moved past her. He and Rory and Alick had done anything and everything they could to help while Geordie was down. She couldn't have managed without them, and she appreciated it.

Aulay gave her hand an affectionate squeeze before she withdrew it from his arm, and then he was past and she was continuing to the bedside.

Smiling at Geordie, she asked, "Are ye hungry or thirsty?"

"Both," he said on a sigh.

Nodding, Dwyn settled on the edge of the bed and glanced over the tray. "Broth, cider or mead first?"

"Cider," he decided, and she helped him drink, allowing him to have more than a few sips this time.

When Geordie said, "Thank ye," she set the cider down and picked up the bowl of broth.

"Aulay said ye've been dribbling broth and cider down me throat the whole time I've been sick," he said as she scooped up a spoonful of broth.

"Aye. I thought ye might be hungry, and ye could no' tell me nay," Dwyn teased, and lifted the spoon of broth to his mouth.

Geordie eyed it with a grimace, obviously not pleased that he had to be fed like a child, but finally opened his mouth for her to slide it in.

"Mayhap ye should just pour it in a mug and help me drink it," he said wryly after the second spoonful. "I feel like a child having to be fed like this."

"It will no' be for long," Dwyn said sympathetically. "Ye'll regain yer strength quickly now ye're awake."

"I hope so," Geordie sighed, and opened his mouth again when she lifted another spoonful to his mouth. After swallowing, he asked, "What happened to yer gown?"

Dwyn paused and glanced down at herself, but the new forest green gown seemed fine. There were no small tears, or stains on it. When she raised her confused gaze to his, he explained, "The neckline's no' as low as I'm used to."

Dwyn's face split into a wide smile at that, and she nodded. "Aye. The women and I have all been sewing while we visited. We managed to get a couple o' new gowns done while ye slept." She noted the dissatisfaction on his face, and frowned with concern. "Do ye no' like this one? I thought 'twas pretty."

"Aye, 'tis," Geordie assured her roughly. "The color suits ye, and the style is nice . . ."

She raised her eyebrows in question when he paused, hearing a silent *but*.

Finally, he admitted, "But I miss the low necklines."

"Ah." Dwyn bit her lip to hold back a sudden grin. "Well, I still have those gowns too, and will be happy to wear them fer ye. But I am a bit more comfortable no' being so much on display around the soldiers and the men in yer family."

"Oh. Aye," Geordie said with understanding, and opened his mouth when she moved the spoon to his lips again. He swallowed the liquid almost before she removed the spoon this time, and as soon as he was able, he asked, "How are yer feet? Aulay said ye injured them again dragging me through the woods and Rory only gave ye permission to walk again yester eve."

Dwyn's mouth twitched with irritation. "He was most annoying about me feet this time. I was beginning to think he'd never let me walk again."

She caught the grin that crossed Geordie's face at her annoyance, and arched an eyebrow. "Ye'll no' be smiling when ye want to be up and about and he's insisting ye stay abed longer."

Geordie's expression dimmed at that, and then he said, "Ye should have left me in the woods and run for Buchanan."

"I'd no' have left ye alone, m'laird. If the other men had come looking for the two men ye dispatched, they'd have killed ye."

"I suspect they did come looking," Geordie said grimly.

Dwyn raised her eyebrows at that. "Why?"

"Because Aulay said their camp was empty when the men found it and they managed to escape Buchanan land before Simon and the other soldiers could catch up," he announced, and then pointed out, "They had to have prior warning somehow, and it seems likely they may have grown concerned, looked for the two men and found them dead. That would have been enough to make them scramble off our land. Although it must have been close else I'm sure they would have pursued us, and with ye dragging me across the forest floor on a plaid, our tracks would have been easy to follow."

Dwyn stared at him, recalling the sound of a branch snapping behind them just before she'd heard Aulay and the other men thundering toward them on horseback. Had one or even two of the men found their comrades and been creeping up on them when they too heard the approaching riders? If so, she was lucky he or they had decided to flee rather than try to drag her off again. She was also lucky they hadn't taken the time to slice Geordie's throat before fleeing, Dwyn thought with horror. Dear God, she shouldn't have left him alone even for those few minutes while she'd run out onto the path to stop Aulay and the others.

"Lass, ye've gone pale. What is it?" Geordie asked with a frown.

Dwyn opened her mouth, and then paused and glanced to the

door when a knock sounded. Sighing, she shook her head and set the bowl back on the tray, surprised to see that it was empty. Standing then, she moved to open the door, unsurprised when Geordie's siblings and their mates greeted her.

Managing a smile, Dwyn backed up and let them in, realizing only then that she hadn't thought to warn Geordie they were all coming up to visit him.

Chapter 14

"I NOTICED THE RUSHES WERE GROWING A BIT STALE LAST EVE when I brought up the sup fer yerself and Laird Geordie, and I was wondering did ye wish me to collect ye some fresh ones? Or mayhap some wildflowers to scent the ones ye have? Or both?"

"Oh, thank ye, Katie." Dwyn smiled at the maid as they walked up the hall toward the room she shared with Geordie. "Fresh rushes and some flowers to scent them would be nice. 'Tis kind o' ye to think on it."

"Oh, well, Mavis most like would have thought on it the next time she came above stairs," Katie assured her easily. "She just has no' been in the room since the first day Laird Geordie woke."

"Ye're right," Dwyn agreed, thinking the room had been too full of Geordie's brothers and sisters for Mavis to get into the room the last three days. They'd had company with them in the room nonstop since shortly after everyone broke their fast until after the sup every day since Geordie had woken. Dwyn had seen Mavis look in on passing a couple times though, and suspected the first time she saw the room empty, or at least with less people, the woman would stop in for a visit. While Mavis had stayed in the background while the other would-be brides had been at Buchanan, once they were gone and Geordie's siblings and their mates had arrived, she'd sat at the high table with them and visited often. It was how Dwyn knew the Buchanan brood saw Mavis as something of a second mother. She also knew the woman loved each and every one of the Buchanan brothers and their sister like their mother. It actually made Dwyn envious. She wished she'd had someone like Mavis as a child.

"Here we are," Dwyn said, pushing those thoughts away as she moved ahead to open the door for the maid.

"Good morning, m'laird," Katie said cheerily as she carried the tray to the bedside. "How are ye feeling this morning?"

"Better, thank ye, lass," Geordie said, but his gaze was on Dwyn as she followed the girl.

Smiling at him, Dwyn let her gaze move over his newly shaved face and damp hair. She'd been concerned when he'd asked her to fetch Rory and Alick up to him when she'd woken this morning, and had waited anxiously in the hall, afraid that there was something wrong. She'd been pleasantly surprised though when Rory had stepped out and explained Geordie wanted a bath and had been asking if that would be all right, and if they couldn't perhaps aid him with it. Dwyn couldn't help but think that was a good sign, and had gone below to speak to Mavis about arranging one.

When the woman had suggested she might like one too, and said she'd have a second bath sent up to her sisters' room for her to use if she'd like, Dwyn had nodded with relief. She hadn't wanted to trouble the servants with a request like that. They were already doing so much for her and Geordie, but she hadn't bathed since a couple days before Geordie woke. She'd been making do with washing up at the ewer since then, but had longed for a bath and the opportunity to wash her hair. She'd enjoyed that bath like none other, and had been grateful for Katie's assistance in washing and rinsing her hair. The maid had even brushed it by the window where a warm summer breeze had helped speed the drying. Dwyn had left it down to help it finish drying, and knew it wouldn't take long at all. It was already swinging around her rather than lying wet and limp.

Her gratitude made the smile she gave the maid a little wider than usual as Katie passed her to leave the room and pulled the door closed behind her.

"Yer brothers shaved yer face," Dwyn said with a grin as she approached the bed.

"Did ye no' like me with a beard and mustache, then?" Geordie asked with amusement.

"Actually, I did," she admitted, her lips curving up as she settled on the edge of the bed next to him. "At least at first. 'Twas short and gave ye a sexy wild man look. But it did prickle a bit when we kissed."

"Aye, which is why I shaved it off. I wanted to kiss ye without scraping yer sensitive skin," he admitted, and then said, "Kiss me, lass."

Her eyes widened, but Dwyn didn't hesitate and leaned forward to kiss him. She sighed the moment their mouths met, and then opened for him when his tongue slid out to slide along the seam where her lips came together, a silent request for entry. She moaned, her back arching eagerly when his tongue filled her, and was pleased to hear Geordie's answering moan. To her it felt like forever since he'd kissed and held her. He had only been awake three days, and was still weak, yet his response and the sudden wildness to his kiss matched her own.

When Dwyn felt his hand at her breast, she almost sucked his tongue out of his mouth with her gasp of shock. Breaking their kiss, she pulled back and stared at him.

Geordie grinned up at her with satisfaction. "I've been working at building me muscle at night, repeatedly raising me fingers, then me hands, then me arms, to regain me strength."

"Oh," she breathed, her eyes wide. His hand had followed her upright and he was toying with one erect nipple through the material of her gown.

"That's no' all I can raise," he added with another grin, this one wider.

"Yer legs?" Dwyn asked uncertainly.

"Aye, I can raise them a bit, but no' as much as me hands and arms yet," Geordie admitted, and then added, "But that was no' what I was talking about."

When she blinked in confusion, he said, "I'm hot, lass. Could ye get these furs off me?"

"Oh, o' course." Dwyn turned to remove the large fur cover from him. It was made of several furs sewn together and very heavy, and the moment she pushed it off of him, the linen underneath popped up to form a small tent.

"Oh," she breathed. First Dwyn stared and then she found herself reaching for the tent pole.

"Nay!" Geordie barked with alarm. When Dwyn glanced quickly back to his face, he smiled wryly and admitted, "Lass, all I've done the last two days was think on loving ye. 'Tis how I encouraged meself to work harder to regain me strength. I'd think on how I wanted to touch ye." Grimacing, he added, "But I fear do you touch me now, I'll no' be loving ye at all."

"Oh," Dwyn repeated, uncertainly this time. Now she didn't know what to do. Geordie did though.

"Undo yer lacings and bare yer breasts fer me, lass. I want to see ye and do no' want to waste what little strength I've built up undressing ye. I'd rather save it fer touching."

Dwyn didn't hesitate. Meeting his gaze, she reached up to undo the lacings, surprised to see her hands trembling. It wasn't shyness. There was very little shyness in her in regards to his seeing her body. Geordie had seen, touched and licked every inch of her before taking the wound that presently had him stuck in bed, and she'd dressed and undressed in front of him several times since he'd woken from that wound. But she was trembling like a virgin on her wedding night. Still, she got the lacings undone, and then quickly shrugged her gown off her shoulders.

"Stand up," Geordie growled as she reached to push her shift off too.

Dwyn stood, allowing her gown to drop to the floor, and then waited as she watched a slow smile spread his lips.

"Damn, I love yer shift," he murmured, and she glanced down at it. While she'd made new gowns with higher necklines, her shifts all still had the very low ones and this one exposed the tops of her nipples. Geordie's voice was a hoarse rasp when he requested, "Take it off too."

Dwyn removed it, pushing it off one shoulder and then the other to let it drop on top of her gown.

"Aye, now climb on me, lass, straddle me stomach," he ordered.

Dwyn's eyebrows rose at that, her gaze moving to his erection, but she did as he asked and climbed onto the bed, swinging her hair over her shoulders first so she wouldn't accidentally kneel on it.

"Ah, lass," Geordie sighed, reaching out to cover her breasts with his hands. "Have I told ye how lovely ye are?"

Dwyn's eye widened, but she couldn't have responded had she wanted to; his touch was sending shivers of excitement through her and she was busy gasping in response.

"Bend down here and kiss me, lass."

Dwyn obeyed at once, leaning down until she could cover his mouth with hers, a groan sliding from her lips into his mouth as he squeezed and kneaded her more firmly. It was a strange position for her to be on top and in control of the kiss, but she liked it. In this position she decided the angle, the pressure and depth of the kiss, and she was greedy after so long without this. Her mouth devoured his and invited him to devour in response as he fondled her breasts, and pinched her nipples. At least, she did at first, but when he turned his head breaking the kiss, Dwyn sat up slightly, panting with the need growing in her.

"Ye're wet already," Geordie growled, and she felt the first flash of embarrassment. She was straddling his stomach, but he hadn't touched her yet, and still he knew she was wet . . . because . . . well, because she was straddling his stomach and he could apparently feel the way her body was weeping for attention.

"I want to taste ye."

Dwyn blinked at those words, as confused now as she had been the first time he'd said them to her, but not for the same reason. "But ye canno'—"

"Straddle me face, wife."

Now her eyes widened incredulously. "I could no' just—"

"Ye vowed to obey me in front o' Father Archibald, our family and God, Dwyn. Are ye no' going to keep yer vows?" Geordie asked solemnly.

"Ye remember," she said with surprise. Until now he'd not said a word about their marriage here in this room the night he was wounded, and Dwyn had begun to worry he didn't even remember it.

"Our wedding?" Geordie asked with disbelief. "O' course I remember. I'm the one who asked Father Archibald to perform it. Now crawl up here and straddle me face, wife. I want to taste ye."

Dwyn's mouth opened, closed, and then she shook her head, but when he shifted his hands to her hips and urged her forward, while she shook her head again, she also started to move. Worried about hurting him, and anxious about what he'd asked her to do, she got to her feet on the bed and then moved forward, grabbed the headboard to brace herself and slowly lowered herself over his face, her knees on either side of his head and calves and feet on his shoulders and chest. Dear God, this was new, she thought with dismay, aware of the view he was getting.

"Lower, wife."

Dwyn shook her head, but lowered herself some more.

"Almost perfect, just a touch farther forward," he instructed.

Muttering under her breath, Dwyn shifted a bit forward and then nearly screamed when his tongue lashed across her sensitive center. Biting her lip to silence herself, she clenched her hands on the headboard, her wide eyes staring blindly at the bed drapes as he clutched her hips and brought her firmly against his face. He used his chin, his lips, his tongue and even his teeth on her tender flesh, his hands moving her hips until she was excited enough to forget her position and start moving herself, riding his face. He murmured what Dwyn thought was approval then, and she groaned and let her head fall back as the sound hummed over her skin and through her body.

Dwyn was on the edge of finding her release when he suddenly urged her back by his grasp on her hips and growled, "Ride me now, lass."

He didn't have to ask twice. Dwyn would have done just about anything he asked at that point, and quickly shifted back down his body to straddle him. She didn't await further instruction, but impaled herself on him with one swift plunge, and then let her head fall back, and groaned as her body adjusted to his filling her again. It had been so long.

"God, woman, I've missed ye," Geordie moaned, his fingers digging into her hips. "I feel like I've come home every time I'm in ye, and it has been a long time since I was home."

Dwyn raised her head to peer down at him, and then leaned forward to brace her hands on the pillow on either side of his head. Her hair fell around them, a pale gold curtain sheltering them from the world as she began to move on him, her breasts brushing across his chest, and their eyes meeting.

Geordie watched her face, his hands running down her body to clasp her behind and help her find the perfect pace, and then he growled, "Did I say home, love? I meant heaven."

"MAVIS SAYS YE'LL BE HOLDING A WEDDING CEREMONY AND feast at Innes rather than here," Katie commented, and then added, "She said that all the Buchanans will be in attendance."

Dwyn glanced up from the chest she was packing and watched the maid strip the bed she and Geordie had left in such a rumpled state this morning. It was a month since he'd woken after his wound. His stitches were out, and he'd worked hard at rebuilding his strength, even before they'd been removed. The man had definitely succeeded there, Dwyn thought with a slow smile as she recalled some of the positions he'd shown her last night and this morning. He claimed it was all to aid in rebuilding his strength to make love to her with him standing up, and her in his arms, her legs wrapped around him as he clasped her under the bottom and raised and lowered her slowly onto his staff. Dwyn was most pleased to help him regain his strength in such ways. After all, it was her duty as wife to aid him in any endeavor.

The thought nearly made her snort to herself with amusement. Help him, or not, she definitely enjoyed the bedding part of marriage. But she enjoyed other aspects too. Just talking and laughing with him was wonderful. Walking in the gardens and orchard. Playing games of Nine Men's Morris and chess. Dwyn had come to the realization that she not only loved the man, she loved being with him and couldn't believe how lucky she was to have him.

"M'lady?"

"Hmm?" Dwyn glanced to the girl, and then recalled her comments and said, "Oh, aye. Well, 'tis no' really necessary, but the people o' Innes should be able to celebrate our union. And Geordie's family wanted to attend it as well."

The maid's eyebrows rose at that. "Ye do no' think marrying in the eyes o' the church is necessary?"

"Oh." Dwyn blinked as she realized the maid had no idea they were already married in the eyes of the church. There had only been her father, Una, Aileen, Rory, Alick, Aulay and Jetta there to witness the ceremony Father Archibald had performed the night Geordie was injured, and she supposed it hadn't probably been discussed afterward. It hadn't exactly been a grand affair, although it had been special to her. Besides, everyone had been so worried about Geordie, especially when the fevers started . . .

"'Tis no' that I do not think 'tis necessary," she began, and then paused and glanced toward the door when it opened.

"There ye are!" Geordie crossed the room quickly when he stepped in and spotted her. Clasping her by the waist, he lifted her into the air, lowered her to press a quick kiss to her lips and then raised and lowered her again for another quick kiss.

"Building yer strength again, m'laird?" Dwyn asked with amusement as he raised her for a third time.

"Aye, but with a purpose. I'm takin' ye to the waterfall," he announced, and set her on the floor, then snatched her hand in his and turned to tug her toward the door.

"The waterfall?" she asked anxiously, dragging her feet.

When he realized she was not following enthusiastically, he turned to peer at her. "What is it, love?"

Dwyn hesitated, but then asked uncertainly, "Is it safe?"

Geordie faced her solemnly. "The men have been scouring Buchanan land ever since the attack fer any sign o' the bandits' return, and have seen nothing. Also," he added. "'Tis daylight. 'Tis always safe there in daylight. And I want to show ye why I love the waterfall so much ere we leave." Brushing his fingers lightly down her cheek, he continued. "Besides, it has been six weeks since the attack, Dwyn. Bandits do no' hang about in one area fer long. They'll have moved on."

Dwyn bit her lip briefly, and then glanced back to her chest and said, "But what about packing? We leave for Innes tomorrow and I still have—"

"We can do that tonight," he pointed out, and then added, "But we canno' go to the waterfall at night." Bending, he pressed a kiss to her lips and then whispered, "Come with me, lass."

It was the almost pleading tone to his voice as he said it that made up Dwyn's mind. Pushing her worries and concerns aside, she nodded.

"That's me girl." Geordie beamed at her, and then turned and hurried out of the room, pulling her with him.

"'Tis so empty now that everyone is gone," Dwyn murmured in a hushed voice as she followed Geordie down the stairs to the great hall. Which wasn't really empty. There were servants and soldiers coming and going, or sitting to enjoy a repast or drink. But they were all going quietly about their business, when she was used to laughter and loud voices.

"Dwyn, love, ye've said that at least ten times a day since me sister, brothers and their mates all returned to their homes, and that was nearly four weeks ago," Geordie pointed out with a chuckle as they crossed the great hall, headed for the doors to the bailey.

"I ken, but it just feels strange still. While yer brothers and sister and their mates were here, 'twas always loud and boisterous in the great hall. Then they left, and—" She shrugged.

"Aye, I miss them too," he murmured with a faint smile. "But we'll see them soon. They're coming to Innes for the wedding,"

Geordie reminded her, and then paused in front of the doors to the bailey to face her as he asked, "Will there be room for everyone at Innes?"

"Innes does no' have as many rooms as Buchanan, but the keep itself is a good size. We'll find room for everyone," Dwyn assured him.

"Aye, we will," he agreed. Smiling, he kissed the tip of her nose and admitted, "I'm curious to see our home, and eager to leave."

"By this time tomorrow we'll be on our way, and in three days ye'll see it," she murmured, because that's how long he'd said it would take to get to Innes. It had taken Dwyn and her family much longer to travel to Buchanan from Innes, but they'd had a wagon and a large party of soldiers with them. She and Geordie were planning to ride straight there at speed, with just a sack of clothes each and Alick and Rory for company. Their chests would follow with her father, sisters and the escort of Innes warriors they'd brought with them and would take twice or perhaps even three times as long to make the journey. She knew her sisters were above stairs seeing to packing their own clothes away in the chests they'd come in.

"Should no' we tell Aulay or Jetta where we're going?" Dwyn asked as he pushed open one of the doors and led her down the keep stairs.

"Aulay was taking Jetta above stairs for a nap when I came to find ye," Geordie said, glancing around to waggle his eyebrows suggestively to let her know what kind of nap he was speaking of. Heading for the stables now, he told her, "Which is what made me think I should take the opportunity to take ye to the waterfall."

"Ah," she said with amusement.

Geordie must have stopped at the stables before coming to fetch her. His horse was ready and just being led out as they arrived. When he caught her about the waist and lifted her into the saddle, Dwyn supposed that meant she was riding with him rather than on her own mount, but didn't mind. Any excuse to have his arms around her always gained Dwyn's approval, and she leaned back into him with a pleased little sigh once he was mounted behind her. Geordie's arms slid around her and he hugged her briefly, and then he took the reins and they were off.

They'd barely put the outer wall at their back before Geordie was shifting his reins to one hand so that he could reach up and caress her breasts with the other. Moaning, Dwyn pressed back into him with her shoulders, her back arching upward into the caress.

"Ye're always so responsive to me, love," Geordie growled, nipping her ear and then sucking it soothingly so that she hardly noticed when he pulled her neckline down to free her breasts to his touch without the cloth in the way.

Dwyn didn't protest it though when she felt his rough fingers on her unprotected skin. Instead, she reached behind her to rub him through the cloth of his plaid and said, "I ken, m'laird. I turn into little more than a slattern with ye."

Geordie released her breast to clasp her jaw and turned her head up and back for a punishing kiss, and then growled, "Fer me, mayhap, and I hope ye always will be."

He returned to fondling her then, so that by the time they reached the waterfall, they were both panting heavily and burning for each other. They undressed each other at the same time, stumbling and fumbling a bit as they tried to kiss and grope each other even as they did it, and then Geordie lifted her up into his arms and she wrapped her legs around him, trapping his erection between them and rubbing against it as he walked out into the water and then under the falls.

Dwyn gasped as the cold water briefly poured over them, and then he set her on a ledge where she was able to lean her upper body back so that it rushed down over her breasts and stomach, but not her face. She saw Geordie through a sheet of water, and then his face joined hers in the safe waterless space and he kissed her as he slid into her.

Dwyn had never experienced anything like it, water was caressing them everywhere as he loved her, adding to his caresses and kisses, and she suddenly understood why he'd wanted to show her this spot. She told him so later as they lay on a plaid in the clearing at the edge of the loch.

"Aye." He ran one hand lazily up and down her back where she'd collapsed on him after he'd carried her out of the water and they'd made love again. "'Twas as good as I imagined 'twould be."

Dwyn lifted her head and raised an eyebrow. "As ye imagined? Ye've never done that before?"

"In the waterfall?" Geordie asked, and then shook his head. "Hell, no. I always feared I'd drown meself did I try it, and I would no' drown meself fer any woman. Except you."

"That sounded like it was meant to be a compliment," Dwyn said thoughtfully. "And yet I just want to slap ye." When he raised his head to peer at her with surprise, she said solemnly, "I do no' want ye to drown fer me, husband. I'd rather ye live fer me, thank ye very much."

Geordie grinned at that and hugged her close, but then admitted, "Well, no' just fer ye, mayhap. I have been imagining doing that almost since meeting ye."

Dwyn smiled faintly, and rested her head on his chest again, but after a moment he sighed and said, "I suppose we'd best head back. 'Twill be time fer the sup soon, and I promised to help ye with packing after."

Her eyebrows rose at that. She didn't recall him promising to help her. Although she had some vague recollection of his saying "they" could pack that night. She suspected though that his helping would end up just slowing her down since they had so much trouble keeping their hands off each other. She didn't point that out, however, but simply dragged herself off of him, and began to gather her clothes.

They dressed in a companionable silence, and then walked to his horse holding hands. Geordie mounted first this time, and then leaned down to catch her about the waist and lift her up before him. He didn't urge the horse to move right away though. Instead, he sat for a moment, letting his eyes sweep the loch, the waterfall and the clearing.

"I shall miss this place," Geordie admitted after a moment. "I grew up here, swimming with me brothers and sister, and . . ." He let his words trail away, and then smiled crookedly down at her, and said, "But there's a whole sea o' water to enjoy at Innes, is no' there?"

"Aye, there is," Dwyn agreed, and pointed out, "And we can visit here as often as ye wish, husband."

Nodding, he bent to kiss the tip of her nose, and then turned the horse to start along the path through the woods.

Geordie didn't appear to be in a hurry to return to the keep. He kept his mount at a trot as they left the clearing and started along the path. She suspected he was saying a silent goodbye to this place that had been home to him for twenty-nine years of his life. That part of marriage had never occurred to Dwyn during her childhood imaginings. She'd never included the part where she'd have had to ride away from Innes, the only home she'd ever known, to go to someplace she'd never seen before, but was supposed to happily accept as her new home. That hadn't happened in the end, but it was happening to Geordie now that he'd married her.

She hoped he didn't resent that. He'd told her he loved her the night they were married, but hadn't repeated it since awaking. Had the declaration been the result of the injury, something easily said when he'd thought he was about to meet his maker, or had he meant it?

Dwyn knew Geordie was happy with their marriage right now, and was even looking forward to seeing Innes. But would he like Innes once there? She bit her lip worriedly at the thought. She loved Innes, but it was in the flat Lowlands while he was used to the majesty of the mountains in the Highlands. And then there was the problem of Laird Brodie. Dwyn had tried to tell Geordie about that to prepare him ahead. They'd discussed much while he'd been healing the last several weeks. But every time she'd tried to bring up the subject of their neighbor, Brodie, he'd interrupted her to say it was fine. All would be well. They were married now. There was nothing the man could do, and did Brodie foolishly try something anyway, he'd take care of it.

Geordie's suddenly stiffening behind her and his arm tightening around her waist drew Dwyn from her thoughts. She glanced ahead, half expecting to see riders approaching. Instead, her gaze fell on a large, dark bundle on the path some fifty feet ahead. It took a moment for her to recognize what the bundle was and even then she wasn't sure until she was able to make out the strong bare legs sticking out of the bundle of cloth. They weren't moving. "Is that a Buchanan soldier?"

Geordie grunted behind her, and she twisted her head around and up to look at his face. His expression was grim, his eyes scouring the trees around them and the path beyond the fallen man as he slowed his mount. Dwyn turned back then, her own gaze sliding quickly around. When she didn't see a horse or anyone or anything that might be a threat, she shifted her attention back to the body. They were closer now and she could make out more detail. The body was large, a man with fair hair, lying on his stomach, his arms raised and slightly curved around his head, his face turned away from them as if looking back toward the keep. He wore a dark green, blue and red plaid she'd noted on about half of the warriors at Buchanan, Geordie among them, and there was blood pooling in the dirt by his chest, but there was no arrow, knife or any other weapon to suggest the source of the wound that had bled so profusely.

They were both silent as Geordie reined in just before the body and dismounted. He turned back then, just in time to catch her by the waist and ease her drop to the ground as she slid off the horse. Once on her feet, they hurried to the man.

Dwyn paused on the near side and peered down at his face as Geordie moved around to the other side. The man looked familiar. She'd seen him speak to Aulay several times since arriving, but it wasn't until Geordie gasped the name, "Simon," that she realized it was Laird Buchanan's second, the man who took over when Acair was too busy to manage his duties as first, which had been a lot of the time lately, she realized.

She waited until Geordie had turned the man over, and then knelt across the body from her husband and lowered her head to the fair-haired man's chest to listen for a heartbeat. Dwyn didn't hear one, but the amount of blood on the ground hadn't given her much hope that she would.

Geordie didn't appear surprised when she shook her head. Sighing, he leaned forward to shift the top swath of plaid aside and tugged the second's tunic out of it to reveal the injury he'd taken. Dwyn frowned when she saw the large gaping wound. The man had been gutted by either a sword or a knife. She raised her head to glance at her husband, and froze, as she saw the man behind him.

Tall, barrel shaped, with iron gray hair on his head, but a beard and mustache both more black than gray, the man was not attractive. He also had cruel eyes that haunted her in her nightmares.

"Brodie!" Dwyn gasped the name with horror.

Geordie started to turn, but it was too late. Faolan Brodie was already slamming the hilt of his sword into her husband's head.

Dwyn's gaze shifted to Geordie with dismay as he collapsed across Simon's chest. Terrified that Brodie would kill him as he had Simon, she instinctively threw herself on top of her husband, protecting his head and back the best she could.

"Take her on yer mount, Garbhan, else I might kill her ere I can wed her."

She heard Brodie's words, but paid them little heed until someone—presumably Garbhan—grabbed her arm and started to drag her to her feet. Desperate to keep Geordie safe, Dwyn struggled violently to break loose and return to her husband. But her struggles were brought to an abrupt end when pain exploded in the back of her head and she lost consciousness.

Chapter 15

Terrible pain was crashing through Geordie's skull when he woke up. Moaning miserably, he squeezed his eyes closed and raised his hands to cover his head, only to suck in a pained gasp when one hand pressed against cloth rather than hair. The touch sent the ache in his head ratcheting up from just terrible to excruciating.

"Drink this."

Geordie heard the order, but paid it little heed until his hands were forced away from his head as he was lifted into a sitting position and something was pressed to his lips. His mouth was open on his pained groans, and liquid poured in at once, choking off the sound. He tried to struggle as a vile-tasting fluid flowed over his tongue, but someone caught his hands and held him still as the liquid continued to pour in. His choice was to swallow or let the liquid slide into his lungs and drown him. Geordie swallowed and continued to do so until his mouth was empty and he was eased back onto a soft surface.

He lay still then, aware that people were talking quietly around him, but was more concerned with trying to control the agony he was experiencing than anything that was being said. It seemed to Geordie that he lay there for an hour suffering before the pain began to ease, but suspected it was probably only a quarter of that. Rory often said it took a quarter hour before his tonics started to work and an hour before their full effect was felt. Hoping like hell that this wasn't the full effect, he finally opened his eyes, wincing when bright sunlight struck his eyes, sending more pain shooting through his head.

"Keep your eyes closed until the pain eases more," Rory instructed, laying something cool and damp across his forehead. "Ye took a mighty blow to the head."

Geordie frowned at the news, trying to recall how that had happened, and then stiffened as he remembered.

"Dwyn!" he growled, sitting up abruptly, and then collapsed back on the bed with a moan as someone stuck a knife through his head. At least, that's what it felt like, though he knew he'd taken no further harm.

The cool damp cloth was returned to his forehead now and Rory said, "Just rest another minute. Let the tonic work."

Geordie remained still, but growled, "Where's Dwyn?"

"The men are looking for her." That was Aulay's voice, solemn with an undertone of anger. "What happened?"

Geordie took a moment to sort his memories, and then sighed. "We were coming back from the waterfall. We saw a body on the path ahead, stopped to investigate . . . It was Simon," he recalled unhappily. "He'd been gutted."

"Simon was already dead when ye got to him?" Aulay asked, and he could hear the frown in his brother's voice.

"Aye," Geordie breathed. "And had been for a while. He was cooling." He frowned at the recollection. "He must have died shortly after Dwyn and I reached the waterfall. He was no' on the path when we rode out to the loch."

"The men said he and Katie rode out almost on yer heels," Aulay told him. "Ye must have ridden by the spot just before the men who killed Simon arrived. 'Tis lucky you are no' the one lying in the path."

"Did Katie see who did it?" Geordie asked at once.

"Aye, but she does no' ken who it was. She said it was a large group o' men—at least fifty warriors rode out o' the trees and surrounded them. She said they did no' say a word, just stabbed Simon. He fell from the horse behind her, and then his mount spooked and ran away with her. She said the men did no' pursue her, and even made room for her to leave, but it took some time fer her to get control o' the mount and get him to turn around. By the time she got back to where they'd been attacked to check on Simon, the men were gone, Simon was dead and ye were lying unconscious across his chest. She managed to get ye on his horse and brought ye back."

Geordie frowned at that, but before he could think on it long, Aulay asked, "Did ye see who hit ye?"

"Nay. Whoever it was crept up behind me while we were checking Simon," he admitted, mouth tight. But then his eyes narrowed as the memory of those moments on the path cleared a bit for him, and he said, "Aye. Dwyn gasped the name Brodie just ere pain exploded in me head."

"Brodie?"

Geordie opened his eyes at that bark. Fortunately, this time while the light hurt, it wasn't as bad as the first time and he was able to see that Baron James Innes stood between his two brothers at the side of his bed. The man was blanching at this news.

"Who is Brodie?" Aulay asked.

"Faolan Brodie," James Innes said grimly. "He's laird over the Brodie clan, our neighbors."

It was Geordie who explained. "Brodie wanted Innes and tried to force Dwyn to marry him so he could get it."

"Aye," James said grimly. "No doubt he still wants Innes, and will be very angry when he realizes he canno' marry her and get it."

"Angry enough to kill her?" Geordie asked sharply.

"That'll no' get him Innes," Aulay pointed out, and asked James, "How bad do ye think he wants yer land?"

James Innes hesitated. "At first, I thought it was his only interest. But when he attacked Dwyn . . ."

"She told me about that," Geordie admitted. "She said he tried to force the issue and her dogs drove him off."

"Is that how she described it?" James asked, his mouth tight.

Geordie's gaze narrowed. "Is it no' what happened?"

"Aye, but . . ." Sighing, he ran a hand over his thinning gray hair, and then said, "I heard it all secondhand from Maon, one o' me men. He was on patrol, and saw it all. He was a good distance away though when it started, and said he never would have got there in time to stop the man when he attacked Dwyn. Maon said she was fighting like a hellcat and screaming for the dogs, but Brodie had her on the ground in seconds, and silenced her by pinning her neck with one arm. He'd already yanked his plaid up over his arse, and was choking her with his weight while he tried to drag her skirts up when the dogs came out o' the woods. The dogs separated when they saw what was happening, coming at him from both ends. Angus went for his throat, but Brodie managed to get his arm up and in the way first, and the dog tore into that instead. But even as that happened, Barra went for his ballocks."

Geordie winced despite himself, and James Innes nodded.

"Brodie did no' see it coming, and likely could no' have protected himself anyway if he had. The beast grabbed hold and shook his head from side to side and came away with meat in his mouth when Brodie kicked out at him and rolled to the side. Moan said Dwyn crawled several feet away and only called off the dogs when Brodie pulled out a dirk and started slashing at them. Angus and Barra listened at once and moved to stand in front of her, their bloody teeth bared as they growled at him. Brodie managed to crawl to his horse, cursing Dwyn and the dogs the whole way. He used his horse to get to his feet and Moan said he was bleeding something fierce, both from his arm and from between the legs. But he managed to mount just as Moan reached Dwyn. Despite me man's presence Brodie vowed he'd make Dwyn pay for what her dogs did that day." His mouth tightened. "Laird of Brodie or nay, Moan could no' stand fer that threat against his lady. He drew his sword and hurried toward him, but Brodie merely put his heels to his horse and left before he could reach him. We have no' heard from the man since."

Geordie ground his teeth together, a muscle in his jaw ticking as he thought on how close Dwyn had come to being raped and forced to marry the bastard.

But James Innes wasn't done, and added, "When Moan went

back to Dwyn, she was ordering Barra to drop what was in his mouth. The beast let it go as he reached her. 'Twas one o' Brodie's ballocks and the end o' his cock. A good two inches o' it."

"Ah, Christ," Geordie breathed, but not in sympathy with Brodie, in fear for Dwyn. If the man blamed her for the dog doing that, how would he punish her? What torment would he think was equal to what Barra had done to him?

Dwyn had tried to tell him, Geordie thought. She'd said the man was dangerous, but in his arrogance he'd assured her she was safe now they were married. Of course, he hadn't known the extent of the damages the man had sustained, but only because he hadn't let her tell him. When she'd tried to, he'd silenced her with kisses and reassurances. He was a fool, Geordie thought with dismay. He knew Dwyn was special. She was not your average woman given to hysterics. He should have known that if she worried about Brodie, there was a reason, and he should have listened and let her say all the things her father had just told them, because he knew without a doubt that's what she'd been trying to do when he'd silenced her with a finger over her mouth the last time she'd tried to tell him.

"We shall have to hope Brodie still wants Innes, then," Aulay said now, drawing his gaze. "It will force him to keep her alive if he wishes to avoid all-out war with eight clans."

"Aye," Geordie said grimly, and then shifting his gaze to James Innes, he assured him, "It does no' matter that I gave up all rights to Innes land should our marriage end by death or any other reason. If he kills her, we will still hunt the bastard to the ends of the earth. We will no' let him try to force Una or Aileen into marriage, or attack Innes."

James Innes blinked in surprise at that, and then turned to Aulay and said, "He does no' ken. Dwyn could no' have told him."

"Nay," Aulay murmured, and reminded him, "Dwyn was going to present it to him after the ceremony as a wedding gift, but we never held it. They were wed right here while Rory was sewing up Geordie's wounds from battling the men by the loch."

"Aye," James murmured with a frown. "Perhaps she planned to tell him after the wedding at Innes."

"What do I no' ken?" Geordie asked with a frown. "What gift?"

Aulay opened his mouth, and then closed it and walked out of the room.

Geordie gaped after him with disbelief and then struggled to sit up.

"How is yer head?" Rory asked grimly, stepping forward to help him get upright, and then stacking pillows behind his back to keep him that way.

"Better," Geordie said through gritted teeth. It was still pounding something fierce, and sitting up intensified that enough that he didn't stand up as he'd originally intended, but it was better. Shifting his gaze to James Innes, he asked, "What the hell is the gift Dwyn did no' give me?"

James hesitated and glanced toward the door as if hoping Aulay would appear there, but when he didn't he sighed and ran a hand through his hair. "In truth, the gift is already given. Ye just have no' been presented with it yet," he muttered finally.

"With what?" Geordie asked insistently, and then movement drew his gaze to the door as his brother returned with a scroll in his hand. Pausing at the bedside, Aulay held it out to Geordie.

"What is it?" he growled, simply staring at the scroll and not taking it.

"'Tis Dwyn's gift to ye, brother." Aulay extended his arm farther and pushed the sealed scroll toward him. "Read it."

"Nay. Just tell me," he said stiffly, almost afraid to touch the scroll.

"'Tis a will. Dwyn's will," Aulay announced, and Geordie closed his eyes, not wanting to hear more. She would not die. He wanted nothing to do with anything that might suggest she could. But Aulay added, "And though she did no' plan it this way, 'twill keep her alive."

That caught Geordie's attention, and he lifted his head to spear his brother with eager eyes. "How?"

"If she dies, Innes goes to you, no' back to me or her sisters," James explained when Aulay hesitated.

Geordie peered at Dwyn's father with amazement. "Ye agreed to this?"

"I had little choice in the matter," he said dryly. "I had already given Innes to the two o' ye in the marriage contract as was demanded in the invitation to come here, and ye had already signed it over to her. It was Dwyn's to do with as she wished. I did try to talk her out o' it," he admitted. "But she was determined ye'd no' be left homeless and landless did she die." Sighing, he added grimly, "And now, it seems a good thing I could no' talk her out o' it. It may save her life."

When Geordie peered at him in question, not understanding why, he pointed out, "If Faolan Brodie wants Innes, he canno' kill Dwyn. Innes would go to you on her death."

Geordie began to relax a little. Brodie couldn't marry Dwyn and couldn't kill her if he wanted Innes. In fact, the only way to get his hands on Innes was to—

"He'd have to kill you to have any chance at gaining Innes," Aulay said even as Geordie thought it. And then he added, "If Dwyn dies ere ye do, Innes goes to you. Does she survive ye and then die, it passes back to her father or her eldest living sibling if he has passed. So, he needs to kill you and either force Dwyn to marry him and change her will, or kill you, and then her and her father, and then go after Una, who would then be Laird Innes's next heir."

"So he'll have to keep her alive and come after me," Geordie said with satisfaction.

"Aye," Aulay and Laird Innes said together.

Geordie considered that briefly and then pointed out, "But he could still punish her for what her dogs did to him. He could torture or—"

"But he canno' kill her," Aulay interrupted firmly. "We can help her heal from torture. We canno' bring her back from death."

Geordie nodded, but felt sick at the thought of the torture

Dwyn might suffer. And the worry that if Brodie tortured her . . . How would she be affected? Would she even be his Dwyn when he got her back?

IT WAS COLD WATER SPLASHING OVER HER FACE THAT WOKE Dwyn. Gasping with the shock of it, she sat up abruptly, and then groaned and raised her hands to her head. Shoulders bowing under the pain presently crashing about inside her skull, she pressed her hands tight to either side of her head above her ears, trying to force the pain back.

"Get up."

Dwyn stiffened at the cold order, not because of the words, but because she recognized the voice. Faolan Brodie. The name slipped through her mind, followed by the recollection of what had happened, or at least what she knew of what had happened. The last thing she recalled was being dragged away from an unconscious Geordie. She had no idea what had happened to him after that. Had they killed him like they had Simon? Was she a widow?

"If ye ken what's good fer ye, ye'll get up." This time the words were hissed in her ear. "And ye'll marry me all obedient-like or I'll make ye sorry."

Dwyn's head jerked up at that, her eyes wide with horror. "Ye killed him, then?"

Faolan Brodie smiled grimly at her dismay. "Who? The Buchanan?"

When she bit her lip and nodded, he shook his head with cold amusement. "Do I look a fool to ye? I've no desire to have the Buchanan brothers with all their clans on me arse. They'd hunt me to hell and back had I killed him." He sounded disgusted at the prospect, as if he didn't understand such loyalty and love for a sibling. "Nay. We left him alive. But do no' be thinking that'll save ye. Once the wedding is done, ye're mine and he canno' do a thing about it. He'll let it lie and find another bride."

Dwyn let out a slow relieved breath at this news. Geordie was safe.

"Now get up. The priest is waiting," Brodie growled, stepping back.

Dwyn glanced around to see she was seated on a pallet in a traveling tent. They weren't at Brodie, then, but she had no idea where they were or how long she'd been unconscious. They could be just beyond the Buchanan border or a day's travel back toward Brodie and Innes. Perhaps even two days' travel away. She had no idea how much time had passed.

"I said get up!" Brodie roared, and backhanded her.

Dwyn swayed to the side under the blow, the pounding in her head increasing briefly so that she still didn't move. Once the worst of it passed, she raised a hand to press it against her stinging cheek and straightened to peer up at him. Voice calm, she said, "I'll no' marry ye, and ye canno' make me."

She expected him to hit her again and braced for it. Instead, Brodie caught her by both arms and jerked her up off the pallet to dangle before him.

"I paid the MacGregors a lot o' coin to camp on their land and get their priest out here today. One way or another, ye will marry me, lass," he assured her coldly. "The question is whether I'll need beat ye till ye agree, or whether ye go willingly to the priest." Smiling coldly, he added, "Do ye go willingly, I'll only let me men have at you after the ceremony."

When her eyes shot to his face, he shrugged. "Someone has to consummate the marriage and those vile dogs o' yers have ensured I canno'." Mouth tightening, he added, "The beasts will pay for that with their lives when we get to Innes."

Dwyn's mouth tightened with disgust. "And that is supposed to convince me to marry ye willingly?"

"Nay," he admitted. "What'll do that is the fact that do I have to force ye out o' this tent and make ye say yer vows, I'll let me men do what they will with you, as well as yer sisters when we get to Innes. I ken how much ye care about yer sisters," he added with the satisfaction of a man who thought he held all the cards.

Brodie set her down on her feet then, and Dwyn stumbled

slightly to the side before finding her balance. Once she was steady, he asked, "What'll it be?"

Dwyn stared at him silently for a minute, and then shrugged with disinterest and turned to walk toward the tent entrance. She heard Brodie chuckle behind her, but ignored it, and stepped out into sunlight to peer around the camp. Brodie had said he'd paid the MacGregors to camp here so she knew where she was. The MacGregor stronghold and land were on the northeast border of Buchanan. She wasn't that far from Buchanan keep if she could get loose and get her hands on a horse . . . Her gaze slid around the camp again, and her mouth tightened as she noted the number of men moving about. Brodie had not brought a small contingent of soldiers with him. There were at least a hundred men that she could see, and every single one had turned to peer at her when she straightened in front of the tent flap.

Her mouth tightened at the leering looks sent her way. She could practically feel their anticipation of her "wedding night," and Dwyn could only thank God that Geordie had married her first. Of course, that didn't mean Brodie wouldn't give her to his men anyway when he learned he couldn't marry her. But he wouldn't do it in front of the priest, she was sure. Raising her chin grimly, she started toward the priest standing by the fire.

"Ye've got balls, lass. I'll give ye that," Brodie growled, apparently impressed with her marching out to meet her fate.

"One o' us should," Dwyn shot back as he caught her arm and forced her to slow down and walk with him. She'd known he wouldn't hit her in front of the priest, but wasn't terribly surprised when his fingers dug painfully into her arm in response to her smart crack. She *was* surprised the bone didn't snap under the viciousness of his grip though. Dear God, it hurt. But she suspected it would be the least of her pains by the time Brodie was done with her.

"Lady Innes, Laird Brodie, come, please. I have other duties to see to," the priest said, his gaze narrowing on her pained expression and then shifting to Brodie's grip on her arm. He frowned as he noted the way her skin had blanched around his thumb and fingers under the pressure, and opened his mouth to say something, but Brodie spoke first, cutting him off.

"O' course, Father. We're eager to be wed and would no' hold ye up any longer than necessary," Brodie said quickly, urging Dwyn the last ten feet to stand before him.

The priest noted the way Dwyn sneered at his suggestion that they were eager to wed, and frowned slightly. "Is aught amiss, Lady Innes?"

"Nay, Father Machar," Brodie said for her. "Go ahead. Let's get this done so we can celebrate this blessed union."

Father Machar gave him a repressive look and said solemnly, "I asked Lady Innes."

"It's Lady Buchanan, Father," Dwyn corrected him gently when the priest turned to her, and then announced, "I married Geordie Buchanan a month past." She managed not to flinch as all hell broke out around her.

Chapter 16

"We shall have to keep ye guarded until we locate and capture the bastard," Aulay announced. "I'll—"

"Or," Geordie interrupted, "we could use me as bait."

"Brother," Aulay began with a frown.

"He has Dwyn," Geordie said sharply. "And the bastard's clever. We had men searching Buchanan for weeks after the attack at the waterfall and he managed somehow to stay hidden in the woods between here and there all that time, evading all of our men."

Aulay's eyebrows rose at the suggestion. "What makes ye think that?"

"Well, how the hell else did he ken to attack us there today?" he asked pointedly.

"That is a good point," Aulay murmured thoughtfully.

Geordie was silent, his own mind mulling over what he'd just said. It was hard to believe that the Buchanan soldiers had missed a small group of men hiding in the Buchanan woods, let alone a larger one the size Katie had mentioned. Yet how else could they have known to be there today unless they'd been there all along? But if they'd been there all along, why hadn't they attacked him and Dwyn on the way to the waterfall? Why wait to attack them on the way back? And why kill Simon? He shook his head. None of it made sense.

"Ye're shaking yer head," Aulay said quietly. "Like me, ye've suddenly realized something is no' adding up."

"Aye." Geordie sighed the word, and raised a hand to run it through his hair, but paused as he recalled the linen bandages wrapping his head and the wound beneath them. Letting his hand drop, he scowled and said, "There is no way Buchanan soldiers would miss even one man on a horse in the woods, let alone a large group."

"Nay," Aulay agreed solemnly.

"So they were no' there all this time?" James Innes asked with a frown.

"Nay," Aulay assured him, and then glanced back to Geordie expectantly.

"Which means they were only there at that time because they knew I'd taken Dwyn to the waterfall and would be traveling that path to return," Geordie reasoned. "They'd no' be likely to risk getting that close to the keep otherwise."

"Aye, they must have kenned ye had taken her there or were going to take her there and set themselves in the woods along the path, ready to ride out and stop ye when ye rode past," Aulay suggested. Geordie didn't comment, but something still wasn't right.

"And they mistook the maid and yer second for Geordie and me Dwyn and attacked and killed the wrong man," James reasoned.

Geordie shook his head at once. "Katie has dark hair, and Simon fair. They could no' have been mistaken for Dwyn and me. We are the opposite. She is fair and I am dark."

"Oh, aye," James Innes said with realization. "Then why kill the man?"

"That is the wonder," Geordie murmured, going back over matters in his head, before glancing to Aulay and asking, "Ye said Katie and Simon left directly behind Dwyn and me?"

"That's what the men on the wall said," Aulay assured him. "Katie was seen coming out o' the keep behind ye and Dwyn, and she and Simon rode out five or mayhap ten minutes after ye and Dwyn did, but no more."

"So, she fetched him for the ride," he said thoughtfully, and then glanced toward the window as the sound of the men on the wall shouting greetings, and the thunder of horses on the bridge, came through the window.

Aulay walked to the window to peer out. The angle he was at allowed Geordie to see the way his eyebrows rose and the smile that pulled briefly at his lips before disappearing. Turning back, he announced, "Saidh and Greer, Dougall and Murine, Niels and Edith, and Conran, Evina and her cousin, Gavin MacLeod, are riding across the bridge with their escorts. The MacKays and Sinclairs are with them."

Geordie knew they were returning for the wedding. He hadn't expected them to come to Buchanan first. Meeting them at Innes would have shortened the journey for them, but he said, "Ye should go greet them and tell them what's about."

Aulay nodded and headed for the door, but as he reached for the handle, Geordie added, "Ask Katie to bring up water and a clean linen for me. I would wash Simon's blood off me. Make sure 'tis Katie."

Aulay's hand dropped from the handle without opening the door and he turned to Geordie, one eyebrow raised.

"She was in here stripping the bed to remake it when I came to fetch Dwyn to take her to the waterfall," he explained, answering that silent question. "She's the only person who kenned where we were going."

"Well, she is no' a very good maid, then," James Innes informed him dryly. "The bed was stripped, but no' made when we got ye up here. The linens just sat there on the bed. Rory and I had to make it quick while Aulay waited, holding ye in his arms."

"Ye think she told Brodie where ye were after he killed Simon," Aulay said on a sigh, and then shook his head. "Ye canno' blame her if she did. She would have been terrified."

"I do think she told Brodie I'd taken Dwyn to the waterfall," Geordie agreed quietly. "But I do no' think Brodie killed Simon. I think she did."

"What?" James gasped with shock.

Aulay merely stared at him, his eyebrows high on his forehead.

"She's the only one who kenned where we were, and the only one who could have told Brodie. But she would have needed a horse to reach the man to give him that information." When Aulay remained silent, he said, "Simon said he and the soldiers followed the path of the men in the woods to the border of Buchanan land. Which border?"

"MacGregor," Aulay answered without hesitation.

"That's two hours on a fast horse," Geordie said thoughtfully, and then nodded. "Simon's horse could do it in less time with a wee lass like Katie on his back."

"How long were ye at the falls?" Aulay asked, stone-faced.

"We left after the nooning meal. Dwyn went up to continue packing, you and I talked a bit and then ye took Jetta above stairs for a nap. That's when I decided I should take Dwyn and show her the falls. I went up to fetch her at once," he told him. "And 'twas nearing time for the sup when I decided we should head back to the keep, so we were at the falls for . . ." He paused to think briefly, deducting the time he thought had passed before he'd gone up to fetch Dwyn, and the time he'd thought they had left before the sup when he'd suggested they leave, and finished, "Mayhap four and a half or five hours."

"Enough time," Aulay said, looking disappointed at the realization.

"Wait a minute," Dwyn's father protested with disbelief. "Ye're suggesting that little maid who brought ye back killed yer second, a big burly soldier, so that she could use his horse to ride out and tell Brodie where to find you and me daughter?"

Geordie nodded and pointed out, "It's more believable than that it took her four and a half or near five hours to calm the horse and ride him back to where Simon was killed."

James Innes frowned at that, but then shook his head. "Nay, it does no'. If she wanted Brodie to kill ye, why would she bring ye safely back to the keep?"

It was Aulay who said, "Because she did no' want Geordie dead."

"She just wanted to get Dwyn out o' the way," Geordie finished, and then added, "How do ye think she got me on Simon's horse?"

"What?" James asked with surprise.

"Dwyn could barely drag me through the woods on a plaid," he pointed out. "Yet Katie claims she somehow got me across Simon's horse's back and returned with me."

James frowned and said uncertainly, "Well, maids are stronger than ladies."

"Dwyn climbs trees and wrestles dogs to the ground who are bigger and heavier than herself. She's no' a weakling," Geordie said firmly.

Laird Innes was silent for a minute, and then asked, "Why would the maid want me Dwyn dead?"

"No' dead, just out o' the way," Geordie muttered wearily.

"Do ye really think she cares if Dwyn is dead or just out o' the way?" Aulay asked, and then pointed out, "If what ye're thinking is what happened, she killed Simon for a horse."

Geordie's mouth thinned.

"Ye did no' answer me question," Laird Innes said now. "Why would she want me Dwyn dead or out o' the way?"

"Because I tupped her," Geordie admitted after a hesitation. But when his father in-law stiffened, he quickly added, "Long ago . . . ere meeting Dwyn."

Laird Innes relaxed at once, but simply said. "Nobles tup servants all the time. It rarely leads to murder."

"Aye," Geordie sighed. "But after tupping her, I was stupid enough to allow guilt to influence me into showing her a kindness she misconstrued."

It was Aulay who explained. "Some time ago Katie and Geordie were mistaken for meself and me wife, Jetta, who does have dark hair like Katie," he added heavily. "Because of that mistake, Katie was shot with an arrow while riding back to the keep with Geordie."

When Aulay paused, Geordie picked up the thread of the explanation and said, "The lass has no family. Her mother was a maid here who came to work at Buchanan when Katie was a wee bairn, and she died some years back. There was no one to tend to her, or even care really whether she lived or died." He took a deep breath and added, "I felt guilty. She'd been injured because o' me family. If I hadn't stopped to take her up on me horse that day, she never would have taken the arrow. It did no' seem fair, or right, so I . . . I stayed at her bedside until she recovered," he finished unhappily.

James Innes raised his eyebrows. "That was a kindness on yer part."

"Apparently, no' as kind as ye'd think," Geordie said dryly. "She misconstrued me actions and decided I must love her . . . and so did everyone else."

"Even I thought he might have finer feelings for the maid," Aulay admitted on a sigh. "I was waiting for him to approach me about taking her as a bride if she recovered. When Katie was well along the path to healing and yet he did no' do that, I brought the subject up with him."

"And that's when I realized what I'd done," Geordie said grimly. "I stayed away from her after that, but she was near to healed by that point anyway, and was below stairs days later. She followed me around after that, giving me calf eyes, always there to fill me mug ere it was even empty, bringing me food at every turn, and offering me herself at every opportunity. 'Twas a relief to get away and go help Conran with his brother-in-law, the MacLeod," he admitted. "When I returned and heard she'd been seeing Simon while I was gone, I thought mayhap everything would settle down now." Grimacing, he scrubbed his face with his hands, and said, "I'm thinking now though that I was wrong."

There was silence for a minute, and then Aulay said, "'Tis possible we're wrong about this instead. She's always been very pleasant to Dwyn in my presence."

"Aye, she has in front o' me too," Geordie admitted. "And while Dwyn probably would no' have said anything, I'm sure Una or Aileen would have mentioned if any o' the servants had been anything but pleasant to Dwyn. But," he continued quickly when Aulay opened his mouth to speak, "Katie offered herself to me after the sup the night after I returned. 'Twas an hour or so ere Dwyn stepped in the glass," he added to make sure they knew which night. He'd returned in the middle of the night before the incident he was talking about. Now he said, "I refused, o' course, but when I said I thought she was seeing Simon now, she shrugged and made it obvious that did no' matter. She'd toss him over for me." He allowed a moment for that to sink in and then pointed out, "Besides, ye said she claimed Simon fell off the horse behind her after being wounded and the mount spooked and fled."

"Aye," Aulay agreed, obviously not understanding what that had to do with anything.

"If she was seated in front o' him, how was Simon gutted behind her by anyone but her?" he asked simply.

Aulay's head went back as if Geordie had punched him. When it came back down his expression was cold. Nodding, he opened the door. "I'll send Katie up with water."

"Ye ken Simon wanted to marry Katie," Rory said solemnly as the door closed behind Aulay.

Geordie turned to peer at his younger brother, amazed to realize he'd forgotten all about his even being in the room he'd been so quiet. "Nay, I did no' ken that."

"He told me that just yesterday," Rory said sadly, and then asked, "What are ye going to do once Katie gets here?"

Geordie was silent for a moment, thinking that this was his fault. That he should have told Simon Katie wasn't faithful and had tried to get him to sleep with her. Perhaps he would have broken off with her. Perhaps he wouldn't have ridden out with her today. Perhaps he'd still be alive and Dwyn would still be here rather than captured by a man who meant her nothing but harm.

Sighing, Geordie straightened his shoulders, and said, "I'm going to get her to admit what she's done and tell me where Brodie has Dwyn."

Rory nodded and began to gather his medicinals. "We should leave, then."

Baron Innes didn't argue and Geordie soon found himself alone, waiting for someone he hoped like hell could tell him where his wife was. Because if he was wrong about this, he didn't know how they'd find Dwyn.

"SURELY YE DO NO' EXPECT ME TO BELIEVE THAT NONSENSE, LASS? Ye're no' married to Geordie Buchanan. Ye canno' be!"

Dwyn tore her gaze from Father Machar, who sat tied up in the corner of the tent, and turned to peer at Faolan Brodie. "Why? Because it disrupts yer plans to force me to marry ye?"

She watched the rage grow on the man's face and braced herself to be hit, but he merely roared, "Nay! Because there's been no wedding! Katie made sure o' it. The last thing she wanted was for you to marry Geordie Buchanan. She wants him for herself. 'Tis why when he started paying ye too much attention she spread glass on the floor outside the garderobe, and why when that did no' work she poisoned yer drink. It was all to keep ye away from Geordie."

"Katie? The maid?" Dwyn asked with amazement.

"Aye, sweet wee Katie the maid," Brodie said with a laugh, and took great pleasure in telling her, "Apparently, yer betrothed was tupping wee Katie not so long ago and then sat at her bedside night and day for two weeks while she was recovering from an injury. She's sure he loves her and that only his brother's disapproval stands between them. She plans on removing that obstacle soon enough, but first she has to be rid o' you ere ye can marry the bastard and steal him out from under her nose. And since I did no' want ye marrying the bastard either, because I wanted ye fer meself, it behooved us to work together."

Dwyn stared at Brodie, but wasn't really seeing him. She was trying to come to grips with the fact that the sweet, smiling maid, Katie, was a murderous, two-faced bitch. She could hardly credit it. The girl had been nothing but kind to her, always eager to help, always carrying trays of food up for her . . . well, food trays meant for Geordie while he was ill, she realized. But Katie was also always offering to fetch wildflowers to scent the rushes in . . . what was essentially his room. Besides, it was probably when she was able to slip away to meet Brodie. Still, she was always nearby, smiling and refreshing their drinks, bringing the platters of food to them . . . Perhaps she'd always refreshed Geordie's drink first, and moved on to fill Dwyn's only when Geordie pointed out her drink could use topping up as well, and perhaps the platter had been held between them and a little closer to Geordie than her, but— Dear Lord, the woman was crazy in love with Geordie, Dwyn realized.

She took a moment to accept that, and then cleared her throat and asked, "How do ye ken Katie?" Dwyn had barely asked the question when another was shooting from her mouth. "And how did ye even ken me family was here?"

Brodie scowled briefly, but then said, "I kenned ye were here thanks to Deoiridh."

Dwyn blinked. "Deoiridh, the chambermaid at Innes?"

"Aye. Her sister married one o' me men some years back and lives at Brodie. The two visit though, and when last she visited, yer Deoiridh apparently told her sister—me man's wife—all about the Buchanan bridal hunt business, and that ye were on yer way here. He, in turn, passed the information on to me. Unfortunately," he added grimly, "that was near a week after ye'd already left fer Buchanan. So, while I gathered me men together and rode out almost at once, ye were already at Buchanan before we caught up to ye. The best I could do was camp here on MacGregor land, and send a handful o' men to lay low in the woods o' Buchanan to watch the keep for an opportunity to steal ye away."

He scowled at the inconvenience of it all, and then continued. "And that is how I encountered the lass."

"You were in the woods with yer men?" Dwyn asked uncertainly.

"Nay." He scowled at the very thought. "But she ran into me

men in the woods the night she poisoned ye." Smiling suddenly, he said, "Apparently, all the Buchanans were fussing over ye while ye were retching, including Geordie Buchanan, which was the exact opposite o' what she'd intended with the poison. She left the keep in a fine dander, and headed down to the loch to try to come up with another way to be rid o' ye. But she got distracted when she met me men. She serviced all o' them fer a coin, and as she did, they asked her a lot o' questions about you. Katie asked questions o' her own in return, and when she realized I wanted to marry ye, she demanded to be brought to me. She told them she could help."

Smiling, Brodie shrugged. "And she did in the end. Katie's the one who came to fetch me with the news that ye were out o' the keep and at the waterfall with Geordie."

Dwyn stiffened at this news, her mouth tightening, and Brodie grinned, obviously recognizing her dismay and enjoying it.

"How else did ye think we came to be there waiting in the woods along the path at just the right time?" he asked with amusement.

Dwyn's gaze narrowed on him grimly. "So ye killed Simon and . . ." Her words trailed off even before he started to shake his head. The timing for that didn't seem right. Simon had been dead for hours when they'd found him. Brodie wouldn't have waited there along the path for hours; it would have been too dangerous. He would have come for them at the waterfall, and got off Buchanan land and back home as quick as he could.

"If Simon is the man who was lying on the path, 'twas Katie who killed him," Brodie said now. "She needed a horse to get to us since me men could no longer hide in the woods after two o' me men were killed and the others chased off. I had to sit idly by and wait here for any news she could slip out to give us when she was supposed to be gathering flowers, or performing other duties."

Mouth tightening, he admitted, "I was angry at her for killing the warrior when I heard what she'd done, but 'twas handy in the end," he said dryly. "It was spying the body on the path that told us ye'd no' yet returned to the keep from the waterfall. The body would have been gone otherwise. But 'twas late, nearly time fer the sup by the time we got to Buchanan, and we feared missing ye did we travel through the woods to the loch to get ye, so we waited in the trees fer yer return."

Dwyn closed her eyes briefly, the panicked worry that she had to get away and get back to Buchanan before Katie poisoned or otherwise killed Aulay Buchanan rushing around inside her head. She couldn't let Katie kill him; she liked Geordie's brother Aulay. Aside from that though, Geordie loved him and would be crushed was he murdered on his account.

"So," Brodie said. "Now ye ken I know ye're no' married. And all ye've managed to do with yer attempt to convince me ye are is anger me further. Because now that the priest kens ye do no' want to marry me, I'll have to bribe him with coin to get him to overlook that fact and get him to wed us. Something else I'll have to punish ye for once we're back at Innes."

Dwyn wanted to think that the priest couldn't be bought that way, but she wasn't sure. She *was* sure he wouldn't marry them though, if he was convinced she was already married. So she opened her eyes, and let her lips spread in a wide smile.

Brodie frowned, obviously knocked a bit off-kilter by her reaction to his threat.

Before he could speak, she said, "The thing I find most amusing is that 'tis the actions o' both you and Katie that actually saw me wed to Geordie Buchanan."

"What?" he squawked with disbelief.

"When me feet got sliced up by the glass ye say Katie is responsible for, I could no' walk. Geordie is the one who carried me everywhere afterward for the next two days and nights, and that certainly pushed us closer together," she told him, and explained, "It was the second day o' his carrying me about that we ended up alone in the orchards so that me feet could dry out in the sun, and that is where he first almost made love to me. He carried me back inside and, although I did no' ken it at the time, while his brother Rory tended me feet, Geordie went to Aulay and me father to have the marriage contracts drawn up."

She let that sink in and then added, "That was when I was poisoned. A terribly unpleasant experience, by the by. I was very sick . . . and 'twas Geordie who tended me and held me while I retched through the night. We fell asleep together on his bed after one such round o' retching, and I woke in the morning still in his arms."

Brodie was starting to flush almost purple with his rage, but she continued. "O' course, having slept through the better part o' the day, Geordie knew we would no' sleep that night. We'd be the only ones awake, and because he's an honorable man, and because he did no' think he could resist anticipating our wedding through that night, he got me father's permission to handfast." She met his gaze as she added, "So ye see, if no' for Katie, I might no' even have handfasted with Geordie."

"The stupid bitch," Brodie breathed furiously.

"Oh, it gets better, m'laird," Dwyn assured him with amusement. "Because that night we knew we'd no' sleep was the night we went to the loch where yer men tried to drag me off, then wounded Geordie before he could kill them both. And that is why I am now married. Because when I got him back to the keep, Father Archibald came to give him the sacraments o' the dying, and Geordie asked him to marry us in case he died." She allowed a moment for that to sink in and then announced, "We were married in his room, both o' us in pain and bleeding, with me father, me sisters and his brothers Rory, Alick and Aulay and Aulay's wife, Jetta, as witnesses."

Meeting his gaze she said firmly, "I *am* married, m'laird. The wedding at Innes is merely to allow the rest o' his family, and me people at Innes, to witness it and welcome their new laird, Geordie Buchanan."

Sitting back, she shrugged. "So ye see, I should really thank both you and Katie. If no' fer what she and yer men did, presumably under yer order, I'm no' sure Geordie and I would be married now at all. We may no' even have been betrothed."

Judging by the fury building on Brodie's face, Dwyn gathered the man finally believed she was married to Geordie. Now she just had to worry that he might kill her for it.

Chapter 17

"OH, GEORDIE, ME POOR SWEET MAN, I'M EVER SO GLAD TO see ye awake and recovering."

Geordie stiffened at those words as Katie hurried into the room, but forced himself to relax. Turning his head, he watched dispassionately as she rushed around to where he sat on the side of the bed with his feet in the rushes.

"Thank goodness I found ye and was able to get ye back here for Rory to heal," the maid said as she placed the ewer and bowl on the bedside table. Turning to peer at him then, she shook her head unhappily. "Ye're soaked in blood."

"Most o' it is Simon's," he pointed out, his voice even. "I'm sorry ye lost him, lass. I ken ye were lovers."

Katie blinked, and toned down the smiling, replacing it with a sad moue. "Aye, well, I liked him well enough, but I did no' love him. No' like I do you."

Geordie ignored that and lowered his head. "I loved him. He was like a brother to me."

"Well . . ." Katie paused and was silent so long he almost raised his head, but then she said with practicality, "Fortunately, ye've six true brothers still alive and well. Here, let me help ye out o' yer clothes so we can get ye cleaned up."

Geordie caught her hands as she reached for the pin of his plaid, and squeezed firmly, barely keeping himself from breaking her fingers as he growled, "And Dwyn is gone. Taken by that bastard Brodie. He's probably torturing and killing her as we speak."

"Nonsense," Katie snapped, trying to tug her hands free. "All he wants is to marry her. She'll be fine. And ye're better off without her. She was no' right fer ye anyway. She could no' make ye happy like I can."

Geordie raised his head and speared her with cold eyes. "But I do no' want you. I want her. And she does make me happy. 'Tis why I married her."

"You— She— Ye're no' married," she got out at last. "The wedding was to take place at Innes. And ye do no' love her. Ye love me. 'Tis only Aulay that made ye end our relationship. I ken that. One minute we were playing Nine Men's Morris and laughing, and then he came to the room and took ye away to talk, and ye never came back. I ken he made ye stay away from me after that. I ken ye love me, Geordie. Ye do no' have to pretend anymore that ye do no'. I've taken care o' everything. Aulay'll no' interfere after tonight, I promise. Ye'll be able to live yer life as ye please and we can marry and ye can love me openly."

Geordie stared at her, his brain suddenly sending out a loud alarm in his head. Releasing her abruptly, he stood and walked to the door. Much to his relief, he opened it to find Aulay and every one of his, as well as Dwyn's, family members standing there. They were waiting in the hall, offering silent support and staying near in case he needed them. They'd probably heard most, if not all, of what Katie had just said. Still, he met Aulay's gaze and murmured, "Do no' eat or drink anything until we ken how she's *taken care o' ye*."

Aulay nodded and then said in a voice low enough it wouldn't carry into the room, "I spoke to one o' the men who were on the wall when Katie and Simon rode out. Ye're right. Katie was sitting in front o' Simon. He could no' have been stabbed, let alone gutted, by anyone but her in that position."

Geordie grunted and closed the door.

"Who were ye talking to?" Katie asked with a frown as he started back across the room. "Who's out there?"

Geordie didn't answer. Instead, he caught her by the throat and drove her backward until she was pinned against the wall. He didn't have the patience to try to trick her into a confession. Besides, she'd already given enough away.

Eyes wide, Katie gasped for the air he was choking off and grabbed at his hand, trying to pull it away.

"I *am* married to Dwyn," he assured her coldly. "Father Archibald married us the night Brodie's man ran me through with a sword. After he gave me the sacraments o' the dying, I asked him to marry us. Because I love her. And he did," Geordie told her grimly. "Now where is me wife?"

"It's no' true," she cried the minute he eased his grip on her throat. "Ye love me."

Geordie smiled coldly. "I do no' love ye, Katie. I never did. How could I love a murdering bitch who would kill a man like Simon? He was a good man, Katie. He cared about ye. He told Rory he planned to ask ye to marry him. I should have told him that ye were sneaking around trying to get back into me bed, but I did no', and ye killed him like he was nothing." Slamming her back against the wall, he growled, "Where is Dwyn?"

"I did no' kill him," Katie cried the moment he eased his grip on her throat, and Geordie immediately tightened his hold again, cutting off her air.

"Ye were seated before him when ye rode out, Katie. No one could have stabbed or run him through without going through ye first. Only you would have been in a position to do that, and no one would have taken four or more hours to calm a horse and return to Simon. Ye killed him. Ye went to Brodie and had him come knock me out, take me wife, and then ye had him or one o' his men lay me over Simon's horse so ye could ride back to Buchanan with the ridiculous story about being attacked. Now." Geordie slammed her against the wall again. "Where's me wife?"

He eased his grip on her throat again, and this time she didn't immediately try to deny what she'd done. Instead, sweet, always smiling Katie snarled, "I hope he kills the bitch."

Geordie's fingers contracted around her throat almost of their own accord, and he might not have stopped this time if someone hadn't started knocking at the door and then opened it.

"Geordie, we know where Dwyn is."

Aulay's voice made him freeze, and then he released Katie and turned to hurry across the room as she collapsed to the floor, coughing and sucking in great gasps of air.

"Where is she?" he growled, striding out of the room.

Aulay pulled the door closed and glanced to Rory. "Can ye guard the door and keep the lass here until I can deal with her?"

"Aye, I'll no' let her out," Rory assured him.

Thanking him, Aulay took Geordie's arm to urge him through his sister and Dwyn's sisters, every one of his sisters-in-law, as well as their friends Lady MacKay and Lady Sinclair. None of their brothers or the other men were there now besides Rory, he noted distractedly, but then shifted his attention to Aulay as they started down the stairs and his brother began to speak.

"Alick was leading a group o' soldiers searching the border between our land and the MacGregor land when he encountered one o' their men on patrol. He told him what was happening here and that he was looking for yer wife, who had been taken by a Lowlander named Brodie, and the MacGregor's man told him that there's a laird named Brodie on MacGregor land right now, that he paid MacGregor to let him camp there. Brodie claimed at the time that he was traveling home to Brodie from Arran when several o' his men became ill from what he suspected was bad meat and they needed to bide a wee while they recovered. The MacGregor soldier said they've been no trouble, but then this afternoon one o' Brodie's men rode up to the keep with more coin and a request for the priest to come to their camp. He claimed it was to give the sick men the sacraments o' the dying, but—"

"Brodie must have sent his man to fetch the priest when Katie got to his camp so that he'd be there waiting when he got back with Dwyn. He's trying to make her marry him," Geordie said grimly as they stepped off the stairs and hurried toward the keep doors. "He does no' ken she's already married to me, then."

"Well, he did no' ken it at the time," Aulay agreed, and then caught his arm, drawing him to a halt as he cautioned, "But he may ken by now."

Geordie's mouth tightened. "If he's hurt her, I'm killing him." He waited for Aulay's nod of assent and then turned to continue to the door, only to pause again when he saw Dwyn's father enter, spot them and move their way.

When Geordie offered the man an abrupt nod of greeting, James Innes said, "Geordie, I ken ye think little o' me, that ye do no' approve o' how I raised me Dwyn and that ye think me a selfish old bastard. But I love me daughter. All o' me daughters," he added, casting a glance to Una and Aileen, who had moved up beside them. Turning back to Geordie, he said, "We have to get Dwyn back, Geordie. Brodie's no' just a brutal bastard, he's no' right in the head. We need to get her back."

"We will," Geordie assured him, clamping a reassuring hand on his shoulder briefly before moving past him to push through the keep doors. He was halfway down the steps before he bothered to glance around, and then he paused when he saw the men all gathered on horseback in the bailey. Nearly every last Buchanan warrior was mounted and waiting, but they weren't alone. There were soldiers carrying the banners from each clan his sister and brothers belonged to, as well as the MacKays, MacLeods and Sinclairs, and of course the Inneses. They were the soldiers that had escorted his in-laws, his family members and family friends here. Combined, they easily matched the Buchanan warriors in number.

"So this is what it means to have the Buchanans backing ye," James Innes said with awe.

Geordie heard him, but he had turned to his brother in question.

It was Saidh who answered the silent query. Moving down another step until she could have put her head on his shoulder if she'd wanted, she said, "Ye did no' think we would no' back ye up, did ye?"

Geordie turned to look at her, noting that the women were all lined up on the steps behind him, Aulay and James Innes.

Smiling at him solemnly, Saidh added, "Rory and Jetta are staying behind to hold down the fort and prepare in case some healing is needed, but the rest o' us are coming too." Grimacing, she added, "Though we have promised to stay back and merely watch and wait to greet Dwyn when you big, strong men free her and bring her to us."

Geordie tried to swallow the sudden lump in his throat so he could speak, but it wasn't moving. In the end, all he could do was nod his gratitude. Turning away then, he continued down the stairs, thinking it was good to have family. And he had the very best.

"I'M SO SORRY, LADY BUCHANAN."

"What for, Father?" Dwyn asked distractedly as she felt her way blindly across the ropes binding the priest's wrists.

"For no' being able to do aught while Laird Brodie beat ye," Father Machar said on a sigh. "I did try to loose me bonds to help ye, but he trussed me up well."

Dwyn was silent for a minute as her split lip and every bruise on her body seemed to ache a little more at his reminding her of the beating. Ignoring her aches and pains, Dwyn turned her attention back to what she was doing, and told herself she'd got off easy. Brodie had punched her several times, in the stomach, the chest and the face. He'd also managed to rip open the top of her gown while at it. Not intentionally. He'd held her with one hand curled around and clutching the neckline as he'd punched her in the face, and the material had torn as her body was forced back under the blow.

Dwyn looked down at it now, and had to hold back a sigh. She wasn't falling out of the dress exactly, but it was holding her about as well as the low necklines of the dresses her sisters had altered did. This dress had been one of the new ones too, and was now, of course, ruined. Dwyn could live with that though, and considered herself lucky that the few blows and a torn dress were all she'd suffered so far. At least Brodie hadn't tossed her out of the tent for his men to pass around and have at. She could survive a beating. She could probably survive being raped as well . . . by one man. Dwyn wasn't too sure she'd survive being raped by one hundred of them though, emotionally or physically. She suspected something like that could kill a woman, or at least make her wish she was dead.

Clearing her throat, she murmured, "Oh, now, there's nothing fer you to be sorry for, Father. 'Tis Brodie who should be sorry. As ye said, ye were tied up."

"Aye, but the MacGregor offered to send warriors to escort me when Brodie's man came to ask me to come to the camp. I refused. Had I allowed the men to accompany me—"

"They'd probably be dead by now," she inserted on a sigh, most of her concentration on trying to unknot the ropes binding the priest's wrists behind his back. Dwyn had managed to force her gag off by using her tongue, teeth and the priest's back to drag it along, and then had removed the gag Brodie had tied around Father Machar's head by using her teeth to tug the dirty cloth out of his mouth and down. While the priest had been quite flustered and embarrassed to have her sticking her tongue in his mouth to hook it under the cloth and drag it to her teeth to pull it over his bottom lip, he'd also been grateful to have the material out of his mouth. Brodie had ripped up a filthy old tunic to make the gags so that aside from the material sucking all the moisture out of their mouths, it had tasted most unpleasant.

"Oh, I'm sure he could no' have managed that," Father Machar assured her. "The MacGregors are fine warriors."

"Aye, but no' expecting trouble, the MacGregor probably would no' have sent more than six or ten soldiers with ye. Brodie brought a hundred," she pointed out.

"Oh, aye, well, that may ha'e been a problem," he agreed with what sounded like a frown in his voice. He fell silent briefly as Dwyn continued tugging at the cord at his wrists, and then said, "Might I ask? Why is Laird Brodie so determined to marry ye?"

Dwyn smiled faintly. Why, indeed, she thought grimly, but said, "He wants me family home and its property. We border

Brodie, ye see, and if he can force me to marry him, he plans to join the two properties and make it all Brodie . . . with him as laird, o' course."

"Oh, I see," he said with an "aha" sound to his voice. "Aye, it makes much more sense now."

Dwyn stopped working briefly, quite sure she'd just been insulted. Although she doubted the man even realized he'd just insinuated that Brodie's desire to marry her couldn't possibly have been just for her person, whereas greed made more sense. Shaking her head, she went back to work.

"Well, I shall have to explain to him that God frowns on greed," Father Machar said now. "Perhaps I could even read him a passage from the Bible on it. Luke 12:15 would be good." His voice dropped to a theatrical boom, and he quoted, *"Then he said to them, 'Watch out! Be on your guard against all kinds of greed; a man's life does not consist in an abundance of his possessions.'* Or," he said, sounding excited, "perhaps Corinthians 6:10. *'Nor thieves* nor the greedy *nor drunkards nor slanderers nor swindlers will inherit the kingdom of God.'"* He barely finished that before he was exclaiming, "Oh! Or I could quote—"

"Father?" Dwyn interrupted gently.

"Aye, lass?" Father Machar asked.

"Ye may want to no' lecture or quote to Laird Brodie. I fear the man is quite mad and like to hurt ye if ye do," she pointed out.

"Oh, nay. Surely not?" he said, the excitement replaced with concern. "Greed may seem like madness, but—"

"He's tied up a priest," Dwyn pointed out dryly. "And he's kidnapped and tied me up as well, and that besides wounding me husband terribly and trying to rape me to force me to marry him ere I came to Buchanan. And the man talks to—"

"Rape? Really?" Father Machar interrupted.

Dwyn couldn't tell if it was titillation she was hearing in his voice, or not. Telling herself of course it wasn't, she said, "Aye. Fortunately, me dogs attacked him and drove him off."

"Ah," he said wisely, and then suggested, "Have ye considered that was God's vengeance? Punishment for his evil ways?"

"I somehow do no' think God would make me dogs bite off the end o' a man's pillicock, Father," she said dryly.

"Oh, dear," he muttered with dismay. "Nay, I canno' see him doing that either." He fell silent briefly, and then in an obvious attempt to turn the subject said with feigned cheer, "So ye're married to Geordie Buchanan?"

"Aye, Father," Dwyn murmured, tugging a bit of cord through another and hoping she was moving it the right way and wasn't simply knotting him up more.

"The Buchanans are fine men," Father Machar assured her. "Good warriors too."

"Their sister, Saidh, is lovely as well," Dwyn pointed out, a little annoyed on the woman's behalf that she hadn't been included.

"Oh?" he asked with interest. "And yet Father MacKenna found her most trying."

"Who is Father MacKenna?" Dwyn asked.

"Father Archibald's predecessor," he explained. "He was the Buchanan priest for years."

"Oh." She tugged on another cord, but when it didn't budge at all, moved on to test the next.

"Aye, and Father MacKenna said Saidh could no' simply accept his teachings, but had to question everything," Father Machar explained as if that were the worst thing in the world a woman could do.

"Is asking questions no' how we learn?" Dwyn asked distractedly.

"Oh, aye, and 'tis even encouraged so long as ye're no' questioning the church."

"I see," she said dryly. "What happened to Father MacKenna?"

"Well, it would seem he met with foul play some years ago. He just disappeared quite suddenly," Father Machar told her with a shudder that suggested he was imagining something of that ilk happening to himself.

Considering he was tied up at present and at the mercy of a madman, Dwyn thought that imagining it wasn't really necessary and the shudder was justified. To distract him, she asked, "Is it possible that was God's judgment on Father MacKenna for speaking so unkindly o' a good, kind woman like Saidh?"

"Oh, nay," he said at once, but then asked with interest, "Do ye think so? He always was rather unkind to me. Perhaps he was being punished for that instead."

Dwyn blinked at the suggestion, and then stiffened when Brodie pushed through the tent flap.

"I've found the solution," the big man announced with satisfaction as he straightened inside the tent.

Dwyn eyed him warily, but said nothing, afraid it would simply draw his attention to the fact that their gags were off. Something he didn't appear to have noticed yet.

It was Father Machar who asked pleasantly, "Oh? And what is that?"

"Oh, I canno' be telling *you* that, Father. Ye'd be scandalized," Brodie announced, and then ordered, "Close yer ears and do no' listen."

Dwyn glanced over her shoulder at Father Machar, wondering how Brodie expected him to do that. She suspected the priest was wondering the same thing, but after a moment he turned his head away from Brodie, giving him the back of his head so that the priest now stared at the tent wall beside them.

Much to her amazement, Brodie grunted with approval at that and then turned his gaze to Dwyn and proceeded as if he thought Father Machar really couldn't hear him. "I'm going to kill Geordie Buchanan."

Dwyn's head jerked back slightly, but she kept her voice calm when she said, "The Buchanans would hunt ye to hell and back."

"Only if they ken I killed him," he responded with amusement.

"They would ken," she said firmly.

"But could they prove it?" Brodie asked silkily. "If his death looks an accident, they may suspect, but Aulay Buchanan is known to be a fair man. If he has no proof, he'll no' act against me."

Dwyn frowned, very much afraid he was right. She'd seen that fairness in regard to Lady Catriona and Lady Sasha. He and Geordie had suspected they were behind the attacks, but hadn't sent them away until they needed the rooms because there was no proof. Mind you, it turned out Aulay had been right to do that. The attacks hadn't been by the two ladies at all, but by Katie. Dwyn still found that rather dismaying news. She'd smiled and chatted with the maid, never knowing how close she stood to a killer and someone who meant her so much harm.

"Me plan is really very clever," Brodie announced, drawing her attention back to him. "I'll send three men separately to Buchanan. One will stay in the woods by the loch Geordie seems to enjoy so much, awaiting an opportunity to drown him and make it appear accidental. Another will camp in the woods on the edge o' the village, and watch for an opportunity to knock him from his horse should he come or go. He'll then make it appear he was thrown from his horse and broke his neck. And the last man will offer his services as a soldier and move right into Buchanan. If they take him on, which I'm sure they will since I've no doubt their men are so stretched right now with their search fer you they could use more help, he can await any possibility to kill him there—breaking his neck and throwing him down the stairs when no one is about so it looks accidental, bumping into him in the training field so he is skewered on his opponent's sword while practicing with the men, a fire in the stables while he is in there." He beamed. "The possibilities are endless."

Brodie turned suddenly as if listening to someone, and then frowned and nodded. Starting to pace the length of the tent, he said, "Aye. O' course ye're right. Finding an opportunity to cause a death that might look accidental could take a while, and we canno' live out here in a tent forever."

She felt Father Machar move behind her and glanced over her shoulder to see that he was staring at Brodie with confusion.

"Aye, dove, again ye're right. It very well might be better to poison the food at Buchanan, or the water, with something that could appear to be the result o' bad meat, or something o' that ilk. But what?" he asked, and then scowled irritably. "What do ye mean ye do no' ken? Why suggest it if ye've no idea what to use to do it?"

"Who is he talking to?" Father Machar whispered with bewilderment.

"I think his dead wife," Dwyn whispered back. That was what she'd concluded the last time he'd started talking to someone who wasn't there. It was while he'd been trying to rape her. Apparently, his wife had been giving him pointers, or urging him on anyway. It was the only reason he hadn't managed the task before her dogs had got to them and attacked. He'd stopped briefly to shout at the empty sky overhead, telling someone that she'd always been a bloody nag, which was why he'd never managed to plant a bairn in her belly. He'd then bellowed out that if she'd been more pleasant to be around, he never would have choked her to death. He'd started foaming at the mouth at that point too. The man was mad.

"Damn woman! Ye're as useless dead as ye were alive. Killing ye was the smartest thing I ever did!" Brodie snarled with frustration.

"Oh dear," Father Machar breathed behind her and Dwyn supposed it was at the realization that the man had killed his wife.

"Oh, leave off, woman!" Brodie barked suddenly. "I shall have to think on this. There must be someone in the area who kens about such things. I will find out."

He didn't even look toward Dwyn and Father Machar then, but simply stormed out of the tent.

"Lady Buchanan?" Father Machar murmured, his voice shaky.

"Aye, Father?" Dwyn asked, returning to trying to undo his bindings.

"I do believe ye may be correct. Laird Brodie is quite mad."

"Aye, Father," Dwyn breathed, and then sighed with exasperation and started to scoot away from him.

"What are ye doing, lass?" he asked, craning his neck around to try to see her.

"I am going to try to get me hands in front o' me," she muttered, and then shifted up to her knees and slid her bound hands under her butt and then forward as she dropped back so that they rested in front of her bottom beneath her upper thighs. Dwyn then shifted her feet so that her bottom was on the floor and her knees were raised with her feet planted on the ground. Pressing her chest as tight to the raised tops of her legs as she could, she squeezed her feet back to press against her butt and slid her hands under her feet until she could push them in front of her feet. It was a bit tight thanks to her overlarge chest, but she managed it, and expelled a relieved breath when her wrists were now in front of her and she could relax.

"My," Father Machar breathed. "That was clever. Do ye think I could do it?"

Dwyn glanced toward the aging prelate and smiled faintly. "Ye can try if ye like, Father, but hopefully I'll be able to get free now and then will free you too."

She turned her attention to the ropes around her wrists, picking out which cord to start with and then raised her wrists to her mouth, bit into the cord and began to tug. Dwyn was aware that Father Machar had pushed himself to his knees and was trying to do what she had done, but didn't look over to see how he was making out. Instead, she concentrated on her ropes. It occurred to her halfway through that she could have simply untied the priest and let him untie her, but she was so close to being done by that point that there seemed little sense in stopping to do it now.

"There," Dwyn said with relief as the rope dropped from her wrists. Shifting her attention to her ankles, she quickly undid those and then turned to Father Machar and blinked in surprise.

"My," she said, biting her tongue to keep from laughing. The priest had managed to get his hands under his behind, but then had toppled over. He was now rolling and flopping about on the ground like a landed fish, but in a fetal position. Shaking her head, she blew out her breath and crawled to him. "Let me help ye, Father."

"IS THAT—?"

"The MacGregor," Geordie said when Dwyn's father hesitated. "Aye."

"Is this good, or bad?" Baron Innes asked with concern, his wide eyes moving over the large army behind the giant, fair-haired warrior who waited just across the small river that marked the border between the Buchanan and MacGregor properties.

"Well, since they're no' attacking, I'd say good," Geordie said dryly, and then turned to signal the men to stay, before turning back and urging his horse forward. He wasn't surprised when Aulay kept pace with him. The fact that Dwyn's father did as well though did surprise him. He knew the man was no' a warrior, but it seemed he was willing to become one for his daughter. It raised his opinion of the man.

"Buchanan," the MacGregor greeted, his eyes on Aulay when their horses carried them out of the shallow river and onto dry land before the man.

"MacGregor," Aulay responded, his face as expressionless as the other man's.

Conn MacGregor turned his gaze to Geordie then. "I summoned me men to come help ye reclaim yer bride. Had I kenned Brodie was up to no good, I'd have refused him sanctuary on our lands."

Geordie relaxed in the saddle, relieved the MacGregors wouldn't be a problem. "We appreciate it."

"Aye, we do," Laird Innes said quietly. "Thank ye."

"This is me wife's father, Baron James Innes." Geordie introduced the two men.

"Innes," MacGregor greeted him with a nod, and then cracked a smile and said, "Ye've made a fine match fer yer daughter. She's in good hands . . . Or will be once we get her back."

"Aye," Dwyn's father said. "I'm coming to see that."

The MacGregor nodded, and then turned back to Geordie and Aulay to say, "Brodie's camp is in a small valley no' far from here. The sides are lined with trees. I'm thinking with the men we have between us—" his gaze skated over the large army on the Buchanan side of the river "—we can surround the valley and just ride down in on the bastard and demand yer woman back, and then kill Brodie and his men or no' as ye like."

When Laird Innes started to speak, and then hesitated, Geordie turned to him in question. "What is it, m'laird?"

"I just worry that Brodie will kill Dwyn for spite if he realizes he is surrounded and has no way out. The man is . . . no' quite right in the head."

"Dwyn said there was something wrong with him as well," Geordie said with a frown. "What makes ye both think he's no' right in the head?"

"He gets so excited when he's angry that he actually foams at the mouth," Innes said with a grimace, and then reluctantly, as if he feared they wouldn't believe him, he added, "And he talks to his dead wife as if the woman is standing beside him."

"That does no' mean he'd kill yer daughter," the MacGregor pointed out.

"Aye, but Laird Innes may be right. He might kill her for revenge," Geordie muttered, frowning as he considered the matter.

"Revenge for what? The bastard kidnapped her, no' the other way around," MacGregor said with disgust.

"Aye, well, me wife's dogs attacked him when he tried to force himself on her," Geordie explained. "One o' them bit off one o' his ballocks and part of his cock. He's been seeking revenge ever since. He most like *will* kill her if he kens he's caught before we can get Dwyn away from him."

The MacGregor grunted at that, and then glanced over the armies on both sides of the river as he considered the matter for a moment. Turning back to Geordie, he said, "Then we should probably sneak in and get her while the men get into position around the camp. Once we have her and me priest out, I'll give the signal and our men can ride in."

Geordie nodded at once. He was eager to go in and get Dwyn, and since MacGregor knew the area better, having his assistance would be most helpful.

"Have yer men cross over and we'll line them up with me men

and yer men interspersed so me warriors can lead them where they need to go," the MacGregor suggested. "And while they do that, we'll look at the map me scouts made o' the camp and decide our best approach."

"Ye had yer scouts map the camp?" Aulay asked with interest.

"Aye, as soon as me man came to tell me what yer brother Alick had said, I sent out men to scout the area. I thought it might come in handy."

"Aye, I'm sure 'twill," Geordie said as Aulay turned to signal their men.

Chapter 18

"Oh, dear, this is most embarrassing."

Dwyn bit her lip to hold back a laugh at that moan from Father Machar. The man was on his back, his scrawny legs in the air, and his black robe gathered around and between his thighs as Dwyn worked at untying his wrists, which were presently pressed tight to the backs of his legs where they met his arse. While the man had got his bound wrists under his bottom, he hadn't been able to get them past his feet, even with her help. Worse still, he hadn't been able to move them back behind his bottom again either when she'd suggested that. He'd complained that the rope was burning his wrists too much to manage it. Hence the awkward position he now found himself in. Fortunately, Brodie hadn't bothered to bind up Father Machar's ankles as he had her. Apparently, he hadn't considered him likely to flee with his hands bound.

"Almost there, Father," Dwyn said soothingly. "Just think o' the story ye'll be able to tell once ye're back at MacGregor."

"Oh, dear Lord, I shall never breathe a word o' this to anyone," Father Machar assured her. "Nay, indeed. Why, I could lose me position as the MacGregor clan priest if anyone learned I had a lady's tongue in me mouth and her hands on me bottom."

"Well, it was no' at the same time, Father," she pointed out dryly. "And 'twas necessary. Besides, me hands are no' on yer bottom."

"Well, something is rubbing me there," he muttered, and lifted his head, straining to look around his raised legs at her.

"Me knuckles," Dwyn explained. "They brush against ye on

occasion and I'm sorry for it. Now please lie back and relax yer muscles again. Ye're pulling yer wrists tight and just making me work harder."

"Oh. Sorry," he muttered, and let his head drop back on the ground with a sigh before saying, "Mayhap we should just give up and wait. I'm sure the good Lord will save us."

Dwyn's eyebrows rose at that. "Or mayhap the good Lord only helps those who help themselves and He expects us to make our escape."

"My dear, our chances o' escaping are quite thin. There are two o' us against a hundred Brodie soldiers," Father Machar pointed out dryly.

"Aye, well, they're no' especially smart soldiers, Father," she pointed out. "No one has checked on us even once since Brodie stormed off to think on how to poison me husband and his family."

"Hmm," Father Machar muttered grimly. "The man is certainly insane, and dangerous as well. Did ye realize he'd murdered his wife?"

"He did mention something of the sort when he attacked me," Dwyn admitted distractedly.

"Why did ye no' write to the king then?" Father Machar asked with dismay. "He could have done something about the man had he known."

"Because 'twould have been my word against his," Dwyn pointed out quietly as she continued to work on the rope. "I had no proof to give the king."

"Oh. Aye," Father Machar murmured on a sigh and fell silent.

"There," Dwyn said with relief a moment later as she pulled the last cord and the rope unraveled from around the priest's wrists. His arms split apart at once now that they were no longer held together, and she nearly got clobbered over the head when Father Machar's legs immediately began to drop as if his wrists had been holding his legs up. Gasping in surprise, she rolled to the side, just avoiding his legs, and then quickly popped to her feet.

"Oh my, this is so much better. Thank ye, m'lady," Father Machar murmured, tugging his robes down to cover his legs and then getting to his feet as well. "What do we do now? I suppose we canno' just walk out, can we?"

While Father Machar asked the question, it sounded to her like he was hoping she had some way that they *could* just walk out the tent flap and into the center of camp, but that wasn't going to get them anywhere. Turning slowly, Dwyn examined the items in the tent with them. Much to her relief it wasn't just where Brodie slept, but where he kept anything of value, she noted as her gaze slid over several weapons. Moving to the table where a dirk, sword, belt, shield and several other items lay, she picked up the dirk and then glanced at Father Machar.

"Which do ye want? The dirk or the sword?" Dwyn asked as he moved to join her.

"Oh, my dear, I canno' carry a weapon. I'm a priest. How would it look?" he asked with dismay.

"Like ye were interested in surviving?" she suggested dryly.

When the priest merely pursed his lips, Dwyn sighed and turned back to the table to lift the sword experimentally. It was extremely large and heavy, of course. Not something she could carry with one hand or swing easily even with two, so she left it and merely took the dirk and moved to the back wall of the tent.

"What are we doing now?" Father Machar asked in a whisper, practically treading on her heels.

"Making a new way out," Dwyn whispered in response, and knelt to slide the dirk into the bottom of the tent about six inches up from the ground, and started to pull it up. Once she had a gash that ran about five feet up the tent wall, she eased the sides apart and slowly stuck her head out to take a peek around.

Much to Dwyn's relief, the only thing behind the tent was woods. They started not far from the back of the tent, and she didn't see anyone to the left or right, but that didn't mean they wouldn't be seen by someone to the side of the tent once they got close to the trees. They'd have to move quickly, Dwyn decided, and pulled her head back in to offer Father Machar a reassuring smile. "I do no' see any soldiers back here. I think we can get to the cover o' the woods if we are quick about it."

Much to her relief, Father Machar nodded assent.

"I'm going to slide out and wait while you slip out and then we'll make a run for the woods together. All right, Father?" she asked.

When he nodded again, she turned and cautiously eased her head out again. Not seeing anyone, she then began to push her shoulders out through the slit. Her chest followed next.

"HE'S PROBABLY KEEPING THEM IN THE TENT."

"Aye," Geordie said in response to that whispered comment from the MacGregor. The men were no doubt already in position farther up the hill in the trees that surrounded the small but deep valley. It had taken he and Conn some time to make their way here to this spot halfway down the hill. Brodie hadn't left the trees unguarded. There were men patrolling to ensure no one snuck up on them, and they'd already taken out five men on their way down the side of the valley. Posting the patrols was about the only smart thing Brodie had done. Choosing to camp in the valley had been incredibly stupid to Geordie's mind. He would have chosen a high flat hill himself, so that he could see anyone approaching for a good distance. But he wasn't going to complain about his enemy making things easier for him. Especially if it raised his odds of getting Dwyn back safe.

"I say we make our way down to the tent, listen fer a minute to see if Brodie is inside and then slice a—"

Geordie glanced to the man with curiosity when he fell silent mid-speech. Eyebrows rising at the startled expression on the MacGregor's face, he then turned to peer back at the tent, his own eyes widening incredulously as he saw that a gash had appeared in the back wall of the tent and a head was pushing out to look around. Geordie knew at once by the pale gold hair that it was Dwyn, and the tightness that had felt like a hand crushing his heart since he'd woken to find her gone eased its grip a bit. She was alive. He couldn't see her well enough from this distance to tell what shape she was in, but she was alive and on her feet . . . and the smart little minx was making her own escape.

Grinning, Geordie watched as she glanced around. When her head disappeared back into the tent, he eased out of his crouched position and began to move silently forward through the trees even as the MacGregor did. They both paused again about twenty feet later when Dwyn's head appeared again through the slit. Geordie immediately scoured the area to both sides of the tent in search of any soldiers who might be a problem for his wee wife. He then glanced back to the MacGregor when the man sucked in a hissing breath. He was expecting to see one of Brodie's men approaching or something else, but there was no one about. Following the man's gaze back to the tent, he saw that Dwyn's shoulders had followed her head out, and now her bosom was framed by the tent as it pushed out as well. The sun had set not long ago, and night was falling. It was that twilight hour when it wasn't quite dark, but not really light either. But what light there was seemed almost to be caught by her pale hair and skin where her gown didn't cover it, and the sight of Dwyn's beautiful breasts swelling over the top of her gown was enough to make him sigh.

"Ye're a lucky man, Buchanan," Conn MacGregor murmured.

Geordie nodded as he watched her stomach and hips slide through the gap now.

"Most lasses would sit about waiting to be ravished or rescued," MacGregor added.

"Me Dwyn's no' like most lasses," Geordie assured him, and they began to move forward again as if by agreement.

DWYN SUSPECTED THAT MANEUVERING HERSELF THROUGH THE slit she'd made in the tent was much like being born, though less messy and probably with less resistance than a body would offer. But then the tent also didn't have muscles contracting to push her out, but she made it through the slash she'd cut, and then stood to the side of it and glanced nervously around as she waited for Father Machar to push his way out as well.

The priest was a slender man, but still bigger than her and seemed to have some difficulty forcing his way through the slit. Dwyn was beginning to think she should cut a cross slit in it to help him out when he suddenly stiffened, his eyes going round with alarm.

"Get back in here, ye bloody bastard!"

Sucking in a sharp breath of alarm at the sound of Brodie's voice, Dwyn caught Father Machar by both hands and yanked with all her might. She threw her whole body into the action, but was still amazed when it worked and the priest suddenly shot from the hole. Dwyn gasped as Father Machar came crashing down on top of her, and then pushed him off and leapt to her feet.

"Come," she hissed, grabbing his arm to drag him to his feet. Brodie was bellowing away furiously, and trying to push his own way through the slit she'd made in the tent. Fortunately for them, he was twice as big as Father Machar and was stuck, at least briefly. Not wanting to stick around to see how long it would take him to break loose and tumble out after them, Dwyn caught the priest by the hand and dragged him after her as she rushed for the trees.

Dwyn wasn't surprised when she glimpsed Brodie soldiers running around both sides of the tent after them. Faolan Brodie was making enough noise that she was sure the entire camp was coming. Refusing to let herself think about what might happen to her if those jackals got their hands on her, she kept her head down and put all her effort into running. Within seconds they were slipping into what little cover the trees offered. Running became more dangerous then, the ground suddenly uneven with roots and fallen branches to trip them up. Dwyn didn't slow though, and didn't look up either until she heard her name shouted over the sound of the gasping breaths she was taking.

Finally raising her head, she spotted two large shapes ahead of her and nearly turned to swerve around the pair, until one of them called out again. "Dwyn, love, this way."

"Geordie," she gasped, recognizing his voice this time. Squeezing Father Machar's hand reassuringly, she managed to put on a burst of speed. The problem then became that she wasn't sure which one of the two large shapes was her husband. Both men were of a size, and she couldn't see features or hair color in the dark woods, so she flipped a coin in her mind—left, right, left, right. Right. Dwyn rushed the man on the right, nearly running right up his body and into his arms. She realized the moment she caught a whiff of his scent that it wasn't her husband. He smelled nearly as nice as Geordie, but different, and she pulled back sharply.

"Lady Buchanan," a deep rich voice full of amusement greeted her, "Conn MacGregor at yer service. Pleasure to meet ye," the man said even as he passed her off to another set of arms.

"Dwyn," Geordie breathed with relief as he held her. She recognized his scent and immediately curled into his arms. He didn't say anything else; he simply started to run with her, heading up the hill.

"Laird MacGregor! Oh, dear!"

Dwyn stretched up to glance over Geordie's shoulder at that surprised gasp and nearly laughed aloud when she was confronted with Father Machar's bottom yet again. The other man, Laird MacGregor, had slung the priest over his shoulder and was hard on Geordie's heels. She was just relaxing when she looked past him and saw how close Brodie's men were. There were a bare few feet between Father Machar's head and the closest of Brodie's soldiers, and their pursuers weren't having to cart another person with them.

They'd be on them in another minute, Dwyn thought with dismay, and then her head swiveled so she could look forward as a thunderous battle cry rent the air. Not one, she realized as she saw the darkness ahead morph into several moving shapes. Many. The air was reverberating with the shouts of countless men on horseback, charging down the hill toward them.

Eyes wide, Dwyn watched the warriors approach, afraid they would charge right over them. But the horses flowed around them and trampled, or engaged, the men following instead, she saw as she swiveled her head again.

"Geordie!"

Dwyn turned forward again at that shout and saw two men on horseback approaching, each leading a riderless mount. The men were nearly on them before she recognized her father and Alick.

"Take Dwyn and the priest to the women," Geordie ordered, setting Dwyn in her father's lap even as the MacGregor helped Father Machar up behind Alick on his mount.

"Husband!" Dwyn grabbed at his hands as he released her. When Geordie paused, his head lifting to hers, she whispered, "I love ye. Be careful."

Geordie squeezed her hand, but then turned to mount his horse as the MacGregor mounted his own. The two men rode into the fray as her father and Alick turned to head back up the hill.

Dwyn had no idea where the women were, or even who they were, and was too busy trying to watch Geordie over her father's shoulder to care much. Unfortunately, it was too dark and the scene too chaotic to see much. She quickly lost sight of her husband in the dark shapes battling in the trees.

"Are ye all right, lass?"

Dwyn shifted her gaze to her father's face. She couldn't see his expression, but he sounded concerned. "Aye, Da, and glad to be safely away from Brodie."

"Geordie'll get him," James Innes said with confidence. "He was most worried about ye. I think he near killed Katie when she would no' tell him where ye were."

"Ye ken about Katie?" Dwyn asked, as surprised at the knowledge as she was over the fact that she'd briefly forgotten all about the woman.

"Aye. Geordie worked it out that Simon could no' have been stabbed without going through her with her position before him, and she was the only one who kenned ye were at the waterfall, so is the only one who could have told Brodie that."

"Oh," Dwyn sighed, and they both fell silent as they rode. She was beginning to fear they were going to ride all the way back to Buchanan when the horses began to slow.

Lifting her head, she glanced ahead, her eyes widening at the sight before them. Several torches had been planted in the ground in a large circle that surrounded a fire and several logs where women sat waiting, or had. They were all getting up now and rushing to meet them as her father slowed his mount and helped her dismount.

"Dwyn!"

Turning, she found herself caught up in a fierce hug by Aileen. Una soon joined them, wrapping her arms around both of them.

"Are ye all right?" both of them asked at the same time, not releasing her.

Managing a smile despite the pain they were causing her by pressing against her bruised chest and stomach, Dwyn hugged them back.

"Aye. I'm fine now," she murmured, and then heard as Father Machar assured the women surrounding him, "Oh, nay, I'm fine, m'lady. Just fine. Lady Buchanan took good care o' me, though she took a terrible beating herself."

Dwyn sensed rather than saw when all eyes turned on her. Sighing, she opened her eyes to glance around in time to see that most of the women were all now moving toward her.

"Brodie beat ye?" Una asked, sounding angry as she pulled back. Reaching out, her sister pushed the hair out of Dwyn's face and inhaled sharply, then breathed, "Bastard."

"I'm fine," Dwyn assured her.

"Nay, Dwyn, you are not fine," a woman she'd never met before said quietly with an English accent. Una and Aileen fell back at once to make room for the newcomer. "You have a split lip, a terrible black eye and a bump and cut on your forehead that look serious. Come over by the fire and let me look at you."

"Dwyn, this is Jo Sinclair," Saidh said, taking her arm and urging her toward the fire.

"Aye," Murine said, urging Father Machar toward the fire as

well as Dwyn was ushered that way. "Ye remember us mentioning her. She is a fine healer."

Dwyn nodded silently. The women had told her all about how they'd met, which had been at Sinclair. They'd been invited there by Campbell Sinclair's mother in the hopes that he'd be interested enough in one of the women to finally marry and produce grandbabies for her. As Dwyn recalled, it was where the women had got the idea to invite all the heiresses to Buchanan. But a fine joke had been played on all since Campbell had arrived at Sinclair with Jo already as his wife. Even so, the women had become fast friends, and Saidh and the others had insisted that Jo and Campbell, as well as Jo's aunt and uncle, the MacKays, should be invited to the wedding at Innes.

"Brodie did this?" Saidh asked as she urged her to sit on the fallen log closest to the fire and looked her over.

"Aye," Dwyn murmured. Noting the grim expressions all around, she was guessing she looked pretty bad at the moment, but then a black eye and split lip would hardly be pretty; add a cut and swollen forehead and she feared her plainness had moved on to just ugly.

"Oh my, it was an adventure," she heard Father Machar saying from a nearby log that the other women had urged him to. "The Brodie gagged us and tied us up back-to-back. It was most unpleasant. The gag was dirty, ye see. But Lady Buchanan got her gag off and then even managed to remove mine as well. She had to stick her tongue in me mouth to do it, but there was nothing lascivious about it. She was just trying to get the gag out."

Dwyn turned to peer at the man with raised eyebrows. She seemed to recall him declaring he couldn't possibly talk about what had happened. What would people think? he'd asked. Apparently, he'd forgotten that concern, she thought wryly as he continued.

"Just as I'm sure there was nothing lascivious when she put her hands on me bum while I had me legs in the air. It wasn't even really her hands, but her knuckles. She was trying to undo me bindings, ye see."

There was a brief silence and then one of the women loosed a giggle. It was short. Whoever it was obviously tried to stifle it, but it was the catalyst that had everyone laughing, and Dwyn felt herself relax a little, and then jerked in surprise when something cool touched her forehead.

"Sorry," Jo Sinclair said apologetically as she smeared something oily over the cut on her head. "I did not mean to startle you. I am just putting some salve on to help prevent infection and reduce the swelling."

"Thank ye," Dwyn murmured, doing her best to remain still.

Jo smeared more salve around her eye after that, and a little on her split lip, and then frowned at the bruises visible on Dwyn's chest, but began to press on her ribs, asking if it hurt.

"I do not think he broke any of your ribs, but you are definitely bruised there. And everywhere from what I can see," Jo said grimly.

"He was angry that I was married already," Dwyn said wearily.

"And thank God ye were," Saidh said grimly. "I canno' imagine ye'd have survived long married to that bastard."

The other women all murmured agreement to that and then Jo said, "You look tired, Dwyn. We brought plaids out with us. Why do you not rest on one until the men return? Or would you rather return to Buchanan and rest in a bed? It could be a while before the men finish and return."

"Nay. Here is fine," Dwyn assured her. She wasn't going anywhere until she was sure Geordie was all right.

Father Machar was still chattering away about his "adventure" as she lay down on the plaid the women spread out for her. She murmured, "Thank ye," when Aileen and Una spread another plaid over her and then allowed Father Machar's excited voice to lull her to sleep.

"ANYTHING?" GEORDIE ASKED GRIMLY, WIPING WHAT HE SUSpected was blood from his forehead with the back of his arm as Aulay and the MacGregor approached.

"Nay," Aulay said. "Brodie's no' among the bodies or the prisoners."

"The bastard appears to have abandoned his men and slipped away in the melee," Conn MacGregor growled with disgust.

Geordie cursed under his breath at the news. He'd wanted to put an end to this chapter of Dwyn's life so she'd never need fear the man's popping up again in the future.

"I'm no' surprised," Alick said grimly. While Laird Innes had stayed behind to guard the women, the youngest Buchanan brother had returned to the fray the moment he'd delivered Father Machar to the women. Geordie had seen him return and had been relieved to know Dwyn and the priest were well out of it. Now his brother said, "What else would a coward do? And any man who beats a woman is a coward."

Geordie's gaze sharpened on his brother. "He beat Dwyn?"

"Badly, by what Father Machar said on our ride back to the women," Alick told him solemnly. "By his account, Brodie was no' happy to learn Dwyn was married to ye and beyond his claiming her." Grimacing, he added, "I got a look at her face once we reached the temporary camp and the light from the torches and fire. She's several bruises and wounds and her gown is ripped. She . . ."

Geordie didn't hear the rest; he had already mounted and turned his horse to head back to the women.

Chapter 19

"Oh, bother," Dwyn muttered, pushing aside a branch that appeared to be trying to yank the hair out of her head. She then paused to survey the darkness around her, unsure she was heading the right way.

Much to her surprise, Dwyn had actually managed to fall asleep for a bit by the fire while waiting for news from the men. When she'd woken up, the rest of the women had been resting while her father stood guard. Dwyn had nodded at him and slipped into the trees to relieve herself. That was why she'd woken up, a desperate need to water a bush. Now she'd finished the task and was making her way back to camp, but was suddenly worried she'd got herself turned around and was heading away from rather than back toward the fire. She was sure she hadn't come so far from camp. Dwyn would think she'd be able to see the fire ahead through the trees by now, but she'd been still half-asleep when she'd stumbled from the plaid and couldn't be sure how far she'd gone.

Grimacing to herself, Dwyn bent to catch the back of her skirt and draw it up between her legs to tuck it into the belt around her waist. She'd just climb a tree and have a look around. That should give her an idea whether she was heading the right way or not. She hoped.

The tree next to her felt a good size, she decided after sliding her arms around the base to test its girth. Stretching up to grasp the highest branch she could reach, Dwyn dug her slippered foot into the trunk and pushed herself upward as she pulled with her arms. She'd just managed to get both feet off the ground and had shifted one hand to a higher branch to continue upward when her ankle was grabbed and yanked downward.

Dwyn cried out in surprise, but instinctively tightened her hold on the two branches she was grasping as she glanced down. All she could see was a dark shape below, but it was too big to be one of the other women or her father, and whoever it was obviously wasn't a friend or they'd have spoken by now. That thought in mind, Dwyn hooked her arm over the nearest branch to give her more stability, and then removed her free foot from the branch it was on, and kicked out at the hand grasping her other ankle.

Her aim was good, and Dwyn heard the man bark out a curse as her foot was suddenly released. Her blood ran cold as she recognized Brodie's voice behind the expletive. Turning her gaze desperately to the branches above her, she began to scramble upward as quickly as she could. Dwyn had just pulled the previously caught foot up to a branch and started to pull up the other when it now was caught and yanked viciously. Her arm was still hooked over the branch, but Dwyn lost her grip on the higher branch and tried desperately to grab on to something else to save herself. Unfortunately, Brodie was still exerting pressure on her foot and before she could save herself her arm slipped and she was falling out of the tree.

Dwyn screamed as she fell, screamed again as she crashed onto Brodie and grunted as they both crashed to the forest floor. She was immediately kicking and scrambling to get away from the man, but he caught her knee in a bruising grip and crawled onto her legs, keeping her from kicking any more. It didn't stop her punching out at him, but Brodie did by grabbing her hands and forcing them to her sides.

Dwyn groaned in pain when his fingers and thumbs pinched into her wrist bones, and then he forced them to the ground and rested the weight of his upper body on her wrists as he dragged himself up on top of her.

"Thought ye'd got away, did no' ye?" Brodie growled once his body covered hers from the waist down. "But I swear I'll kill ye if it's the last thing I do."

He released one of her hands then to grab her throat instead, and Dwyn struck out at him with her free hand as he began to choke her. She went for his eye, her three longer fingers extended and squished together. Grim satisfaction ran through her briefly as she hit her target.

Brodie roared in pain and fury, and then released her other hand to punch her in the face, but the hand at her throat remained, continuing to choke off her air. Dwyn was flailing at him now a little wildly. A buzzing had started in her ears, her body was beginning to tingle and it felt like her tongue was swelling in her mouth, though she knew it couldn't be. Even so, she was starting to fear she would not escape him this time and he really would kill her. Dwyn had barely had that panicked thought when he was suddenly gone.

Gasping for air, and coughing violently, Dwyn pressed one hand to her throat and tried to drag herself away, pulling with her other arm and digging her feet into the dirt to push with her legs. The sounds of curses and grunts and the thuds of fists hitting flesh followed her and she glanced warily back to see one large, dark shape rolling across the forest floor behind her. Even as Dwyn watched, however, the shape shifted and rose slightly and a snapping sound filled the air. It wasn't very loud, but seemed to be in the silence that followed, and then the shape shifted again, part of it dropping to the forest floor and the other disengaging itself as the man stood.

"Dwyn?"

She'd turned to start crawling again, but paused and turned back at the sound of Geordie's voice and then he was kneeling beside her, raising her shoulders to hold her against his chest.

"Are ye all right, lass?" he asked anxiously, his hands moving over her as if checking for broken bones or wounds.

"Aye," she got out in a shaky rasp.

"Oh, thank God." Geordie scooped her into his arms and held

her close, his head resting against hers. "I came back and yer da said ye'd slipped away to find a handy bush. I was going to wait patiently, but then I heard ye cry out. God," he breathed, pressing a kiss to her head. "I think me heart stopped."

Dwyn slid her arms around his chest, holding him as he shuddered against her.

"I love ye, Dwyn," he said solemnly. "I truly do, and I do no' ken what I'd do if I lost ye."

"I love ye too, Geordie," she whispered.

He found her face with his hands, and tried to kiss her, but stopped at once when she winced in pain as his mouth covered her split lip.

"I'm sorry, love," Geordie said at once, and then gathered her in his arms, and pushed to his feet, murmuring, "I'd best get ye back to the fire."

Dwyn glanced over his shoulder at the dark shapes on the forest floor. In truth, she couldn't tell which shape was Brodie and which were just bushes.

"Is he dead?" she asked.

"Aye, I broke his neck," Geordie said, his voice grim. "He'll no' be bothering us again."

Dwyn merely nodded, and rested her head against his chest with a little sigh. She believed him, but didn't really believe him if that made any sense. She'd been so afraid and worried about Brodie for so long it would take a while for her to accept she had nothing more to worry about.

"Ye found her!"

Dwyn blinked her eyes open and glanced around at that relieved cry from Aileen, surprised to see that they were already back at the small makeshift camp where the women had waited. She hadn't been that far away, after all. The woods here were just so thick she hadn't been able to see the fire for the trees.

While the women had all been sleeping when she'd slipped away several moments ago, they were all up now. Many of them were busy tending to the wounded making their way to the camp, but Aileen and Una were rushing toward them as Geordie carried her toward the fire.

"Aye," Geordie grunted in response to her sisters as they rushed to his side. When Aulay and Alick appeared on his other side, he added, "Brodie had made his way back here and found her."

"Is he dead?" Aulay asked, offering Dwyn a smile as he waited for her husband's answer.

"Aye. I snapped his neck," Geordie said grimly as he sat on the log nearest the fire, and adjusted Dwyn to sit in his lap. "He's about twenty feet into the woods."

"Alick and I'll take torches and go find the body to be sure," Aulay said, and moved away with the youngest Buchanan brother following.

Geordie grunted at that, and then clasped Dwyn's upper arms and murmured, "Now, let me see ye, love."

Dwyn turned from glancing around the now-busy camp and raised her face for him to see it.

"Oh, sweet Jesus," Geordie breathed, running a finger gently over her cheek as his gaze took in the various bumps, bruises and cuts on her face. As his gaze dropped to her chest, he growled, "I should have taken me time killing the bastard."

Dwyn tucked her chin in to look down and grimaced at the large ugly black bruises visible on her chest. It was where some of Brodie's punches had landed when he was beating her after learning that she was married.

"Yer dress is ripped, lass. Did he . . . ?" Geordie's voice was soft but grim and he seemed incapable of finishing the question. Dwyn figured out what he was asking from that and shook her head at once.

"Nay, he did no' rape me," she assured him, her voice still just a raspy whisper. Dwyn's throat was sore, and she was sure it would bruise as well from his choking her, if it hadn't already started. Still, she pushed on. "He just hit me. I'm fine, husband, truly."

Geordie swallowed, and managed a small relieved smile, but

then he sighed and shook his head. "I want to hug and kiss ye, but am afraid I'll unintentionally hurt ye if I do."

"Here."

Dwyn gave a start and glanced around as something cold brushed her chest. Una and Aileen were beside them. Una was trying to press a cold, damp cloth to her throat while Aileen stared at her with a combination of dismay and concern. Dwyn lifted her head so Una could press the compress to her throat, her eyes widening as she found herself meeting the gaze of a large, fair-haired mountain of a man now standing on Geordie's other side.

"Lady Buchanan," the man growled, solemn eyes moving over her bruised and battered face. "'Tis a pleasure to meet with ye again."

"MacGregor?" she whispered in query.

She immediately thought it doubtful that he could hear the word over the noise around them, but he did, and said, "Aye. 'Tis glad I am ye're safe now. I apologize fer allowing Brodie to camp on me land. Had I kenned what he was up to, I would have captured him and brought him to Buchanan meself."

"'Tis fine," Dwyn whispered, but noticed that his gaze had wandered to Una as she continued to hold the cold compress to her throat.

"Here, hold this, Dwyn, and I'll fetch ye something to ease yer throat," Una said now.

Dwyn reached up to take over pressing the cloth to her throat and noted the way the MacGregor watched her sister move away.

"That's Dwyn's younger sister Una," Geordie announced with amusement, apparently having noticed the MacGregor's interest. "She's only sixteen and betrothed."

The MacGregor turned back at the news, and asked, "Who's her betrothed?"

"Laird Graham's eldest son, I believe," Geordie answered.

Dwyn nodded when he glanced her way for verification, and then shifted her surprised gaze back to the MacGregor when he snorted with amusement.

"Alpein Graham," he said, obviously knowing the Graham clan, or at least who the eldest son was. "Poor lass'll live a lonely bairnless existence does she marry him."

Dwyn frowned with concern, and opened her mouth to ask why, but he saved her the effort by explaining, "The man prefers men. To the point I doubt he'll even be able to consummate the marriage. He'll leave her in the keep and ride off on 'hunting' trips with his 'friends.'" He shook his head with disgust. "'Twould be a waste o' a lovely lass did she marry him." He watched as Una started back with a mug in hand and added, "I canno' abide a waste like that and may have to do something about it."

He turned and walked away and Dwyn stared after him with amazement, and then glanced to Geordie in question.

"He's a good man," Geordie assured her solemnly. "He'd never hurt a lass."

Dwyn was just relaxing when he added, "He'll ask me permission first and wait until she's a little older to steal her to bride."

When she turned wide, dismayed eyes to him, Geordie shrugged. "Would ye rather yer sister was with a man who preferred men and neglected her, or someone who would fill her with bairns and make her happy?"

Dwyn couldn't answer. Aside from the fact that her throat hurt too much to respond just then, Una had reached them by that point and she didn't want her sister learning what Conn MacGregor had said and worrying unnecessarily. But she was definitely going to be discussing this with Geordie later, Dwyn decided firmly as she smiled at Una and accepted the mug she held out.

DWYN WAS DOZING FITFULLY WHEN THE SOUND OF THE BEDchamber door opening and closing stirred her. She opened her eyes to see that the sky was lightening with the rising sun. Dawn was coming and Geordie was just finally joining her, but it had been quite late when they'd got back to Buchanan. After looking her over here in Geordie's room, Rory had given her a potion to soothe her aches and pains, and then Geordie had helped her undress and get into bed. Pressing a kiss to her cheek, about the only place on her face he could kiss her without causing her pain, he'd told her to rest and he'd be along as soon as he finished dealing with things.

Dwyn hadn't made him explain what these things were. She knew. They included figuring out what Katie had done to "handle" Aulay, and deciding what to do with the maid as well as Brodie's soldiers, at least the ones who had survived the battle.

Curious about those things, she lay on her side facing the window and listened as Geordie disrobed and then slid into bed behind her. When he started to curl around her, his arm reaching over her and then stopping uncertainly, she took his hand and pressed it to her breast with his palm over her nipple.

"'Tis the only spot that is no' bruised," she explained with amusement when he went still with what she suspected was surprise.

Geordie relaxed then and pressed a kiss to her neck. "I did no' expect ye to be awake yet."

"I drowsed fer a bit," she admitted, scooting back until he was spooning her. "But I was curious to learn when we are leaving for Innes."

"Everyone's decided to delay fer a day so we can rest up after what happened. I thought ye may prefer fer us to travel with yer da and the others so ye can rest in the cart while ye heal."

"Nay," she said without hesitation. "I can ride."

"Are ye sure?" he asked with concern.

"Aye," she assured him. "Me bottom is no' bruised. Besides, riding in a wagon would be more torture than rest."

"Ah," he murmured with understanding.

"What will become o' Katie?" Dwyn asked after a moment.

Geordie pressed another kiss to her neck, but then sighed and admitted, "She is dead. We left her locked in the room with Rory guarding the door, and she chose to jump out the window rather than face whatever punishment might have been meted out."

When Dwyn stiffened and turned her head in question, she was able to see him nod in the light cast by the rising sun.

"He did no' mention it when we first got back because he did no' want to upset ye," Geordie explained.

Nodding, Dwyn turned to peer out the window again as she asked, "Did ye figure out what she had done to 'take care' o' Aulay?"

"Aye," he murmured, his hand moving lightly across her nipple, in what she suspected was an unconscious action. "There was poison in the whiskey in his study. Rory did no' think anything else had been tampered with, but Aulay had everything in his study thrown out just to be safe."

"Probably a good idea," Dwyn said a little breathlessly, wiggling her bottom closer to the hardness she could feel growing and pressing against her. "What about Brodie's men?"

"We've decided to release them," Geordie admitted, rolling her nipple between thumb and finger now, which definitely wasn't unconscious. Leaning up again, he began to nibble at her neck as he pointed out, "They were only following their laird's orders, so they're being escorted off Buchanan land as we speak and sent on their way . . . without their horses."

"Without them?" she breathed as he nipped at her ear and then sucked on the tender flesh briefly, before shifting his mouth to her neck and nipping and sucking lightly there as well.

"Aye." His voice had deepened in direct proportion to the hardness growing between them, and Geordie shifted, rubbing himself against her. "They had to be punished somehow and walking home to Brodie seemed— Damn, Dwyn," he interrupted himself on a moan of despair. "Ye've been beaten and abused and I should be just holding ye and offering ye comfort, and instead I want to . . ."

"Come home?" she suggested gently when he broke off.

"Aye," Geordie breathed apologetically, and then kissed her gently on the shoulder, and eased back from her, retrieving his hand from her breast to rest it on her hip instead. "But I love ye and wouldn't want to hurt ye, so I can wait."

Dwyn hesitated for a minute, and then reached down and back

to clasp his hand. "While we canno' kiss just now with me mouth sore as it is, and the only safe places to touch me are me breasts and right here." She drew his hand between her legs and pressed his fingers against her. "I'd like ye to come home, husband. That would comfort me."

"God, I love ye, Dwyn Innes Buchanan," Geordie growled, kissing her neck again as his fingers began to slide between her folds to caress her. "Ye're brave and ye're smart, and ye're funny . . . Ye're just perfect. I think God surely must have made ye just fer me."

Dwyn opened her mouth to assure him she felt the same way, but a gasp slid out instead as his fingers glided over her sensitive core.

"Ye're wet fer me, love," he breathed with awe by her ear.

"I'm always wet fer ye, husband," Dwyn moaned. Her hips moving into his caresses, she reached back to clasp his hip. "Please love me, Geordie. I want to feel ye inside me while ye touch me. I need ye to make me ferget today, and—" Her words ended on a groan as he shifted and slid into her, filling her even as he caressed.

Within moments, Geordie's steady thrusts and caresses had Dwyn forgetting about Brodie and what had happened that day, along with pretty much everything else as he kissed her neck and shoulder and patiently but slowly drove her toward her release. It was different this time though, Dwyn noticed. The passion was still there, but he was being extremely gentle and careful with her. Geordie was making love to her, rather than just loving her, and she quite suddenly understood what he meant. She too felt like she'd come home.

Epilogue

WITH THE SOUND OF THE WIND BLOWING AND THE WAVES crashing on shore, Dwyn didn't hear the horse. It was Barra's excited bark that told her someone was approaching and who. Smiling wryly at the dog, she turned, unsurprised to see Geordie riding up on his mount.

"I can never surprise ye with those beasts around," Geordie said on a laugh as he reined in and dismounted.

"Nay, ye canno'," she agreed with a grin, shaking her head when Barra immediately rushed excitedly to her husband the moment he was off his horse and standing in the sand. The dog licked his hand, and then dropped to the ground and rolled about excitedly on his back, showing submission even as he invited pets. Clucking with irritation, she said dryly, "That dog used to be mine."

Geordie chuckled at her jealous comment, and bent to run his hand over the dog's belly, before giving him a pat and straightening to approach Dwyn where she stood next to a much more dignified Angus. Much to her relief, he, at least, had not abandoned her, and had remained seated obediently at her side.

"We're all yours, love," he assured her, bending to pet Angus now as well.

"Hmm," Dwyn murmured dubiously.

Geordie grinned at her expression. "I'm sorry, wife. Are ye feeling neglected? Shall I rub yer belly too?"

Dwyn laughed softly when he did just that, rubbing the small bump where their child grew. Her laughter turned into a soft moan though when he kissed her, his tongue thrusting into her mouth.

"Damn," Geordie sighed a moment later when he managed to make himself break the kiss. Resting his forehead against hers, he confessed, "I'll never get enough o' ye."

"That's a good thing," she breathed, resting against his chest.

They were silent for a minute, just holding each other while they waited for their passion to ease a bit, and then he pulled back to peer down at her and announced, "Rory and Alick are here."

"What? Why?" Dwyn asked, and then worry knitting her brow, she asked, "Is there trouble? Do your sister or one o' yer brothers need ye?"

"Nay," Geordie assured her, hugging her briefly. "He's here to check on you. He'll be visiting us often to check on yer progress growing our child, and then staying the last month or so ere ye have him, her or them." He pulled back again then and said seriously, "I'm no' taking any chances with yer health, love. I'm too happy here at Innes with ye to risk losing ye on the birthing bed."

Dwyn grinned, but asked, "Are ye? Happy here, I mean? Ye do no' miss yer Highlands too much, do ye?"

"I'm very happy," he assured her solemnly. "I love ye, Dwyn. I love you, I love our dogs, I love our home, I love Innes and I love having the ocean at me back door." Cupping her face, he added seriously, "I love our life together, Dwyn Innes Buchanan, and do no' miss the Highlands. Ye're the best thing that ever happened to me, lass, and I canno' even imagine me life without ye."

Dwyn breathed out a relieved sigh, and smiled. "I love you too, husband, and canno' imagine life without ye either."

"And ye never will," he assured her, bending to kiss her again. This time Geordie didn't stop when their passion ran away with them, but lowered her to the sand.

"What about Rory and Alick?" Dwyn gasped after tearing her mouth from his.

"They can wait," he growled, sliding one hand up under her skirts and running it up her leg, pushing her skirts before it. "I've a mind to—" He paused on a groan as her hand found his growing erection through his plaid.

"Come home?" she teased softly, caressing him.

"Aye, lass," Geordie said seriously, and then told her, "Ye may laugh that I call it that, but home is where the heart is, and ye've had me heart almost since the first moment I met ye. You are home to me, love."

Dwyn's face lost its teasing expression at those words, and she pressed a hand to his cheek as she said solemnly, "Then come home, husband."

Read on for a look at

LOVE IS BLIND,

a fan-favorite Lynsay Sands historical,
reissued in a beautiful new package!
Coming July 2020

Chapter 1

London, England, 1818

"'LOVE IS A FEVER . . . IN MY BLOOD.'"

Clarissa Crambray winced as those words trembled in the air. Truly, this had to be the worst of the poems Lord Prudhomme had recited since arriving at her father's town house an hour ago.

Had it been only an hour? In truth it felt more like several days had passed since the elderly man arrived. He'd entered brandishing a book, announcing with triumph that, rather than go for their usual walk, he thought perhaps today she'd enjoy his reading to her. And Clarissa would have, had he chosen to read something other than this poppycock. She also would have appreciated it more were he not acting as though he were doing her a favor.

For all his words, Clarissa was not fooled. She knew the reason for the sudden change in plans. The man was hoping to avoid calamity by restricting her to sitting decorously on the settee while he read aloud from his book of poems. It would appear that even the aged and sympathetic Prudhomme was growing tired of her continued accidents.

She couldn't really blame him; he'd been terribly forbearing up until now. Almost a saint, to be honest. Certainly he'd shown more understanding and fortitude than her other suitors. He'd appeared to accept and forgive all the times she'd mistaken his fat little legs for a table and set her tea on them, had given a pained smile through her tendency to dance on his feet, and had even put up with her stumbling and tripping as he led her on walks through the park. Or so it had seemed. But today he'd found a way to save himself from all that. Unfortunately, his choice of reading material left much to be desired. Clarissa would rather be making a fool of herself in the park and stumbling face-first into the cake table than suffering this drivel.

"'It gives me wings like those of a dove.'" Lord Prudhomme's voice quavered with passion . . . or possibly just old age; Clarissa wasn't sure which. Truly, the man was old enough to be her grandfather. Unfortunately, that didn't matter to her stepmother, Lydia. The woman had promised to John Crambray that she'd see his daughter well married if it killed them both. Lord Prudhomme was the last of the few suitors still bothering with her. At this point, it looked like they were safe from dying. However, Clarissa was in imminent danger of finding herself married to the elderly gentleman kneeling on the floor before her and waving his arms wildly as he professed undying love.

"'I shall vow my' . . . er . . . 'my'— Lady Clarissa," Lord Prudhomme interrupted himself. "Pray, move the candle closer if you please. I am having trouble deciphering this word."

Clarissa blinked away her ennui and squinted toward her suitor. Prudhomme was a dark blob in her vision with a round, pink blur of a face topped by a silvery cloud of hair.

"The candle, girl," he said impatiently, all signs of the charming suitor momentarily replaced with irritation.

Clarissa squinted at the candle on the table beside her, picked it up, and leaned dutifully forward.

"Much better," Prudhomme said with satisfaction. "Now, where was I? Oh, yes. 'I shall vow my undying . . .'" He paused again and his nose twitched. "Do you smell something burning?"

Clarissa sniffed delicately at the air. She opened her mouth to say yes, actually she did, but before the words left her mouth Prudhomme released a shriek. Pulling back with surprise at the sound, she watched in amazement as the man suddenly leaped to his feet and began to hop madly about, his blurry arms flying and appearing to thrash at his head. Clarissa didn't understand what was happening until the white blur that was his wig was suddenly removed and beat furiously against his leg. She blinked at the pink blob that was his head, then at his actions, and realized she must have held the candle too close—she'd set his wig aflame.

"Oh, dear." Clarissa set the candle down, not releasing it until she knew it was safely on the table surface. Her vision blurred and her sense of distance beggared, she nearly knocked the little man over as she leaped up to help him.

"Get away from me!" Prudhomme yelled, shoving her backward.

Clarissa fell back in her chair and stared at him in blind amazement, then glanced sharply toward the door as a rustling announced the arrival of someone.

Several someones, she amended, squinting at the array of colors and shapes standing just inside the door. It looked as if every servant in the house had heard Prudhomme's shrieks and come running. No doubt her stepmother was there as well, Clarissa thought, and heaved a small sigh at the subsequent shocked silence. She couldn't see well enough to know if those by the door were staring at her with pity or accusation, but she didn't need eyesight to guess at Prudhomme's expression. His rage was a living thing. It reached out to her across the few feet separating them, and then he exploded with verbal vitriol.

He was so angry, most of what Prudhomme said ran together into one mostly incomprehensible rant. Clarissa managed to decipher bits here and there—"clumsy idiot," "bloody disaster," and "danger to society" amongst them—but then, in the midst of his rant, she saw his dark arm rise and descend toward her. Clarissa froze, afraid he might be lashing out, but she wasn't at all sure. It was so hard to tell without her spectacles.

By the time his fist got close enough that Clarissa could see that he was indeed attempting to strike her, it was too late to avoid the blow. Fortunately, the others had apparently suspected he was winding up, and had moved closer while he spoke. Several of them descended on the man midswing, preventing the blow. There was a blurry blending and shifting of color before her as they struggled. Clarissa heard Prudhomme's curses and a grunt from one of the shapes, whom she suspected was Ffoulkes, the butler. Then there was much cursing as the kaleidoscope blur of bodies began to shift toward the door.

"Fie! Shame on you, Lord Prudhomme," Clarissa's stepmother cried, her voice clearly distressed as her lilac blur followed the mass of other colors to the door, then she added anxiously, "I hope once you calm down you shall see your way clear to forgiving Clarissa. I am sure she did not mean to set your wig on fire."

Clarissa sank back in her chair with a sigh of disgust. She couldn't believe that her stepmother would still hope to make a match with the man. She'd set his wig on fire, for heaven's sake! And he'd tried to hit her! Though Clarissa should have known better than to think that would put Lydia off making a match. What did her stepmother care if she ended up married to an abusive mate?

"Clarissa!"

Sitting up abruptly, she turned to peer warily around as the lilac blur that was Lydia reentered the room and slammed the door behind her.

"How could you?"

"I did not do it on purpose, Lydia," Clarissa said at once. "And it would never have happened at all if you would just let me wear my spectacles. Surely being graceful, even with spectacles, will get me more suitors than—"

"Never!" Lydia snapped. "How many times have I to tell you that girls with spectacles simply do not find husbands? I know of what I speak. It is better to be a little clumsy than bespectacled."

"I set his wig on fire!" Clarissa cried with disbelief. "That is more than a little clumsy, and really, this is beyond ridiculous now. 'Tis becoming dangerous. He could have been badly burned."

"Yes. He could have. Thank the good Lord he was not," Lydia said, sounding suddenly calm. Clarissa nearly moaned aloud. She had quickly come to learn that when her stepmother went calm, it did not bode well for her.